# THE LINEHOLDER

By Laura McGhee

THE LINEHOLDER. Copyright @ 2020 by Laura McGhee.

All rights reserved.

No part of this book may be used or reproduced in any manner whatsoever without written permission except in the case of brief quotations embodied in critical articles or reviews.

This is a work of fiction. Unless otherwise indicated, all the names, characters, businesses, places, events, and incidents in this book are either the product of the author's imagination or used in a fictitious manner. Any resemblance to actual persons, living or dead, or actual events is purely coincidental.

ISBN: 978-0-578-76443-6

*For my nieces,*

*Amelia, Charlotte, Danika, Hannah, and Paige.*

*Don't shatter the glass ceiling, soar above it.*

*"Any girl can be glamorous. All you have to do is stand still and look stupid."*

Hedy Lamarr


*"All a girl really wants is for one guy to prove to her that they are not all the same."*

Marilyn Monroe


*"The truth will set you free, but first it will piss you off."*

Gloria Steinem

# BEFORE

# Chapter One

Dinah needed 73 hours. That was it ... just 73 measly hours and her life could change.

But then the rich man offered to pay for her type rating in a Gulfstream 400 series if she would have a threesome with him and the flight attendant.

Type rating training in aircraft was very expensive, anywhere between $20,000 - $50,000. Most pilots didn't have that much coin just sitting around. And if they ever did, much of it had likely been allocated to supporting former spouses. As in, most pilots didn't have just one.

You see, the rich man presently owned a Phenom 100, which was a baby jet. Since his ego and his bank account had outgrown it, he was looking to trade up. And that's what it was all about, wasn't it? Trading up. Because if you weren't trading up, then you were pleading down.

Dinah had been flying for the rich man for about three months, dodging his digits and innuendo, both equally clumsy in nature. But she had it easy, compared to poor Fatima. While Dinah was busy working the controls, Fatima was hapless in the cabin, with nothing to occupy herself with after getting the rich man his Diet Dr. Pepper.

"Come on, whaddya say? I'm offering you a great opportunity," he said.

"The type rating or the threesome?" she responded.

He guffawed. "You're funny! I like that – it's good to have a skill and not just coast on your looks."

Dinah had no idea of her attractiveness – she had been raised in a household that placed no importance on physical appearance. Her parents emphasized – in what now seemed a quaint and archaic set of tenets – intelligence, compassion and yes, humor. So, she was never able to use her looks to her advantage, like some female pilots did. Like Britney, who got her first jet job with barely 300 flight hours because she was dating the CEO of the flight company. Dinah hated the Britneys of the world. They made it so much harder for the rest. No, for Dinah, her beauty was like having a trust fund and not knowing about it. Constantly annoyed and confused by offers and solicitations that were a "great investment in your future."

"I already asked Fatima. She's cool with it. She's here on a work permit."

The rich man then stopped talking, which was a rarity, and stared at Dinah expectantly. He had dried wing sauce on his chin and sweat stains under his breasts. Recently, his plugs had grown to a length that he could now use product on them, and he had … generously. The silence was marred only by a sudden pocket of turbulence that disturbed the carton of gun parts that the rich man was taking to the trade show.

Dinah's initial instinct was to tell the rich man to go fuck himself, but she had done just that to other men in the past and it had not ended well. Instead, she took a deep breath, which was completely audible through her Dave Clark headset, and diplomatically explained to him that while she was flattered and grateful for his proposed sponsorship, she felt that it was prudent to keep their relationship professional and also that it was important to her that she progress in the world of aviation purely on merit.

The rich man fired her on the spot.

When they landed at LaGuardia, after walking away from Fatima's forlorn face in the open cabin doorway, Dinah had to purchase a one-way ticket back to Los Angeles on American Airlines. The ticket cost $375. The rich man hadn't paid her yet this month – he was going to square up with her after the gun show - so she put the ticket on her Visa. Not the Chase one, it was maxed out, but the Wells Fargo Visa. She sighed a breath of relief when it successfully went through. This time her breath was inaudible because she wasn't wearing her Dave Clarks.

Her Dave Clarks!

Shit!

She left them on the plane.

***

After a five-hour flight, Dinah waited another thirty-five minutes at LAX for the Van Nuys Flyaway bus.

A bus appeared after 15 minutes but it was full and sped right past the platform of tired and cranky travelers … tired and cranky being redundant when used to describe the aforementioned group. By the time the next bus pulled up in front of them, there was some passive-aggressive jostling and dirty looks. Mostly by the bus driver.

Dinah sat beside a baggage handler, who lived in the same apartment building as her. The baggage handler was a regular on the Flyaway. He took it back and forth every day to his job at Southwest. He groaned slightly as he sank his thin rounded frame into his seat.

"Your back still giving you trouble?" she said.

"Just on marine layer days."

"Did you go to that chiropractor I told you about? The one on Sepulveda?"

He shook his head. "Not covered under my insurance."

"Of course, it's not."

The baggage handler nudged Dinah in the side. "I think you're being watched."

Dinah looked across the aisle, where an elderly lady in a Chico's ensemble stared intently at her. As soon as she made eye contact, the lady exploded.

"My name is Linda Parks and Delta lost my luggage!" She looked at Dinah expectantly. "Well … can't you just look it up on your phone or something?"

"I'm sorry," Dinah replied. "I don't work for Delta."

The baggage handler leaned across her. "And she's a pilot."

A young man in a wool cap – it was 85 degrees out – and an artisanal beard chimed in. "Yeah, and how come the WiFi never works on those flights?"

"I'm a pilot," Dinah reiterated.

"I specially ordered that luggage. It had my face on it!" Linda lamented.

The baggage handler shuddered. "You sure you want to work for an airline?"

Dinah sighed. "More than anything. Anyway, what are you going to do about your back?"

"Taken care of. I just lay down on the kitchen floor and got Ines to walk on my spine," the baggage handler said.

Dinah's eyes widened.

He smiled. "I know, I know, Ines is a generously proportioned woman. But honestly, having my nuts squished took my mind off my back pain."

They were temporarily interrupted by the bus driver announcing that vaping while on the bus was strictly prohibited – likely in response to the fact that the young man in the wool cap had pulled out an E-cigarette.

"What are you doing back so soon? I thought your trip ended on Sunday," the baggage handler asked.

"I got fired," Dinah replied.

She explained what had transpired, 35,000 feet in the air.

Linda leapt back in. "You shouldn't dress like that. Sends the wrong message."

"She's wearing a pilot uniform," the baggage handler said pointedly.

Linda rolled her eyes, and they turned back to their own conversation.

"Are you going to sue the asshole?" he inquired.

Dinah shrugged. "What's the point? It would be my word against his. Plus, I don't want to damage my professional reputation."

"But what about other women?" he retorted. "You know he'll do it again."

"Even if I win, I'm *that* female pilot … the kind that makes an issue of her gender and causes interpersonal problems at work. Ultimately, it will hurt my career."

The baggage handler frowned with disapproval. She averted her gaze and attempted to mollify him.

"Look, I'll be fine, there's a pilot shortage so it will take me about a minute to find another gig. Or I can just go back to flight instructing," Dinah said.

"Yeah, I keep hearing about this shortage," he said. "I thought since 9/11 it was tough going."

"It has been," she replied. "But all the baby boomers are starting to retire … finally. When they raised the mandatory retirement age at the airlines from 60 to 65 that really jammed everyone up for a few years."

The bus pulled into the parking lot. People began to line up in the aisle before it had even come to a full stop. The driver noticed this in his rearview mirror and hit the brakes a little more sharply than necessary. Linda, who was one of the first to spring into action, fell into the young man in the wool cap. She didn't apologize.

***

Dinah and the baggage handler lived just a few blocks from the bus station, so they walked home together, down Woodley Avenue. Their building was a 1970s stucco monstrosity on Sherman Way. Every building on Sherman Way was a 1970s stucco monstrosity. But the rent was under $1,400 a month for a one-bedroom, which was a great deal, even in the Valley. And the building was clean and well-maintained.

Their building manager waved to them from the rental office, with its little sliding plexiglass window. Kristina ran a tight ship. She was known to lurk in the hallways and courtyard area, seeking out illegal pets and horseplay in the pool. Some of the tenants had assigned her the unkind nickname, "Apartment Nazi," which hurt and confused her because she was from Lithuania.

"I'm not even German!"

The two of them got on the elevator – which always lurched demonically and smelled of boiled cabbage – and got off at the third floor. They knew Kristina liked them because new tenants were only ever able to lease apartments on the first floor, regardless of which floor they requested. Then after a probationary period, a vacancy on the third floor would magically manifest itself. There were rumors that the entire second floor was a Russian brothel, but again, a one-bedroom for under $1,400 a month.

In the Valley.

Dinah said goodbye to the baggage handler and continued down the hallway to her place. She put the key in the lock. It jammed, she took it out and tried again, wiggling it this time. The key turned and she dragged her carry-on bag through the door.

Her apartment didn't have air conditioning, so she hurried to open all the windows and turn on the two floor fans she had – one in the living room and one in the bedroom. Then she opened the freezer and took out the carton of Tillamook Mudslide Ice Cream. Also, a bottle of Stoli Vodka she had in there. And that was dinner. Then she wheeled her suitcase into the closet because it was important to her that it was out of sight when she wasn't working.

Thankfully, Dinah had already paid rent this month so that left her almost three weeks to find another job.

She stripped off her now soggy and revolting pilot uniform and put on her favorite grey sundress, made from soft, well-worn t-shirt material. She truly didn't mind wearing a uniform. It took the agonizing decision-making quotient out of business attire. The tie was a little constrictive and there was a female tie option, but it was a weird Colonel Sanders-type affair that reminded her of the Deep South and specifically, Confederacy. So, she toughed out the red rings that appeared on her neck after a few hours. Then came the best part, the unleashing of the tight regulatory bun that she twisted her long blond hair into every day. Loose hair was a no-no in flying – both from a safety perspective and because it inevitably turned into a messy, rat's nest within a few minutes of arriving on the ramp. Facial hair was also a no-no – it interfered with the seal on the crew oxygen masks but thankfully, Dinah figured she had a few more years before she had to deal with unwanted facial hair. She was only in her early thirties. And from a Scandinavian background.

Dinah grabbed her iPad and updated her resume, adding a definitive end date to her employment as a corporate jet pilot at Iceman Enterprises. *Top Gun* really had so very much to answer for in aviation culture. At her last flight instruction job, a young, newly minted instructor had nervously fessed up to having never actually seen the movie and was immediately socially ostracized.

"Dude, then how did you know you wanted to be a pilot?"

She logged onto a website for aviation jobs called, *Climbto350* and started to scroll. First, she narrowed the search engine to jobs in California. Most of the better jobs were elsewhere in the U.S. California was the most competitive job market in the country so any decent positions usually went to far more experienced pilots than her with at least 3,000 hours compared to her measly 1,427. And most of the companies were either "Part 135," or *shudder*, "Part 91."

The Federal Aviation Administration grouped commercial aviation into three categories: "Part 121," which were basically the airlines; "Part 135," which were the corporate flight companies and "Part 91," which was the shitshow that encompassed everything else. As would be imagined, "Part 121" was the most heavily regulated by the FAA. "Part 135" allowed for some weaselly loopholes that characterized some flight companies colloquially as "Part 134 ½." And "Part 91" was Guantanamo Bay, without the charm.

One had to be diligent in recognizing the scams inherent in the job listings. Some positions were advertised perennially, never seeming to be filled, which was suspect. And then one also had to parse the verbiage. Many jobs entailed *other light duties*, which meant picking up dry cleaning and detailing luxury cars amongst other things. One of Dinah's friends from flight school did a lot of cat sitting … and he didn't have a cat. Another buddy was offered free accommodation … which essentially involved sleeping on the aircraft and serving as a makeshift security guard. And so, it went.

Dinah's eyes searched the listings for anything that had the *new* icon next to it. Ah, here was one. It was a small, family-run charter company that operated out of John Wayne Airport in Santa Ana. There had recently been a movement afoot to have his name removed due to the Duke's long history of racist and homophobic comments. There was probably a children's amusement park nearby, named for another racist, homophobic, and misogynistic celebrity that could use a good rebranding as well.

The charter company flew single-engine Cirrus aircraft, which Dinah had instructed in and King Airs, which were twin-turboprops. Dinah had her multi-engine rating but building flight time in multis was always a challenge. And the airlines wanted to see a sizeable number of multi hours. Twin engine planes were expensive to maintain so not that common and just as expensive to rent yourself. She had never flown a King Air, but the company was advertising that they were willing to pay for the training if you signed a two-year contract. If you left prior to two years, then you had to pay them back for the training costs. This was a standard condition in aviation though many people questioned the enforceable legality of the contract. Still, a vast improvement from a few years back when pilots habitually had to pay out-of-pocket for their own training and type ratings.

Some ads put the salary right out there. Sometimes it was a yearly salary, sometimes an hourly wage. Part 135 companies usually provided benefits and health coverage. Part 91 companies hardly ever. And Part 91 job ads usually stated that the salary was *negotiable*, which loosely translated meant that they were going to make an earnest attempt to exploit the hell out of you.

Sunny Skies Aviation – ugh – was a Part 91 company. But they were located in Southern California. And Dinah was qualified for the position. And rent was due in three weeks.

After today's fateful flight, her updated logbook said that she had 1,432.5 hours.

She attached her resume and pressed *submit*.

Less than five minutes later, her cell phone rang.

Oh, how she wished she hadn't answered that call.

## Chapter Two

The owner of Sunny Skies Aviation, was born and bred in Orange County and despite having no money, maintained residences in Huntington Beach and in Lake Havasu, Arizona.

This phenomenon was directly attributable to the unbridled piggy bank that was his father - his father, being one of the O.C.'s preeminent gynecologists. In a crude way, Sunny Skies Aviation was a flight company built by vaginas.

The owner had never wanted for anything in his hedonistic life. He grew up in a home overlooking the beach, where he spent his summers surfing, while his classmates had summer jobs at In-N-Out. He drove a '69 Mustang Coupe that his father had paid to be driven out from Columbus, Ohio because he took a semester off to backpack – to five-star hotels – in Europe.

And when he announced that he had decided not to finish his Associate Bachelor's Degree in business analytics at Loyola Marymount, his father put down his fork, then picked it back up again and asked if there was some other area of interest that his son might like to pursue … praying ardently that it wasn't surfing.

It was aviation.

The owner had, for many years, been a zealous fan of "Microsoft Flight Simulator X." And he was good. His belief, like so many others, was that if he could fly this simulator so adeptly, then he could fly the real thing just as well. Even though actual flight was in three dimensions, with no pause button and you could die if you made a mistake. But still. His father bought him an introductory flight lesson and he killed it. The flight instructor had to help him a little bit with the landing, and the takeoff and climbing and descending. But still. He was hooked. So, his father paid for him to get his private pilot license and his instrument rating, followed by his commercial license and his multi-engine rating. That was really all he needed to plant himself in the aviation industry, but he also decided to get his tailwheel endorsement and a seaplane rating. Many student pilots ended up taking out loans to do their training – many with interest rates higher than those of credit cards. But the owner was fortunate in that his father bankrolled the more than 80 grand that all that training entailed. He didn't *feel* fortunate, but he was.

The next hurdle was how to amass flight hours. The owner didn't want to do any of those experience-building jobs, he wanted to go straight to the airlines. And this was a problem because even a regional airline wouldn't even look at you with less than 1,500 hours. The owner had 322.

He tried incessantly to have his father intercede on his behalf with the Chief Pilot at a well-known regional – they were racquetball cronies – but to no avail. Ever since the Colgan Air crash, the FAA was pretty persnickety about that 1,500-hour rule. Before the fateful event, a pilot could get a job with a commercial airline with just 250 flight hours. Then came Colgan.

Fifty people were killed when a Dash-8 entered a stall and crashed into a house on the way into Buffalo. The crash was attributed to pilot error, specifically that neither the Captain nor the First Officer took the necessary steps to recover from the stall, partly attributed to inexperience and partly attributed to fatigue. As a result, there was a large-scale enquiry and Congress ultimately enacted stricter regulations with regards to safety, training, and rest requirements. One of these new rules was that pilots needed 1,500 hours to work for an airline.

It took years to build 1,500 flight hours and the options for new pilots were limited. A lot of pilots became flight instructors, where you were paid very poorly to allow people to try and kill you every day. Others became banner towers, flying perilously low to the ground attempting to hook a banner that you then hauled up and down the Malibu coastline for hours. If you had an engine failure, your choices were putting it down between swells in the Pacific Ocean or flipping it over on the sand. These jobs usually paid in the ballpark of ten dollars an hour.

The owner didn't want to engage in either of those vocations so he got his father to buy him a plane so that he could just build his hours on his own. His father thought that an older model Cessna 172 would be sufficient, but he talked him into a Cirrus SR-22 Turbo because there really was no comparison. And in no time at all, mostly flying himself and his buddies to Mammoth and back, the owner had his 1,500 hours and his interview with his first regional.

He didn't get that job because there was a Human Resources component to the interview, and he didn't get the next one. But he got the one after that.

The owner made it through training in St. Louis, passed his flight exam, called a checkride, the second time he took it and started flying on the line as an official "lineholder." He absolutely loved strutting through the airport in his uniform. When it first arrived, the shirt was a bit baggy and the trousers hung a little low in the crotch, but he had it professionally tailored until it fit like a glove.

Everything was going along swimmingly – there was even talk about him upgrading to Captain, mostly emanating from him – when he got the *ramp check*.

The FAA could show up unannounced, wherever and whenever they pleased and conduct a safety check. Traditionally this usually happened on the airport ramp before or after the flight, thus the name. Usually paperwork and licenses were proffered upon demand, planes were inspected, and crew members were obliged to do an impromptu drug test, which involved peeing into a cup in the nearest restroom or sometimes, at an offsite drug testing facility. The latter option was especially empowering because one usually found oneself sitting in a waiting room with a bunch of people on parole.

When the owner was handed his cup, he had no choice but to refuse. He told the FAA inspector that he was happy to provide a sample in another 72 hours. This ultimatum accomplished two ends. Number One, he was not subject to any criminal charges because he had *not* technically tested positive for drugs. Number Two, he was immediately dismissed by the airline for failing to comply with the test.

So now what? Well, that was when the owner decided that all airlines sucked and that flying was bullshit. But surfing definitely deserved a second look.

His father was about to retire but kept his practice open so that he could help his son open his very own charter company, flying passengers on demand to wherever their hearts desired. He had advocated vociferously for a mid-sized jet but after taking out a second mortgage on their family home, his father had to relay the heartbreaking news that they could only afford a King Air.

Over the last few years, the owner had predominantly been the only employee at Sunny Skies Aviation. Other pilots had come and gone at an alarming rate due to a combination of sporadic business and the owner's personality. In fact, he kept the ad going in *Climbto350* continuously because even when he had freshly hired someone, he anticipated it wouldn't be for long.

He was in his lakefront cabin in Arizona, heating up some sake, when Dinah's resume pinged on his screen.

He logged off *match.com* and punched in her number.

*\*\*\**

"So, how'd you get into flying?" he asked.

"Sort of by accident, really," Dinah said. "Somebody bought me a flying lesson for my birthday, and I fell in love with aviation."

"That's unusual. Most pilots have a history of aviation in their families or flew in the military."

"What about you?"

"Yeah, definitely. Anyway, your resume says that you have Cirrus experience."

"I used to instruct in one. I have about 200 hours dual time."

He laughed. "That's awesome. Most of the asshats I've hired in the past can't handle the horsepower."

She laughed too. "It does tend to veer off the runway on takeoff if you don't hit that right rudder."

A doorbell sounded in the background.

"For sure, for sure. Oh shit, can you hold on a sec? Forgot I ordered sushi."

"No problem."

She heard him walk over and open his front door. There was a brief but heated exchange with the delivery person. They had forgotten his California roll. As a result, there was no tip.

He picked up his phone. "Sorry about that."

"Are you a vegetarian?" she asked.

"Nope, nope, I'm a red-blooded American male. Just try to tear me away from a good Korean barbeque. What about yourself?"

"Um, I guess technically I'm a pescatarian."

"You're a mermaid?" he laughed again.

"No, I have two legs, last time I checked. Which is a good thing … you know … on account of the rudder pedals."

Dinah heard him chewing his sashimi. She wasn't sure if he was using chopsticks but, in her heart, she felt that he was.

"Right, right, on account of the torque. Very clever. So Deenah – "

"Dinah – "

"Sorry, Dinah, let me ask you something. It says here that you live in Van Nuys. That's kind of a long way to drive. Would you maybe be able to move closer? It's okay if you need to check with your husband."

There was a long pause borne out of frustration at one end and anticipation at the other.

Dinah answered carefully. "I might be able to look at relocating in the future if the salary allows. Right now, I'm in a rent-controlled apartment. You understand."

The owner made several sounds that indicated that he did, in fact, understand.

"Sure, sure. And of course, you'd be more than welcome to crash on my office sofa, anytime you're too tired to drive home."

"That's very kind of you," she said, because she knew he expected her to.

"Well, I'm frequently accused of being a softie. Guilty as charged!"

They both laughed. In Dinah's case, it was taking an increasing amount of effort. Then, out of nowhere, there was a sudden expression of rage from the owner.

"Is everything okay?" she asked.

"Yeah, fuck. I just spilled soy sauce on my Keds. Fuck," he whined.

"I'm sorry – are they …?"

"Yeah, they're fucking white."

She put on her most empathetic tone. "I'm really sorry."

"Me too. Hold on a sec, I'm just going to toss these out," he said.

This time he was gone almost ten minutes. Dinah stared out the window at some kids who were playing with foam noodles in the apartment pool. They were hitting each other over the head. It looked like fun.

When the owner returned to the phone, he seemed to have collected himself. He resumed the conversation with gusto.

"So, no husband?"

She shouldn't have been taken aback. But she was.

"No, no husband. No wife, either."

He let that last part slide, without commentary.

"Yeah, it's hard to have a relationship in this industry. You're never home," he said.

"I mean, I had a boyfriend, but we broke up last month," she said.

"What happened there? Did he cheat on you?" he ventured.

"No, no, nothing like that. He was just really jealous."

"Of other guys?"

"No, of my career. He's a pilot too and when I got that jet job, he couldn't handle it."

The situation was actually a lot more complicated than that. Her ex was still flight instructing when she got the position with Iceman Enterprises and he was furious. He had more hours than her and accused her of having only gotten the job because she was a woman. And then she had a higher income than him, which he said made her bossy. Before that, he had been making more money than her and he complained frequently that she wasn't pulling her weight financially. He refused to have friends over because he was embarrassed about their apartment on Sherman Way. For some reason, he seemed to be of the opinion that poverty was a character flaw. Dinah felt like she couldn't win in this gender dynamic. To have a higher salary made her emasculating, to have a lower salary made her a burden. She didn't understand why a man's degree of success couldn't stand autonomously and conversely, always had to be relative to hers.

It ultimately came as a relief when the relationship ended after three years. They were staying at the Hotel del Coronado in San Diego when the tension finally became untenable. The hotel was an American icon, designed by a Canadian architect and built by Chinese laborers in 1888. The movie, *Some Like It Hot*, had been filmed there in 1959 and there were photos of Marilyn Monroe and Tony Curtis and Jack Lemmon in drag on the walls in the lobby. Dinah always felt profound sadness whenever she looked at Marilyn Monroe. To her, she represented the danger of having your sexuality used as currency – she was a tragic, cautionary tale. Dinah and her boyfriend couldn't afford a weekend getaway at that time, but he had been insistent, so she succumbed. There was a cornhole game set up beside the pool and after more than a few Dos Equis, he had challenged her to a match. And unfortunately, she had won. Soundly. He was livid but containing his rage. Until the father and adult son who had been watching, stuck it to him. He exploded like an apoplectic piñata. And that, as they say, was the end of that.

"I like being single," Dinah said.

The owner quickly adjusted. "Oh, me too. I really value my freedom."

She felt a crippling fatigue begin to descend upon her coupled with a lack of will to continue.

"Did you have any questions for me about flying?" she asked.

"Um ... for sure, for sure. How about this? What do you do if you get carb ice?"

She answered quickly. "Cirrus aircraft are fuel-injected, they don't have carburetors, so they don't get carb ice."

She could hear his smile.

"Nailed it! That was a trick question."

"Yay, me," she responded weakly.

And then without warning, he was all business.

"Okay, look, here's the deal. I'm looking for someone reliable, who will stay long term. I keep losing pilots to the airlines."

"Oh, I have no airline aspirations," she assured him.

She totally did.

"Good to hear. I don't know why people get their panties in a bunch about airline jobs. All airlines suck scrotum. Also, I'm looking for someone with people skills like me. We really strive to offer personalized, concierge-style service to our clients, many of whom are regulars."

He had never had a repeat customer.

"I understand that Southern California is a very distinct demographic," she replied.

"It is, it is. We fly folks to resorts in the Baja Peninsula, to wine tastings in Santa Barbara, you name it."

"Would that be in the King Air?" she asked.

There was an almost imperceptible pause.

"Mostly we're using the Cirrus right now."

"But you would train me in the King Air?"

"Oh of course. We'd start you off in the Cirrus and then get you trained up in the King Air."

"Okay," she replied dubiously.

"Now, do you have any questions for *me*?"

She had already given him several, but she forged ahead anyway.

"How many pilots do you have working for you?"

"Right now, it's basically just me. But I'm interviewing like crazy," he answered.

"Okay, well I'll wait to hear from you after you speak to the other candidates," she offered magnanimously.

He almost cut her off, seemingly afraid that she would hang up.

"Actually, are you available tomorrow?"

"For an in-person interview?"

"No, for a flight," he responded.

She didn't answer right away so he elaborated.

"I've got this couple who want to go to Napa, and I'm stuck out here in Havasu."

Dinah was certain she had misunderstood him. "You want *me* to fly them? But I haven't even been checked out in the aircraft."

"I trust you. You're an instructor."

"But don't you need to do a checkout flight for insurance purposes?"

She could feel the wink.

"I won't tell if you won't."

She did not want to do this, so she threw up another roadblock. "But how would I get the keys?"

"I keep a set in a lockbox by the plane. The combination is 1,2,3,4."

Of course, it was.

"Honestly, I'm not sure if I feel comfortable … "

He put on his most earnest tone. "You'd be really helping me out of a jam. I've got a guy coming to install a new surround sound system and I need to be here. How about I pay you a day rate of $800?"

The going day rate for a charter was $500, which was considerably less than his offer.

And rent was due in three weeks, which she now had to cover completely on her own.

And he hadn't asked why she left the jet job after only three months.

And she had 1,432.5 hours.

So, she said yes.

The clients were not a couple. And they weren't going to Napa. And there was definitely no wine involved.

## Chapter Three

They were sod farmers from Merced. They needed to fly up to inspect their fields. When Dinah arrived after driving three hours in morning rush hour traffic, they were waiting impatiently at the FBO, which stood for Fixed Base Operator. A Fixed Base Operator was an organization that provided services for aircraft and passengers at airports. The good ones had freshly baked cookies and the bad ones had Red Vines.

The sod farmers were wearing jeans, cowboy boots and cowboy hats, which threw Dinah for some reason. Maybe because they were in Southern California. They were the same fair coloring, and the same physical build, skinny and tall – a pair of eerie, incongruous twins. It was as if Sam Shepard had written, *The Shining*.

Dinah led them out to the plane, which was filthy, and of course when she opened the lockbox, the keys weren't inside.

She was just about to call the owner when one of the sod farmers stopped her.

"Hey, the door is unlocked," he said, pulling it open.

"I'll bet the keys are under the seat," the other one said.

They were. Unbelievable. This was a $700,000 aircraft.

After a game of rock paper scissors, to decide which sod farmer got to sit up front with her, they taxied over to Runway 20R and took off. It was a beautiful day, with no marine layer at all, so Dinah was able to fly VFR – Visual Flight Rules – all the way up to Merced.

The sod farmers weren't very talkative. Other than asking if she could fly up the coastline so they could take some photos, that was about it. She accommodated them until she got to Vandenberg Air Force Base, which was restricted airspace. At that point, she headed inland.

Dinah was pleasantly surprised by how well she had remembered how to fly the SR-22. She hadn't flown one for a few months and was worried it wouldn't come back to her. The last thing a passenger wanted to see was a pilot stumbling and fumbling around an aircraft with a visible lack of familiarity. She *was* having a little bit of trouble reaching the rudder pedals. At 5'3", this was not an uncommon problem for her. Dinah made a note to bring a cushion with her for the next flight.

When they started to approach Merced - KMCE, she began to self-announce. Merced Airport didn't have a control tower, so pilots made their own position reports on a common radio frequency. It was kind of surprising how many uncontrolled airports still existed in California – some in extremely busy areas. Compton was her least favorite. She used to go there to practice takeoffs and landings in the traffic pattern and it was Thunderdome.

But out here, it was relatively flat and empty, which made for easy, stress-free flying. The winds were light and even though she was a little nervous about landing the plane, Dinah put it down so gently that the sod farmers gave her a brief round of applause.

"Was that dumb?" the one in the back asked her.

"Not at all," she replied. "All positive feedback is appreciated. And any pilot who says that they've never had a bad landing, is a liar!"

They parted ways at the FBO – which had Red Vines.

"We'll be back around three p.m.," said the other sod farmer.

It was 11 a.m.

Dinah ambled over to the reception counter.

"Excuse me, is there a restaurant on the field?"

The young man who had fueled the plane for her after they arrived, was also working the counter.

"No ma'am, there's not. We have vending machines."

"How far is town?"

"About 15 minutes, give or take."

"Do you have a crew car I can borrow?"

It wasn't unusual for FBOs to have one or two cars that they would lend to flight crews to use to go and run errands or get a bite to eat.

His face became apologetic. "We do have one but it's in the shop. Sorry. We have vending machines."

"Okay. Thanks."

She turned away from the counter.

"Ma'am?"

"Yes?"

"How would you like to pay for the fuel?"

She crossed her fingers.

"Does Sunny Skies have an account here?"

"No. Sorry."

Of course, they didn't.

"Visa. I guess."

So, it was Fritos, Netflix, and credit card roulette for the next few hours.

***

Dinah was contemplating her second Sprite, when the door from the parking lot burst open and the two sod farmers hustled through it.

One of them was carrying a baby goat.

They were frantic.

"Someone poisoned our goat!" the one not carrying the goat cried.

Dinah was confused. "Who would poison a goat?"

They both looked at her incredulously.

"Lots of people," the one carrying the goat said. "We have to get her to our vet in Carlsbad."

"Wouldn't it be better to take her to a vet, here?" Dinah asked.

"We had a falling out with the vet in Merced," the non-goat-carrier said.

"We didn't care for his recent leanings towards naturopathy," the goat-carrier explained. "Please, get the plane ready, quickly!"

And so, they took off from Merced, with the one in the back holding the goat – whose name was Cleopatra – in his arms.

No rock paper scissors this time.

Cleopatra was somewhat lethargic for most of the flight. The two sod farmers tried desperately to keep her awake, which was fine. But they also made every effort to have her vomit the poison out of her system, which was not fine. Fortunately, when the sod farmer sitting shot gun tried to stick his finger down her throat, she bit it. There were no further attempts.

It wasn't until Dinah was flying over LAX, using a special procedure, called "The Mini-Route," that the goat began to become agitated. Cleopatra started to squirm and then kick, trying to free herself from the sod farmer's embrace.

"Maybe you should let her go," the one up front said.

"That's not a good idea," Dinah responded.

But he did anyway and several seconds later, the goat came through the middle console, kicking the throttle forward to max power. The nose of the airplane shot up and Cleopatra fell backwards. Her left hoof landed squarely in Dinah's right eye socket, temporarily blinding her with tears. She somehow managed to throttle back to idle without busting the 2,500-foot altitude, that she'd been assigned.

"You're going to have a shiner there," the one up front said.

"I've got her!" the one in the back exclaimed.

But he didn't and by the time that Dinah, was able to land at John Wayne ... and this time the landing wasn't even remotely gentle ... the goat had eaten most of her headrest. The sod farmers apologized profusely and sped off with Cleopatra.

It wasn't until Dinah was tying down the plane that she noticed the slim, elegant gentleman getting out of the silver BMW that was parked, with the engine running, a few feet away from the aircraft. He was none other than the owner's father, the O.C.'s most renowned gynecologist. Dinah recognized him because she had checked out his website, partly out of curiosity and partly out of boredom. But mostly for the Yelp reviews. He had come to the U.S. in the late 1970s from Iran, to escape the violent upheaval that resulted from the Shah being deposed. And he had been able to preserve his wealth so he could set up his medical practice in Southern California.

Her pulse rate increased when she saw him approaching, but he was there to pay her.

In cash.

He also reimbursed her for the fuel and was extremely understanding about the headrest.

"Do not worry," he said. "I will take care of it."

And the goat lived. Ironically, the headrest probably saved her life because it slowed down the metabolizing of the poison in her digestive system. And it was determined that the poisoning had been accidental. Cleopatra had eaten deadly nightshade during her midday graze. No charges were laid.

***

Dinah entered the lobby of her building four hours later, with a hunger so intense it felt like her stomach was consuming itself. The baggage handler was already on the elevator when the door opened.

"What happened to your eye?" he asked.

Dinah glanced in the mirrored elevator panel. Her eye had swollen up and turned black.

"I got a new job."

"Sparring with Conor McGregor?"

"No, with a goat."

"Is that a euphemism for something?"

"I wish. Hey, I'm going to go to Beeps. Can I treat you and Ines to some comfort food?"

He wagged his finger. "You shouldn't eat that garbage. It's not good for you. Don't you have to pass an aviation medical every year?"

She wrinkled her nose. "I'm not worried."

"You should be. All you chubby Americans with your diabetes. You should take better care of yourself."

The elevator door opened on their floor.

"So, that's a *no* for you?" she asked. "What about Ines?"

The baggage handler opened his apartment door.

Dinah called out through the opening. "Ines, do you want anything from Beeps?"

A disembodied voice, surprisingly deep for a woman, came back to her.

"Large fries."

"No," said the baggage handler. "She doesn't need it."

He waved goodbye and closed the door.

***

At Beeps Diner, her black eye didn't even warrant a second glance. It was Van Nuys, unfortunately. Dinah surrendered completely to her cravings. She got a veggie burger with Swiss cheese, onion rings, fries, and a chocolate malt. Even though she was exhausted, she jaywalked with a skip in her step across four lanes of traffic and a grass median, ignoring the resentful horns.

Outside the baggage handler's door, she set down a bag of large fries, pounded the doorknocker and scurried away.

Back in her apartment, Dinah inhaled her meal in front of the tv, watching the news. Another heatwave was on the way. It was going to be 104 degrees by mid-week. And she didn't have air conditioning.

She had taken the big wad of cash she'd been paid, out of her pocket before she went to Beeps. It was Van Nuys, unfortunately. It was sitting in the middle of the dining room table.

Dinah stared at it, feeling her mood improve as her blood sugar stabilized. Suddenly the wad moved. A cockroach wriggled out from beneath the pile of bills and crawled across the table. It scurried down the leg and disappeared into the galley kitchen.

She had 1,437.4 hours.

## Chapter Four

Dinah was just getting out of the shower when she heard her phone ring. She ran to the bedroom to grab the call, leaving a trail of wet footprints on the very well-worn Berber carpeting.

It was the owner, whom, she still hadn't met in person.

"Hey, beautiful, what's your schedule looking like?"

"For when?" she asked.

"Today, in about two hours," he answered blithely.

"I'm at home so I don't know if I can get to the airport in two hours."

"Well, just do your best."

"Who is the client?"

"Oh, they're great. You're going to love them."

And then he was gone.

Her uniform was dirty – she hadn't been able to do laundry because someone had tried to wash a comforter in the communal washing machine and broken it. So, she put on a white golf shirt and some khakis with a pair of dress flats. Good enough.

Dinah took the elevator down to the parking garage and had backed out of her designated spot – which non-designated people parked in quite regularly – when she remembered she needed a cushion. Back she went up to the apartment, to get it. There was now a half-eaten sandwich on the floor of the elevator. It looked like ham.

Two and a half hours later, Dinah pulled into the parking lot. And wanted to keep driving when she saw who her passengers were.

They were *Triple Ws* – Wealthy, White Women – the most feared demographic in aviation charters. Any pilot who had even flown charter flights for a minute, had a battle story involving *Triple Ws* and *PTSD* – Post Traumatic Socialite Disorder. One was forced to drive 20 miles to an organic juice store to get a particular type of pomegranate nectar for the flight while everyone waited back at the plane. He was not reimbursed. And ultimately the *Triple W* didn't even drink it. Another pilot had to gently explain to a *Triple W* that she had brought too much baggage for her Thanksgiving trip to her third home in Hawaii. The aircraft would be over the weight limitations, so she would need to leave some things behind. Perhaps the two suitcases of cashmere sweaters? The *Triple W* refused and told him to remove some fuel instead. When the pilot explained to her that they would be flying over the Pacific Ocean with nowhere to refuel, she screeched that that wasn't her bloody problem. And one of Dinah's old flight instructors had once flown three *Triple Ws*, one at a time, to three different destinations, on the same day. And they were all dating the same investment banker. They hadn't been aware of each other's existences until that fateful moment. That charter flight had been the catalyst. And the pilot had been the only man in sight. And their collective captive audience. He was formally deposed at the hearing. Missed a full day of work.

Dinah's clients were a mother and daughter, trendsetter tag team. They were wearing Lululemon yoga pants and Versace sunglasses and carrying the types of purses you had to loop over your forearm instead of slinging over your shoulder.

Their blond highlights had been surgically applied and their skin had no pores.

Dinah guessed that their names would start with the same letter.

Chrystal and Cat – Cat was the mom and Chrystal, was the daughter – were having a besties day. Chrystal's prom was fast approaching, and they needed to get her a dress. They wanted Dinah to fly them to La Jolla, so they could get something of quality in the Girard and Prospect area. Apparently, there was a nagging concern that Chrystal might be unlucky enough to show up in the same dress as a classmate. And there was some sort of meme that people loved to create that had a "who wore it better?" caption, which was the absolutely worst thing that could ever happen to a woman other than tan lines.

La Jolla was less than an hour's drive from where they were. But Chrystal and Cat *refused* to sit in traffic, so they decided to fly instead to Miramar Airport.

The flight was 12 minutes.

On the plus side, when Dinah introduced herself, Cat looked her up and down and said, "A girl pilot. How fun!"

Both women, put their hands out to allow Dinah to help them into the plane. Chrystal was up front because Cat wanted her to witness a strong female role model. Dinah, started to tear up, not from the flattery but from the suffocating cloud of Le Labo. Chrystal kept referring to the brand mistakenly as "Le Labia," which peeved Cat more than it should have. Maybe it wasn't a mistake.

"I have to say, the fact that you fly planes, is so supremely badass, I can't even," Chrystal said.

Dinah tried her best. "It *is* pretty exciting. Much better than sitting in an office."

"No doubt. Do you have kids?"

Cat, who had been animatedly texting someone from the backseat, popped her head forward to quickly diffuse what she must have thought was an indelicate query.

"Chrystal!" she chastised, "I'm sure that Dinah doesn't have time for a family. She's probably never home."

"Actually," Dinah countered. "Lots of female pilots have kids."

Cat placed her hand supportively on Dinah's shoulder. "Are you not able to conceive?"

"No! I mean, I'm able to, I just don't want kids."

"At this stage of your life?"

"No. I mean, I just don't want to have kids. Period. Ever."

If Chrystal had been smitten before, this most recent revelation put her over the top into a deep state of girl crush. She beamed at Dinah with diluted pupils.

"See, I just don't understand that," Cat said. "Why would you not want to be a mother? It's the best job in the world. And who is going to look after you when you're old?"

"At this point, probably the State," Dinah said.

Chrystal chortled.

"You know what? I just decided that I'm never having kids either," she stated. "Especially if it deprives *you* of the opportunity to become a GILF."

She turned and stared pointedly at her mother.

"What's a GILF?" Dinah asked.

Cat waved her off, so Chrystal leaned over and wrote down the definition on Dinah's kneeboard.

Dinah gasped.

Cat and Chrystal both howled.

"I'd make a damn good one too, if I say so myself!" Cat bragged.

"You need to say so yourself, Mother, cause *no one* else is going to!" Chrystal returned.

Now it was Dinah's turn to laugh. She was kind of enjoying herself. What was happening?

Chrystal turned her attention back to Dinah.

"You know, you have great bone structure." She turned to get Cat's take. "Doesn't she have great bone structure?"

"She does," Cat affirmed.

"Ooh! We should totally get your eyebrows threaded!"

Again, Dinah didn't know what they were referring to.

"OMG, don't you have any girlfriends?" Cat asked.

Truth be told, Dinah didn't really have any girlfriends. Working in a male-dominated field, surrounded by men all day meant that most of her friends were guys. Mostly due to proximity but also because she shared interests and experiences. She never seemed to have much in common with most women. And she always felt like a hot mess next to them with their elegantly coiffed hair and ensembles that somehow looked both meticulously put together and casual at the same time. One of the loneliest moments Dinah had ever had, was attempting to apply false eyelashes for a Christmas party. Only one of them had made it anywhere near her eye. The other one ended up stuck to her cheek. And there was glue everywhere. The other barrier was that a lot of women were intimidated by Dinah because she was a pilot. They felt marginalized because they saw her as so accomplished.

She had a brief friendship with a life coach named Shirley that she had met at the gym. But when she tweeted that she had just gotten her multi-engine rating, with a photo of her in front of the plane, Shirley had tweeted the following comment, "I just need you to get fat and fail at something."

So no, Dinah didn't really have any girlfriends.

And that was largely why she let the *Triple Ws* drag her into La Jolla and to a prohibitively expensive salon, where not only were her eyebrows threaded – which entailed an esthetician using two actual threads in rapid motion to remove unwanted eyebrow hairs and help shape the ones that were left and yes, it hurt like hell. But also, she had new makeup professionally applied.

"See!" said Chrystal triumphantly. "I told you, you had good bone structure."

"You said that she had *great* bone structure," said Cat.

"Mother, don't you have a bartender to seduce, somewhere?"

"Yes, but your boyfriend doesn't get off work until two a.m."

Dinah dropped her new bag of makeup on the cobblestones, she was laughing so hard.

"Hall of Fame burn, Cat! I bow down to you."

And she did.

Then they suited her up in a pair of Lululemons and a darling halter tee because her original outfit was tragic and gave off a strong lesbian vibe, an observation that Dinah asserted was insulting to lesbians everywhere. And then they took her to Jamba Juice to show her off, and also to hydrate her because her skin was dry. No lesbians approached Dinah at Jamba Juice, so their collective efforts must have paid off.

Somewhere in the midst of all these festivities, Chrystal managed to find the prom dress of her dreams. Quite honestly, Dinah thought that it looked like the same $30 hooker dress that the teenagers in the Valley got from Ross Dress for Less. But when Chrystal emerged from the dressing room and did her fairy tale twirl, Dinah gushed just as vocally as Cat.

When they arrived back in Santa Ana, Cat refused to take a penny for any of Dinah's new purchases and in fact, tipped her 100 bucks.

"We've had a blast with you, today!" she said

"A total blast!" Chrystal added.

"I had such a wonderful time with you as well," Dinah said.

And she meant it.

"Thank you again, for your generosity."

"You see how polite she is," Cat said to her daughter. "You should pay more attention to that."

"Mother, you should pay more attention to your rapidly falling ass."

Dinah nodded in solidarity. "Solid burn."

"Solid," said Cat.

"I'll give you that one," surrendered Chrystal.

They both gave her the most genuine hugs she had received in ages and then, in a puff of $3,000 perfume, the *Triple Ws* were gone.

\*\*\*

The building manager, Kristina, was cleaning up all the flyers that people had dumped on the floor of the mailroom, when Dinah went in to get her mail. She did a visible double take when she saw her.

"You look very nice today," Kristina said.

"Oh. Thank you. Feelin' cute."

"You should make an effort more often. I'll bet your boyfriend would finally propose. I've been married for 27 years … in a row," she said proudly.

"Um, actually we broke up."

"That's a shame."

Not really.

"Yeah, thanks."

"So, he moved out?" Kristina asked.

"He did. About a month ago," Dinah answered.

Kristina stuffed a bunch of flyers into the garbage bin and then folded her arms, looking suddenly very official.

"Well, that changes everything."

Dinah could feel herself tensing up.

"It does?"

"Yes. Your boyfriend was on the lease with you."

Dinah relaxed a bit.

"Oh, okay – not a problem. You can just take him off the lease."

Kristina made an unpleasant sound in the back of her throat. "No, that's not possible. We will have to do an entirely new lease."

"I can do that."

"That's fine then. You will need to provide pay stubs or a bank statement showing that your income is two-and-one-half times the amount of your monthly rent."

This stipulation was not unusual for renters in L.A. County. It was such a transitory environment, with such little accountability. And the laws really erred on the sides of the tenants. It habitually took a landlord over a year to have a tenant evicted for non-payment of rent. One of the servers who worked at the airport café took full advantage of this. He would lease an apartment, pay the first month and the security deposit and then never pay another cent. After about a year, he would be evicted. One would think that this blight would mar his financial reputation and make it difficult for him to lease another apartment. But he would simply forge new records and voilà, he'd be hosting another housewarming party. So, Dinah understood why so many landlords were paranoid and overcompensated in the screening process. But it was a frustrating roadblock for the honest, hardworking facet of society.

Dinah gulped. "The thing is, I just started a new job, so I don't have any way to show income yet."

"In that case, you would have to have a co-signer," Kristina said.

Shit.

"I don't know anyone that could do that, unfortunately."

Shit, shit.

Kristina thought for a moment. "Let me contact the management company about your options. Perhaps a letter from your new employer would be sufficient."

Shit, shit, shit.

She had 1,437.6 hours.

## Chapter Five

Tammy didn't have a pilot's license, but she flew all the time. She was just extremely vigilant. No scud running (flying close to the ground), no bad weather flying (so she didn't have to file an instrument flight plan) and no landing at airports with control towers. Which, in Northern Ontario, was not really a huge obstacle.

She lived in Kapuskasing, Ontario, Canada. "Kapuskasing" was a Cree word, that meant, "bend in the river," in this case, the eponymous Kapuskasing River. Kapuskasing was about 800 kilometers north of Toronto, which was about 500 miles and home to both the Lumberjack Heritage Festival every July and the River Walleye Tournament in August. For most of the remainder of the year, it was home to a shit ton of snow.

Tammy's family owned a convenience store in town, called Smythe's. Their last name wasn't Smythe but the man they had purchased it from when they immigrated to Canada was named Smythe. And it simply cost too much to get a new sign.

They didn't live in town, instead opting to enjoy a few acres of land on a farm that Tammy's dad had used the very last of their savings on. They had chickens, a rooster, two pigs and an extraordinarily vain cow. They also had a barn ... that housed a 1978 Piper Cherokee, which was cleverly hidden away between flights. The penalty for flying without a license was a six-figure fine and the possibility of spending several years in jail.

And yet, in rural areas, a startling number of pilots never got their licenses. Many of them were older men who flew in the war (pick one) and couldn't be bothered to make themselves legit. They flew to inspect their crops or cattle. It was extremely difficult to catch them unless you saw where they landed or could somehow note their tail number. And you never heard their voices on the radio. Some of them learned to fly planes before there *were* radios.

In Tammy's case, there simply wasn't any money for her pilot's license. You had to train for a minimum of 40 hours and get signed off for your checkride with a Certified Flight Instructor and then pay to write a Transport Canada flight exam, and then do a private pilot checkride, comprised of an oral exam and a practical exam in the aircraft, with a Designated Pilot Examiner. None of this was cheap, even if you could use your own aircraft – which had to be registered and certified as airworthy. Which the Cherokee wasn't.

The farmer who had sold them the property, had taught Tammy to fly. He had Parkinson's disease and moved into a care facility in town. Tammy's family had been kind enough to temporarily house the plane while he "tried" to sell it, entailing no effort on his part whatsoever. Her parents worked long hours at the store, which left Tammy to her own devices, which for a 14-year-old, was really rolling the dice.

One gorgeous summer day, the farmer dropped by unexpectedly, because he had also unwisely been left to his own devices and came upon her sitting in the plane.

"You're sitting on the wrong side," he said.

She scrambled to get out of the plane, thinking he was going to tear a strip off her. He put up his hands.

"You're grand, don't fret. Just slide over there to the left seat."

Tammy shimmied over on one cheek, getting temporarily snagged on the flap lever between the seats.

The farmer pulled himself up onto the wing – it took several tries – and entered through the only door, which was on the right side of the aircraft.

She stared at him shyly, but her eye had a gleam in it. He saw it, he recognized it and he shared it.

"She's a pretty sweet girl," he said, gently patting the glareshield, which on a car would be called the dashboard.

"She's a girl?" Tammy asked.

"Sure, she is. Boats and planes are always females."

"How come?"

"Because they cost a lot of money to maintain."

He laughed with the timing of someone who had clearly had many occasions to deliver that line. Tammy kind of wanted to laugh too but for some reason felt that she shouldn't. So instead she asked what the plane's name was.

He smiled. "Her name is Hedy. After Hedy Lamarr. You're too young to know who that is."

"Hedy is a girl's name?"

He nodded. "Short for 'Hedwig.' Hedy was a real beauty from Vienna."

"And she was a pilot?" Tammy asked.

"No, she was an actress. She played Delilah."

"From *Samson and Delilah*. The one where she gets him to cut his hair!"

"You bet," he said. "Taking away all of his manly strength. But did you know, she was also an inventor?"

"Well I didn't even know who she was until 30 seconds ago, so no."

"Don't be a smarty pants. Hedy Lamarr invented a frequency-hopping spread spectrum that became the foundation for your WiFi and your Bluetooth."

"Are you serious?"

"Dead on."

"That's impressive. How come more people don't know about this?" Tammy asked.

"You got me. She was better known for being a looker. And being married six times."

Tammy whistled. "That's a lot." She thought about it for a moment. "But she was beautiful and talented and smart."

"Exactly. What man could live up to her ideals? She was too smart for her own good."

The farmer ignored her look of confusion.

"Do you want to take her up?"

Her eyes widened. "Like, right now?"

"No time like the present."

"Should I check with my parents?" she said.

"Hell, no," he responded. "Hold tight for a wee minute."

He pried himself loose and climbed down to the right, rear side of the aircraft. He opened the small baggage door and retrieved a set of keys. He called up to her.

"Do you want a parachute?"

"Huh?!"

"I'm pulling your leg. There's no parachute."

The farmer walked around to the front of the plane and grasped the propeller. With a certain amount of huffing and groaning he slowly began to pull the plane out of the barn. Twice, he slipped and lost his footing, disappearing temporarily from view.

"Should I get out?" she called.

He waved her off impatiently.

Eventually they were clear of the barn and he managed to insert himself back into the right seat.

"Okey dokey," he said. "She hasn't flown in a while, so we'd best give her a prime."

She looked at him blankly.

"You see that silver knob there, to the left of the yoke?"

"What's the yoke?"

"The steering wheel thingy," he clarified. "Yeah, that's it. Just pull that out and push it back in, let's say, three times."

"It's really hard to push," she moaned.

"Put some muscle into it."

She began to count. "What does this do?"

"It's putting a little extra fuel right into the engine, so it'll be easier to start. The trick is not to do it too much or it'll flood."

"And then it won't start?"

"You got it. Okay, that's just fine. Now, I want you to take this red knob – it's called, the 'mixture knob' and push it all the way in. It controls the ratio of air to fuel going to the engine. You want it all the way in to start – that's called, 'full rich' – full rich, just like you like your men, right?"

He elbowed her jovially and she sneered at him.

"I'll remind you that I'm 14."

"Okay, smarty pants, put the key in the ignition – don't turn it yet."

She did as she was told.

He continued. "Good job. Now, you see that double switch there?"

"Yup."

"One side is the battery and the other side is the alternator. Push it up."

"Is that like, the same as a car?" she asked.

He looked surprised.

"Exactly! Well, the older ones anyway. So, the electrical system and the starter are going to be powered by the battery and then …"

"And then after the engine is running, the alternator will do it," she finished.

"You got it! Okay, let's fire this bad girl up. I want you to turn the key all the way to the right and then let it go. Keep your right hand on the throttle." He pointed to the smaller black knob beside the mixture knob. "And after the engine catches, I want you to pull that back a scooch."

"How much is a scooch?"

"More than a titch but less than a smidge. Okay, let 'er rip."

Tammy did as he had instructed and the engine sputtered up, the propeller spraying debris everywhere. The body of the plane vibrated, and the noise was deafening. The farmer pointed to a headset that was hanging from the yoke.

"Put that on," he yelled.

She did and he did the same on his side. He showed her how to position the microphone in front of her face.

"Can you hear me?" he asked.

She nodded.

"No, say something back so I know if your headset is working."

"What should I say?"

"Good enough."

The plane was starting to creep forward on its own.

"Okey doke, I want you to put your feet on the rudder pedals. Can you feel them? It's just like the brake pedal in a car."

"I don't drive yet."

"Why the hell not?"

"Again, I'm 14."

"No excuse. No matter, so your brakes are on the tip toes of the pedals. Go ahead and press both of them with your toes."

She did it and the plane stopped moving.

"It worked!" she said excitedly.

"Miracle of miracles. Okay, here's the big difference between this and a car. In a car, you steer with the wheel. In a plane, you steer with your feet. If you want to go left, press the left rudder pedal. You want to go right, press the right one. Go on, try it out."

He pushed the throttle in a little bit to give the plane some momentum and it started to roll, initially in a straight line and then lurching left and right as Dinah worked the pedals.

"Is this right?" she asked.

"Not even close," he responded. "Head over to that field over there."

She looked. The cow was grazing contentedly. "But Gretchen is there."

"She'll move."

The plane lurched along like Frankenstein's monster until it eventually got to the field.

"Good for you – we made it before dark," he said. "Ready for takeoff?"

"Ready."

She took her hands and feet off the controls.

"Oh, *you're* doing the takeoff."

"I am?"

"Hell yeah. I sure as tootin' don't need the practice."

She suddenly looked terribly ill at ease. He took note of it and adjusted his tone.

"Look, it's easy as pie. Push the throttle all the way in and keep the plane straight. She's going to want to torque to the left a little because the propeller is spinning to the right, so press the right rudder pedal."

"The left rudder?" she asked nervously.

"The *right* rudder. Not the left one. The right one."

"When do I take off?"

"That's the easiest part. You're just going to let the speed build up."

"How fast?" she asked, looking at the airspeed indicator.

"Ignore that. I want you to feel when she's ready to go. She won't want to be on the ground anymore and she'll start to float on up," he described.

"And then do I pull back on the yoke?"

"No," he said. "This is a grass field so you're going to hold the yoke back and then when she starts to leave the ground, push forward a little bit so that we can build up enough speed to start climbing. Then let her ease up into the air. Folks always want to rail back on that yoke, but this girl will fly herself into the air, if you let 'er. You're just going to help her out a little bit. Sound good?"

"Sounds good," she said.

"Okay," he said. "Cleared for takeoff."

She did nothing.

"That means 'go'."

Tammy pushed the throttle all the way in and then it all happened exactly as the farmer had said it would. One minute, they were bouncing violently down the field and the next minute, the plane just floated up off the ground and Gretchen was below them, having begrudgingly moved out of their flight path at the last possible moment.

That was also the moment that Tammy knew she was going to be a pilot.

***

That evening at dinner, Tammy was so depleted she could barely lift her fork. Every ounce of adrenaline had drained from her body, hours ago.

"I'm going to need you to come to the store with us this weekend," her father said. "We have to do inventory."

Tammy agreed without putting up a fight, which raised her parent's suspicions.

"Are you feeling well?" her mother JoJo inquired.

"I'm just tired," she answered.

Her father snorted. "What on Earth do you have to be tired about?"

She wanted to tell him, so desperately, but she knew if she did, that would be the one and only time she would ever fly a plane.

"Nothing. I don't know."

"What did you do all day?" JoJo asked.

"I played with Gretchen."

"Gretchen's a cow. She doesn't know how to play. She eats, she sleeps, and she swats flies away."

"And she's not altogether successful with the flies," her father added.

"Why don't you call some of the girls in your class?" her mother asked.

"Because they all have summer jobs," Tammy replied.

"Well, we're not having this discussion again. We need you at the store and to help out here at home," she said. "Did you get the laundry done?"

"Almost," Tammy said. "It's in the dryer."

Her mother pushed back her chair. "No, no, no. You have to get to it the second it turns off or everything wrinkles."

She exited rapidly.

Tammy's father took a long sip of iced tea and considered her. She decided to beat him to the punch.

"Teenagers!! Am I right??"

He patted his mouth with his napkin.

"You know, young lady, it would be nice to see you show some initiative."

So that's exactly what she did.

## Chapter Six

Dinah had called the owner four times asking him if he could give her a letter of employment for her landlord. She still hadn't heard from him. She'd been playing hide-and-seek with Kristina, the building manager, for days. It was a pain to come in the back entrance and climb three flights of stairs so that she didn't have to pass by the rental office. She was sick of feeling like a kid sneaking in after curfew. So, she texted him.

He didn't text back, but her phone rang about five minutes later.

"Hey, beautiful, what's your schedule looking like?" he asked.

"Did you get my messages?" She ignored his query.

"Sure, sure, no problem, we can absolutely get you a letter."

"Oh, thank you so much. This has been a big headache," she said gratefully.

He chuckled. "Don't worry about it. I understand what a nightmare a landlord can be. I'm one myself."

"So, how will I get it?" she asked.

"Get what?"

"The letter. How will I get it from you? Can you email it to me?"

"Even better, I can give it to you in person."

"Oh?"

"That's why I was calling. How would you like to log some time in the King Air?"

"By myself?" she asked warily.

He laughed. "No, no, in the right seat. But I'll let you log the hours. I have so many at this point in my life, I stopped counting ages ago."

She *really* wanted to.

"I'd really love to, but should I go without any training beforehand?"

"Of course, of course, safety first. No, I meant, you can observe me flying and work the gear and the radios. It'll be a great orientation opportunity for you."

She relaxed a little.

"Oh, okay. That'd be fantastic. I really appreciate it. I won't log the hours though if you're flying."

"Your call, beautiful. So, see you bright and early tomorrow morning at five a.m.?"

Jesus.

"Perfect! Looking forward to meeting you in person."

She shouldn't have said that.

"Me too!" he responded, his tone instantly brightening.

"Well, I'll let you go," Dinah said. "Oh, where are we going, by the way?"

"Aspen."

Fuck.

***

Aspen, Colorado had one of the dangerous airports in the world.

Aspen-Pitkin County Airport – also known as Sardy Field, a lot of airports had two names – had an elevation of over 7,800 feet above sea level. It was in a small valley, north-west of the city of Aspen. And it was surrounded by mountains on all sides.

There was basically one way in and one way out. The runway was 8,000 feet long, which wasn't unreasonable but aircraft approaching had to stay up high enough to clear the mountains and then "chop and drop," which meant pull back the power and push forward aggressively to lose altitude in order to descend to the runway in time. It was extremely difficult to keep your airspeed down under those conditions and more than one plane had gone off the end of the runway at Sardy Field.

The mountains presented such an acute hazard that instrument approaches were prohibited at night. If you couldn't maintain visual contact with the ground, then you were out of luck. You had to go find an alternate airport to land at.

Dinah hated Aspen.

So, she opted not to eat anything before the flight. Her stomach had been churning since the night before and she hadn't slept well. Not a great start.

Their clients were two actors from a CW show about sexy vampires, who were going to Aspen for snowboarding purposes. They were extremely put out that Dinah didn't know who they were.

"But we've been in syndication for two years," the lead actor protested.

She had no idea what he was talking about.

He was traditionally handsome in the most non-descript, unmemorable way. His bro and co-star – they kept referring to him as the "second lead" – had a tiny body and a huge head, like a Bobblehead doll. They explained to Dinah that proportionally this was ideal for television screens. They were also so skinny that she could see their ribs through their thin but pricey t-shirts. On camera, this translated to looking "ripped." All *women* looked obese on camera, no matter what. This indisputable fact was communicated with great empathy by the second lead.

The three of them waited over two hours for the owner but the lead and the second lead were both super stoned, so time was nothing but a false construct for them.

The owner apologized profusely when he did arrive. There'd been an accident on the 210. Wait, that meant that he had *driven* in from Arizona. Which was a four-and-a-half-hour drive. Which meant that he'd been up since at least two a.m.

Awesome.

And Aspen was approximately 626 miles from John Wayne Airport, which in a King Air 200, would take about 3 hours each way. So, six hours of flying total after driving for four hours and change and being awake since the middle of the night.

Awesome.

And the forecast for Aspen was increasing clouds and snow, with possible windshear in the vicinity.

Awesome.

You couldn't tell the owner was fatigued by his demeanor. He was the very definition of affable, fist-bumping the vampire actors and showing them around the aircraft, like an excited kid.

"What do you think, beautiful?" he asked her, giving the right main tire a playful kick.

"It's a gorgeous plane," she enthused.

And she meant it. Her anticipation of flying in this model for the first time, temporarily distracted her from the stressful circumstances of the flight.

The King Air was a twin turboprop, made by the Beechcraft manufacturing family, who were legendary in aviation. Walter and Olive Beech were aviation royalty, whose marriage had just as many ups and downs as a trip over the Rockies. On one occasion, Olive walked out on her husband in New York City and boarded a train back to her home in Wichita, Kansas at Grand Central. Somewhere, in the Midwest, the train was brought to a sudden halt. Walter had flown after Olive and landed his plane in the middle of the tracks in an effort to win her back.

It worked.

In 1950, after Walter passed away unexpectedly of a heart attack at the age of 59, Olive took over as CEO of Beechcraft. It was absolutely unheard of to have a woman as CEO of anything in the day and she actually signed her name as, "O.A. Beech" on all correspondence, in order to deflect any gender issues. Olive was a champion of female aviatrices and sponsored them in cross country races. One winning team, comprised of record-setter, Louise Thaden and Blanche Noyes, left New York and landed in Los Angeles a full 45 minutes ahead of the 2nd-place team.

When Olive took over the company, it was worth $6.5 million. She ran it for 30 years and then sold it. For $800 million.

Awesome.

"So, are you guys ready to hit it?!" the owner asked.

"Let's do it to it!!" the lead actor howled.

They boarded the plane, and the owner pulled the cabin door closed and locked it.

The actors made a big show of choosing which of the 13 seats to stretch out in.

The second lead touched Dinah on the arm. "Excuse me," he said. "Could I possibly get a spring water?"

The lead actor looked embarrassed on his behalf.

"Bro, she's not the flight attendant," he chastised his buddy.

"Oh man, I'm sorry. I'm such an asshole," he said apologetically. "Are you the pilot's girlfriend?"

"No, I'm also a pilot," Dinah said.

"That's so dope!" he enthused.

"So monstrously cool!" the lead actor added.

"The beverages are in that fridge," Dinah called over her back as she made her way up front. "Help yourselves."

***

It wasn't until they were airborne, that Dinah had a chance to really get a good look at the owner.

He was very exotic-looking. He was clearly of mixed race but which races, she couldn't have told you. His jet-black hair was professionally coiffed and had just the right amount of product in it, which for male pilots, was a rarer occurrence than an eclipse. He was wearing jeans, but they had been ironed and were designer jeans and a light purple dress shirt that looked like it had an astronomical thread count. And his jaw was cut so square that it looked like it could slice a tomato. He should have been extremely attractive.

But he wasn't.

There was something off in his eyes. He never looked directly at you and there just wasn't anything there when you looked at *him*. Just emptiness.

It was unsettling.

"Hey, do you want to land it?" he suddenly asked.

"Oh, I thought that you were going to do all the flying and I was going to observe," she said hurriedly.

"You bet. Here's the thing … I haven't been to Aspen in over a year."

Aspen was a special qualification airport in that you had to have done at least one takeoff and one landing within the last 12 months to have airport currency.

Fuck.

He took her silence for hesitation.

"You know what? Don't worry about it. I got this," he assured her.

"Okay, thanks," she said for some reason, like he was doing her a favor.

Speaking of favors.

"Oh, I almost forgot. Did you bring the letter?"

He snapped his fingers. "Totally slipped my mind. Not a problem, I'll do it for you when we get back to John Wayne. What does it need to say again?"

"It just needs to verify that I work for Sunny Skies Aviation ... and that my monthly salary is $4,000." She grimaced at the last part.

The owner laughed out loud. "Wow! I am very generous."

"Sorry. It just needs to *say* that – you don't have to *pay* me that much."

"Not a problem. Seriously."

"Actually, if you're uncomfortable, you could just take my checking account info. We could set up direct deposit and then I could just show them my bank statement and see if that works."

She could tell by his expression that he did *not* want to do that.

"Yeah, we're really more of a cash business. It's better for us for taxes that way."

"Oh sure, I understand."

"But we'll definitely get that letter taken care of."

"Thanks again."

He gave her a playful punch in the arm.

"Stop apologizing so much, you'll make me think that you're Canadian!"

"Close," Dinah said. "I'm from Minnesota."

"Minne-sohhhda," he exclaimed. "How did you end up in California?"

She hung her head. "I don't want to tell you."

"Well now you have to."

She took a deep breath. "I absolutely abhor snow. Winter is my personal nightmare. I despise it all – the back-breaking shoveling, the filthy slush, the biting cold."

He turned and studied her.

"What about winter sports?"

She snorted.

"Name one."

"Hockey?"

"Concussion."

"Skiing?"

"Broken leg."

"Snowmobiling?"

"Frostbite."

"Ice skating?"

"Sixteen stitches."

"Damn! Curling?"

"You have to use a broom."

"That's fair," he agreed. He snuck a look over his shoulder. "Well, do me a favor and don't slag winter sports to these goons. They're paying $1,200 an hour to rent this plane!"

Dinah also snuck a look into the back.

It sounded awfully rowdy for just two guys.

"I think they've drank that much in whisky." She looked again, and alarm crossed her face. "Do you have a dart game on board?"

"Do I look that stupid?"

"Then they must have brought their own. Who brings a dart board from home?"

The owner turned around and his eyes widened.

"Grab the controls."

He unbelted himself and went back to talk to them. The plane was on autopilot so there wasn't much to do except monitor the instruments. A short time later, the owner slipped back into his seat.

"They said they'll cool it."

Dinah turned around one more time. Now they were throwing the darts at each other instead of at the board.

Awesome.

"So," he said, settling back into their conversation. "You're not a fan of winter. What *do* you like to do?"

She thought about it.

"You know, I'm not sure how to answer that. Ever since I can remember, I've worked at least three jobs, so I never have any free time. Whenever I have a day off, I just do laundry and catch up on errands. And sleep. God, I love sleep."

That evoked a big smile from him.

"You know, that's the problem with California, everyone has to have three jobs to survive. And three roommates. SoCal is the only place I've ever seen where 40-year-olds have roomies."

Dinah nodded. "It's so expensive. But … location, location, location."

"Can't argue with that," the owner said. "Well, beautiful, I'll share the same sage words my father shared with me. And that is, 'work to live, don't live to work'."

Easy for you to say.

"Good advice," she said.

They were interrupted by the lead actor, who struggled to hold himself upright by grabbing the back of Dinah's seat.

"Everything okay?" the owner asked.

"We need to make a quick detour," he slurred.

"To where, exactly?"

"Albuquerque."

\*\*\*

They had to change their flight plan so that they could land in New Mexico. And then file a new one from Albuquerque - KABQ to Aspen - KASE. The reason for the deviation was a model named Mercedes.

The lead actor had met Mercedes at the SXSW Festival last year and when she texted him en route to Aspen, he couldn't resist inviting her to tag along. The only person who seemed to be excited by this change in plans, was him. The second lead now became a third wheel and the whole bros' weekend theme was obliterated.

After they picked Mercedes up, he sulked recalcitrantly in the back of the plane. Mercedes, for her part, didn't seem to notice. Or if she did, didn't seem to care. But the lead actor did. He kept trying to engage the second lead in conversation but to no avail. Eventually he gave up and focused all his attention on the six feet of legs sitting beside him.

Dinah was expecting the owner to be similarly attentive, but he was uncharacteristically quiet after they left Albuquerque. He clearly hadn't wanted to modify their travel plans and looked annoyed with himself for giving in. At least she hoped he was annoyed with himself and not her.

While they were waiting for Mercedes to arrive, she kept checking the deteriorating weather in Aspen.

"It'll be fine," the owner assured her, but he frowned when he saw the visibility was forecast to be less than a mile.

The other issue was the rapidly disappearing day. Daylight Savings hadn't kicked in yet, so sunset was going to take place at about six p.m. And Mercedes had taken quite some time to make her way to the airport. She looked really good when she got there, though. So, there was that.

By the time they were ready to shoot the approach into Sardy Field, the wind was gusting over 35 knots, which was about 45 miles per hour. They were getting tossed around nicely, which wasn't a deal breaker for Dinah and the owner. But there was a lot of whimpering coming from the back.

Mostly from the second lead.

The lead and Mercedes had been dry humping for the last hour and seemed quite committed to that activity.

Dinah dialed in the radio frequency for the weather at Aspen Airport, a service called the ATIS – Automatic Terminal Information Service. She listened to it on a second radio so that the owner could still listen for air traffic control instructions on the first radio.

"I'm back," she said, after the broadcast looped back around.

"What's it looking like?" he tried to ask casually.

"The viz is one and three-quarters."

Which meant that the visibility was being reported as one and three-quarters of a mile.

"What do we need for the approach?"

"Exactly *that*."

That meant to be able to fly the most sophisticated approach for this airport – which required GPS equipment – the visibility could not be less than one and three-quarters of a mile. Otherwise, legally you could not initiate that approach. Never mind the safety considerations in play.

"We're golden!" he said.

And so, they began the RNAV (GPS)-F Approach into Aspen.

And there was no way the viz was one and three-quarters.

"We could divert to Eagle County," Dinah suggested.

"That's 25 miles away," the owner said.

And?

"I really think – "

"Sterile cockpit," he asserted.

That was his way of telling her to shut up.

So, she started watching the altimeter. The minimum altitude they could go to without breaking out of the clouds and seeing the runway, was 10,200 feet mean sea level, which was about 2,400 feet above the ground.

She watched.

13,000 feet.

12,900 feet.

12,500 … no runway.

11,500 … nothing.

11,000 … still no runway.

10,500 … her stomach hurt so bad.

10,400 … 10,300 …

10,200.

She called it. "Missed!"

Which meant that he needed to abort the landing and fly a missed approach.

He shoved the throttles up and started to climb.

"Gear up," he ordered.

She pulled the gear lever and the landing gear retracted.

"Should I let them know that we're going to Eagle County?" she asked.

He peered out the window. "No, it looks like the ceiling is coming up. I'm going to come around and try it again."

But now it was dark out.

"But it's too dark now," she protested.

"It's still dusk. We're good."

It wasn't dusk. It was night.

"But – "

"Call them. You know what? Never mind, I'll do it."

So, the owner called up air traffic control to initiate the approach again while Dinah sat there, stupefied. How lucky were the three in the back, completely ignorant of how much danger they were in? Or maybe they would have preferred to know that they were enjoying – well, the second lead not so much – the last few minutes of their lives?

This time Dinah braced for impact all the way down. No one was more surprised than her when they slammed down on the runway. The owner fishtailed for a few hundred feet before he got the aircraft under control.

She was worried that the owner would want to spend the night in Aspen. In the past, she had been asked to share a hotel room to cut down on costs. She usually ended up paying for her own room. There was no way she'd be able to afford anything here. And she doubted that they'd let her sleep in the lobby.

So even though she was numb with exhaustion, Dinah supported the owner's plan to head back to Orange County immediately after dispensing the passengers.

The departure procedure was not as dire with regards to the weather requirements. Before too long, they were back above the clouds and benefitting from a nice, healthy tailwind. That would cut at least a half hour off their flight time.

Dinah was expecting a redressing for being verbally resistant to the owner. But instead he patted her knee.

"Glad to have you with me on that one," he said.

"I don't know how much help I was," she answered. "I have zero familiarity with the plane."

"Not what I meant," he divulged. "I'm not exactly instrument current at the moment."

To be legal to fly on an instrument flight plan – IFR (Instrument Flight Rules), which they had just done, a pilot had to log six approaches (along with some other maneuvers) within six months. Otherwise, they had to have a safety pilot with them. And if they were flying in actual instrument conditions (IMC – Instrument Meteorological Conditions), that safety pilot had to be instrument-rated and have currency.

"So, I was your safety pilot?"

He patted her knee again.

"Thanks, buddy!"

That meant that if anything had happened, Dinah was technically the PIC – Pilot in Command of the aircraft. And it would have been her ass in a sling. And her career out the door.

Awesome.

When they got back to John Wayne, she slept in her car in the parking lot.

The owner left without giving her the letter of employment.

She still only had 1,437.6 hours.

You know what? Screw it.

She now had 1,443.5 hours.

And her phone woke her up the next morning at six a.m. at the exact same moment that the airport security guard did.

She thought the owner was calling to apologize about the letter.

But he wasn't.

## Chapter Seven

Dinah saw the urn first.

The widower was in his early sixties, with thinning grey hair that stuck out in all directions. His face was deeply lined – he looked like a former smoker. Or maybe a present smoker. She forgot that there were people who still smoked in Southern California.

She quickly called the owner back.

"Hey," she said. "Is this guy planning on scattering some ashes?"

"Wha???" he answered. "If he is, he certainly didn't mention it to me."

The widower had absolutely told the owner the purpose of the flight.

"Well, in addition to being a violation of the California Health Code ..."

"Wait – that's a thing?" he asked.

"It's a thing," she responded. "But beyond that, it's not going to be physically possible."

He thought about it for a few moments.

"Oh, because of the prop wash. Not a problem – just idle the engine and fly downwind."

She had foolishly given him the benefit of the doubt.

"No ... we'd be going in the Cirrus, right? The windows don't open," she pointed out.

While most single engine planes had windows that you could open, even when you were in the air - up to certain speeds - the SR-22 did not. All Cirrus aircraft had doors that flipped up, like a DeLorean. Usually, Dinah kept her door open for ventilation while she was taxiing. She closed it just before takeoff and then the air became cooler as she climbed. It was extremely inadvisable to try and pop a door in the air. Even if it popped by accident, the slipstream was strong enough to hold it closed. Sometimes her flight students wouldn't shut their door firmly enough and it would open slightly as they gained altitude and the air pressure changed. They would always panic, and Dinah would have to reassure them that they weren't going to fall out. No one fell out of a plane who didn't want to.

"Damn, you're right," he acknowledged. "Let me think."

Uh-oh.

"Maybe, I could suggest to him to scatter the ashes on the beach?" Dinah put forth.

"Or how about this? I've got a buddy who rents Cessnas on the field. Let me hit him up real quick. Call you back."

He hung up and Dinah turned to the widower with dread.

"Again, I'm so sorry for your loss."

His eyes began to water. "Thank you. Are we going to be able to make this happen?"

"We're just working out the details. Can I ask? Where did you wish to memorialize your dearly departed?"

"What?"

"Her ashes. Where did you want to scatter them?"

His crinkled face registered recognition.

"Over Catalina. It was our special place."

"Why don't you just take a boat over there?" Dinah asked.

"Oh, Fanny *hated* boats."

Her phone rang. The owner had it all arranged. Dinah could borrow one of the Cessna 172s – which had fully functioning windows –

for an hour. She just had to go up with his buddy for a quick assessment flight before he gave her the aircraft.

"Did you tell him about us scattering the ashes?" she asked.

"Thanks for your discretion on this. I owe you one!"

And he was gone. Again.

So, while the widower waited, becoming more distraught with each passing moment, Dinah went up into the traffic pattern above the airport and did three takeoffs and three landings with the owner's buddy. Each time they taxied past the widower, who had transferred the urn to a small gym bag and was sitting despondently on a bench by the hangar, the owner's buddy waved enthusiastically at him, not understanding the gravity of the situation.

Dinah was judged to be competent, so the buddy got out and the widower got in and off they went.

It was always a risk to have an emotional passenger on board. Emotional people were unpredictable, which could be hazardous. A few years earlier, Dinah had had a frightened pharmaceutical rep try to grab control of the plane on landing. She had managed to calm him down by talking to him, but other pilots had been forced to physically strike passengers in order to get them off the controls. And in one tragic circumstance, a female instructor had died when she was teaching a male firefighter how to get out of a spiral dive, and he became so terrified that he locked on the controls and she couldn't get him off. He flew them right into the ground.

Dinah immediately engaged the widower in conversation.

"So, Catalina was your special place?"

He beamed. "It was indeed. We used to go there all the time to hear Lynda Carter sing at my favorite club."

"Lynda Carter? As in *Wonder Woman*?"

"She has a fabulous voice. And she's aged very well. She's still a stunning woman."

"I did not know that – the part about the singing, I mean. Do you work in the music industry?" she asked

He looked slightly abashed.

"No, I sue people for a living," he replied.

"You're an attorney?"

"Not exactly. What I do is, I take photos and post them on the Internet. People assume the photos are public domain and use them. Then I sue them for copyright infringement."

She wasn't quick enough to hide her initial look of disgust. He noticed.

"I know, it's not the most noble profession. It was the reason Fanny left me."

He started to cry again.

"Wait." She gestured towards the urn. "This is your *ex*-wife?"

He nodded.

"Why didn't you just find some other way to make a living?"

A sob caught in his throat. "I know, right? She was the love of my life. And I let her slip through my fingers. You never appreciate what you have until she's gone!"

He bent over and sobbed. Dinah couldn't help but feel badly for him. She patted his back.

"You're not alone in that sentiment. Trust me, it's an exceptionally large men's club with a worldwide membership."

***

When they were directly over Catalina Island, Dinah asked the widower if there was any specific place he had in mind for the "ceremony."

"Right over there," he said. "Where the buffalo roam."

He meant it quite literally.

Bison had been on Catalina Island since 1924, when they were imported for the filming of a Western, called *The Vanishing American*. When the production company wrapped production, they just left the animals there to fend for themselves. Showbiz!

"The buffalo was the official mascot of our marriage. Not many people know, this but they're very passionate."

Most of the ones on Catalina Island were inbred.

"Could you get a little bit lower?" he asked.

"I'll try," she said. "Legally, I have to be at least 500 feet above the ground."

The FAA regulation was 1,000 feet above a populated area and 500 feet above an unpopulated area. Dinah wasn't sure where a populated area of bison fell within that regulation, but she figured she had some latitude.

She told him to get ready. The widower reached into his bag and extracted the urn. He unscrewed the lid.

And began to sing.

*"Home, home on the range / Where the deer and the antelope play"*

He then reached into the bag again and withdrew a large wooden spoon and began to spoon Fanny's ashes out of his window.

*"Where seldom is heard a discouraging word"*

A moment too late, Dinah realized that the right rear window had been left open. As the widower spooned the ashes out the front window, they blew right back into the plane, coating the upholstery.

"Stop!" Dinah yelled.

He stopped singing.

"No! Stop with the ashes!" She reached back and closed the window, coating her bare arm and hands with the remains of Fanny.

*"And the skies are not cloudy all day"*

***

On the way back to the airport, the widower's cries devolved into silent shaking.

"Are you okay?" Dinah asked him as gently as she could.

"I am," he said, wiping his nose with his sleeve. "You've been exceedingly kind. Thank you."

"You're welcome."

"And thank you for taking me up on such short notice. My situation was very time sensitive," he confided.

"Was that for religious reasons?"

"Not at all. I grabbed the urn during the visitation at her second husband's home."

"Wait, what?"

He nodded.

"I really needed to unload the contents before they caught up to me."

She gripped the yoke and tried to control her breathing.

"Fanny's family doesn't know you did this. You didn't have their permission?!"

He grinned like a Cheshire cat, "Romantic, right?"

***

As they taxied in, Dinah prayed she wouldn't see irate family members waiting for them on the other side of the fence. But luckily, the coast was clear. Not so luckily, the owner's buddy was out front when they parked the plane and he was volcanic when he saw the backseat. He called the owner an "asshole," and went on a short rant, professing that this was par for the course for him and that he should never have let his guard down.

Dinah felt awful and she offered to clean the plane. He left and returned, dragging a Shop-Vac. She spent the next two hours sucking up Fanny.

Finally, after wearing the same clothes for approximately 32 hours, Dinah did her best to dust herself off and crawled into her car. Mercifully, traffic wasn't too bad, and she reached the Valley in under two hours.

She needed to get her mail – it had been a few days – so she had to risk a Kristina encounter. But luckily, the office was dark, and the door was closed. Small blessings. Oh wait, it was Sunday, that's why the office was closed. Dinah didn't even know what day of the week it was anymore.

As she walked down the hallway towards her apartment, she could see a package had been left in front of her door. It was from Ines. Another work of art.

Ines was a talented painter who had never caught a break. Raw talent had so little to do with an artist's success anymore. If you didn't know someone who could open doors for you then they remained permanently shut, regardless of your ability. Cronyism and nepotism were the flavors of the day. Bye bye, Schwab's Drug Store. Adieu, Andy Warhol. Lately, Ines had been creating a series based on the same theme. She had shared with Dinah that her favorite work was Edvard Munch's *Der Schrei der Natur* – better known as *The Scream*. So, she had self-commissioned a series of her favorite female celebrities, all painted in the style of *The Scream*.

And she had been extremely generous with her bestowments. Thus far, Dinah had a scream version of Jennifer Aniston, Angela

Lansbury, and Oprah Winfrey. They were all in her closet because her ex-boyfriend couldn't stand them – he called them "feminist bullshit," and said they creeped him out. She carried the newest addition inside and unwrapped it. The face of Dolly Parton screamed back at her.

Inside the apartment, even though she was filthy and numb with fatigue, Dinah got a hammer and her picture-hanging kit from under the kitchen sink, carefully scouting for roaches before she reached in. She hung all four pictures, giving Dolly the place of honor over her bed. If there was an earthquake, she would get smacked in the face by Dolly Parton. Not a bad way to go.

After a shower and a nap, she updated her logbook.

She had 1,445.2 hours.

## Chapter Eight

The farmer was having an extremely earnest conversation with Gretchen the cow when Tammy caught up with him.

"Sorry," she apologized. "It took my parents forever to leave."

Earlier that week, Tammy had ridden her bike to the care facility to make the farmer an offer he couldn't refuse. She found him in the middle of a massive group coloring circle. A poster, depicting Homer's *Odyssey*, was laid out on a large, round craft table. The farmer was coloring in the Sirens.

He didn't look at all surprised to see her.

"What can I do you for, Amelia Earhart?" he asked.

"Funny that you should ask, "she said. "I want you to teach me how to fly."

"You do now, do you?"

"Yes. But I'm not sure when I can train or how often. And I don't have any money."

"So, what you're saying is that you're a typical flight student."

He didn't say "no", so she took that as a "yes" and sure enough, here he was, on the day and time she had texted him. The farmer had texted back. He had texting on his phone. She was stunned to discover that nugget of information.

"Ready to go?" she asked him.

"That'll be the exact question the priest asks me. And the answer will be the same."

As they walked over to the barn to pull the plane out, Tammy became curious.

"What were you and Gretchen talking about?"

"Our mutual love of soymilk."

***

"Okay, level off here." The farmer pointed to a nice flat area below. There wasn't a cloud in the sky today and the bumpiness had evened out as they had climbed through 4,000 feet.

Tammy eased the nose forward and gave the speed a few moments to catch up before she pulled back on the throttle.

"Good girl!" he said. "You didn't take the power off right away."

"You said not to, right?" she replied. "Otherwise the plane will start descending again."

"Exactly, and you'll be chasing that 4,000-foot altitude all day long. Now trim it out."

Tammy leaned over and moved a small black plastic disk that lay between the seats. The elevator trim took over some of the pressure so that she didn't have to hold the yoke so tightly.

"What are you going to teach me today?"

He rubbed his hands together. "How to get out of a stall."

"Is that like, when the engine stalls and you have to turn the key to restart it?"

"Nice try, but no. That's technically an engine failure and we're going to do that next."

"What??"

He ignored her.

"A stall is when the wing stalls and then it no longer provides lift and down you go."

She frowned. "How does that happen?"

"All kinds of reasons. Maybe your nose is too high, maybe you're going too fast and you hit turbulence, maybe you're turning too steeply and there's too much g-force – 'g' meaning gravitational. See the leading edge of the wing out there?"

He had her look out the window to her left.

"Yes."

"Okay, well the air has to hit that leading edge at the perfect angle to provide lift – that's called the 'angle of attack'."

"The angle of attack," she repeated.

"If the 'critical' angle of attack – which is usually about 16 degrees - is exceeded, then the wing stalls. I'm going to teach you how to recover from that."

Tammy furrowed her brow. "Wouldn't it just be easier not to ever stall the airplane?"

The farmer guffawed.

"It would, but we *are* talking about pilots here. Some of them are not the sharpest tools in the shed."

"I thought you had to be really smart to be a pilot," Tammy said. "Like, good in science and stuff."

"Young lady, the very first time that I soloed, I went to pull the throttle back and instead I accidentally pulled the mixture knob all the way out and shut off the fuel supply to the engine."

"You did?!"

"I did. Darwinism is a common theme in aviation. Learn that."

The farmer had Tammy slow the plane down and then he extended the flaps – which slowed it down even more. He told her to keep raising the nose until the plane started to buffet and the stall warning horn went off.

It made a loud piercing noise.

"That's an upsetting sound," Tammy complained.

"It's meant to be – it's letting you know that you're about to stall. You don't want it to sound like Streisand."

After that came the scariest part. The nose of the plane suddenly dipped down. Tammy found herself staring at the ground.

But instead of pulling up, the farmer instead pushed forward on the yoke. He added full power with the throttle and then slowly eased the nose back up, brought the flaps up a little at a time and levelled the plane back off again at 4,000 feet.

"Okay, I did not understand that at all," she said.

"Simple, the only way to break a stall is to push forward on the yoke. What happens if I pull back?"

She ruminated on this.

"If you pull back more, then the angle of attack gets bigger and the stall gets worse."

"Yes! By pushing forward slightly, you are decreasing the angle of attack and reengaging lift over the wings. Okay, now you do it."

Sweat broke out on her upper lip.

"That's okay. I'm good."

He smiled. "I know you're scared. Everyone is at first, nobody likes stalls. But I promise you it will get easier and one day, knowing how to get out of a stall will save your life. That's an important part of being a pilot – knowing how to get yourself through stressful situations – no matter what life throws at you."

She took a deep breath.

"Okay, but could I build up to it? Could we just fly straight and level for a while first?"

"I've got nowhere to be," he said.

So, they flew a racetrack pattern while Tammy screwed up her courage.

"How come your family decided to come here?" he asked.

"To Canada?"

"Oh no, I get why people come to Canada, it's the best country in the world. I meant, why *Kapuskasing*? We don't get a lot of ... um ..."

"Tan people?"

"Your words, not mine but yes. We're pretty far north up here. Your family didn't want to be in Toronto with all the other folks from India?"

"We're not Indian. We're Sri Lankan."

"Isn't that kind of the same thing?" the farmer asked innocently.

"Do you like it when people think you're an American? Isn't *that* kind of the same thing?"

"Jesus Murphy, no!"

Tammy smirked.

"My family was sponsored to move here by the Kapuskasing Lion's Club," she said.

"Well that was pretty nice of them."

"So, they keep reminding us. We wonder at what point we will be able to stop saying, 'thank you'."

This last comment evoked a small smile from the farmer.

"But why didn't you want to stay in Sri Lanka?" he queried.

"It's not that we didn't want to, it's that we couldn't – it wasn't safe."

She banked the plane gently to the left.

"Wait, isn't Sri Lanka still under British rule?"

"Not since 1972, when it was Ceylon. Then it became a republic, but the trouble started long before then. The British always gave preferential treatment to the Sinhalese population and basically shafted the Tamil people. So, the Tamils started fighting back. And then the Sinhalese retaliated and so on and so on. Thousands of people have been massacred," Tammy explained.

"And your family is …?"

"We're Sinhalese."

She banked again.

"Well I hope you feel safer here, you and your parents," he said.

"We do, thank you. Sometimes it feels uncomfortable to be so different. But you also get to feel unique and special. And you Canadians love to overcompensate. Your country is kind of like an insecure teenager. It's like you want to feel superior to everyone else but you're also super insecure and need to be liked. Here in such a small town, that works for me. I feel like the Buddhist Britney Spears. In Toronto, I would disappear into the crowd. And unfortunately, it is still somewhat dangerous there."

"In Toronto? Go on!" he exclaimed.

"It's a sad thing but the fights that existed back home, are often brought with us to our new country. The Tamil and Sinhalese gangs are still going at it here."

"Sometimes, it's not enough to change your physical location to start fresh. You have to change things up here." The farmer tapped his temple.

Tammy nodded.

"Okay, enough stalling from the stalling. You ready? I'll put you in one, okay? And then when I yell, 'recover,' you get out of the stall."

The farmer stalled the aircraft.

"Recover."

Tammy pushed forward on the yoke so hard that they both hit their heads on the roof of the plane. The aircraft was facing straight down. She screamed and the farmer laughed and took control.

"Darn near everybody does that the first time," he explained. "I want you to just release the back pressure – don't push so hard. You just need to break the stall, not break the airplane."

"I need a minute."

She flew straight and level. She was breathing quite hard and beads of sweat rolled down her temples.

"So, *you* like it here. How about your parents?" He tried to distract her from the blood that was likely thundering through her ears.

"I guess. I mean I never ask."

"They sure are hard workers. Old Man Smythe never kept the hours they do."

She nodded proudly.

"Sri Lankans have amazing work ethic. Some of my cousins work in restaurants down in Toronto. They never miss work and if for any reason they must, they never call in sick. They send another cousin to take their place."

The farmer chuckled.

She blushed.

"I know – it's weird. And they all have multiple jobs. My oldest cousin, worked in two different restaurants - one lunch shift, one dinner shift – seven days a week and after two years, he was able to buy a small house and send for his bride."

"That's really something. I admire folks who want to make a better life for themselves. It shows the highest degree of integrity."

Tammy blushed again.

"Well, they're not about the integrity 24/7. They're not saints."

"How so?" he asked.

"Probably shouldn't tell you this but my cousin told me that they all share the same TTC Pass."

TTC stood for Toronto Transit Commission and was the public transport company in Toronto. Residents paid a monthly fee to get a "TTC Pass" that allowed them to travel as much as they wanted or needed to by bus, streetcar, or subway. The passes were government subsidized but they still kept going up in price. Presently a monthly pass was almost $130.

"How do they do that?" the farmer asked.

"Well, my cousin and all his friends work different shifts, so they just hand the pass off to each other at the station."

"And that works?"

She nodded.

"Apparently. My cousin says that if Canadians are too stupid to tell them all apart, then why should they spend all that extra money on more passes."

The farmer almost choked.

"You know what? I think your cousin should run for Prime Minister."

She laughed.

"Okay, ready for Round Two?"

She gulped. "Nope."

"That's what I like to hear."

This time when he yelled, "recover," Tammy tried her best to control her adrenaline and pushed much more gently on the yoke. The plane eased out of the stall.

"There ya go! Nicely done!"

"Was that better?" she asked.

"That was darn near perfect."

"Oh good. Can we stop doing stalls then?"

He snapped his fingers, like a genie.

"Your wish is my command," he said and then paled. "Oh bugger, was that racist?"

"Aladdin was Arabian so that was probably racist, just not racist towards me." She grinned cheekily at him.

"Phew."

"Still racist though."

"Duly noted."

The farmer quickly glanced outside to orient himself and then reached out and pulled the throttle all the way out.

"What's going on?" Tammy cried.

"Engine failure time!"

"Can we go back to doing stalls??!!!"

# Chapter Nine

**A** new client had booked a series of regularly scheduled flights with Sunny Skies. And the woman had specifically requested a female pilot. Ironically, Dinah was never flattered by these types of requests – it felt like tokenism. She arrived at the airport, in her usual wary state as the owner had given her little information beyond that.

When she saw the head scarf, she instantly understood.

Sherry actually apologized for booking the flights.

"I've been driving to chemo but lately I've been feeling so weak, it's quicker if I fly."

Dinah was extra gentle belting her in.

On the flight into Santa Monica Airport, the apologizing continued.

"I hope my requesting a female pilot, didn't antagonize you," Sherry said.

Dinah grimaced. "Usually, that request is followed by another request that I show up in a pencil skirt and high heels. With the hat on."

Sherry gasped. "You're not serious?"

Dinah nodded affirmatively.

"Jesus. What is wrong with the world?"

"Everything," Dinah replied.

"You know what? You're right," Sherry agreed. "When I was in college, I worked on a cruise ship in one of the dance shows. We had a weekly weigh-in to make sure the costumes still fit."

"What happened if it didn't?" Dinah asked.

"It was cheaper to find another dancer who fit the costume than to alter it."

"What is wrong with the world?"

"Everything!" Sherry reiterated. "So, full disclosure, the reason I asked for a woman is that I never know how I'm going to feel afterwards, and I figured a guy wouldn't be able to handle it."

Dinah felt strangely flattered.

"Of course, whatever you need."

"Thank you. I appreciate it."

There was a brief lull. Somehow Sherry knew exactly what Dinah was hesitant to ask.

"It's Stage 4."

Her heart sank for this woman.

"I'm so sorry."

"Well, it could be worse. I'm not married and don't have kids. Parents are both dead and I'm an only child so at least I'm not leaving behind a lot of mourners."

"Pets?" Dinah asked.

Sherry shook her head. "I travel too much for work. Well, I *did* travel too much … until recently."

"Well, I know you're not a pilot since *I'm* flying *you*. Do you work in the airline industry?"

"I was a lobbyist," Sherry responded.

"Oh," Dinah exclaimed. "I don't know much about that. For the oil industry?"

"Worse," Sherry said. "Sugar."

Dinah's brow furrowed. "Sugar is worse than oil? I didn't know that."

Sherry smiled wryly. "Sugar is legalized cocaine. It's the most powerful lobby in America."

"That's fascinating. And slightly terrifying. Forgive my ignorance, but what exactly does a lobbyist do?"

"Whatever is necessary. We push the positive aspects of sugar, the economic benefits. We try to get federal funding wherever and however we can. We wine and dine senators so that they'll push our bills through. We're basically political pimps."

Dinah was slightly shocked at Sherry's candidness and it must have showed.

"Don't worry, I lost my soul a long time ago. You literally can't offend me. Go ahead."

Dinah still tried to choose her words carefully. "But did you like your job? I mean, is that what you always wanted to do?"

Sherry's scarf had started to slide back on her head, and she adjusted it before she continued. There was not a trace of self-consciousness in her action.

"I *wanted* to be a seal trainer. But there's not a lot of money in that. Plus, the whole captivity thing bothered me. So, I headed to Washington."

Dinah pressed her.

"Do you ... did you ... like it?"

Sherry pondered a moment before answering.

"I certainly liked the paycheck. And all the fringe benefits. The travel ... the lifestyle. And I was good at it. It's so gratifying to know that you excel at your job. I could convince anyone of pretty much anything. I liked the hunt and honestly, the rejection was just a challenge."

Dinah shuddered. "I've never been any good at sales."

"Yes, but that's the thing isn't it? We're all selling some aspect of ourselves in whatever job we have. We either become effective at self-promotion or we don't progress."

"I've always had a problem with confidence," Dinah confided. "Not to mention the pressure to 'represent'."

Sherry snorted. "Welcome to being a woman. We inherently seem to have a need to please when really the only people we should be pleasing are ourselves. In my case, I just refused to listen to that voice in my head. And I fed off every scrap of success and grew bigger as a result. The problem is that success is addictive." She held up a finger. "Not as addictive as sugar, but still. And especially being one of the few women on Capitol Hill, you start to feel like a pioneer, which feeds your ego even more. Which then demands more success. So, you're never satisfied, constantly restless instead."

Santa Monica Pier was just coming into view. Dinah drew an imaginary line inland from the west, like she always did, and there was the runway.

"You know what, you just reminded me of?" she asked, not expecting an answer. "Audrey II, from *Little Shop of Horrors*."

"The plant?" Sherry asked. "'Feed me, Seymour!' I was also in the drama club in high school."

"So ... seal trainer/dancer/actor?" Dinah joked.

"Yes ... and in a way, that's exactly what I became."

\*\*\*

There was a volunteer from the Cancer Society waiting at the airport to drive Sherry to UCLA Medical Center. Dinah chatted with her while Sherry used the restroom.

"This is so kind of you," Dinah commented.

The volunteer was a slightly built woman in her mid-twenties with purple hair in an adorable bob. Her name was Nell.

"Hey, somebody did it for me. Got to pay it forward," Nell said.

Something was nagging at Dinah.

"I'm curious – and please let me know if this is too personal – but cancer is so intense ... would you not have preferred a spouse or family member, you know, someone close to you, to take you to treatment?"

"No, quite the opposite," Nell answered. "You're already dealing with so much. And then you've got all the emotional baggage that comes with family getting involved ... the guilt, feeling like a burden, feeling resentful that they're not handling it as well as you are. Sometimes it's just easier to have a total stranger help you with your problems."

Dinah felt like an explosion had just gone off in her head.

"My God, thank you for your honesty. That's so courageous."

"Family is really a double-edged sword. They are a great support system but that support system does not come without strings attached. Strangers equals no strings."

Sherry returned from the restroom and the two headed off after Dinah reassured her that it was no trouble at all to wait for her to return.

"I'll grab a bite of lunch at the Spitfire Grill," she said.

The Spitfire Grill was across the street from the airport. There used to be a fantastic restaurant right on the field, called Typhoon, but it had shuttered, following the closures of most of the flight schools and many other businesses that had been located at the airport.

Santa Monica Airport had a tempestuous history. It was opened in 1928 and used as a staging airport during World War II. After the war ended, when it was still called Clover Field, it was the base of the Douglas Aircraft Factory. But with the boom that came after the war, houses and businesses built themselves up around the airport and the residents began complaining about the noise and safety issues. And the proliferation of jets exacerbated the issue.

Dinah had always advocated that the airport was there first and if you got a $3 million house for $800,000, you shouldn't be surprised that it was because it was under a flight path. But there was a lot of wealth and influence in Santa Monica and there was sufficient pressure to chase airport businesses away.

Those who remained, dealt with a lot of caveats. There were strict time constraints on when you could land and take off and strictly monitored noise restrictions. On weekends and holidays, pilots couldn't practice in the traffic pattern and the rest of the time, they were charged $20 each time they landed. Dinah had a student solo at Santa Monica last spring, and it cost him $160 in landing fees. Some pilots tried to outsmart the system by doing low passes and never touching their wheels down, but the cameras recorded their tail numbers and invoices were issued anyway.

Santa Monica Airport also couldn't seem to catch a break. Every time, its proponents gained traction on its behalf, there was another crash, furthering the opposition's case. It didn't help when it was a high-profile celebrity having to do an emergency landing at nearby Penmar Golf Course. Or the day that a student pilot had bounced off the end of the runway and crashed into a neighboring home. Some housepainters had pulled him clear of the aircraft – he had a broken leg – but the crash had gotten a lot of airplay and it renewed the battle. The painters had gone so far as to sue the flight school that dispatched the student, claiming that the fuel fumes from the plane had caused them health issues. House painters ... who painted houses ... and ingested paint fumes ... for a living ... every day ... all day long.

The federal lease on the land was due to expire on Dec. 31, 2028 and it was likely the airport would close permanently at that time. There were stipulations as to how the land could be reallocated subsequent to that. It could only be a park, recreational facility, or an open space. But it was such a prime pocket of land – just a few blocks from the beach – that developers would likely find some palms to grease and the eventual "park" would have a multi-million-dollar condo complex in the middle of it.

Dinah enjoyed one of the last "Howard Hughes" salads – it was just a Caesar – she would likely ever have at the Spitfire. After she finished, she wandered back across the street and sat on one of the observation benches so she could judge the landings of other harshly.

Which was a favorite hobby of all pilots.

Shortly after 2 p.m., Nell's white Fiat pulled into an open parking spot, of which there were many these days. The engine turned off. But nobody got out.

This was not a good sign.

***

The chemo session had been an especially brutal one.

Sherry had been sick twice in the car on the way back to the airport. Dinah helped Nell clean it up while Sherry lay down in the nearby grass, apologizing profusely yet again.

Nell seemed reticent to leave them.

"We're fine," Dinah assured her. "We'll just sit until she feels well enough to go."

"Okay then, if you're sure," Nell capitulated. "See you same day and time in a few weeks, yeah?"

Sherry gave her a shaky thumbs up from her prostrate position.

Dinah helped Sherry over to the bench, so they could watch the planes.

"I'm really sorry about this," Sherry said. "If you have to go …"

"Are you out of your mind?" Dinah exclaimed. "The second I leave some skeevy private pilot will be all over you."

Sherry looked down at herself. The clothes that were hanging so loosely on her were stained with vomit.

"You know," she said, "I used to be so obsessed with how my body looked. I thought I had fat ankles, so I used to walk around with ankle weights on. And I existed on a diet of cigarettes and Wheat Thins.

It seems so silly now. I took my beautiful healthy body for granted. I'd give anything to have that body back now."

Dinah made an effort to raise her spirits.

"Will you go back to lobbying after you go into remission?"

Sherry gave her a sympathetic glance, recognizing the charade but graciously and silently agreeing to play along.

"I don't think so. That rat race doesn't appeal to me anymore. And let me tell you, there was never a more apt term."

"Back to the seal training then?"

"The seals are on their own. The one good result from working myself to death for the last few decades is that I am very comfortable financially. Comfortable enough that I never have to work again."

Dinah sighed. "I wish."

She blushed with shame at the thought of expressing envy towards a woman with Stage 4 breast cancer.

"When people say that money doesn't buy you happiness, they may be wrong but what it does buy you is peace of mind. And more importantly, it buys you options. And that's key. Because life without money isn't living, it's just surviving."

Sherry doubled over in pain. Dinah rubbed her back.

"I'm okay."

They heard a screech of tires and looked over at the runway.

"That landing sucked," Sherry said. "At least I'm not that guy."

"Totally pancaked it," Dinah added.

Dinah watched Sherry's labored breathing carefully. Eventually Sherry raised her head back up and looked Dinah right in the eye.

"I'm not afraid, you know," Sherry said.

"Of dying," Dinah assumed.

"No, dying's the easy part," Sherry clarified. "When I first got the diagnosis, I was afraid, not of dying, you know but that I had wasted my life. Our society is so goal-oriented, you know. And social media has made it so much worse. We're all judged for our material achievements. We can only estimate our own worth by the valuations of others."

Dinah nodded her head vigorously.

"It's like Maslow's Pyramid," she said. "I studied it in my Fundamentals of Flight Instructing course."

Sherry pointed to herself. "Minored in psychology in college. How does it go again? First are *physiological needs* – like food and sleep. Then *safety needs* – physical and financial."

"Exactly. Then *love and belonging* and after that *esteem*."

"And the top of the pyramid is *self-actualization*, right? But we all seem to have plateaued at *esteem*. We can't achieve our full potential as human beings because we just mirror ourselves back to everyone else."

Dinah thought on this. "Do you think that's why people are so unhappy?"

Sherry responded slowly. "Partly. Honestly, I think happiness is a false Western ideal. Who decided that we're supposed to be happy all the time? And that if you're not, then you are clearly doing something wrong? Life is supposed to be a series of ups and downs. Do you think that cavemen sat around wondering why they didn't feel fulfilled all the time?"

"Now you sound like a Buddhist."

"Maybe I am. I thought I was an atheist but I'm kind of chickening out in the 11th hour. I've just always abhorred organized religion … talk about your pyramids … they're the worst pyramid scheme in history."

Dinah stared at her. Rapt.

"So, Sherry, as an atheist guru …"

Sherry laughed which degenerated into a coughing fit. Dinah grabbed her hand.

"I'm good … maybe agnostic," Sherry assured her.

"I'm quite serious, as an *agnostic* guru, how should I live my life so that I can achieve the top of the pyramid … the summit of self-actualization?"

"If I could do it all again," Sherry asserted. "I wouldn't worry so much about leaving a mark, you know. Really the only person your life needs to matter to, is you."

Dinah made a fireworks sound effect.

"Words to live by," Dinah said.

"And do everything you can in that life to maximize the mirth and to minimize the misery."

Dinah was quiet this time.

"Words to leave by," Sherry said softly.

And the two women sat there for another 40 minutes, holding hands, and watching planes, some making good landings and some making bad ones. One hand was sunburned and muscular and the other hand was trembling and veiny. Yet both hands were somehow equally strong.

1446.0 hours.

## Chapter Ten

The deejay was 14 when his mother brought him to Irvine, California from Seoul, South Korea. They were supposed to be visiting for two weeks but at the end of two weeks, his mother, Jin, went back to South Korea by herself and he was left with his auntie, Hee-young.

That was simply how it was done.

When he was 16, he and his cousin took a bus for 2 hours in each direction to work in a box manufacturing warehouse for 12-hour shifts. He did this for three years. He never went back to Seoul because he couldn't. But his mother visited once more during those three years. It was to deliver his younger brother, who was also left behind to pursue a better life.

At the age of 19, the deejay was fortunate enough to be sponsored for a 3-year work visa by the manufacturing company – by then he had moved into production design. And from that he attained his green card. He was one of the lucky ones. Qualifying for a green card was difficult. You could do it through marriage, but a green card marriage was pricey and risky. And he didn't have time to do it the old-fashioned way. You could invest in real estate or start your own business – so long as you had $1.8 million. You could qualify under the category of, "an alien of extraordinary ability," but that was reserved for Nobel Prize recipients and Emmy winners. People who worked in box factories or won People's Choice Awards did not typically make the cut. Or you could get a work visa, and piggyback that to a green card but it had to be under the auspices of a specific company. And it was only valid so long as you continued to work for that company. Many companies wanted no part of sponsorship. It cost them $5,000 per employee to apply and it opened them up to scrutinization by the USCIS – United States Citizenship and Immigration Services. Other companies used the process as a means of sanctioned slavery – knowing that the visa holder was beholden to them to stay in the country legally. But the deejay had been well-briefed by his relatives and he avoided all the pitfalls, got hired by an ethical, equitable company, worked his ass off, didn't cause any trouble and ultimately got what he came for.

That was how it was done.

You had to have your green card for five years before you could apply for citizenship – unless you got it through marriage, then it was only three years. The deejay filled out the application himself – lawyers were too expensive – and reported to a USCIS center to have his fingerprints taken. A few months later, there was an interview and citizenship test. During the interview, the immigration officer tested him on his written and spoken comprehension of English and then there were a series of questions taken from a 100-question knowledge bank.

Applicants had to get seven out of ten questions correct. Some of the questions were extremely easy, like: "What body of water lies to the west of the United States?" Some were a little more challenging, like: "How many amendments are there in the Bill of Rights?" Some were outright offensive, like: "During the Cold War, what was the main concern of the United States?" After the deejay got the first seven questions, without any problems – of course he had studied extensively and been stringently tested at home - the immigration officer congratulated him and commented that no one who was *born* in America would be able to pass that test. And then he winked at him.

Once the deejay had his citizenship then he was able to sponsor other immediate family members to come to the United States.

Because that's how *that* was done.

A few years later, his mother, his sister, Yuna, and his grandmother, Mi-kyong, moved to Irvine as well. None of them could work however, so he was the chief breadwinner in his family.

He was 23.

The deejay stuff really began by accident. Like a lot of teenagers who came to the U.S. from other countries, he was eager to embrace the culture of America. Or in his case, specifically the culture of Orange County. He downloaded Spotify – not the version you paid for, the free one – and listened to everything he could get his hands on. Truth be told, he didn't like a lot of musical genres or rather just couldn't relate to them. But there was one … oh, there was *that* one that to him, defined the sunny beach lifestyle that embodied life in the Golden State. And that genre was "yacht rock." Boz Scaggs, The Doobie Brothers, Steely Dan, Ambrosia, Seals & Croft, England Dan and John Ford Coley, Hall & Oates – any smooth 1970s to early 1980s easy listening sounds that were made by white men *for* white men – sated his soul.

His mother would come into his room, utterly confused.

"What is this?"

"It's yacht rock."

"Why?"

"I don't know. I guess because rich old white guys listen to it on their yachts," he surmised.

"But you are not rich old white guy. And you don't have yacht," she puzzled.

He just shrugged and turned up the sweet sounds of "Baby Come Back" by Player.

His friends were equally mystified.

"Dude, what *the* fuck?"

\*\*\*

It wasn't until he heard Beastie Boys', "Sure Shot" one evening at Tito's Taco Stand that he was hit by a bolt of lightning.

He started looking on Craig's List for mixing and sampling equipment and cruising yard sales for old turntables. And he began creating a sound. A sound that was fluffy, soothing, and superfluous with an underlying beat that was raw, aggressive, and unrelenting.

And it was genius.

He took it slow. First playing for his friends in his room.

"Dude, what the *fuck*?!"

Then he did some backyard parties for family acquaintances.

And then someone booked him for a Korean quinceañera – that was a real thing in California.

One of the guests owned a club in Huntington Beach. The deejay became a featured act every other Saturday. Then other clubs started requesting him. After that, he started getting fans. He had a fanbase. They followed him from gig to gig, selling out venues.

And before long, the gigs moved to larger venues and bigger cities.

He appeared at Playhouse, right on Hollywood Boulevard. Quite honestly, he was under the impression that the booker might have thought he got a really good deal on Steve Aoki but hell, he liked what he heard and gave him a regular monthly spot so who cared.

At this point, the deejay was still living with his family, and extended family. He started to hint at maybe getting his own place, but his mother, Jin, teared up just at the mention of it, so he delayed his emancipation plans.

But he spent progressively less and less time at home. Instead, he flaunted his new-found financial freedom and popularity up and down the coastline. He had had to behave so exemplarily for so many years, while other young men his age raged. While he had been illegal, he couldn't do anything that called attention to himself. He lived under the radar, always in fear of being made an example of. He was quiet, perennially polite, always exercised self-control, never made eye contact. Any time a police cruiser was nearby, his stomach flipflopped and he held his breath until it was gone. He played it smart, so he never had any trouble.

Until Labor Day weekend.

It started at Tony's in Redondo Beach. Tony's was this really cool bar right on the pier. And if you ordered one of their top-notch mai tais, you got to keep the souvenir glass that it came in. Which was also really cool. By three in the afternoon, the deejay had six of these glasses.

Then one of his buddies suggested that it might be really cool to rent a couple of jet skis. And the three bikini-clad girls – Amber, Ashley and Ainsley – that they had met at Tony's also thought this would be really cool.

Without debate, the deejay was smart. But he was also having fun, which he never got to do. Even when he was deejaying, he was still working, it was everyone else who was having fun. He never got to have fun. Never. Just this once. Just this once, he wanted to be like everyone else on Labor Day. So just this once, he wasn't smart. He was very, very stupid.

He was only a few hundred yards from the shore when the Harbor Patrol nabbed him. Even though it was his first time on a jet ski, he got the hang of it quickly. But he wasn't as adept at the turns. He kept turning too abruptly. And the third time, he tried it, one of the "A's," maybe Ainsley, fell off the back. She was fine, she laughed when she eventually surfaced but the officer was not equally amused.

The deejay thought he would just be ordered back onto land or that they would tow the jet ski, but it ended up being much more serious than that. He was cuffed, put in the back of a police vehicle, and transported down to the station, where he was charged with impaired driving.

He didn't even know you could be charged with drunk driving a jet ski.

His friends downplayed the event, emphasizing that everyone in SoCal had at least one DUI. Welcome to the club.

*Dude*, what the fuck!

He did his best to retain his composure and not lose face in front of his group. But truth be told, he was petrified. After the Lyft dropped him off in front of his aunt's house, he slunk back into the carport and cried. That was about enough fun for the moment.

The deejay managed to withhold this shameful event from his family. And he was lucky. He got off with a four-month suspension and mandatory enrollment in a DUI Education course. He worked through his ignominy and self-loathing by listening over and over to Christopher Cross' "Sailing."

He was about two months into his suspension, when he had a huge plum drop into his lap. Omnia, in Vegas, had had a last-minute cancellation and needed someone for a residency. And it was a lot … *a lot* … of money. More money than all his other gigs combined.

Obviously, he couldn't drive to Las Vegas, but he was smart, he'd figure something out.

The first gig was that night. In six hours.

\*\*\*

Dinah was so tired of getting these last-minute calls to fly.

She intellectually understood that it was the nature of the business, but it was also inconsiderate as hell. She was sick of never having any control over her time and an inability to plan anything.

Plus, she was on the first day of her period and the cramps were particularly painful this month. This was one of the times she hated being one of the only 5% of pilots who were women. Male pilots were incredibly squeamish about anything relating to the female reproductive system. One oblique reference to Midol and they would fall apart, deflecting the conversation immediately to that time they got food poisoning in Des Moines. Or their faces would look like the Nazis' at the end of *Raiders of the Lost Ark*. On one occasion, she had been so ill that she had no choice but to send her ex to CVS for supplies. He had been mortified to have been tasked with such an unmanly quest and returned at the speed of light with a package of Depends, having grabbed the first thing off the shelf that looked viable.

So, Dinah didn't feel like bleeding and bouncing around over the broiling hot desert.

She tried to say, no.

She was unsuccessful.

Then a TFR popped up on her *Foreflight*.

*Foreflight* was a ground-breaking aviation app that had weather, charts, flight planning, you name it, on it. You could even pay extra to have your aircraft show up on the chart or airport diagram for increased situational awareness. *Foreflight* would put colored rings around geographical areas where there were TFRs – Temporary Flight Restrictions.

Temporary Flight Restrictions could be imposed over certain areas for emergencies, like fires or large assemblies, like sporting events or presidential visits, like that afternoon.

Presidential TFRs didn't come up with much notice, on purpose, for security reasons. The circle started out in yellow, when it wasn't yet active and turned to red when it was active. This TFR was over all of Las Vegas, including McCarran International and the other two airports, North Las Vegas, and Henderson. And it started in an hour and lasted until 6 p.m.

If a pilot violated TFR airspace, it was an automatic 30-day suspension of their aviation license. After that, there could be other penalties. You could spend up to a year in jail or have a $100,000 fine or have your license permanently revoked.

As soon as Dinah saw the TFR, she tried to call her client, some douche nozzle who just "had to get to Vegas." Nobody "had to get to Vegas." Not even Celine Dion.

But when she got through, it was his voicemail and the automated message said his voicemail was full.

Douche nozzle.

Well, it looked like he was going to be late for whatever pressing matter he had to attend to in Sin City.

***

He was so nice that she felt like a complete asshole.

He was completely understanding about the TFR and suggested that they wait it out at Starbucks, his treat. The deejay had one of those smiles that instantly transformed him from non-descript to devastatingly handsome.

He didn't seem to have a car with him, so Dinah drove. The deejay noticed the hot water bottle in her backseat.

"Are you okay?" he asked.

"Oh, yeah, no, not really," she said. "Just feeling a little under the weather."

"Let's just cancel. I can get a bus or something."

"What time do you need to be in Vegas?" she asked.

He told her and then he told her why he had to be there.

"You absolutely can't take a bus!" Dinah exclaimed. "I'll rally. Trust me. I've dealt with worse."

When they got to Starbucks, he got himself a Grande Coffee Frappuccino and a Venti Iced Latte for her. Then he quickly excused himself and ran across the street to Walgreens. When he returned, he had a bag for her with Extra-Strength Pamprin and a heating pad in it. And a Hershey bar. No nuts. *King* Size. Even chocolate adhered to the patriarchy.

She almost cried. But she didn't.

"I have a sister. And four girl cousins," he offered in the way of explanation.

"This is beyond kind," Dinah said. "I'm a bit embarrassed."

"Why on Earth would you be embarrassed? I'm the one who should be embarrassed ... dragging a sick pilot to Vegas so that I can spin records for a bunch of tourists trying Molly for the first time."

"You're downplaying it," she said. "No pun intended."

He laughed. "For serious, my jam is laughable compared to what you do. You fly planes! Do you have any idea how impressive that is?!!"

She smiled with gratitude.

"I'm so impressive that I almost didn't notice that TFR, which would have been the end of flying planes for me."

He took the straw out of his drink and removed the lid, sipping it directly from the cup.

"Is that a common thing? For pilots to violate a Temporary Flight Restriction. I mean, it sounds pretty serious."

Dinah opened the bottle of Pamprin and chugged one down with her latte.

"Pilots bust TFRs all the time. Some of the stories are hilarious, actually."

He leaned his elbows on the table.

"Tell me your favorite."

"Okay, well, a couple of years ago, there was a Presidential TFR that started on a Thursday at 2 p.m. local time and lasted until 11 a.m. the next day. This was a big one and it included LAX, Burbank, Van Nuys and Santa Monica."

She started giggling, which made him start giggling too.

"Okay," he managed to get out. "What happened?"

"So, around 2:30, Air Force One was taking off from Santa Monica Airport and a Cessna 172 basically flew right across its flight path."

"No!"

"Oh yes. So, two military fighter jets forced this Cessna down at Long Beach Airport."

"They didn't shoot it down?"

"The pilot was lucky they didn't shoot it down. They could have," she said.

"What happened when they got to Long Beach?" the deejay asked. "Did they arrest the guy? Wait, was it a guy?"

"It was a guy alright. And this guy was flying down the coastline from Bellingham, under 2,000 feet all the way."

"Because …"

"Because radar surveillance starts at 2,000 feet."

He frowned.

"I don't get it."

"When the Secret Service and the FBI arrived at the plane and opened it up …"

She started giggling again.

"What??"

"This is so good," she gushed. "When they opened it up, the seats had all been removed and the Cessna, was packed, I mean, *packed*, full of weed!"

He doubled over.

"Dude, no!!"

"Can you imagine this poor guy, flying along with his stash and then suddenly he's surrounded by the Air Force?!"

"He must have been thinking, 'how did they know?!'"

"How did they *know*?!" she echoed.

"What an unlucky bastard!" he lamented.

"And the moral of the story is – "

"Don't smuggle drugs in a 172," he interrupted.

"The moral of the story is," she continued. "If you're going to smuggle weed, be a professional. Check your TFRs."

And she did an ostentatious bow.

"Superb," he said, his eyes sparkling. "Just superb."

\*\*\*

The deejay's fascination with Dinah continued once they were finally airborne.

"You are seriously amazing," he said. "How did you learn all of this?"

"Flying is a pretty steep learning curve," she admitted. "But you just kind of embrace the suck and eventually you stop screwing up every single thing and only screw up every other thing."

He laughed. "Like the radios, for example. They talk so fast and I can't understand a thing they're saying. And how do you know when they're talking to us?"

"You learn to listen for your call sign. And trust me, if you miss a call, you'll know it. You get yelled at. And everyone else on the frequency hears you getting yelled at. Like I said – steep learning curve."

"This is fantastic! This is such a trip!" he enthused.

She looked over at him.

"Do you want to fly it?"

"Dude, seriously?"

"I'm also an instructor. Put your hands on the yoke."

The deejay barely rested the tips of his fingers on the controls.

She smiled encouragingly. "It's not a rattlesnake. You can grab it a little more firmly. Just don't do the death grip."

He exhaled loudly. "If I screw up, you can just override my controls with yours, right?"

"No, actually, that's not a thing. The controls are equal so whoever is strongest, wins."

"Well, I'm a slightly built Asian deejay and you're Wonder Woman so I'm clearly outmatched and over-powered."

She hadn't thought about her cramps in half an hour.

He looked over at her with a huge grin on his face.

"And I'm totally comfortable with that. I'm flying a plane!"

"You're flying a plane!" she said.

"Wait, I *am* flying it, right? I mean, you don't have it on autopilot or anything?"

"I would never do that to you. Yes, you are actually flying this plane."

"I'm flying a mothereffing plane!"

His enthusiasm was so infectious.

"You're flying a mothereffing plane!"

***

Somewhere over Victorville, she had to tell him, they were going to be late. There was a strong headwind and their groundspeed was ridiculous. Dinah looked down and saw cars passing them on the 15 Freeway.

The deejay was magnanimous about it, but she could tell that he was upset. Still, he didn't take it out on her. He texted the booker and then proceeded to use the extra time to go over his set list.

"What kind of music do you play," she asked. "Or is that a stupid question? Sorry, I don't know very much about deejaying."

"That's not a stupid question at all," he assured her. "Well, ideally every deejay has their own unique sound, that's what keeps people coming back."

"So, you're not just playing original songs?"

"Back in the old days, that's definitely how it worked. But deejaying has really evolved into its own art form." He blushed. "Sorry, that sounded pretentious."

"Not at all," she countered. "I can see how animated you are about it. So, tell me how you create your own sound."

He showed her on his laptop. Dinah put the radios on speaker so that she wouldn't miss any calls from ATC – air traffic control. The deejay's screen looked like a cardiogram for an airline executive.

"So, what you do is ... you take samples from songs that you like, and you create your own underlying tracks or mix different tracks to create something new or to reinvent something that already exists," he explained.

He played a few moments of his opening track for the gig that night. Dinah's face lit up with recognition.

"I know that song! It's Poco – 'Crazy Love.' Am I right?"

A look of incredulity crossed the deejay's face. "How in the hell did you know that?"

Dinah could feel herself gearing up.

"Nerd alert, but when I was a kid, I used to spend my summer vacations with my Grandma Helen, at her cabin on Boyer Lake. She had this transistor radio on the window shelf, in her kitchen. It was always on – I guess she liked the company. And the station never changed. Grandma Helen worshipped easy listening."

"It sounds like Grandma Helen knew where it was at," he surmised.

"You know, at first, I would change the radio to another station. She never said anything, but she always changed it back.

Eventually, I learned to like it. Now, it has great sentimental value to me."

"See, that's what is so great about music," he enthused. "It can have such emotional impact on people. That's why I love it."

"You're absolutely right. To this day, if I hear a little Pablo Cruise, you know I'm going to start to get misty."

He gasped. "Whoa! Okay, you are seriously blowing my mind right now."

She giggled. "I was going to mention, Ace, but I wasn't sure if you could handle it."

The deejay grabbed the left side of his chest and feigned a heart attack.

"'How Long'!"

"One of my favs," Dinah admitted.

He started typing rapidly on his keyboard. "Can I play something for you really quick? I just finished this."

He pressed "play" and Dinah heard the Steely Dan song, "FM." But it wasn't just "FM." It was like the original song was just a starting point. The deejay had put a punk beat underneath it – The Clash's "Should I Stay or Should I Go" - that transformed the song from a kind of funky laid-back tune into something entirely different ... something with a hard-driving sexuality. She loved it.

"I had no idea. I really didn't. You're a *composer*," she exuded.

The deejay's smile was so wide, it looked like his cheeks might crack.

"Thank you for saying that."

"I mean it!"

Any further admiration was immediately cut off by the fact that they had now descended out of the mountains and were directly over the Mojave Desert. The Cirrus was behaving like a yoyo - gaining and losing altitude quickly.

The deejay grabbed the handle to the upper right of his seat.

"Is this normal?" he asked nervously.

"Totally," she answered. "It's always bumpy coming into Vegas. It's a combination of the cold air higher up mixing with the warmer air as we come down. There's also mechanical turbulence, which is caused by the wind coming through the mountain passes. That's why on summer days I fly in here early in the morning and leave late at night. Otherwise, these single-engine planes take a shit-kicking!"

"Wonder Woman," he marveled again.

Despite, the roller coaster ride, Dinah expertly piloted the plane into McCarran Airport, flying in the traffic pattern, first parallel to the runway and then turning onto the base leg – which was perpendicular – at the Stratosphere and then onto final approach. It wasn't her best landing but fortunately for her the deejay had no frame of reference for landings in small planes.

After they parked in front of the Signature FBO, Dinah, despite his protestations, helped the deejay with his gear. She was in no hurry to leave. And not just because the day had reached peak heat.

"Listen," he said. "I don't know what your plans are ..."

"Oh, I don't have any," she quickly answered.

"Good! I was hoping you would say that," he finished. "I would be so honored if you would come to the show as my guest."

"Where is it?" she asked.

"At Omnia at Caesar's Palace," he said. "And they're comping me a hotel suite so it wouldn't cost you anything." He blushed. "You'd have your own room so you wouldn't have to worry about any pervy stuff."

"I accept. Thank you for the invitation." Why did she sound like a Victorian spinster suddenly? "Plus, this way I can tell the booker that it was my fault you were late, so they're not pissed at you."

"That's very chivalrous of you," he joked.

"Oh, I'm all about the chivalry," she said.

***

The show was transformative. Besides just really enjoying the music, Dinah felt so included, bobbing up and down with a roomful of other easy listening acolytes, dancing until she was dripping sweat and not even caring. With the atmospheric lights and the incredible sound system, the entire venue vibrated. It felt like a sort of communion. And naturally, the "Yacht Rock Messiah," was up there on his pulpit, under an appropriately ethereal spotlight.

Dinah watched a constant stream of lovelies approaching him all night long. Some were subtle, some were not so subtle. The deejay was polite and respectful to them, but they were all turned away. Sometimes you could only tell they were offended by the ireful swish of their long hair as they turned back to the dance floor.

And he was true to his word. Dinah had a room to herself and she was left alone until morning. Truth be told, she was grateful that he hadn't obliterated her initial impression of him. But she was also a little disappointed that he turned out to be as chivalrous as she was.

They went downstairs for the famous Bacchanal Buffet for breakfast and then waddled back to the plane.

Back at John Wayne, they both lingered in the parking lot after landing.

"So ... I'm back at Omnia in two weeks ..."

"I'm absolutely available," she said quickly.

"Okay, cool," he said just as quickly. "That makes me really happy."

Dinah looked around the parking lot.

"Where's your car, by the way? Oh wait, do you not drive?"

"I do," he answered. "My car's in the shop so my brother is picking me up."

She told him that if his car was still in the shop next time, she would drive him home. He thanked her. And then he kissed her hand.

He kissed her hand.

***

Back in Van Nuys, the bubble burst when Dinah was in the mailroom of her apartment building. She hadn't been receiving payment from the owner on a regular basis and after chasing her tail in circles, she had finally had to resort to contacting his father. The father apologized on his son's behalf and asked for her mailing address so that he could send a check.

Dinah opened her mailbox. The check hadn't arrived. There was nothing but flyers and credit card applications.

"Hello, good afternoon."

The building manager had snuck up behind her like a ninja, while she was getting the mail. She hadn't even heard the door open.

"Hi Kristina, I'm sorry I haven't – "

Kristina cut her right off. "Are you and your boyfriend back together again?"

"Um, why do you ask?"

"Because I thought I saw him in the lobby the other day."

Dinah grabbed the lifebuoy.

"We are. We are back together. We managed to work out our problems. Giving things another try."

Kristina smiled. "That's wonderful to hear. You look much happier today."

"I am happy. Thank you for noticing."

Kristina opened the mailroom door and then turned back.

"I guess I won't be needing that letter from your employer then after all."

"I guess not."

Kristina held eye contact for a second longer and then she was gone.

It looked like chivalry was in heavy supply at the moment.

Dinah had 1453.8 hours.

## Chapter Eleven

The baggage handler was sitting on the bench in the lobby when Dinah came down for work two days later. He was sitting hunched over, staring at the carpet.

"What kind of flower is that?" he asked.

Dinah had a good, long look.

"I don't think it's a flower, I think it's just an abstract pattern."

"Oh."

Dinah studied him for as long as she had studied the carpeting.

"So, what's going on? Oh, I almost forgot – can you thank Ines for that awesome painting? I love Dolly!"

He sighed as she imagined Rodin's *The Thinker* would have if he could have moved.

"Those paintings – mierda! I would make more money selling the supplies and the blank canvases," he lamented.

Dinah sat down beside him.

"Can I help?"

"Not unless you have 200 extra dollars lying around."

"You're short on rent again?" she asked.

He nodded. "I worked double shifts all last month too. But Ines had a flare-up and missed a lot of work. She's lucky that her manager at Target is so nice."

Ines had severe asthma and the smog in the Valley sat there sometimes like a thick layer of brown sludge. Dinah could see it as she flew into Van Nuys and it was disgusting to think of people breathing that in.

"I wish that I did, you know that I'd give it to you," she said. "Are you waiting to talk to Kristina?"

He nodded miserably.

"They don't consider it late until the 6$^{th}$, so I've still got a couple of days but …"

"Okay, well, hang in there. Maybe something will come up," she said with as much encouragement as she could muster.

The baggage handler ran his hands through his hair.

"I hope so. Because I'm too old to hook." He smiled wryly.

Dinah smacked him lightly on his knee as she got up.

"Shame on you!" She walked towards the door. "You're never too old to hook."

\*\*\*

Dinah's next client wasn't a client. He was a flight student. The owner had called her and begged her to take him on. She really didn't want to drive all the way down to the O.C. to flight instruct – she could do that at home in Van Nuys. Flight instructing was just so much more work than flying the plane yourself. And you built hours so slowly that way. But the owner said this guy was a personal friend of his and that he was a natural – a real "stick and rudder" guy. He would progress so quickly that it would be painless and productive.

When would she learn?

Dinah's new flight student worked for U.S. Customs and Border Patrol. He was a tall, physically imposing man with a crew cut. It was a good thing she was training him in the Cirrus – he probably wouldn't have fit in a Cessna.

As she walked him through the training syllabus for the private pilot program, he seemed to disengage quite quickly. A lot of guys had the same reaction. They seemed to think that flying was like a Learning Annex course. You came in on a Saturday and then on Sunday you got your private pilot license. They were always so annoyed that the process was more involved and lengthier than they had anticipated.

One time, she was giving a ground lesson on aviation weather to the CEO of a fabric company and he yawned in her face and said, "Just so you know, this is really boring." This was an adult who ran his own multi-million-dollar company.

"Are you wanting to get your license so that you can fly for Border Patrol?" Dinah asked.

Personally, she couldn't imagine a more loathsome application of her ability. Flying along the border, trying to track down tired, desperate immigrants. Just thinking about it was physically reviling.

"Not exactly," he revealed slowly. "Okay, full disclosure, I'm actually terrified to fly."

What?

"I don't understand," Dinah said. "Then why would you want to take flying lessons?"

"Here's the thing," he added. "I was on a United flight a few months ago. I was going to visit my mother. And as soon as they shut the door, I had a massive panic attack. I mean, the whole nine yards. I was sweating, shaking, I couldn't swallow."

"Oh dear."

"Yup. It was so bad, that they let me deplane. And I haven't flown since."

"I'm so sorry. But you don't have to fly to travel. You could drive, take a train. You're not alone. Lots of people are afraid to fly. It's nothing to be ashamed of."

"But my mother lives in Athens, so none of those are possible. And she's getting older. I won't have that many more years with her. I can't allow my fear to keep us apart."

Dinah thought about alternatives.

"Okay, but what about some psychological help? You know, they have specific programs for people who are afraid to fly."

He nodded. "I talked to my therapist about that, but his opinion was that it was just like slapping a band-aid on a gunshot wound."

"It treats the symptom, but doesn't address the root of the problem," Dinah said.

He raised his right index finger.

"Exactly! My therapist seems to think that the deeper issue here is a feeling of lack of control. That's why he thought that if I could actually fly a plane myself – "

"Then you would have a sense of control over the situation," she said, finishing his sentence.

"And then it would be a piece of cake going back to being a passenger." Dinah didn't say anything. "Look, I know how stressful this might be for you as a teacher so if you're not into it, I totally understand. I'm going to test your patience. I know that. But I'll also be very generous with payment. I promise it won't be a waste of your time."

"Not at all. Helping people is never a waste of my time. My only potential issue is that I have no idea how you may react up there and my chief priority is keeping you and I and the plane safe. If I get you in the air and you have another attack, or you react adversely in some other way then our security is jeopardized."

"I get it. I absolutely do. Would you like to take some time to think about it? Or get to know me a little better?"

Dinah smiled. "That's okay. I've gotten fairly good at assessing people quickly in this job. As I said, my life can sometimes depend on it."

He smiled too. "In a way, you're somewhat of a therapist yourself."

"You're not wrong. People learn new things – especially things outside their comfort zone – in different ways. And everyone has different coping mechanisms. I had one student who had to complain about his live-in mother-in-law for 15 minutes before every flight. It was like he needed to get it out of his system so he could focus on the flying. And I had another student who threw up before every flight for at least the first ten lessons."

"Did he quit?" the border agent asked.

"No, he was determined. He said it was a bucket list item for him and he would be crushed if he couldn't see it through," she said.

"Did he finish?"

Dinah grinned. "He's a Captain with Air Canada now."

The border agent clapped his hands.

"Tremendous!"

"I'm so proud of him for persevering." She paused. "You know what? Let's give this a try and see how it goes."

She got up from the table and indicated that he should do the same.

"And we'll take it slow?" he asked.

"We'll take it slow," she said.

\*\*\*

For their first lesson, they walked out to the plane. They looked at the plane. And then they walked back into the terminal.

She still had 1453.8 hours.

But he gave her 300 dollars.

When she got home, she got an envelope, put 200 dollars in it and slid it under the baggage handler's door.

***

Their second lesson consisted of walking out to the plane, opening the door, getting into the plane. And getting right back out again.

1453.8 hours.

And another 300 bucks.

***

Lesson Three: they walked out to the plane. They got in the plane. They started the engine. And shut it down.

Holding fast at 1453.8 hours.

300 dollars and a cronut from DK's Donuts & Bakery. Eating their feelings.

***

By the fourth lesson, the border agent was comfortable with the sound and vibration of the engine … sort of. They taxied out to the runway. And then cancelled their takeoff clearance and taxied right back in.

"I'm really sorry," he said.

"Nothing to be sorry about. We're making progress."

He sighed. "At this rate, I'll be lucky to get to Athens for my mother's funeral."

"Hang in there," Dinah said. "I want to say, Rome wasn't built in a day but that doesn't seem pertinent in this scenario."

He exhaled. "Greeks and Romans. Don't get me started."

"Do you want a cronut?"

"I do. I really do."

Off they went.

The Hobbs meter, which recorded flight time, started ticking the second the engine turned over and they started moving, so Dinah was actually able to log some hours on that lesson.

She began the day with 1453.8 hours.

And ended it with 1453.9 hours.

\*\*\*

The border agent cancelled the next two lessons, citing problems at work. Dinah didn't buy it. As a seasoned flight instructor, she had heard it all. Headaches, stomachaches, car accidents, running out of gas, work issues, family issues, pet issues, mugged on the way to the airport issues, bear in the swimming pool issues and her personal favorite – couldn't find the airport so got frustrated and just went home issues.

All of these were excuses. Excuses to avoid a challenge that people were nervous to address. Dinah used to tell her students that the hard part was already done – making the decision to rise to a goal that was outside their comfort zone. That already distinguished them from everybody else. All the people who talked and talked about stretching their horizons and then never did. And always … *always* … regretted not having acted on their aspirations.

She gave the same speech to the border agent, the next time he texted to cancel, citing a reticence to go flying when the heat was so debilitating. He didn't feel it was safe.

It was 78 degrees out.

Also, the winds were coming up. It was getting gusty.

It was three knots ... which wouldn't dishevel your bangs.

But what about the tire treads? They had been looking pretty worn last time.

The tires were fine. When they got to the point that they were no longer effective, a gold thread would show through on the treads. That's when they needed to be replaced.

Dinah talked him off the ledge and into his car, agreeing to meet him at 2 p.m.

"And no cronuts this time. We're going up in the air. And you're going to get such a rush of endorphins, you'll only want a salad afterwards."

***

She got there around 1:45 p.m. By 2:30 p.m. he still hadn't arrived.

She called him.

No answer.

She texted him.

No response.

So, she got a glass of cucumber water from the FBO refreshment area and sat there, trying to decide what to do. If she left now, then she'd get caught in rush hour. And she would have driven all the way down there for nothing.

It was while she was considering her options that the owner sashayed through the automatic doors with a florid retiree behind him.

"Hey, beautiful!" he said. "What's up?"

"I'm just waiting for my student, he's late."

"Shame on him for keeping a lady waiting," said the retiree.

The owner draped his arm around the portly man.

"Too bad you're booked. We're headed down to Rosarito for a week."

The retiree's cell rang.

"The Mexican Mistress calls!" he wandered off, cooing into the phone.

"Seriously, it's too bad," the owner continued. "He's putting us up at Las Rocas Resort & Spa for seven days. All expenses paid!"

Dinah's left eye started to twitch.

A trip to Rosarito and back would be between five and six flight hours.

Of multi-engine time.

With no snow and no mountains.

The eye continued to twitch.

Dinah's phone pinged. It was the border agent, apologizing for being late. He was stuck in traffic. But he was coming. He was within 15 minutes.

She gave her regrets to the two men and sent them on their way, both making revolting jokes about worms and tequila as they disappeared around the corner of the hangar.

Dinah waited another 90 minutes for the border agent. He never showed. So, she drove home in rush hour traffic. Which took almost four hours and two tanks of gas.

After she had dragged herself through the door of her apartment and summoned enough energy to toss a Lean Cuisine into the microwave – which had begun sparking intermittently – she collapsed on her IKEA sectional and flipped on the Canadian show, *Air Disasters*. For some reasons, pilots could never get enough of watching other pilots in the shit. Maybe it was educational, a cautionary tale or maybe it was schadenfreude, better him than me, but regardless, it was required viewing.

He called her at 11:45 p.m. She was in bed.

"I'm really sorry," he started with.

"Okay."

"I'll pay you for your time."

"That's not the issue and you know it." She wasn't letting him off the hook.

"I know it's not," he concurred. "Can I just explain the events leading up to today?"

Dinah was so tired of dealing with other people's problems.

"Go ahead," she said.

"I don't know if you know this, but a lot of people look down on border patrol. They think that we're militant scumbags who are just hunting illegals like animals. But some of us are good guys. Some of us became agents for the *right* reasons."

"Why did *you*?" she asked.

"I actually wanted to protect these people. The drug cartels terrorize and exploit them, and these coyotes extort them and then essentially leave them for dead. The smugglers and the traffickers are the reason I became a border agent. Unfortunately, the immigrants often become collateral damage. Yesterday the collateral damage was bad. Worse than usual."

"Do I want to know?"

"Probably not. But you should. It was an entire family – Dad, Mom, two boys under the age of ten and a baby girl. They burned them so badly that -"

"Okay, I can't," she interrupted.

And sometimes the excuses for not flying weren't excuses at all. They were legitimate reasons.

She counselled him that perhaps the flying therapy should wait. Wait until there was a better time. When things were less complicated.

"Like when?" he posited.

"Good point," she countered.

The border agent cajoled her into coming down to John Wayne, one more time for him.

"If I 'no show' next time, you can ghost me," he said.

"If you 'no show' next time, I'm going to come to your house," she returned.

"How do you know where I live?"

"Your student pilot file ... remember, I had to scan your driver's license?"

"Oh shit, that's right. Then I guess I'd better show up."

She wasn't kidding. She would go to his home. And she wouldn't have cronuts with her.

***

He was early, that was a good sign. And even though he was his usual sweaty, shaky self, there was an underlining determination that day.

Dinah explained to him that once they got in the air, if he changed his mind and wanted to go back, she wouldn't be able to land immediately. She would have to fly a lap of the traffic pattern at Santa Ana, which involved flying upwind of the runway until at least 500 feet off the ground before she could turn. Then she'd have to turn left crosswind, fly away from the runway a little bit, and then level off at pattern altitude, which was 1,000 feet above the ground. She would then have to fly downwind, alongside the runway until the runway was about 45 degrees behind them. Then she could start to descend back down and turn base in preparation for landing. After turning final, she would have to get landing clearance from the tower before they could touch down on the runway. And if for whatever reason, the tower cancelled their landing clearance and told them to go around, they would have no choice. They would have to comply. And then it would start all over again.

"So, what you're saying is, once we're up, there's no turning back," he said.

"Not unless we have an engine fire," she added.

"What?!!"

Dinah winced. "The second that was out of my mouth, I regretted it. We're *not* going to have an engine fire. Or any other malfunction."

"But if we do?"

"If we do then I am trained to deal with it. That's ingrained. As a pilot, every single time I taxi onto that runway, I expect the best, but I am prepared for the worst."

"How long does the traffic pattern take?" he asked.

"Typically, about 10 to 15 minutes. Do you think you can hold on that long?"

"I can do this." His hands formed fists.

"You can do this."

She gave his shoulder a little squeeze and led him outside.

The border agent embraced all the classic stalling and avoidance techniques. He insisted on doing the preflight procedure himself and quite literally crawled around that plane. There was a moment of concern when he found a small screw lying beside the nosewheel but it wasn't from their aircraft so Dinah pocketed it so that they wouldn't run over it. When she finally coaxed him inside the plane – he got back out twice with a dipstick to check the fuel in the wings – he couldn't seem to remember how to put on his seatbelt. Which was similar to the seatbelt in his car. Dinah reached across and got him belted in. Then he started having trouble closing his door. Cirrus doors were a pain to close. You had to give it a good slam and then you moved the door handle all the way forward to seal and lock it. It took a few tries, and a diatribe about not wanting to close the door too aggressively in case he broke it, but ultimately, he got it closed.

When they got out to the runway, it was just as Dinah feared. A nice calm, sunny day in California brought out all the GA – General Aviation – pilots. There was a long wait for takeoff. The border agent started to sweat profusely so Dinah had no choice but to let him open his door again. While they were waiting, she burned some carbon deposits off the cylinder heads by leaning out the mixture as much as she could without killing the engine and then running the power up to almost full throttle. The revving of the engine and the consequential shaking of the plane didn't seem to affect him at all.

Which wasn't a good sign, because it meant he was glazing over, which was a coping mechanism. His brain was checking out in order to protect his nervous system.

Should she go back?

Something told her not to.

When they were next for takeoff, Dinah told him to close his door. This time he slammed it so hard that the whole plane shook. In her head, she apologized to the Cirrus.

They were cleared for takeoff and approved for left closed traffic.

Dinah pulled out onto the runway.

"Ready?" she asked him.

He swallowed several times and then managed to squeak out, "Ready."

She lined herself up with the centerline, applied a little pressure to the right rudder pedal and smoothly pushed the throttle all the way in.

She tried her best not to look at him because she needed now to concentrate on flying the aircraft. But she could feel the heat coming off him and she could sense him trembling.

When the aircraft lifted off the ground, the border agent whimpered a little.

"Are you okay?" she asked.

He didn't answer. He just stared straight ahead.

She kept flying upwind. The tower gave her an early turn. They wanted her out of the way so that they could clear the next plane for takeoff. Dinah banked the plane as gently as she could. She glanced over quickly, and his hand was gripping the armrest so tightly, the foam had given way.

When she was adequate distance from the runway, Dinah turned downwind and reduced power to level the plane off. She had a brief respite now before the prelanding procedure needed to happen.

"How are you doing?"

The border agent swiveled his head painstakingly towards the airport.

"Is that the runway?" He pointed down.

"It is. You're halfway there! You're doing it!" she said.

"I'm doing it."

"You're doing it!

"I'm doing it!"

He was still sweating buckets, but the wildly darting eyes had ceased, and the shaking had lessened. He was also licking his lips a lot but that wasn't uncommon on a first flight.

Dinah reduced power as gently as she could and started to put some flaps down. Sometimes, the tower extended your downwind leg if the pattern was busy but today, she lucked out and they told her to turn base at the normal spot.

When she turned, she saw the Cessna 152 turning base from the opposite direction. The Cessna was given landing clearance ahead of her. She was told to follow it. She was Number Two.

Crap.

They should have put the Cessna behind her. It was much smaller and slower than her. If she couldn't slow her speed down enough then she would have to pull up and go around. This is what drove her nuts about air traffic controllers. Most of them weren't pilots so they often didn't understand the finer nuances of spacing. And you couldn't just magically make a 310-horsepower plane go slower than a 160-horsepower plane.

The border agent looked like he was going to be able to hold it together for now, but she didn't want to risk another lap of the pattern. Dinah pulled the throttle all the way back to idle and dumped down full flaps to help slow herself down.

The Cessna was now on short final – about a quarter mile to the runway. It was taking *forever*. It looked suspended in the air. She was getting too close. The tower was going to tell her to go around.

She asked if she could do some "S-turns." An S-turn was just that – a gentle turn in an S-pattern, designed to buy time. She was approved.

"I'm going to do an S-turn, okay?"

"What's that?" He was fidgeting now. Starting to become agitated.

"I just need to create a little more spacing between us and the guy ahead of us. Don't worry, it happens all the time."

They did three turns and then the Cessna was on the runway.

Good.

But then it just kept rolling out. It went past the first taxiway and didn't exit. Then the second.

It was illegal to land while another aircraft was on the runway.

Crap.

"We're going to have to go around, okay?" she told him.

She was just about to push the throttle in and bring up the first notch of flaps when the Cessna veered off at the next taxiway. The tower cleared her to land.

Dinah did a short field landing – which meant touching down within the first few hundred feet of the runway and got off at the first taxiway. She stopped when she was clear of the runway and brought her flaps up. She switched from tower control to ground control and asked to taxi back to the hangar.

The border agent was hyperventilating by the time she parked the aircraft. She shut it down quickly and popped his door, unfastening his seatbelt as she leaned across.

"Do you want to get out?" she asked him.

He shook his head.

"I just need to sit for a minute."

"No problem."

She unfastened her belt and started to deplane. He grabbed her arm.

"Don't leave, okay?"

"Okay." She sat back down.

The airport was busy so you could hear a cacophony of engines. But you could also hear the cicadas, underscoring the less subtle symphony.

And then another sound, superseded the other two.

The border agent was crying.

It didn't faze Dinah in the least. Generally, the bigger they were, the harder they fell. That societal machismo paradigm and the equating of vulnerability with emasculation was all too common to her. But the truth of the matter was that every human being, regardless of gender, experienced emotion. And if that emotion built up and up and had nowhere to go, it was like water up against a dam. You only needed one little crack as a catalyst for a deluge. Dinah had a neighbor named Carol, when she was growing up, who ran a waxing salon out of her home. The first and only male client she ever had was a Marine. The Marine's girlfriend had been complaining about his excess back hair and persuaded him to have it waxed off. Carol only had the opportunity to rip the first one off before the Marine burst into tears. He sobbed violently for the better part of 20 minutes, while she held him. And then he left, with his back looking like a short, narrow landing strip in the middle of a shag carpet.

When the big, tough guys eventually and inevitably lost control of their emotions, it was usually in front of a woman. Carol always maintained that the reason for that was that they felt more comfortable showing their sensitive side to a female. Dinah believed the anti-thesis to have greater validity. She believed that it was more important for them to show testosterone-fueled impenetrability around other men because a man's opinion of them was more important than a woman's opinion. Dinah had experienced this with her ex. He would often behave in a manner that he knew wasn't popular with her so that he could save face with a male counterpart. Even seeking approval from a man that he didn't know usurped his desire for approval from an intimate female partner who shared his life.

Dinah knew exactly how to handle this situation. And it wasn't her first time at the rodeo.

"Oh, please don't be sad," she said. "You should be so proud of yourself right now. You overcame your fear and achieved your objective. I have so much respect for you."

He wiped his tears with the back of his hand.

"I'm not crying because I'm sad. I'm crying because I'm so goddamned happy right now!!"

He reached over and hugged her so tightly that he almost cracked her rib. And this sudden intimacy wasn't odd or inappropriate at all. Because flying was this profoundly emotional experience that bonded human beings in a way that few other arenas matched.

"You did it!!" she declared.

"You have changed my life," he stated.

Sometimes aviation had no limits. Sometimes it soared celestially.

1454.3 hours.

## Chapter Twelve

**H**e told her that her landings blew.

"Don't feel bad," the farmer reassured her. "Everybody's landings blow – it's the hardest part of learning to fly. And any pilot who tells you that they've never had a bad landing is a full-fledged psychopath."

"When will my landings stop blowing?" Tammy asked.

"Never."

"Seriously?"

"Seriously. Landings are a cycle of suck. You suck, you suck, you suck, then you get good at them for a while. Then you suck again, then you're good again for a bit. And then the suck returns. It's a never-ending lifelong cycle. Welcome to being a pilot," he said gleefully.

"Is that why they all seem to have such big egos?" Tammy asked. "They have to inflate themselves to compensate for their insecurities?"

"Jaysus and Joseph, what have you been reading Dr. Freud?"

"Simone de Beauvoir. She's a French feminist writer. She wrote a book called, *The Second Sex*. One of my teachers recommended it. He said I was too smart for the school curriculum."

"Young lady, I think you might be too smart for the world's curriculum," he laughed. "What does that mean – 'the *second* sex'?"

"It means that men are considered the first sex and then women come behind them."

"Oh, I get it. It's like, when Henny Youngman says, 'Take my wife, please!' – his catchphrase."

"I don't know who that is."

"He was a very popular comedian in my day," he said haughtily.

"I don't think I like those old comedians," Tammy surmised. "All of their jokes are about insulting women. My parents made me watch *Nick at Nite* with them. It's how they learned English. Not my deal."

"Okay, well what about the girl ones? Like Phyllis Diller and Joan Rivers?"

"Well, all of their jokes seem to be about insulting themselves."

"Okay, smarty pants, who do you like, then?"

"I like '*South Park*'."

"I don't know who that is."

That day, instead of their usual routine, he decided they were going to head over to the airport in Hearst.

"It's a paved runway, which will be easier for you to practice on and there's no control tower to deal with," he explained.

Hearst was about an hour away in the Cherokee. The farmer had her practice her cross country skills by timing legs between visual waypoints to see if her groundspeed was faster or slower based on the winds and then had her calculate her revised estimated time of arrival. And also, the corrected track that she needed to fly contingent upon the wind direction to remain on course. All of this was accomplished with a simple and timeless device called an E6B – a small metal contraption with a wheel that turned, commonly called a "whiz wheel."

"You know they have flight computers for all of this stuff now," she chided him.

"Do they now?" he replied. "And what happens when the battery on your flight computer is dead or heaven forbid your screen overheats? I'm telling you – old school is the way to do it. Pilots have been using E6Bs since the U.S. Army introduced them in 1940. They're tried and true. And you can use them no matter what happens. I'll betcha even the Night Witches used whiz wheels."

Tammy frowned. "Is that another one of your old comedian bits?"

The farmer frowned right back.

"You don't *know* about the Night Witches?" He shook his head. "I can't believe what they're not teaching in the schools these days." He pointed to the heading indicator. "You're 10 degrees off-course. Try a heading of 310."

She turned slightly to the right.

"Who are the Night Witches?" Tammy persisted.

"I don't know if you're ready to hear about the Night Witches," he teased. "Maybe you should finish reading that French lady stuff first."

"Come on. Who are they?"

"They *were* a regiment of Russian bomber pilots in World War II – all women. They flew all their missions at night – on the Eastern front. And get this – they would idle their engines and then glide down to release their bombs."

"Why did they do that?" Tammy asked.

"So that no one could hear the engines coming ... like witches on broomsticks."

"That's pretty incredible," she commented.

"You think that's incredible? They didn't wear parachutes because of the low altitude flying and the weight of the bombs. They flew wood and canvass planes in winter conditions, eight or more missions a night, with no defense ammunition and they had to hand prop the engines to get them started again. In the air."

"Holy moly!"

"The holiest."

Tammy shook her head. "That should be taught in every history class, ever."

Hearst Airport became visible in the distance.

"Do you see the airport?" he asked.

Tammy looked. "No. I never see the airport. It's so frustrating."

"Okay, I'm going to help you. Don't look for the runway first. You're too far out. Look for an empty area. Do you see one?"

She pointed excitedly. "There!"

"Good. And at night, look for the flashing beacon first. Then the runway."

Tammy got set up for landing. She always got so nervous on final approach. The farmer noticed that she had stopped breathing and that her shoulders were up around her ears.

"Okay, take a deep breath for me and then let it out," he said.

She complied.

"Never hold your breath. Now roll your shoulders back. You're too tense. You can't land an airplane when you're all bunched up like that."

Her shoulders slowly sank back down.

"Now, I want you to look at the threshold of the runway. Is it moving up or down or is it just getting bigger?" he asked.

"It's moving up," she answered.

"Good. What does that mean?"

"It means, I'm sinking, and I need to add some power."

"Well done. Good call. Okay, now as soon as you are over the threshold, I want you to shift your eyes to the end of the runway. And when the end of the runway starts to line up with your eyeline, I want you to start to pull back a little bit at a time on the yoke – that's the flare – until the main wheels touch down."

Tammy took another deep breath.

"Last time we hit really hard."

"That's because you flared too high. If you're looking straight down, you're always going to flare too high. That's why you need to look at the end of the runway."

Tammy added another little burst of power.

"That's looking really good," the farmer commented. "You're right on the glidepath. Okay, now cut your power – throttle all the way back – and now – start the flare."

Tammy did as he said, pulling back a little bit, letting the plane settle, a little bit more, settle, a little bit more until she felt the main wheels touch down on the runway.

Then she let go of the yoke and the nosewheel slammed down.

"Oops," she said. "Sorry."

"Don't apologize to me. Apologize to the plane," the farmer advised.

"Sorry Hedy."

"Never let go of the yoke. Keep the back pressure up and gravity will bring the nosewheel down on its own. And much more gently than that. Okay, taxi off and let's head back around and go again."

"How many landings are we going to do?" Tammy asked, not wanting to be a glutton for punishment.

"As many as it takes."

They did 15. Tammy bounced it, she pancaked it, she came in high and floated halfway down the runway. She landed right of the centerline, she landed left of the centerline, she landed on one main wheel first and then the other. But around Landing Number Nine, she started to get it.

"That's it," he assured her. "There are no shortcuts to good landings. You just gotta keep hammering them out until you get better at them."

"I'm getting pretty tired," Tammy said.

So, they did six more. And the last four were textbook. They were perfect. And suddenly she wasn't tired anymore.

"We'd better start heading back," the farmer said, looking at his watch.

Tammy couldn't help noticing that his shaking had worsened considerably since the last time they had flown.

"Are you feeling all right?"

"Let me tell you kid, do not get this disease. It's awful not having control of your own body."

"Parkinson's ... that's what Michael J. Fox has, right?"

Now, it was the farmer's turn.

"I don't know who that is. Is he one of your little teeny bopper crushes?"

Tammy considered her thoughts for a moment before deciding to share something with him.

"Actually no. I don't like boys. I like girls."

She felt like the wind was suddenly sucked out of the atmosphere. It had been a mistake to share this information. Then he spoke.

"How do you know you like girls?" he asked.

"How do you know *you* like girls?" she asked back.

"Ah, fair enough. Well, I guess if you're going to be a gay -"

"Lesbian."

"If you're going to be a gay lesbian, then Canada is definitely a better place for you than Sri Lanka."

She breathed a sigh of relief.

"That's a fact. I'd probably be in jail in Colombo."

The impact of that statement and the perfunctory nature of its delivery were not lost on the farmer.

"Well, I'll tell you what. People always say that life is short, but it's not, it's long. And it's a lot better if you can find someone to share it with. Someone who can love the hijinks of cats as much as you do and get just as mad when there's no parking spots at the mall around Christmas time. Someone who can take care of you."

"Was that like your wife, sorry, what was her name again?" Tammy asked.

"Darla. Yup, Darla took care of me for 40-some years. And then she had the stroke and I had to take care of her. And I'd never taken care of anyone before that, so I had to learn. Did you know that you can't microwave dry spaghetti?"

"No, you have to add water otherwise it just catches fire."

"It sure does. It sure does."

They both reflected on that as the Cherokee flew straight at the sunset, blinding and breathtaking at the same time.

"You know, we always held hands when we went to Church and one day, the choirmaster said he thought it was so endearing that we still held hands. And do you know what Darla said?" Tammy shook her head. "Darla said, 'Don't kid yourself, we're just holding each other up!'"

He chortled and Tammy joined in, genuinely enjoying the moment and Darla's wit.

"Your wife should have been a stand-up comedian. I think I would have liked her act," she stated.

A few miles ahead, Tammy could see the red barn that characterized their family property. It was almost dusk, but she still could make out everything she needed to, to navigate visually.

"Would you like to take the landing?" she asked the farmer hopefully.

"Not a chance."

She sighed. Okay, one more ... she could do one more.

It was probably because the adrenaline had worn off and she was having to concentrate on psyching herself up to enable enough focus to get them down safely on the ground one more time, that she didn't notice.

She didn't notice until they only had about 50 feet left to go.

Both of her parents were standing on the edge of the field, staring up at them with a combination of astonishment and rage.

## Chapter Thirteen

Dinah had 1476.3 flight hours.

That was it. She just couldn't build any more no matter how hard she tried. And oh, how she had tried.

The sod farmers had never returned. Probably because they were embarrassed about the headrest. Which still hadn't been replaced. Dinah would forget sometimes on flights and go to rest her head back and suddenly be staring at the roof of the aircraft.

She had done two more trips with Cat and Chrystal – one to Palm Springs for The Palm Springs Film Festival and one to San Carlos, so that they could go shoe shopping in San Francisco. They tried to buy Dinah a pair of Louboutins, but she had never learned to walk in heels and knew that the $500 would be wasted on her so she made up an excuse about bunions. Because she knew Chrystal would give her a very public walking lesson, that her ego, frankly, just couldn't take.

There had only been one more flight with Sherry for chemo. She had developed an infection and had to postpone the remaining treatments. Dinah had kept in touch with her. During the last phone call, Sherry's voice had sounded so weak.

There had been no repeat business from the widower – thankfully – and also no subsequent fallout from that fateful first flight – thankfully. The last thing Dinah's career needed was a rap sheet that included illegal disposal of a body.

Ditto, for any more multi-engine time. Dinah had reached out to the owner, several times after she had to miss the flight to Rosarito. He always responded that there was nothing on the books, but she'd be his first call. And there was no more mention of formal training. She knew he was full of shit because there was an app called *FlightAware*, that allowed you to input an aircraft's tail number and it would show you the flight path of any recent or present trips. The only condition was that the pilot had to request, *Flight Following*, from air traffic control. That meant that you were going to fly a visual flight but instead of being on your own out there in the wild blue yonder, ATC monitored your flight and basically babysat you from your departure to your destination.

Dinah had once soloed a student to Santa Barbara with *Flight Following*, and he had been too afraid to land there so he had merely circled the airport a few times and flown back to Van Nuys. She had been able to see the circling patterns on *FlightAware*. The student had been flabbergasted when she somehow magically knew that he had bailed on the landing.

According to *FlightAware*, the owner had flown several times in the last few weeks. Dinah figured that he didn't want her on board after the Aspen trip.

She had, happily, made several excursions to Vegas with the deejay. And he had made several excursions to Van Nuys. In Southern California, there was no greater show of affection and commitment than the willingness to brave traffic from one county to another. Dinah knew several people who flat out refused to date anyone who lived more than a 30-minute drive from them.

Swipe left.

The border agent had done one more flight in the traffic pattern – this time she got him to go around twice – but he had contracted bronchitis, a condition that he had ignored and tried to "power through," and now he had pneumonia. He was likely down for the count for at least a month or two.

So that was that. 1476.3 hours and not counting. Dinah had run out of ways to accrue more unless she wanted to shell out her own hard-earned money to rent a plane and build them by just flying around L.A. Which she would have done except that she didn't have any money to allocate to that end. She needed 23.7 hours. The cheapest plane she could find to rent was a Cessna 150 for $115 per hour. Which would require $2,725.50. She had the 50 cents. It was the remainder of the balance that was the sticking point.

What was she going to do?

Stewing in her juices in her apartment, she glared out the living room window. They were in the pool.

The cyclists.

A few weeks ago, she was woken on a Saturday morning by the sound of encouraging shouting and Taylor Swift. A resident named, Aunjanue, had taken it upon herself to start conducting stationary cycling classes in the community pool ... a complete and utter violation of her lease. You weren't permitted to conduct business operations at a private residence. There were liability issues not to mention the infringement of privacy rights of the other residents. Yet here she was, with nine other women, monopolizing the pool and *shaking it off*.

Dinah waited for someone to come and pull the plug – literally and figuratively. But no one did. And the classes continued the next week and the week after that. It irritated her more than it should have. Sometimes it felt like she was the only one following the rules while the rest of the world got a free pass.

It was while she was debating whether to go down there and either complain or try to recruit new flight students that her phone rang.

It was one of her old instructors.

"Hey," she answered. "Long time no hear."

He had been flying cargo up in Alaska.

"Guess where I am?" he asked.

"Fairbanks?" she guessed.

"I'm at FlightSafety in Denver."

She knew what that meant, and her heart leapt for him.

FlightSafety was a training conglomerate that many of the airlines and commercial operators used. They had enormous warehouses throughout the country, filled with simulators for all the different types of aircraft. They also supplied their own instructors if your employer didn't care to supply their own.

"You got an airline gig?"

"You bet I did! With SkyQuest – I started training two days ago."

"Oh, I'm so happy for you! Way to go! See, I told you all that hard work would pay off."

She could tell he was grinning at the other end of the phone.

"You did, you did. And now I'd like to pay it forward. SkyQuest is offering a $2,500 referral bonus for pilots. If you like, I could walk your resume in and then we could split the bonus."

He had *no* idea how good that sounded.

She groaned. "God, I would absolutely love you forever for that, but I still don't have the hours."

"Well, what have you got?"

She sighed. "I only have 1,476."

Dinah waited for the polite and dismissive "so long."

"Dinah, you can do a Restricted ATP."

A Restricted ATP was a loophole that Congress had recently created due to the pilot shortage. It allowed pilot candidates to still be hired with less hours than required for an ATP certificate, with certain limitations in place. Once the requisite hours were attained, the restriction was lifted, and it just became a regular ATP certificate.

"Are you sure? I didn't think that the regionals were doing Restricted ATPs?"

"Yeah, a lot of them are now. And SkyQuest is for sure," the instructor said. "You have your Associate degree in Aviation and trained at a Part 141 school, right?"

A Part 141 flight school was overseen by the FAA with respect to its curriculum, syllabus, and lesson plans. It was generally a more structured training environment. Conversely a Part 61 flight school had more flexibility. Students could learn at their own pace and instructors could develop their own curriculum and tailor them more towards the learning needs of each client.

"That's right."

"Then you only need 1,250 hours," he said.

The buzzing sound that had been in Dinah's ears for the last three days, suddenly subsided.

"This is amazing. Yes! Thank you, thank you, thank you! I'll email you my resume right now. Thank you!"

He laughed. "No probs, buddy. It's all good karma, right?"

Dinah did a little shaking it off of her own and then ran to her laptop.

\*\*\*

Two days later, she received a call from Courtney in Talent Acquisition at SkyQuest Airline. This call was considered to be the initial interview. A brief and superficial "get to know you" conversation had Dinah explaining how she got into aviation and elaborating on some of the positions on her resume. Then came the HR questions. These questions were all looking for responses that showed good pilot decision-making and/or personal growth. Dinah had her stock answers. Every pilot did. She was also asked what she liked to do when she wasn't flying. She answered the same way she always did … with volunteer work and surfing.

Yup, *volunteer work* and *surfing*.

The call went well and a few hours later, Dinah received an email inviting her to a presentation and interview the next Monday afternoon at the Hyatt Regency by LAX. She was told to bring originals of all her certificates and her passport as well as all logbooks and a copy of her first class medical.

Damn.

She only had a second class medical.

Every pilot had to pass an aviation medical exam which could not be administered by just any doctor. It had to be a physician who was specially certified by the FAA. They were called AMEs – Aviation Medical Examiners. Many of them were pilots as well. Almost all of them, in Dinah's experience, were over the age of 80. And men.

A third class medical was what most General Aviation pilots got. If you were under the age of 40, it was good for 5 years. Over the age of 40, you had 2 years. A second class medical was for most commercial pilots and involved a few more tests and stricter parameters. It was valid for two years, regardless of your age. And a first class medical, was generally for airline pilots. If you were under 40, it was good for a year. Over 40, only 6 months and you had to have an EKG – electrocardiogram - every year. The system was presently in flux, as the FAA had recently modified the criteria at the third class level to make it more conducive for private and recreational pilots to keep flying. Now they could go to their family physician every four years with some FAA paperwork to fill out and they had to take an online certification course every two years. It was called *BasicMed* and that was only for third class. First class was still a "First Class Pain in the Ass."

Dinah hated going for these medicals. And they weren't covered under any insurance or compensated by most employers, so it was out of pocket. Most of the time, you got what you paid for. The better – and more evolved – the medical examiner, the better the experience and the higher the price. There was a delightful AME she used to go to in Westwood who told her stories about flying with Barron Hilton and joked that her urine sample had tested positive for cocaine. And then she would counter with the quip that they both knew flight instructors couldn't afford cocaine. And then they'd have a shared experience chuckle. But he charged $220. And he was retired. Then there was a guy at Compton Airport that did medicals out of the trunk of his car between hangars. $75. Cash. He wasn't around anymore. Like, at all.

Dinah's choices were last minute and limited. She googled and selected the closest one, without even glancing at the Yelp reviews. He answered the phone himself, barking out the name of his practice.

She asked if she could come the next day at 11 a.m. He barked again that it was fine but to remember to bring her confirmation number. And then he hung up without saying goodbye.

What the hell was the confirmation number?

Oh right, they had changed the system so that you filled the paperwork out online on a website called, *MedXPress*. Then it gave you a confirmation number that you presented to the AME and they were able to go online to access your records.

Dinah quickly went online and filled out the forms. And then she made sure she didn't eat anything with poppyseeds in it. You know, just in case.

***

The doctor's office was packed. Why did he give her that appointment time if he was already overbooked?

Another itinerant pilot told her that the doctor never said no to an appointment, so it was really luck of the draw. Sometimes, you arrived at an empty office and sometimes you waited two hours.

One of the worst parts of waiting was that Dinah had drunk a copious amount of water in preparation for the urine test and was now in quite a lot of discomfort verging on a loss of control. She tried to distract herself by looking at all the autographed photos of celebrities who were also pilots. Patrick Swayze's retro '80s headshot beamed at her from high up on the wall. As well as his wife's, Lisa Niemi – who was also a pilot.

The doctor finally reappeared in the little half window. He looked exactly like Jerry Stiller. It took everything Dinah had not to wish him a "Happy Festivus." She gave him her confirmation number and he waved a pink plastic cup at her.

"You can go in the restroom and take care of this. It needs to be at least to this line."

He drew a line about a third of the way up the cup with a black magic marker.

Dinah grabbed the cup from him. "Okay, thank you, sir."

"Leave it on the shelf above the toilet when you're done. Don't forget to wash your hands."

Who wasn't washing their hands?

When she got into the restroom, Dinah quickly filled the cup to overflowing, despite also peeing all over her own hand. She dumped half of it down the sink and then left it on the shelf with the three other cups, labelled with male names. Her cup was labelled, "Dinah Shore."

Whatever.

Dinah went back to the waiting room. A few minutes later, the doctor's voice boomed from the back.

"What's Junel?"

All the other pilots looked at each in confusion.

Dinah's face reddened.

Oh, God.

She got up quickly and scurried to the half window. The doctor was peering over his bifocals at his computer screen. Her application was up.

"It's ... uh ... birth control," she whispered.

"What?" he bellowed.

Dinah could hear snickering behind her.

"It's my birth control."

"What kind of birth control?"

Still bellowed.

"It's the Pill. I'm on the Pill."

He turned and looked her up and down.

"Come back here. Bring your purse. People steal."

The snickering stopped.

Another waiting pilot touched Dinah's arm.

"Hesopeg," he said softly.

"I beg your pardon," she said.

"Hesopeg." He nodded knowingly.

When she followed the doctor to the back of the office, he had her stand against the wall, and he measured her height.

"How tall are you?" he interrogated.

"I'm five foot three inches."

"You're shrinking."

She believed him.

Then he told her to stay there and cover up her left eye. Then her right.

"Read the smallest line you can on the chart," he instructed.

Dinah took a moment to orient herself and then strained to make sense of the lowest line. She thought it said – oh! – H-E-S-O-P-E-G!!! Bless that sweet guy's heart. What a solid.

Then there was a color test in a machine that looked like it predated the Gutenberg printing press. Dinah couldn't really figure out how it worked so she just started guessing which number the red and green lines went through.

"Number Three and Number Seven?"

"You sure?" the doctor challenged.

"Yes?"

It must have been close enough because she was then allowed to be weighed – he wouldn't let her take her shoes off – and he took her blood pressure.

"It's on the high side," he observed.

"I rushed to get here," she compensated. "Could you possibly take it again at the end?"

He harrumphed.

Then he took out his stethoscope and had her jog on the spot while he listened. He grabbed the skin on each side of her neck and waddled it. It returned to its original position, so she assumed she had passed the all-important supple neck skin test. At this point, she wouldn't have been surprised if he ushered a kangaroo in for her to box.

Instead he told her to take off her shirt and pants and lie down on the examining table. The door to his examining room was wide open and had a clear sightline to the busy waiting room.

She walked over and closed it.

On the table, the doctor hovered over her with the EKG pads.

Dinah didn't need an EKG; she wasn't over 40.

The doctor started placing the pads on her legs, stomach, chest, and arms. The pads were extremely sticky, and he kept dropping them and then swearing a blue streak.

"Hold still," he commanded her once he finally had them in place.

The entire process had lasted longer than the Gettysburg Address.

"Doctor -"

"Shh. Don't talk."

"But I -"

"It's important that you are quiet."

He watched his nearby monitor with the focus of a dog at a glass dining table and then turned to her.

"It's good," he adjudicated.

She had no idea what specifically was good, and she didn't care. He told her to meet him outside. And he left the door wide open again.

Dinah gingerly pulled the pads off. It hurt much more than she thought it would. The last three she tore off as quickly as she could. And then she slipped back into her clothes and grabbed her purse. She still had no idea if she had passed or not. And the doctor hadn't taken her blood pressure again, like she'd asked.

Whatever.

When she got back up front, the doctor was printing out her first class medical certificate. He shoved it in front of her.

"Sign this," he ordered.

She gratefully complied.

Then he printed up her invoice. "It's going to be $130. I had to raise my prices because I just signed a ten-year lease on this place."

A ten-year lease? Seriously?

Dinah was worried he would expire before the lease did.

She swiped her bank card and grabbed the receipt.

As she turned to leave, he said, "See you in a year."

She had a year. 12 months.

## Chapter Fourteen

**D**riving down to the interview, Dinah was nervous but manageably so. Her instructor had given her "the gouge," which helped her confidence immensely. In aviation, every type of interview, test and checkride usually had a gouge. A gouge simply meant that some humanitarian had written down all the questions that had been asked along with the accompanying answers. That way, candidates had something concrete and specific to study. People were generally lazy, so it wasn't surprising how rarely the questions changed.

When she got to the hotel, the parking lot attendant informed her that parking was $25 but that SkyQuest would validate her ticket at the end of the interview.

Uh-huh.

She walked into the lobby and a cardboard sign on an easel directed her to Conference Room A. When she arrived, there was a table set up out front and Courtney, a pretty woman with long black hair and a big smile, greeted her.

"You must be Dinah!" she exclaimed.

"I am! So nice to meet you."

"We're so glad you were able to join us today." She handed Dinah an embossed SkyQuest folder. "We'll be starting the presentation in about 20 minutes and we've got a nice buffet lunch for you. Please, please, please help yourself and enjoy!"

Dinah opened the door and entered Conference Room A.

There were about 30 candidates, all male, all wearing various degrees of business attire. Some had full three-piece-suits on, some had dress shirts and slacks, a few had khakis and golf shirts and one guy ...

one guy had shorts and a t-shirt with flip flops and a pair of sunglasses that were pushed up on his head. They were seated at long rectangular tables, facing the front of the room and another long table against the far wall had lunch items on it.

They all turned and looked at her when the door opened and then turned back to their food.

Dinah wandered over to the lunch table. There were pasta salads, green salads, cold cuts, buns and bread, a cheese plate, and a large bowl full of fresh fruit with an assortment of yogurts.

Nope.

She couldn't imagine eating anything. For one thing, her stomach was already churning. For another, she was worried she would spill something on her business suit, newly acquired from TJ Maxx. For yet another, she knew that if she ate so much as a morsel, even if she chewed it at the back of her mouth, she would end up with a big piece of something green sticking right between her two front teeth.

So, nope.

She got a glass of water and found a seat, right up front, where the only available seats were left.

Nobody talked to her.

That was normal with pilots.

Nobody talked about her.

That was *not* normal with pilots. Must be an unusually classy crowd.

About 15 minutes later, a salt-and-peppered Captain in his sixties stood up and walked to the front. She guessed he was in his sixties, because after the age of 65, you couldn't fly anymore at Part 121 airline jobs. So, a lot of these guys moved into the training or recruitment departments. Or their wives made them move into the training or recruitment departments because they couldn't stand having them around the house all day.

He was clearly not comfortable with public speaking.

The Captain started by telling them all a little bit about himself. He was a retired Navy officer.

They were almost always ex-military, these guys.

He had a wife and three boys.

She bet that none of them flew.

None of them flew. One was a civil rights attorney, one was getting his structural engineering degree, and one was a musician.

That last one must have hurt.

Then he talked about how long he'd been with SkyQuest – 15 years - and how difficult the transition had been from military to civilian flying. And how equally difficult the transition had been to more technologically sophisticated and automated aircraft.

"I'll tell you what," he said. "I didn't think I was going to make it through training. I got to my seventh SIM session of seven and I was completely in the weeds. Can't teach an old dog new tricks, if you know what I mean. But I give props to SkyQuest. They hung in there with me. They gave me extra training and helped me across that finish line. That's one of the many reasons, I've stayed with this airline – they invested in me, so I invested in them."

After that, the Captain attempted to roll out a PowerPoint presentation, but he couldn't get it to work. Which was odd because this was their second day of interviews and he had already done the presentation once that morning. Anyway, once they called a hotel IT specialist in, the presentation was up and running. It had been compiled in the early '90s and not updated. It talked about the bright, limitless future of aviation and bragged that even in the roughest of economic quarters, SkyQuest had never furloughed a pilot. Not even after 9/11. It boasted of healthcare, dental and vision insurance. It dangled employer-matched retirement savings contributions. And stock options.

And it insinuated that flying for SkyQuest was the most expeditious way to get to the majors – airlines, that is – since SkyQuest pilots were the elite. The best and the brightest.

She looked back at the guy in the flip flops.

The video ended with a montage, heavily embellished by synthesizer soundtrack, of ticket counter agents and baggage handlers, waving at the camera. Then flight attendants offering various snacks and beverages towards the camera. And then some shots of the flight deck, showing white male Captains but a panoply of minority and female First Officers.

"Anyway, I know there are a lot of choices out there, but I hope you choose to join us here at SkyQuest," the Captain summarized.

Dinah didn't understand why these recruitment sessions always seemed like they were trying to sell you a timeshare in Boca Raton instead of vetting you for a job. The choice was not going to be hers. It was going to be theirs.

Courtney stepped forward and announced that the Captain and their Assistant Chief of Recruiting – she gestured to the back of someone's silver-haired head as they disappeared through the rear door of the conference room – would be conducting the technical interviews in Meeting Rooms 8 and 9. One of them would come and get you when it was your turn. The technical interview would last for about 40 minutes.

In the meantime, she said, gesturing to her left, one of SkyQuest's newest FOs – First Officers - was in attendance to answer any of the day to day operational questions they might have. The FO stepped up to the front, from the porn set he had clearly left. His uniform was sprayed on. It was so form-fitting that Dinah could see the outline of his scrotum. It was ridiculous.

Some pilots were pilots because they wanted to fly.

Some pilots were pilots because they wanted everyone to know that they flew.

The FO seemed to be there under duress. And he couldn't answer a single question. He kept throwing them back to Courtney who piped up that she would "resource" someone or other and get back to them. Eventually it was revealed that the FO was on reserve and had only flown twice since he'd been hired.

"It's great though," he said. "I've actually got a military contract, so I fly Hawkers with them and I'm still on the payroll with SkyQuest."

Courtney was shaking her head at the back of the room.

"Of course, you would need SkyQuest's permission to do any outside flying. You know, for insurance reasons, conflict of interest, etc. … which I'm sure he does," she asserted.

The FO nodded vehemently. "Oh, for sure."

He totally didn't.

The Assistant Chief of Recruiting came back into the room and called out a name.

A tall Aryan fellow got up and followed him out. He didn't push his chair back in or dispose of his lunch refuse.

"Any other questions?" the FO asked.

The guy in the flip flops raised his hand. "Yeah, a lot of regionals are offering hiring bonuses. Is SkyQuest?"

The FO looked to the back of the room. Courtney shook her head.

"No, we're not offering hiring bonuses presently. SkyQuest doesn't feel like they need to, to be honest. The honor of working at the best regional in the country with the best long-term career prospects is more valuable than a monetary bonus."

Courtney had a – wow, he really pulled that one out of his ass – look of surprise on her face.

The Captain opened the conference room door and stuck his head in.

"Dinah Sorley." He pointed at her. "Is that you?"

"What are the odds," she said.

He laughed. "Got to be politically correct. It's a *Brave New World*."

She followed him out into it.

***

The Captain interviewed Dinah for over *three* hours. In the time it took for her to answer all his questions, the Assistant Chief guy got through the entire remainder of the applicants. At one point, Courtney stuck her concerned head into the room, to see if everything was okay.

He gave her the thumbs up.

The Captain tested her on air law, on weather, on departure and approach procedures, on navigation, on aeromedical factors. He asked her about coffin corners and Mach buffet and wing aspect ratio. And when he was done with that, he asked her to draw a diagram of the fuel system for the last aircraft that she had flown. He asked her to do math calculations to figure out top of descent points and speeds and to identify and explain different types of icing.

What was a cumulonimbus cloud?

What did ADS-B stand for?

How did TAWS work?

What happened to John Denver?

If you crashed with a Chilean soccer team in the Andes, would you eat them?

Finally, Dinah had to excuse herself to use the restroom. When she came back, he had turned the screen of his laptop to face her. There were two icons on the screen – a red button and a green button.

"Welcome back," he said hospitably. "You're probably wondering what I have here."

She was wondering when the hell she was going to be allowed to leave.

"Are you going to test me for color blindness?" she asked instead.

He smiled broadly. "That's a good one. It's important to have a sense of humor in aviation – helps diffuse stress. So long as it's not too irreverent. The company monitors social media accounts." He returned her attention to the screen. "No, what I have here is our recommendation template. If I think it would be a good idea to recommend a candidate, I press the green button. And if a recommendation is not forthcoming then I press the red button."

For real?

"Did you press one yet for me?" Dinah inquired.

"Not yet. I thought I'd ask you – which one would you like me to press?"

For *real*?

"Well, obviously I'd like you to press the green button."

"And why is that?"

*For REAL!!*

"Well, I think I'd make a positive addition to the SkyQuest family."

"Well, I think you would too!"

He jabbed his finger at the green button. It didn't take. He jabbed it again. Nothing. He tried a third time, shifting the pressure point. It began to pulse.

And with that, she was green lit.

With 1,476.3 flight hours … earned the old-fashioned way … excruciatingly.

## Chapter Fifteen

When Dinah called the owner to give him her two weeks' notice, he reacted exactly as she expected he would – like she broke up with him two weeks before prom. He accused her of abandoning her clients, of leaving him in the lurch, of being ungrateful. He never once congratulated her or expressed happiness for her on acquiring the job at SkyQuest. He did however take the opportunity to denigrate the entire airline industry once again and SkyQuest specifically. He told her it was a horrible company that treated its pilots like garbage. It was like a pilot puppy mill there.

"Give it a few months," he capitulated. "You'll come crawling back." He also added that she would never get LAX as her base, she'd have to commute halfway across the country to work. And that she'd be sitting reserve for at least three years. She'd never see the actual flight deck. But she'd see plenty of the crew lounge. And did he mention the shitty pay? Sure, they promised a lot, but the actual base salary was only $36,000 a year. Good luck living in L.A. on that. "You know your timing really couldn't be any worse. I just got a fantastic new client who needs to fly to Sacramento twice a month for check-ins. He's a registered sex offender but he's a really nice guy."

Buh-bye.

Dinah called each of her previous clients personally, partly because she was a conscientious professional and partly because she wanted to get to them before the owner did. Without exception, they were gracious about her departure and genuinely excited for her. Chrystal gave her the name of a hairdresser in Denver who did killer highlights. The border agent said that he would miss her but was excited to fly on one of her SkyQuest flights.

"I think if I know the pilot it will help my nerves," he said.

"Yeah, that usually has the opposite effect on me," Dinah teased.

"Not funny. Not at all funny."

And the deejay. The deejay. The deejay.

"I have three questions," he said. "How long is training? Can I come visit? Will you still talk to me once you're a fancy ass airline pilot?"

"Training is ten weeks."

"Ten weeks! Why so long?" he exclaimed.

"Because we're not learning to crochet. It's a large passenger jet. Plus, I have to do the Airline Transport Certification class before I can even start training. That's 32 classroom hours, a written test and 10 hours of flight simulator training."

"But are there breaks? I mean, do you get days off?"

Dinah looked at her schedule. "It looks like the first week is something called, 'Indoc' – I guess that's short for 'Indoctrination'."

"Well that doesn't sound like a cult at all."

She laughed. "It's not. It's learning about how the company operates and all their rules and regs."

"Sure. What about the other nine weeks?"

"We have two weeks of ground school – learning about the aircraft. Then something called 'DTS Training' – I have no idea what that is. That's a week. Then another thing called 'GFS Training' – I think that's like a no frills, two-dimensional simulator where they teach you the basics. Then they put us in the actual SIM."

"Ooh – I want a photo of that. Those look cool as hell – like the AT Walkers in *Star Wars*."

"That's actually the part I'm most nervous about. A lot of people don't make it through the SIM training," Dinah admitted.

"Well those losers aren't my girlfriend, so it sucks to be them. Is that it? After SIM you're done?"

"No, SIM is a couple of weeks. First you learn the basic maneuvers in the plane. Then you have to pass a Maneuvers Validation test. Then you do a LOFT."

"What's that?" the deejay asked.

"Line Oriented Flight Training – they put you in the SIM and have you fly an actual flight in real time. And they usually throw an emergency or two at you as well, to see how you can handle it."

Her skin started to prickle.

"Tight. Just like a video game," he said.

It wasn't at *all* like a video game.

"I guess. We've got to pass the LOFT validation. And then we have our FAA checkride."

"And if – sorry, *when*, you pass that, you're done?"

"Not quite. Then we need to get through IOE – Initial Operating Experience. You have to fly a minimum of 25 hours in the actual plane with an LCA – Line Check Airman."

"Jesus, aviation has a ton of acronyms."

"I know. It's the worst. So, after 25 hours, if the LCA thinks you're ready, they give you a line check and then you are officially signed off and you can start as a regular employee. Except you're on probation for the first year," she finished.

"Is the IOE in an empty plane?" he asked.

"No, they can't afford to do that. It'll be with passengers."

He cackled. "If they only knew about the newbie up front!"

"I know. It's kind of surreal to think that my first actual landing in this plane will be with actual people on board!"

"You got this. Okay, so they have to give you days off, right?"

Dinah looked at the schedule more closely. "It looks like we have one day off a week, but it changes every week, depending on where we're at in the training."

"Okay, so can I come visit?"

"Um, let's play that by ear, okay? I've heard the training is brutally stressful and intense. People keep using the term, 'fire hose technique,' which is not at all reassuring."

"Absolutely babe, no pressure."

But he sounded slightly put off.

"But hey, listen, I'm not allowed to sublet my apartment, so it'll just be sitting empty. Why don't I drop you a set of keys and then if you want to crash here, you know, whenever you like …"

He didn't answer right away.

"Sure, that's really generous of you. Let's play that by ear as well, okay?"

"Okay. No worries. Oh, and as to your final question … there's no way I'm going to talk to you once I'm a hot ass airline pilot. See ya wouldn't want to be ya!"

He groaned but not unpleasantly. "Yeah, that seems fair. More than fair."

"I'll remember you fondly though," she offered in the way of compensation.

"Speaking of remembering fondly," he said. "I'm going to make a flight training mix for you. Starting with 'Danger Zone.' Love me some Loggins."

"Maybe I won't remember you *that* fondly," she declared.

*\*\*\**

On the bus down to LAX to catch her flight to Denver, she was so excited she could hardly contain herself. It was a stark contrast to the last time she was on the Van Nuys Flyaway. As a special bonus, the baggage handler was on the same bus.

"I'm honestly so happy for you," he said. "This is an amazing accomplishment."

Dinah waited for the requisite admonishment or advice that followed along but nothing.

"How's Ines doing these days?"

"She's good. I slept on the couch last night. She's good."

He fell against her as the bus lurched across three lanes of the 405 to get into the carpool lane.

"What did you do?" Dinah asked suspiciously.

"Nothing. Why do you have to assume? I've just been so grumpy lately. Must be all the extra hours and the fact that I have to use money that was slid under my door to make rent. You wouldn't happen to know anything about that, would you?"

Dinah shrugged. "I have no idea what you're talking about. Maybe the teenage burnout in Number 321 got confused again and thought you were his meth dealer."

The bus suddenly screeched to a halt and they both smacked into the seats in front of them. Dinah looked out the window. They were at the point where the 101 empties onto the 405 – it always bottlenecked there. And then crawled through Sepulveda Pass. The pace would improve once they got into Santa Monica.

The Flyaway usually smelled slightly of diesel but the fumes were especially pungent on this trip. Dinah's eyes were watering, and she felt slightly nauseous.

"I'm going to be late for work." The baggage handler slumped down in his seat. "I hate this job. How am I going to do this for 30 more years? This life, chica."

Dinah felt guilty that her life was on the upswing while a friend's life was not.

"Is there anything else you can do? What did you go to school for?"

"Nothing. I barely made it through high school. I'm a grunt for life."

"There's nothing wrong with manual labor. It's honest work," Dinah attested.

"Yup, it's honestly low-paying and honestly demeaning and honestly backbreaking," the baggage handler said sardonically.

The bus crept forward a few feet and then stopped abruptly when a black Maserati veered across the double lines and cut it off.

"Let me ask you this - what would you like to do for a career? What interests you?"

He raised his left eyebrow. "Well, *guidance counsellor*, I've always been interested in engines ... car engines, motorcycle engines, *plane* engines."

Dinah clapped her hands. "Ooh – maybe you could become an A&P."

An A&P was an Airframe and Powerplant technician – in other words an airplane mechanic. It was a great career choice and a lot more stable than the pilot hiring pool. Dinah loved A&Ps. For women, the aviation industry perennially expected you to be lacking when it came to correlative knowledge pertaining to the inner workings of an aircraft. Every single A&P that she had ever met had allowed her into the hangar to examine engines and so forth and had patiently and respectfully answered any questions she had or clarified confusion without making her feel stupid. They seemed excited to show someone else who was excited, all about their world.

"Actually, I would be into that. But there's no money for the training."

"Maybe I could look into scholarships for you," Dinah said.

But mechanic scholarships were akin to pilot scholarships. They were a gesture at best. Most pilot training scholarships were anywhere from $500 to a few thousand dollars. To get to the point that Dinah was at, she estimated that she had spent in the area of $90,000 on training. Those scholarships bought a few flight lessons at best. And in North America, aviation training was much more financially feasible than a lot of other countries. In Europe, only the wealthy could even conceive of becoming pilots.

The bus had emerged from the pass and was starting to gain speed.

"That's okay. Nice of you though," the baggage handler said dejectedly.

"Maybe Ines will sell some of her paintings," Dinah suggested.

The baggage handler snorted. "At least I didn't waste my money on a degree in art history."

"Come on now, all college degrees have their value. Just … some might be a little more marketable than others in the present economic climate."

He looked at her sideways. "Did you get a degree in diplomacy?"

It was her turn for the side eye. "No. Film studies if you must know."

"Film studies??!! Dios mío!!"

"Shut up."

Howard Hughes Parkway was coming up and the bus veered back across the same three lanes in the other direction in preparation to exit. The baggage handler grabbed the filthy armrest and Dinah grabbed the window handle.

"Film studies! How on Earth did you afford to become a pilot?" he asked.

The look on her face changed the tone of the conversation immediately.

"From the car dealership my parents owned."

"They sold it so that you could study symbolism in *Back to the Future*?" he said cheekily.

"No. They died. In a car crash, ironically. Or maybe not ironically since they were around cars all the time. The business was left to me."

"I'm so sorry. I had no idea. When was this?"

"About six years ago. That's why I'm a little older than most new pilots. I worked with them at the dealership until … you know. Then I asked myself the question I just asked you. And the answer was, I want to fly planes."

"Your parents would be so proud of you."

"I hope so. Choices that major are such a risk. And there have definitely been moments when I thought I've screwed up my entire life and squandered my whole inheritance for nothing. But there's no turning back, you know? I'm not qualified to do anything else. So, I have to hope that this will work out."

"Because it has to?"

"Because it has to."

Now they were snaking around the entrance to LAX and pulling up in front of Terminal 1, which was where the baggage handler was getting off for Southwest. The bus stopped and everyone for Terminal 1 got up and started to exit.

The baggage handler remained seated.

"Hey, I think what you're doing is amazing. You're going after what you want. Not many people do that – and it's kick-ass of you."

He rose and he shook her hand.

"That's really kind of you to say. Thank you. And hang in there, okay? I'm sure your situation is just short term. I guarantee you that six months from now, you'll probably be blown away by how much has changed."

He nodded and gave her a half wave as he walked down the aisle towards the front of the bus and then exited.

The Flyaway pulled away from the curb and merged – i.e., forced its way back into airport traffic. It stopped at every single terminal. It was a good 20 minutes later when it pulled up in front of Terminal 7.

Dinah got out with her knapsack and then waited patiently for the driver to unload her larger suitcase. She gave him a dollar. And she brought her boarding pass up on her phone and got her passport out of her purse.

The lineup at security was long. She got in it, buoyed by the knowledge that in a few months, she would never have to line up here again. She'd be able to use the KCM – Known Crewmember – entrance to the left, which was blissfully empty.

She couldn't wait.

## Chapter Sixteen

Dinah was over half an hour early for her first day of Indoc. She had already breezed through the ATP – Airline Transport Pilot course. A considerable portion of the 32 hours in the classroom were taken up by watching videos of crashes and people hijacking planes with nail clippers. One particularly memorable montage showed how you could disable an attacker with a rolled-up newspaper by hitting them like an aberrant dog. When the classroom course was over, she was sent to a testing center to do her FAA written test. They had all been given test prep software to study with, so she felt well-prepared. In fact, a great number of the questions on the actual test were taken verbatim from the study guide. She got 98%.

The ten hours of simulator training were a complete blast. There was nothing evaluative involved. The instructor just had to cover the requisite subject areas of high altitude and high-speed operations and the like. Dinah was put into a Boeing 737 and then they had some fun. The instructor turned her upside down, let her land in Singapore, failed one of her engines, all kinds of crazy stuff. And there was no pressure. Which of course, made her fly better than she ever had. In fact, the instructor was surprised to hear that this was her first time on a large aircraft.

So, when she arrived at FlightSafety at 7:30 a.m. for an 8:00 a.m. start, she was feeling buoyed and confident. But also cognizant of the fleeting nature of those feelings. Cockiness always tended to bite you in the butt in aviation.

The cheerful young gent with the precision part in his hair at the reception desk, welcomed her, told her where she could get complimentary coffee and tea and then told her to go to Classroom 3. Dinah went up the stairs and got a mint tea, putting the cup inside two other cups to prevent herself from being scalded. Then she went down a carpeted hallway and turned left and there it was – Classroom 3.

She opened the door and went inside.

There was no one else there yet so she chose a seat about halfway back and waited expectantly.

Gradually people began to filter in, and Dinah was surprised to see at least ten other women in the class. That was unheard of. And then she got the shock of her life.

"Oh my God! Dinah?"

Dinah turned and saw that the owner of the voice was none other than Fatima, the flight attendant from her ill-fated jet job.

She rose and gave the woman a huge hug.

"Fatima! I'm so glad to see you! And to see that you escaped that predator's clutches."

"Barely," Fatima replied. "I had to stay for a few months after you left because I needed the work permit. I managed to fend off his advances until SkyQuest hired me and got me a new work permit for here."

Dinah furrowed her brow. "I'm a bit mixed up – did you become a pilot? Cause that is so cool!"

Fatima frowned. "No, this is a flight attendant class. Did they send you in here?" She shook her head. "They just assumed you were an FA. Typical."

Panic overtook Dinah. She quickly gathered her things.

"I'm in the wrong room?! Listen, I'm so happy to see you again. I've got your number, right?" Fatima nodded. "Perfect! Let me get settled in and we'll have a proper catch up!"

They hugged one more time and Dinah sped out into the hallway and tracked down the correct classroom.

When she walked in, she saw there were no other women. It was mostly white guys in their early twenties with short, all business haircuts. But right up front there was a tall, skinny fellow who looked like he was from the Middle East somewhere and a slightly pudgy guy with a baby face and a side part who waved at her with the friendliest smile.

Bullseye! Those were her people. Pilots from unpopular countries and pilots from unpopular sexual persuasions. Along with female pilots, they formed their own little aviation *Breakfast Club*. And it was a great reminder that no matter how difficult things could be, no matter how much adversity you had to face, things were always more difficult for someone else. At least they could be united in their mutual disenfranchisement. She hastened over to grab the seat in between them.

"Hi, I'm the brown guy," the tall pilot said.

Dinah smirked. "I'm the girl."

The pudgy pilot swept his bangs to the side. "I'm the token homosexual. Are you *also* the token lesbian?"

"No, unfortunately they weren't lucky enough to hit two birds with one stone this time out," Dinah answered.

That was all the meet-and-greet they had time for. The septuagenarian instructor swept into the room and called them to attention. SkyQuest preferred to use their own instructors and lease the classroom space and simulators from FlightSafety. So, this was their best and brightest in the training paradigm.

The first thing he did was have them all get up and then rearrange their seating according to seniority, starting in the front row to the far right and snaking back to the last row to the far left. Seniority at an airline was based on two criteria – your date of hire and your age. If someone was hired before you, it meant everything. They got better work schedules, better pay, better benefits and better advancement and upgrade opportunities. If two or more pilots shared the same hiring date, then seniority came down to age. Whoever was older, had more seniority. Dinah was fairly certain that she would be Number One in her hiring class but there was a guy over 40 who had a consulting firm and his mid-life crisis involved giving that up to become an airline pilot. So, she was Number Two. She lost her seatmates, who were both now several rows back.

The septuagenarian instructor then explained to the front row, how much harder it was to learn how to fly these new technologically advanced aircraft when you were older.

"Learning becomes more difficult with age," he said. "New concepts don't solidify as quickly and focusing can be more of a challenge."

Then he addressed Dinah directly.

"Also, you'll have to forgive me – I'm an old man who often doesn't know when he's not being PC." And he put the PC in air quotes. "Please feel free to call me on it. You're never too old to learn a thing or two about women, am I right?" He winked at her.

Then Dinah was treated to eight hours of instructional slides on the "Whos, Whys and Wheres" of SkyQuest Airline. They had a 10-minute break at the top of every hour because, "Psychological testing had shown that people's optimal absorption rate for active learning was about 55 minutes." The septuagenarian instructor quite literally read the slides out loud to them. Occasionally he would pepper the presentation with anecdotal stories from his long career. Two stories involved crashes caused by incompetent female pilots. One cautionary tale pertaining to human resources hinged upon a female passenger giving a male passenger a lap dance during a flight from L.A. to Newark.

"I'll bet that was a flight that he never forgot!" the septuagenarian instructor raved. "Seriously though, you can't be letting people do sex acts on your flights. It's not sanitary. Plus, there might be kids around."

Then they moved into stress mitigation. Job-related stress, sure, but also external stress and how that can negatively impact your performance as a pilot and possibly affect the safety of a flight. His example of external stress was, "the wife nagging you for being away from home so much."

After lunch, they delved into crew management and crew resources. The septuagenarian instructor visibly rolled his eyes as he explained to them that the FAA really wanted them to focus on communication and teamwork as opposed to the more archaic model of deferring to the Captain in all matters. Studies had shown that this outdated crew model had been directly responsible for many fatal crashes throughout the years. Underlings were afraid to speak up or challenge bad decisions and the results had been catastrophic. He cited a famous crash in San Francisco from 2013. A 777 had crashed into the seawall short of the runway. The Captain flying was going too slow and stalling out the aircraft and the rest of the crew were too intimidated to speak up.

SkyQuest had really run with the new FAA model and had adopted a crew briefing checklist and check-in for various phases of flight that was designed to both improve the quality and effectiveness of communication between crew members. It was also designed to encourage crewmembers to speak up without impunity, whether they were Captains, First Officers or Flight Attendants. Everyone had a place of value. Except the septuagenarian instructor didn't refer to them as "flight attendants"; he called them, "the gals in the back."

At the end of the first day, he assigned them some reading – there would be a stage check, which meant a test, at the beginning of every subsequent day of training, based on the material covered the previous day. If you failed one test, they did remedial training and had you take it again. If you failed more than two tests, then you had to go and meet with the Head of Training. Nobody knew what that entailed.

As they were packing up, the septuagenarian instructor came down from behind the podium where he'd been teaching and sat on the edge of Dinah's desk.

"How'm I doin'?" he asked.

She looked him right in the eye and said, "I think you should bring donuts tomorrow."

***

It was only when Dinah started ground school the following week that she thought fondly upon Indoc.

Now the new hire First Officers were joined by all the former First Officers who were upgrading to Captain on the same aircraft. The seniority shuffle began anew. The upgrading Captains were senior, so they got all the seats at the front of the classroom and Dinah and her boys were relegated to the back few rows. The Captains looked utterly annoyed to even be obliged to share a room with the newbies.

And then something horrifying happened.

The ground instructor – an ineffectual, pasty young waif – who was teaching because he was on medical leave, announced that they would be sorting out their SIM partners over the next few minutes.

All the simulator training was done in pairs. Anyone who was upgrading to Captain, would sit left seat and learn to fulfill all the Captain duties. Anyone becoming an FO, would sit right seat and do the same for the FO duties. The actual learning of flight maneuvers would be identical but performed from their respective seats.

The ground instructor explained that all the Captain upgrades would be paired with new hire FOs. And this was how it was going to be done ... he was going to put 15 minutes on the clock, and he wanted everyone to mix and mingle, get to know each other, and find a suitable SIM partner. Ultimately the final decision was the Captain's since he had more seniority.

Oh, and also, each couple would bid on a SIM time and be awarded one based on the seniority of the Captain. The available SIM slots were 6:00 a.m. to noon (brief at 4:30 a.m.), 2:00 p.m. to 6:00 p.m. (brief at 12:30 p.m.) and 8:00 p.m. to midnight (brief at 6:30 p.m.) ... and go!

It was worse than speed dating. Some of the First Officers made a beeline for the most senior of Captains, both for the experience and the better shot at a decent SIM time. All the military vets found each other quickly. A few suitors were turned away. It was so awkward. And a couple of wallflowers just sat there, paralyzed with social ostracism. The first few pairings seemed to take forever. After that, the rest fell into place.

At the 12-minute mark, the only remaining "singles" were – big surprise - the token brown guy, gay guy, and girl guy.

"Always the bridesmaid," sighed the pudgy pilot.

"I want my mom," said the tall pilot.

"This is ridiculous," Dinah said under her breath. She stood up. "Okay, which of you Captains still need a SIM partner?" There was no eye contact. Eventually two older pot-bellied men with bulging eyes stepped forward.

"I'll take him," said the pot-bellied Captain on the left, pointing to the tall pilot.

"I guess, him," said the pot-bellied Captain on the right, indicating the pudgy pilot.

Nobody else stepped forward so the ground instructor intervened.

"Who's left?" Nobody responded. "Dinah, you still need a partner, correct?"

"Yes," said Dinah, shaking with anger and humiliation.

Every sports team participation *ever* reverberated in her nervous system.

The ground instructor's eyes swept the room and settled on a Captain with a shaved head, sitting in the second row. "Do you have a partner?" An imperceptible shake of the head ensued. The ground instructor pointed at him. "Dinah, here you go."

The shaved head slowly rotated his pate around to look at Dinah, like Robert Patrick in *Terminator 2*. He was not pleased. Dinah clenched her bladder as hard as she could. She heard an exhalation of breath behind her.

"Sweet Holy Fuck," said the tall pilot.

"I want his mom," said the pudgy pilot.

The seats assignments were shuffled around yet again. Now, the SIM couples had to sit together, based on the Captain's seniority. A sign-up sheet was passed around for the SIM sessions. Dinah's Captain had low seniority amongst the others so of course they got the 6:00 a.m. slot.

Brief at 4:30 a.m.

Then plastic clickers were distributed. These were for testing purposes. There was going to be a test at the end of each hour of content to make sure that the material was being absorbed and retained. Just a casual "check-in" according to the ground instructor. Upon completion of a unit of study, a series of multiple-choice questions appeared on the screen at the front of the classroom. You selected your answer of choice on your clicker. Then after everyone had "voted," the correct answer was shown along with the number of persons who had selected it. The wrong answers also showed how many folks had chosen badly.

"Is this anonymous?" asked the pudgy pilot.

"Oh, thank you for reminding me," exclaimed the ground instructor. "I need you to fill out this form I'm going to pass around with your name and the serial number on your clicker. That way we can log your progress."

Another form was passed around. And then the main event got underway. Dinah did okay on the first couple of clicker tests but there was just so much material to take in and the items that began the unit were hard to retain to the end and not be displaced by fresher material. And as the day wore on, her focus flagged.

The other inherent problem was that, like so many exams in aviation, the exams were set by people who did not necessarily have a subtle grasp of the English language in its written form. The questions were often confusing and ambiguously worded, especially in their attempt to be clever. It was virtually impossible to ascertain the correct answer when you didn't even know what the question was asking.

The cherry on the icing on the cake was Couple #15. There weren't enough clickers to go around, so the last Captain/FO pairing had to share a clicker and decide on their answer as a group. While everyone else sat silently trying to figure out which button to press, Couple #15 argued incessantly about what their collective choice should be. At one point, mid-afternoon, they began physically fighting over the clicker and the ground instructor had them step out for a few moments to cool down and get a beverage. When they returned, they appeared to have reached a stalemate. After that, they treated the clicker like the buzzer on a game show ... whoever hit it first, got their answer in there.

That was Day One.

Ground School was ten days long.

\*\*\*

Every night at the hotel, they congregated in the dining area to study. At the end of ground school, there was a 125-question multiple choice exam. If you got less than 80% on it, they sent you home. The exam was divided into sections: fuel system, hydraulic system, engine, etc. An additional proviso was that if you scored 80% overall but less than 80% on any specific section, then that was also counted as a failure. So, ostensibly, you could get 96% but if you didn't know how the air control system worked, you were toast.

Dinah and her *Breakfast Club* buddies, studied their tails off. A paralyzing fear of public failure was their motivation. The tall pilot had come from Syria and was the pride and joy of his family. They were quite wealthy and had allocated a large portion of that wealth towards the furtherment of their only son. Originally, he was to have become a physician but due to the undeniable fact that he fainted quite easily at the sight of blood, he was permitted to change dreams.

"No pressure though," he said wryly.

The pudgy pilot had an equally compelling tale. He had started out as a flight attendant and became intrigued with life at the front of the plane. He started taking flying lessons from one of the pilots who was also a flight instructor and gradually transitioned.

"Was it hard to change jobs within the same industry like that?" Dinah asked him.

"Definitely. People didn't want to take me seriously."

"Good for you for hanging in there."

"I had to. Honestly, people treat flight attendants like peasants. They don't understand that we're there primarily for their safety. I once had a woman throw a cup of coffee in my face because I accidentally put real sugar in it instead of Splenda," he said.

"I'll bet closing and locking that flight deck door is going to feel extra sweet to you, no pun intended," the tall pilot said.

The pudgy pilot giggled. "No doubt. Bye bye airport drunks, screaming babies and emotional support iguanas."

"Well, first we have to get through this nightmarish training program," Dinah said. "Does anyone have the latest version?"

Like everything else in aviation, there was a gouge for the ground school exam. Or eight of them to be exact. SkyQuest was concerned that their trainees were scoring too highly on the tests, so they made it their mission to perpetually change the questions. They had their academic minions working on new versions of the exam constantly. Every class was given a different version.

Dinah wondered if Fatima was having a similarly troublesome time. She had only seen her a few times since their reunion. They had the flight attendants staying at a different hotel. Rumor was that they did it intentionally so that the pilots had fewer distractions. The last time she had run into Fatima in the lobby of the training center, getting their badges. Fatima had looked quite stressed.

"Are you okay?" Dinah inquired.

"We're doing safety drill training today," Fatima explained. "I have to go down the slide."

One of the training components involved the experience of egressing the aircraft via the inflatable slide that deployed from the cabin entrance in the case of an emergency.

"No problem," Dinah said. "You got this."

"Last week somebody broke their ankle going down it," Fatima said. "And our health insurance doesn't kick in for 90 days."

Then she showed Dinah a photo of a classmate who had quite severe skin abrasions from her trip down the slide.

"Just make sure you wear long sleeves and keep your arms tucked in," Dinah said.

"At least I haven't *popped* the slide yet," Fatima said.

One of the other components of safety drill training was learning how to open and close the main cabin door without accidentally deploying the emergency slide. It was harder than it sounded. There were several handles on the door, and they had to be dealt with in a specific order or out the slide went. There was no way to avert it once the process had begun. Maintenance had to be called to come and repack it and if the slide was damaged it cost thousands of dollars to replace.

Dinah wished Fatima the best of luck and then brooded on the fact that she herself would have to do the same training at some point. She would also have to put out fires with a halogen fire extinguisher, effectively don and inflate a life vest and learn how to use emergency oxygen. She would *not* have to learn how to avoid being injured by a heavy beverage cart at the volatile back end of an aircraft during unexpected turbulence.

Flight attendants did not have an easy time of it.

The night before the ground school exam, Dinah didn't sleep very well. She was afraid she would sleep through the alarm. She also forewent the complimentary breakfast the hotel provided. She couldn't even watch other people eat the powdered eggs and microwaved bacon. She grabbed a coffee and started trudging down the street to FlightSafety.

They had just logged into their tablets to begin the exam when someone who looked extremely official came into the classroom and asked to speak to the tall pilot for a moment outside.

He never returned.

After the exam, which she passed with 93% overall and a low mark of 88% on the flight instrument system, Dinah asked the ground instructor about him.

"I'm not sure," he answered. "I think there was an issue with his TSA approval."

Since 9/11, any pilot who was not a U.S. citizen had to get TSA – Transportation Security Administration - approval for flight training. The program was called, AFSP – Alien Flight Student Program. Foreign students had to pay a fee of $130 and submit an application to train. Whatever entity was training them was then contacted for confirmation and approval. Then the student had to get fingerprinted and a background check was conducted. Only after receiving official approval could an individual begin training in an aircraft or simulator. Sometimes the approval came within a few days. Sometimes it could take weeks. There was no predictability.

Dinah tried to call the tall pilot, but his number had been disconnected.

"I heard that they kicked him out because he was Syrian," the pudgy pilot confided.

"What?!"

"Yeah, they have a strict 'no Syrians' policy."

"How is that legal?"

He shrugged. "Flavor of the month. Who knows who'll be next?"

"Well, we can be fairly confident it won't be the Russians," Dinah dryly observed.

They never saw or heard from the tall pilot again.

***

And then the real work started. The DTS – Data Training Simulator and GFS – Graphic Flight Simulator were torture devices in hermetically-sealed rooms. The DTS was simply a desktop program that was designed to teach pilots how to do all the programming in the plane. The initialization was the most arduous. You had to input all the flight variables ... the route, the passengers, the baggage, the weather etc. Then there was additional programming based on the data that spewed out resultantly with respect to runway distance required and speeds. Every morning they were assigned a different hypothetical and given a time limit to accomplish the programming. The computers were quite old and would frequently freeze and then crash. That meant that any data you had input up to that point was deleted and you had to reboot the computer and start all over again.

"Yeah, these computers are problematic," the DTS instructor said. "We complain all the time, but they never replace them."

In the afternoon, they were positioned in front of something called a "paper tiger" in order to learn their "flows." A paper tiger was simply a visual representation of the flight deck in poster form. It was taped to the wall. During each phase of flight, there were procedures that the Captain and First Officer had to perform in a very specific physical order. They were similar in format really to choreography. They had to be done completely by memory so you had to practice them repeatedly with the paper tiger and know them cold – like the programming – before they would allow you to progress to the GFS.

They were tested on the final day on both. They were given another hypothetical trip on the DTS and timed and evaluated on their programming. Dinah made a mistake on hers – forgetting to input the correct temperature but because she finished quickly enough, the instructor allowed her to go back and rectify it. But he also made a big deal out of this act of altruism. Then she scooted across the hall and demonstrated that she knew all her flows in front of another instructor. She was also timed on this.

The next week, as Dinah was introduced to the GFS, she wished she could go back to the DTS. It was a two-dimensional simulator that taught you to amalgamate all of the programming and flows that had been learned up to that point in real-time flights. The controls moved but they didn't work – they were there to teach muscle memory. Dinah also had to begin incorporating "call outs" – which were the verbalizing of certain physical components of the flight that were necessary to facilitate communication between crewmembers – for example, the pilot flying calling for "gear up," which prompted the non-flying pilot (the pilot monitoring) to move the gear lever up, once the aircraft had established a positive rate of climb. They were difficult to remember, especially during the takeoff phase because so much was going on at once. The multi-tasking was overwhelming and exhausting. She went back to the hotel every day with a massive headache and hours of preparation for the simulated flight the following day.

Her GFS instructor was an arrogant Italian Captain who somehow commuted from Bologna to Denver. Whenever Dinah asked him a question, his response was the same.

"We don't have time for this. Look it up in your manuals."

And then he would somehow have time to tell another long-winded story about how much better of a pilot he was than everybody else. Like the time he was flying in a snowstorm in the Italian Alps and saved everyone by overpowering the other pilot on the controls, who had no idea what he was doing.

Why were they flying in a snowstorm in the Italian Alps?

He also had a habit of interrupting her. And whenever she was doing something incorrectly, he would pace behind her and cluck disapprovingly.

Which was often.

The GFS had a touchscreen feature, which only worked if you pressed the desired button with precisely the right amount of pressure. Otherwise the plane would not respond. You could walk by any GFS lab and hear pilots cursing the GFS to high heaven as they angrily jabbed at the screen while their aircraft flew merrily into the nearest mountain or collided unabashedly with the ground.

Dinah's errors were half and half. Sometimes it was because she had misunderstood how to program a flight maneuver and sometimes it was because the screen did not respond. The Italian Captain refused to acknowledge the technical glitch.

"Pilots are always blaming others for their own shortcomings," he lectured. "You need to be accountable for your own learning."

On the day of her GFS validation, he had come down with a cold. And still showed up. Which meant that Dinah was going to come down with a cold.

He gave her the flight information and started the timer. Everything was timed. It was imperative to stay on schedule. He was vocal and rude – berating her all the way through the flight. He kept telling her time was running out and that she was two minutes away from failing. She could feel his breath on the back of her neck.

Peppermint Altoids.

Dinah knew that he was going to give her a localizer approach. Some approaches gave both lateral and vertical guidance down to the runway. A localizer approach only gave lateral guidance. You had to step the aircraft down yourself. Dinah had repeatedly forgotten to change the approach mode in the programming for these approaches. She remembered just as the plane was about to intercept the localizer to final.

"One more second and I would have failed you," the Italian Captain proclaimed.

Then she had to keep the plane descending but level it off at various intermediary altitudes. This necessitated anticipating when to stop and start the descent, which was tricky to time. You couldn't be more than 100 feet off – plus or minus. She could feel the sweat dripping down her back.

"20 more feet and you fail," he caroled.

By the time she got the plane on the ground, her hands were visibly shaking.

"Congratulations," he keened. "You almost failed."

And then he asked her if she wanted to go to Wild Wings with him.

Except that due to his thick accent it came out like, Wild-uh Wings-uh.

Jesus Christ-uh.

\*\*\*

The alarm went off at 3:00 a.m. for Dinah's first SIM session. When she got to FlightSafety, her SIM partner – the Captain upgrade with the shaved head – was already there. Once she chatted with him for a few minutes, she realized he was actually a pretty decent guy. He was a good ole boy for sure – born and bred in Texas, former Ranger but he was low key and had a good sense of humor. She liked his drawl and she didn't mind that he kept addressing her as, "darlin'." Dinah had been told that a SIM partner could make or break you so that was a good sign. She had heard many stories about SIM partners not getting along and torpedoing each other right out of training.

Their SIM instructor was about ten minutes late. He was her SIM partner's doppelgänger except for a small putting green on the top of his head. When he reached the top of the stairs, her SIM partner broke into a huge grin.

"Well, who let this piece of shit into the building?" he bellowed, patting the SIM instructor on the back.

The SIM instructor patted him back. "I guess they couldn't find a monkey to upgrade to Captain," he returned.

Dinah guessed they knew each other.

Which was a good thing?

They both continued to ignore Dinah. She stood off to the side, observing in silence.

"For serious," her SIM partner said. "How in the hell did they rope you into this?"

"I've got two alimony payments to make every month, that's how!"

Dynamite. Another instructor who was devoted to teaching.

The SIM instructor had them move towards the briefing room. The two men walked in front, continuing to catch up while Dinah straggled behind.

The SIM brief was to last 90 minutes, in which the instructor was supposed to go over what they would be doing on the SIM that day. Then they would be in the SIM for four hours – they would each fly two hours and be "pilot monitoring" the other two, which meant doing all the radio calls, most of the checklists and moving the landing gear and flaps into position. Then there would be a 30-minute debrief. Dinah was hoping that she'd be able to fly first. She was concerned about fatigue and lack of focus if she went second. Her SIM partner had already been flying the aircraft for three years as a First Officer but absolutely everything was new to Dinah.

She was told that the Captains always flew first. No explanation why. Her SIM partner said he didn't care if he went first or second. But Captains always flew first.

The two of them continued to bust each other's balls and bitch about the airline industry in general and SkyQuest in particular until the 90 minutes were almost up. Dinah still had no idea what they were going to be doing in the SIM.

"Don't sweat it," the SIM instructor said. "He'll go first, and you can watch what he does. Let's take ten minutes and then we'll get set up in the SIM."

The two of them wandered off together and Dinah frantically reviewed the academic lesson on her tablet. But like most physical skills, it was difficult to learn by looking at diagrams and reading descriptive text. One had to have the tactile feel of the controls and verbal coaching in the moment.

Dinah didn't have a clue once she got in the SIM – she was so flustered and intimidated. She didn't know how to put on the seatbelt or move the seat back and forward or up and down. She didn't understand how the bracket for the tablet worked or how to turn any of the lights on. She should have spoken up, but she didn't. And the two men didn't notice her struggling.

She never figured out how to adjust the rudder pedals.

Every time the Captain finished a maneuver – like steep turns, which were turns with a 45-degree bank angle – the SIM instructor reset the SIM, which repositioned the screen. The Captain saw that the sudden blurring and then change of locale was making Dinah nauseous.

"Darlin' you need to look down or close your eyes while he does that or you're gonna puke."

There was a lot of shooting of the shit between maneuvers so by the time it was Dinah's turn to fly, there was just a little over an hour left. And the pacing of the syllabus was such that it afforded enough time to basically do each maneuver twice. Which wasn't a lot. Especially if you had never flown the plane before.

Dinah was all over the place and didn't finish everything she needed to get signed off on. The SIM instructor shouted out vague encouragements occasionally.

"Fly the plane!"

Once she looked back while she was trying to recover from a stall and thinking she wasn't applying enough forward pressure and the SIM instructor was texting someone on his phone.

Her SIM partner tried to help her by pushing his own yoke forward. "There ya go, hon."

At the sound of his voice, the SIM instructor looked up. "Sorry guys – hold on a minute. This bee-yatch thinks she's getting our boat."

During the debrief, he acknowledged that Dinah was a bit behind but not to worry, they would catch her up.

The next day was more of the same. Again, she had a little over an hour. There was no review of what they had done the previous day. She was told the SIM was so expensive to use that time didn't allow for it.

By the time they got to Day Four of Five, Dinah had only been signed off on a third of the maneuvers she had to do for the Maneuver Validation test the next day. Her SIM partner tried to step in where he could, to help. He gave her verbal coaching a few times until the SIM instructor shut him down.

"Don't prompt her," he admonished him. Then he blew up at Dinah. "You do realize that he's completely carrying you? You don't know how to do anything on your own!"

She was so shocked that she sat there in silence, afraid to open her mouth to defend herself.

"Now, she'll be alright. This is her first big aircraft. She's just gonna need a few extra sessions," her SIM partner said.

He really was a gentleman in disguise.

Her SIM instructor sent her downstairs to meet with the Head of Training about extra SIM sessions, which were in high demand and short supply.

***

"Lots of initial hires need extra SIM sessions. There's a lot of stuff crammed into those lesson plans," said the Head of Training, a man who looked like he should be selling ties.

"That's a relief to hear," said Dinah.

"We probably should just have eight sessions instead of five. The problem is scheduling. I don't have any SIM availability for the next three days. I'll get someone from the Training Department to reach out to you."

Dinah rose to leave. "That's great. Thank you."

"Of course, this means that we'll have to put you on a *Special Track*."

"Wait. What does that mean?" she asked warily.

The Head of Training waved dismissively. "It just means that we keep a file on you detailing your training *issues*. And instead of doing recurrency training with the rest of your class every year, you'll have to do it every six months."

Special.

She held it together until her cell started ringing on the walk back to the hotel. It was the deejay. The second she answered, and he asked how she was, she started to ugly cry. And as she was ugly crying, she explained to him that she was fine and that's how women dealt with stress. By crying. It wasn't because she was emotionally weak.

"I'm getting on a plane," he stated.

And she didn't stop him.

***

When he walked into the lobby of the hotel, 14 hours later, she clung to him like moss. Once they got to the room, she had to let him go because he needed to pee. Once he emerged from the restroom, he sat her down on the sofa.

"So, what's going on? Talk to me."

Instead of telling him about getting short-changed on flying time and not receiving adequate instruction, Dinah told him that she couldn't do anything right.

"I'm the worst pilot ever!" she whined.

"Said every pilot, at one time or another, I would assume," he replied. "Okay, let's break it down. What are you having the most trouble with?"

"The V-1 Cut."

"That sounds weirdly like deejay jargon. What is a 'V-1 Cut'?"

Dinah made a face that was filled with revulsion. "They fail an engine on you on the takeoff roll. The plane starts veering off the runway and you have to get it under control, take off and then climb without flipping it over or letting it veer into a mountain. I've red-screened it twice."

"What is 'red-screening' it?" the deejay asked.

"It's when the simulator simulates that you've crashed the plane. The entire screen turns red, like blood."

"That sounds cool."

"It's not. I can't do this."

"Yes, you can."

"No, I can't."

"Yes. You can."

The deejay had her walk him through every single maneuver she had to do for the Validation Test. Then they started chair flying – which literally meant, sitting in a stationary chair, physically miming the maneuvers, and verbalizing everything. Gradually, Dinah started to calm down and feel a bit more confident.

Her email dinged. The Training Department couldn't fit her in for another SIM session for five days. But they could use her as a seat sub in the meantime for the Captain who had lost his partner when the tall pilot disappeared from the program.

"That's great!" said the deejay. "Now you can get extra SIM time and learn without any of the pressure! See it's going to be okay."

"Will you stay though? Just until the test?"

"Sure thing. I've never been to Denver before. I'll do the tourist thang while you're training and then we'll relax and have some fun. Take your mind off the stress."

"You're the best." Dinah tucked herself under his chin.

"Hey, is this a new bald spot?"

"Don't even!"

\*\*\*

Dinah needed two extra SIM sessions after she seat subbed several times. She had been separated from her SIM partner. She was told they needed to "keep moving him forward," so she had no idea who would be flying with her.

When she got to FlightSafety and saw the pudgy pilot waiting nervously in the hallway leading to the SIM, she ran up and gave him a squeeze.

"I hate this place," she said.

"Me too. My rosacea is coming back. Why are you here?"

"I can't do a V-1 cut. You?"

"Fucking crosswind landings. I've gone off the runway twice."

Crosswind landings were a challenge. You had to crab the wings into the wind on the approach and then just as you were about to touch down on the runway, you had to press the opposite rudder pedal to line the plane up. Sometimes people forgot to do that. But more often, they got the rudder input in there but neglected to hold the ailerons into the wind and the plane was blown sideways.

Dinah frowned. "But the maximum crosswind they should be giving you is 15 knots. That's not strong enough to do too much damage."

The pudgy pilot raised one eyebrow. "Yesterday he gave me 40 knots."

"That's bullshit. Do we have the same instructor today?"

"I don't think so. I challenged him to a fist fight, and he called me the 'F-word'."

Dinah gasped. "He did not!"

The pudgy pilot nodded vehemently. "He did. He called me a 'Flight Attendant!' Fucker!"

Their SIM instructor du jour walrused his way down the hall towards them, chewing on his moustache.

"You my 2 p.m.?" he asked them. They nodded. "Let's go." There were no briefings now because they were rehashing previously covered material. So, they went right into the SIM. The pudgy pilot went first. Dinah thought he did okay but the instructor du jour was brutal on him. "You can't over-compensate with the other aileron. You need to have more control. You're fishtailing all over the place."

But at least he kept the crosswind to 15 knots.

In Dinah's case, he screamed at her not to rotate the plane off the runway until she was back on the centerline and had it under control. Which was hard to do when you could see the end of the runway quickly approaching.

The pudgy pilot whispered to her. "Don't use the ailerons much. And press the rudder as hard as you can. Then when you get it airborne, trim the hell out of it so you don't have to press the pedal as hard."

Dinah tried it and the next one was better. Not great but better.

At the end of the session, during the debrief, the instructor du jour was blunt.

"Look, based on your training records, it looks like today, you both made some progress. The problem is the progress isn't happening quickly enough."

"I was told that a lot of initial hires need extra SIM sessions and SkyQuest is okay with it," Dinah said.

"Up to a point. You can have up to two extra sessions, no harm no foul."

The Head of Training hadn't mentioned a two-session limit when Dinah met with him.

The pudgy pilot raised his hand. "Excuse me, is that two extra ones for the Maneuvers and two extra ones for the LOFT?"

"No, two extra - total. So, if you use them up in Maneuvers that's it. Then if you have trouble during the LOFT training, you're out of luck," he said, turning his palms up.

"What happens then?" Dinah asked with dread.

"They terminate you, which goes on your permanent record for all potential future employers to see."

The two pilots looked at each other.

"So, we shouldn't do any more extra sessions?" the pudgy pilot asked.

The instructor du jour sighed. "Honestly, I don't know what to tell you. Right now, I can't sign you off on the maneuvers. You would need at least one more session each. But then you don't get an extra session during LOFT. And if you don't get signed off tomorrow, then you're fired."

"What are our options?" Dinah asked.

"If I were you, I'd probably go back to flying Cessna 172s. If you resign before you use up all your SIM sessions, then it's voluntary and nothing negative goes on your employment record."

Dinah turned once again to her *Breakfast Club* buddy. "What do you think we should do?"

His face turned to stone. "I am not walking away from this with nothing!"

"So, I guess I'll see you tomorrow," the instructor du jour said.

Dinah didn't reply but tagged along with the pudgy pilot back to the hotel. She introduced him to the deejay and then the three of them went to have pie and whisky for dinner. When they discussed their options, the deejay was in complete agreement with the pudgy pilot.

"No way! You guys have worked so hard! They clearly have a training problem, not a pilot problem."

The pudgy pilot chased a big bite of lemon meringue with a swig of Crown Royal and turned to Dinah. "I like him. Don't screw it up."

"I'll tell you what you do. You both go in there tomorrow and kick some ass!"

"Do you have any brothers?" the pudgy pilot asked him.

"I do, but he's straight. Sorry," the deejay said.

"That's okay. Most of the pilots who hit on me are straight and married with kids."

"Isn't that interesting," Dinah noted.

The pudgy pilot licked an errant spot of meringue off his thumb. "Isn't it, though?"

***

They did it. Somehow, they got through it. Dinah felt energized by the pudgy pilot's determination. She could feel his strength seeping into her from the other seat. She did her first V-1 cut perfectly.

The pudgy pilot clapped his hands. "Yes!!"

The instructor du jour stared at him balefully. "Okay, I hate to admit it, but that was good. But I need to see one more just in case you got lucky."

The pudgy pilot glared at him. He looked like he was about to say something, and Dinah patted his hand and shushed him. She did another V-1 cut. The second one was a little wobbly on the climbout, but it was still within acceptable standards, so the instructor signed her off.

Then came the crosswind landings. The first one was off the centerline but not excessively so. Dinah thought the instructor du jour might give it to him, but no. She could see how livid the pudgy pilot was.

She whispered to him. "Just keep saying 'aileron' to yourself as you kick the rudder in, so you don't forget."

He nodded. The instructor du jour set him up one more time on an approach into Dallas and let it rip. Dinah could hear the pudgy pilot mumbling to himself and she joined in.

"Aileron. Aileron. Aileron."

Bam! Right on the centerline.

"That was a thing of beauty!" the instructor du jour exclaimed. With a sneer.

"Fucking right it was," the pudgy pilot said.

And he signed them off on their Maneuvers Validation.

"But that was your last chance, guys," he reminded them. "No extra SIMs on the LOFT training."

\*\*\*

The best part of all this was that they got to stay together as SIM partners. And after more stressing and sleepless nights, their LOFT ended up being somewhat of a non-event. They had to do an entire flight in real-time from Houston to Dallas and back, once as the "pilot flying" – PF - and once as the "pilot monitoring" - PM. And there was an emergency each time.

The benefit to the flight being simulated in real-time was that they could pace themselves and confer and communicate like an actual crew. And they absolutely had each other's backs, which was pivotal to their success.

And most importantly, they only had to do one goddamn takeoff and one goddamn landing each.

The pudgy pilot flew first. His emergency was a failed autopilot, so he had to hand fly the entire flight. Dinah was really impressed with his stick and rudder skills. He was an excellent pilot. She did everything she could to take as much of the workload over from him as she could so that all he had to do was fly the plane.

Their LOFT instructor commented on how well they worked together as a crew.

Then it was Dinah's turn to fly. She forgot to call for the flaps to come up after takeoff, and the pudgy pilot asked her if she wanted the flaps up.

Good man.

About halfway through the flight, red warning lights started flashing and alarms started going off.

Engine fire. On the left engine.

The pudgy pilot verbally acknowledged the emergency and did a few immediate action checklist items from memory – which was required. They extinguished the fire and shut the left engine down and then he declared the emergency over the radio and started running through the next checklist in the QRH – the Quick Reference Handbook – that was stored in the console between the two seats.

After that, they had to get set up for landing on one engine. They ascertained the new approach speeds and went over a game plan in case they had to go around and climb back out on one engine. Lord knew that Dinah had had enough bloody practice at that.

The hardest part about the landing was that the slower the plane got, the less input you needed on the opposite rudder pedal. But

Dinah felt in control – she didn't let the plane get ahead of her. And she was nice and easy on that pedal.

A little bit.

A little bit.

A little bit.

When she heard the automated voice call out, "50 feet," she started to ease back on the yoke.

And nailed the landing. Absolutely nailed it.

"Go back to flying 172s, my fine ass!" the pudgy pilot said.

They were both signed off on their LOFT training. Almost there. They were so close it physically ached.

Shortly after arriving back at the hotel and having an extremely adorable group hug with the deejay, they both received emails concerning their final FAA checkride.

It was in two days.

At 6:30 a.m.

And an FAA inspector was coming for a "ridealong." Which meant that the FAA was sending one of their guys to examine the examiner who was examining them.

At 6:30 a.m.

In two days.

# Chapter Seventeen

**H**e died.

When the farmer didn't show up for their lesson, or reply to her texts, Tammy rode her bike into town. It was too late. At the care facility, she was told that he had taken a fall going into dinner the night before. His head had hit the tile floor really hard and there was a resultant blood clot. The paramedics had come quickly but there was little the doctors could do for him by the time they reached the local hospital.

Tammy started to cry. "Can I see him? In the hospital?"

The orderly put his arm around her shoulder. "Hon, he had a DNR."

She looked visibly confused. "I don't know what that is."

"It's a do-not-resuscitate order. They took him off life support a few hours ago."

Her crying intensified. "Why? Why would he have that?? That's basically giving up!!"

The orderly put his hand under Tammy's chin. "He was older, and he had no family left. I suppose he didn't want to be a burden."

"He had me! And he wasn't a burden. He was my friend!"

"It sounds like he was an incredibly fortunate man, to have a friend like you. Can I call someone for you, hon?"

Tammy shook her head. "I should get home." She started to exit the lobby and then turned back. "Actually, I left something in his room. Is it okay if I just run back really fast and look for it?"

The look on the orderly's face told her that this was clearly a violation of some policy or other, so she hung her head and wept a little harder.

"Okay, just be quick, yeah?" He looked around vigilantly. "Go right now."

Tammy sped back to the farmer's room and there, right on top of his bureau, were the keys to the plane.

After they had landed and been busted by Tammy's parents, holy hell had ensued. The farmer had been escorted off the property and told not to come back.

"But technically I own the place," he pointed out.

Tammy's mother, JoJo, crossed her arms stubbornly. "Then *we* will leave. You can stay and we will leave."

Tammy's father scowled. "But I like it here. And I've just fired up the barbeque for the roti."

"Shh."

Tammy interceded. "Mom, Dad, please, it's not his fault. I badgered him to teach me to fly. Please don't take it out on him."

The less than amicable compromise was that the flying lessons would cease immediately, and the farmer would only visit in the future in his capacity as a landlord. Tammy put up a full-blown adolescent level of resistance, but her parents were immovable. They also didn't approve of the incongruous friendship.

"It's not normal for a young teenage girl to be friends with an older man," her mother said disapproving.

"You're being ridiculous! I should be able to be friends with whoever I want!!" Tammy yelled.

For his part, the farmer went quietly, waving goodbye to Tammy and sharing a look with her that intimated that this would merely be a temporary situation.

And now it was to be permanent.

Tammy hightailed it out of the care facility and rode like the wind back to the farm, with the keys gripped tightly in her left hand.

When she got there, she dropped her bike recklessly in the front yard and went straight to the barn. Gretchen watched her from the field, chewing her cud and contemplating her existence. Tammy opened the barn doors and pulled the plane out into the open.

Gretchen mooed loudly.

"Shut up, Gretchen!" Tammy called.

\*\*\*

Just after liftoff, Tammy realized that perhaps her decision to solo might have been the slightest bit rash. Leaving the earth was not the hard part. The hard part was going to be coming back down. And that damn cow's eyes had never left the plane. Gretchen watched her circling the farm's perimeter, with brash bovine judgment.

After about 30 minutes of her sweaty hands slipping off the yoke, Tammy decided she'd better have a go at landing. She pushed the mixture knob all the way in, reduced power by pulling out the throttle. She put the first notch of flaps down. She peered around and then turned onto final. Second notch of flaps. Slower. Last notch of flaps. The farmer had taught her how to land on a grass strip, but she hadn't really got the hang of it yet.

That probably wasn't good.

She talked through the steps. Just before touchdown, she was going to add a tiny bit of power so that the plane wouldn't settle on the runway too abruptly. And then as soon as the main wheels touched down, she was going to pull out the power and maintain the back pressure on the yoke so that the nosewheel would come down on its own, as gently as humanly possible. It was kind of like popping a wheelie down the runway. If she touched down too fast or too hard then she could have a tail strike or a prop strike or snap the nose gear.

Tammy got about 20 feet off the ground before she chickened out and did a go-around. She aborted the landing by pushing the throttle all the way in, and bringing the flaps back up in stages. And she started to climb back up. She told herself that that was good pilot decision-making – she had been high and fast.

The next time she went around because she was low and slow.

The third time because Gretchen distracted her, and she wasn't lined up properly.

Then the sun was in her eyes. And a sudden wind gust flustered her. And then the sudden calmness of the wind flustered her.

And then the low fuel light came on.

That was one of the first things the farmer had ever taught her. You never got into an aircraft without checking how much fuel you had. And by checking, he meant you didn't trust the fuel gauges – they were notoriously unreliable. You unscrewed the fuel tank caps on the wings and tested the level with a dipstick, so you could visibly see how much fuel was in each wing. He had told Tammy story after story about "Darwin Award Winners" who had jumped into planes without checking and ran out of fuel just a few minutes later. His favorite had been a car salesman in North Bay who had run out of fuel and had to make an emergency landing on Main Street. Fortunately, no one had been injured. At least at the scene. After the salesman and his passenger were on the six o'clock news, it was Armageddon. Because the passenger was his girlfriend. And he had a wife.

"Again," Tammy had said. "I don't know how appropriate that story is for a teenager."

The farmer had wagged his finger at her. "Look, my point is, you don't want to be on the news for something like that. You want to be on the news for saving a litter of puppies from a burning building."

Tammy grinned. "What about saving your wife *and* your girlfriend from a burning building?"

"I just can't imagine how that would end well for anyone."

And now here she was, no puppies, just annoying Gretchen there to witness her life going up in flames.

Okay, no more nonsense. Even though she could do a power-off landing, like she was in a glider if she had to, she did not want her first solo landing to be without power. You only had one shot to get the plane down in that scenario – there were no go-arounds.

As she turned onto final, Tammy gave herself the talking-to that all pilots do from time to time. That fact had been verified by the farmer. She could hear his voice in her head.

"Pilots have conversations with themselves all the time. Sometimes you do something stupid and you have to call yourself a 'dumbass,' sometimes you have to give yourself a pep talk. You know, a 'you can do it,' kind of encouragement and sometimes you talk to yourself because you get lonely up there in the big ole sky."

Tammy said it out loud. "Come on dumbass. You can do it."

She put the last notch of flaps down and noted that the "runway" was just getting bigger in her windscreen, not moving up or down. That meant she was right on the glidepath. And then it all seemed to happen at once.

Throttle to idle – eyes at the end of the runway.

Add a little bit of power back in – eyes at the end of the runway.

Hold the yoke back a little bit, little bit more, little bit more.

Mains touched down – power to idle – hold the yoke back.

Let the nosewheel come down – and then taxi off the runway.

That's how it should have gone.

Instead, Tammy added too much power and started floating down the runway. Then she pulled it all off and because she had so much back pressure, the plane dropped and landed hard. And then it bounced. And then it bounced again. And the next bounce wasn't as big and eventually the bouncing stopped. As did the plane.

Tammy sat there gripping the yoke. And then she screamed. And laughed. And cried.

And gave Gretchen the finger.

***

Tammy was so emotional that her parents were afraid *not* to attend the farmer's funeral.

"Honestly, would you have guessed that she would ever be this upset about an old white man?" her mother said to her father in the church as Tammy went up front to pay her respects.

"I think that might be a racist thing to say," her father admonished tentatively.

"Don't be ridiculous. Only white people can be racist."

Tammy was comforted by how many people were at the funeral. It looked like almost everyone from the care facility was there as well as a lot of other townspeople. In his casket, the farmer had been dressed in his best – and probably only – suit. A dark brown number that must have fit a lot better in his younger days. Someone had worked a miracle to get that jacket button done up. His hands were folded in front of him and clasped in them was a photo of his wife, Darla. It looked like one of those Sears Portrait Studio specials.

It was perfect.

After the ceremony, there was a wake in the church basement. Finger sandwiches and vegetable platters. Tea and coffee. And Tim Hortons donuts.

Some Canadian stereotypes were charmingly accurate.

A short stocky man with bright yellow hair approached Tammy and her parents. He extended his hand to Tammy. Her mother gently elbowed her, and Tammy took his hand and shook it.

"You must be the famous Tammy," the short stocky man said.

"I'm famous?" she said, surprised.

"Well as far as your buddy was concerned, you were. He quite enjoyed you. When I met with him last, he called you a 'real sparkplug'."

Tammy's mother spoke up because her father was knee-deep in a Bavarian cream. "I'm sorry – who are you?"

"Beg your pardon," he answered quickly. "I'm his lawyer." He handed Tammy his card. "I wondered if you might be able to come by my office tomorrow at 10 a.m.?"

"For what?" Her father jumped in now with a mouth full of donut and chocolate flecks lodged in his moustache.

"The reading of the will, of course."

\*\*\*

He left her his plane.

## Chapter Eighteen

The FAA inspector looked exactly like Dinah thought he would. Thinning white hair, skinny legs but a belly that hung over his belt and an inordinate number of burst capillaries on his face. He exuded authority from every pore. When they spotted him in the lobby, the pudgy pilot exhaled so strongly that his breath moved Dinah's hair.

Their checkride examiner looked like the model for a SkyQuest recruitment poster. He was a blond Adonis, with a square jaw and piercing blue eyes. When he smiled at them, she heard the pudgy pilot suck his breath back in.

"Now, I don't want you guys – sorry, girl and guy – to be nervous about the FAA being here. It's just going to be a regular old checkride. No tricks up my sleeve. Promise!" he said.

"You don't have sleeves," the pudgy pilot said cheekily.

But he did have bulging biceps.

"You're right!" the examiner returned. "So definitely no tricks! Look, we know you're both ready for this. Otherwise you wouldn't have been signed off for the ride, right? So, let's just treat this like a formality of sorts and get you out on the line, yes?"

Dinah relaxed just an iota. She liked how this examiner tried to diminish the stress for them. He didn't have to do that. He could have compounded it.

That was a good sign.

The FAA inspector added his two cents. "Just ignore me. Act like I'm not even here. Like my wife does!"

He laughed at his own joke.

The examiner joined him.

Then the pudgy pilot.

Dinah smiled weakly.

The checkride began with the examiner verifying their identification and FAA licenses and their medical certificates. Then there was a brief and relatively painless oral exam. He alternated questions between them about the different systems of the aircraft. And there were a few regulatory questions from back in Indoc pertaining to rest period requirements and weather with respect to takeoff and landing diversions. The examiner treated them like a crew. If Dinah didn't know the answer to a question, he permitted the pudgy pilot to jump in and answer it and vice versa. After about 45 minutes, he closed his tablet.

"Okay, I'm satisfied. You know your stuff. Why don't we take ten minutes and grab a coffee and then we'll hit the SIM. Have you decided who's going to fly first?"

"Oh God, can I please go first?" the pudgy pilot asked.

Damn.

"Sure," said Dinah.

"Good stuff. Now, this flight will be similar to your LOFT so again, nothing to stress about. We'll start with the required maneuvers that you have to do and then we'll do a short flight that may or may not have an emergency." He winked. "You can pretty much count on an emergency. And then we'll take another break, switch seats and then Dinah will fly. Sound good?"

They nodded.

It sounded like the Boston Marathon.

With an FAA inspector watching.

Just then, the FAA inspector's cell phone rang. "Excuse me." He went out into the hallway to take the call. When he returned a minute later, he grabbed his windbreaker from the back of his seat.

"Everything ok?" the examiner asked.

"I'm awfully sorry about this but I'm going to have to scoot. That was my granddaughter's school calling. She's come down sick and my daughter's away on a business trip. I need to go and pick the poor little gal up and take her home."

He shook their hands and departed.

"Do we have to reschedule the rest of the checkride?" Dinah asked.

"Nope – we keep on rocking and rolling," replied the examiner.

The Boston Marathon suddenly became a 10K.

\*\*\*

The examiner hadn't lied. The checkride was truly just a formality. He didn't seem to be looking for perfection. He just wanted to make sure that they were knowledgeable, proficient, and most importantly, safe.

And he had such a relaxed style. He didn't rush them. Dinah felt like he was on their side. Like he wanted them to pass.

How rare.

How refreshing.

And he engaged them in light banter to try and diffuse the tension.

"So, you're from Minnesota," he addressed Dinah. "Do you say 'soda' or 'pop'?"

"Pop," she answered promptly. "Because I'm not an animal."

He grinned.

"I like Diet Coke," chimed in the pudgy pilot.

"Yup – Diet Coke's a good, solid choice," the examiner responded mercifully.

After they both got through the maneuvers with only a little difficulty – the pudgy pilot rolled out of his steep turn just a little too soon and Dinah took a second too long to respond to being placed in an unusual attitude – they moved on to the flight leg portion. It was virtually the same as their LOFT flight, with the exception that Dinah got the failed autopilot and the pudgy pilot got the engine fire.

Score.

After the examiner had them shut down the SIM, he said the magic words. "Congratulations. You both passed!"

Dinah tried her best not to cry.

Don't cry.

Don't cry.

She and the pudgy pilot took turns taking pictures of each other seated in the SIM, with dorky "thumbs up" poses. Then they went to the office with the examiner and he logged onto IACRA – Integrated Airman Certification and Rating Application – which was the online FAA website for aviation paperwork and filled out their forms. After he was done, he printed out their temporary permits, which were good for a couple of months, until their permanent licenses came in the mail. And then he stood up, came around from behind the desk and high fived them. Dinah had learned early on that if you didn't care for high fiving, you had no place in aviation.

"You both did great," he said. "Initial Operating Experience – IOE - will be where the real training begins. Good luck!"

Dinah and the pudgy pilot didn't speak until they had fully exited the building, almost like saying anything out loud would jinx them. As if the examiner might come running after them and admit that he made a mistake and that in actuality they failed their checkrides. They kept pace as they left the premises.

"What a class act, that guy was," Dinah said when they were free and clear.

"Agreed. He belongs to the NGPA. I've seen him at some of their events. He was at Sun 'n Fun last year in Florida," said the pudgy pilot.

"What's the NGPA?" Dinah asked.

"The National Gay Pilots Association."

Dinah nodded. "That's a good thing."

"Thank you, Martha Stewart."

Dinah blushed. "Why don't you ask him out? I didn't see a ring."

Women always noticed that type of thing … especially at work.

"Because I'm *way* out of his league."

And they sashayed in a triumph of two back to the airport hotel in Denver, Colorado.

*\*\*\**

IOE – Initial Operating Experience – kind of took Dinah by surprise. She had really viewed the checkride as crossing the finish line but couldn't have been more mistaken. Now she had to fly the actual plane, with actual passengers and an actual line check airman sitting to her left. She had to do everything she had done in the SIM but in real conditions.

And she was nervous beyond belief.

Her alarm in L.A. went off at 4 a.m. She got the Flyaway to LAX and then took a four-and-a-half-hour flight to Chicago. She was technically still in training so SkyQuest got her a ticket to fly to her base. This was called "positive spacing." Once she was finished training, Dinah was on her own. She could still fly for free, but she had to fly standby so if the flight was full then she didn't get to work. It was an unbelievable hassle and yet over 50% of pilots commuted and didn't live "in base."

Once Dinah reached O'Hare Airport, the FAA rules decreed that she could fly a maximum of between eight and nine hours per day, depending on when her duty time started. But that didn't include reserve periods and "deadheading" – which was when the airline flew you from one city to another city to start your day. So, all told, you could legally work up to 16 hours a day. And commuting wasn't included in that tally – that was on you. Dinah's flight in Chicago was at 3:15 p.m. Mentally calculating, she deduced that she was going to have an 18-hour day.

And this was after the rest period rules were ratified subsequent to the Colgan crash.

She put her uniform on for her first ever flight and sweated through the shirt in five minutes. Even though it was winter, she just kept on perspiring. Her hat also kept getting blown off, but she was determined to wear it. Because it was cool as hell.

When she arrived at O'Hare, nervous and way early for her flight, she stopped for a moment to get out her passport and make sure her newly minted crew i.d. badges were still around her neck. This was going to be her first time using the Known Crewmember security entrance – better known as KCM.

A disheveled man made a beeline for Dinah so that he could yell at her because his flight was delayed. His flight was with another airline, but Dinah apologized anyway for his inconvenience.

She was from Minnesota.

Then two more passengers stopped her to ask for directions – one to the airport shuttle area and one to the International Terminal. She happily answered their queries. She quickly realized that in her uniform she was now also both an ambassador and an information booth.

And she loved every minute of it.

She went through KCM with a big smile on her face and on the other side, a toddler pointed at her.

"Are you going on a plane?" she asked him. He nodded and clapped his hands. "That sounds awesome! You have fun, okay?" More nodding and clapping.

It took her a few tries to put in the correct code for the crew room door, but she finally succeeded and her LCA was waiting for her inside. Dinah assessed which of the three Captain categories he fell into: The Codger, The Lecher or The Nerd. It sounded like the title of a Peter Greenaway movie from the early '90s. If he was a "codger," then your best course of action was to behave like a humble and grateful protégée. If he was a "lecher," then you survived by withstanding the constant flirting and sexual innuendo with aplomb. The "nerd" was the best. Nerds became pilots because they genuinely loved flying and generally also had at least one other ardent interest that they enjoyed chatting about. The LCA was reading a Philip Dick paperback. Dinah loved sci-fi.

"Can you believe how many movies have been made from Philip Dick novels?" she commented.

The LCA smiled and nodded. "I think of him more as a prophet than a writer!"

It was going to be okay.

She had to fly at least 25 hours and could extend up to 50 hours if needed and that was it. If she couldn't demonstrate proficiency in programming the plane, communicating on the radios and flying the aircraft then despite passing her checkride, she would be asked to leave.

Her first shock was how little time they had to get ready to go. The incoming aircraft arrived late and yet they were still expected to get out on time – which barely left them 20 minutes to preflight the aircraft, do all the programming and the flows and checklists and get their clearance to push back. A big digital clock above their gate counted down their time remaining.

No pressure.

And O'Hare Airport was a special type of purgatory. You had to talk to "ramp control" who then told you to call "metering" who then told you to monitor "ground control." But just "monitor" – Lord help you if you initiated a radio call to ground control on your own. You'd be torn a ceremonial "new one." When ground control got around to talking to you, they gave you your taxi instructions so quickly that there was no hope of retaining it all or writing it down quickly enough. One of Dinah's classmates from Alabama had asked for them to repeat the taxi instruction.

"Ma'am, I'm from the South, I'm going to need you to slow that right down for me," he drawled.

"This is Chicago. We don't go slow!"

The other dragon's lair at O'Hare was that the entire airport was essentially surrounded by two loops – Alpha Loop and Bravo Loop. Alpha Loop went clockwise. Bravo Loop went counterclockwise. And you were expected to just keep on circling until an opening presented itself.

And don't stop.

Don't ever stop.

Or you'd be sent to the Penalty Box – an area off to the side of the airport that was actually designated as the "Penalty Box" on charts, where you would languish in ignominy until they decided to take pity on you and let you back in the taxi flow.

"Don't worry about it," her LCA said. "You're gonna get yelled at, at some point. Just take it in stride. Try not to take it personally. Everybody screws up here."

Dinah did okay with her flows and checklists. She had some difficulty with the programming because it was different from training where they were merely able to simulate some of the protocols.

"Sorry," she kept saying.

"You're fine," he answered. "The first couple of flights are always a clusterfuck but I guarantee you by this time, three weeks from now, you'll be an old pro at this."

He told her that she should fly the first leg – to Charlotte, North Carolina – because the winds were going to be light there. And he would fly the leg back to Chicago, which was always windy – true to its nickname. Also, by that time, it would be dark.

When they got their takeoff clearance, the LCA taxied the plane onto the runway, lined it up with the centerline and then stopped.

"Your controls," he said.

"My controls," Dinah replied shakily.

She put her feet on the brakes and her left hand on the thrust lever. She held the yoke with her right hand. Then she spooled up the engine, pushing the thrust lever forward about a third of the way initially and then all the way up. The engine vibrated beneath her, building up to 14,000 pounds of thrust.

"This is so freaking exciting!" she said before she could stop herself.

"Hell, yeah it is!" her LCA concurred. "Let's go!"

They rumbled down the runway and when he called for her to rotate and she took off, it was everything she could do to not yell out, "Whee!!!!" The first few moments were super busy but once they reached their cruising altitude of 37,000 feet, she got a brief reprieve. One of the flight attendants called up to the flight deck and the LCA had him bring them two coffees and lunch – which was a pasta dish with artichokes and sun-dried tomatoes. With a baby baguette. And a piece of flourless chocolate cake. Dinah balanced the tray precariously on her lap and tore a chunk off her baguette as she took in the incredible view. If you had ever flown on an airliner as a passenger, you could appreciate the gorgeous panorama from the cabin window. Imagine seeing that from the front.

"Not a bad office, right?" said the LCA.

No kidding!

About 200 miles from Charlotte, they started programming again for the landing and briefing the approach and how they would taxi to the gate there. Charlotte was a much smaller airport than Chicago, so it wasn't as complicated to navigate.

"Am I going to land it?" Dinah asked him.

"Of course!"

"But you'll be on the controls with me?"

"Not unless I need to. You got this. The winds are calm, so you won't need any crosswind correction. When you hear '50 feet' start easing back on the yoke. Then when you're down, throw out the thrust reversers. Make sure you pull the levers up for both the right and the left one at the same time or they won't deploy. I'll take control of the plane when you get to 60 knots, okay?"

This guy had nerves of steel. Flying an $85 million aircraft with a full load of passengers and a complete novice at the controls. Dinah couldn't even imagine shouldering that kind of responsibility.

Even if this guy did have two alimony payments to make every month.

She didn't ask.

Her landing in Charlotte was hard. Really hard. Dinah was surprised how differently the real aircraft handled compared to the SIM. The controls were a lot heavier and took longer to respond. When she thought she was pulling back on the yoke, it was barely moving, and the plane responded – or rather didn't – accordingly.

"That was bad, wasn't it?" she queried.

"Naw, it was okay – just a little firm," he assured her. "Trust me, I've had landings that slammed down so hard, I felt like my spine compressed. Next time just pull back a little more assertively and keep the back pressure coming. You'll get it in no time."

*** 

On her next landing, the following day in Roanoke, Virginia, Dinah floated because she pulled back too much too soon.

"Remember," her LCA said. "You've got to get it down within the first third of the runway or that's a definite go-around. And that's no harm, no foul if you need to do that. Safety first, you know?"

"Okay," Dinah said thankfully. "This is a lot different from the SIM."

"You're doing great. You're right on track. We'll knock this out in 25 hours for sure."

She sighed. "That's so nice to hear. Full disclosure – my SIM instructors made me feel like I couldn't do anything right."

He snorted. "You know what? Fuck those guys. Most of them have never even flown the actual aircraft."

She gasped. "Are you serious?"

"Nope – they have zero time on the plane. I wouldn't dwell on their toxicity. There's the SIM and then there's real life. And this is real life right here. And you're handling it like a boss."

Even though the next leg was technically his to fly – because crewmembers usually alternated – he told Dinah to fly it so that she could practice another landing, this time into Atlanta, Georgia where they would be staying overnight.

"My first official overnight!" Dinah exclaimed.

He laughed. "Trust me. Those will get old, quick. You'll love being at home. You'll never take a washer and dryer or a stove for granted again."

"Oh, speaking of, what's a 'slam clicker'?" she asked.

"Me, I guess. A 'slam clicker' is usually someone who's been doing this for a while and when they get to the hotel, they stay put. They 'slam' the door and they 'click' the lock."

"Oh good. I was afraid to ask anyone what is meant because I was sure it was something rude."

He laughed again. "Any other questions?"

"Bidding! How? Why? When? How?"

"Honestly, bidding is harder than flying the plane," her LCA admitted. "Okay, crash course – bad choice of words – every month they put out however many flight lines – which are different monthly flying schedules - they can, and you bid on them in order of preference. And you are assigned one based on your seniority. And if your seniority isn't high enough to be a *lineholder* then you are put on reserve. Which sucks because then you just sit around the airport or your apartment waiting for a call if someone else doesn't show up or calls in sick. Most new hires are on reserve for a long time. When I started, I was on reserve for three years."

"Three years!" Dinah squealed.

"I know. But it's the nature of the beast. Gotta pay your dues."

He paused the conversation for a moment to answer a radio call.

"I guess I'll be on reserve," said Dinah.

He shook his head. "Maybe not. Chicago is a new base for this aircraft. And they just announced that they're going to be taking delivery of 30 new planes over the next few months. You picked a great time to go to the airlines. You're pretty much going to be able to write your own ticket."

Dinah's spirits rose immediately. "That would be so awesome. My base seniority in Chicago is 62."

Her LCA pulled out his phone and swiped a few screens. "You're golden. It looks like there are going to be 75 lines next month and if you're Number 62, you'll get one for sure. Talk about being in the right place at the right time. You have no idea how lucky you are."

"I'm going to be a *lineholder*!!" Dinah exclaimed.

"Okay, lineholder, let's brief the approach. Now Atlanta has coded taxi routes based on colors, like pink and black. So, you just bring the right one up on your tablet and follow along."

"Why is every airport different?" Dinah asked.

"One of the great mysteries of life, truly."

Her landing in Atlanta was "right on the money" according to her LCA so he told her that on their leg back to Chicago the next morning, that she would fly again and that would be her official line check. If she passed, then she was officially done with training and would be able to bid on a line for the next month.

\*\*\*

When Dinah got on the shuttle van the next morning, she remembered that the two flight attendants from the day before were swapping out with a new crew because they lived in Atlanta. She could not have been more delighted to see that one of the new flight attendants was none other than Fatima.

"Ahhh! So nice to see you," Dinah said. "You made it through training! Right on!"

"I just finished IOE," said Fatima.

Flight attendants had their own Initial Operating Experience that they had to successfully pass.

"I'm doing my line check today," Dinah said nervously.

"I'm not worried for you," Fatima said confidently. "You should have seen the boy I flew with last week. He landed so hard that the passengers screamed. And that flight deck door stayed closed. It never opened after we landed."

"He didn't want to do the walk of shame," Dinah said sympathetically.

"He didn't want to pay all of the chiropractor bills," Fatima said saucily.

Dinah gave her arm a squeeze. "I'm so happy to see you!"

"Me as well!"

When they got to the plane, things started out just fine but then when Dinah went to adjust her seat, she realized the track was broken.

"Can you reach the rudder pedals?" her LCA asked.

"Not even close. Maybe I can stuff my jacket behind me?" Dinah suggested.

"Fuck that. You're at the airlines now. Shit needs to work. Go on out and preflight the plane and I'll call maintenance."

Dinah walked around the plane, with her stomach in knots. If they couldn't fix the seat, then she wouldn't be able to do her line check today. She was all geared up for it and really didn't want to have to put herself through it again another day.

Why did stuff have to break on planes at the worst possible moment?

When she got back onboard, a gargantuan maintenance technician was lying on his belly on the flight deck, working under the seat. His ass crack was completely visible. Fatima was standing in the galley.

"Don't look at it and it cannot hurt you," she advised.

A last-minute passenger got on board and shoved his carry-on baggage at Dinah for her to stow. Fatima moved past Dinah to reprimand him. Dinah stopped her.

"It's no problem. Not like I have anything better to do," she said.

"Give me that," Fatima demanded. "You are an airline pilot now. Start acting like one."

Dinah obediently relinquished the bag and Fatima shoved it roughly into the closest overhead.

The maintenance technician gave them the thumbs up a few minutes later and then they had to wait a few more minutes for the paperwork to be signed off and filed and then they were cleared to go.

"Are we late?" Dinah asked her LCA.

"We're absolutely fine. No need to rush. Take your time. I've got your back."

She had a slight crosswind from the left on takeoff, but she remembered to steer into it with the ailerons. Air traffic control amended their final altitude by a thousand feet, but she caught it. And as they approached Chicago, the reported winds were only ten knots, which was fantastic.

Only one landing away from the end.

It was almost over.

Almost.

And then the wind did a strange thing. It suddenly changed direction and started gusting to 25 knots.

This landing was the only thing stopping her from crossing the finish line.

The finish line!

So, she put her big girl pants on and got that damn airplane down in the first third of the runway, right on the centerline. And nobody needed a chiropractor afterwards.

Her LCA shook her hand – she really did love the congratulatory handshaking – and told her she had officially passed her line check.

When they opened the flight deck door, Fatima was literally stopping every single passenger on their way out to inform them that the female First Officer had been responsible for that fantastic landing. Most of the passengers couldn't have cared less but a few verbally thanked her and an older lady with a walker stopped shy of the doorway.

"I didn't even know that there were lady pilots," she said. "Good for you, dear!"

After the last person had deplaned, Fatima came out to the ramp with Dinah and took a picture of her in front of the aircraft in her uniform ... and hat.

It was the proudest moment of Dinah's life.

The date was January 6, 2020.

**AFTER**

## Chapter Nineteen

Money.

When you didn't have enough, it permeated every pore of your being. In your waking hours, it was all you ever thought about. I need more money. How can I get more money? Why does that cost so much? Can I do without it? And you did without everything and anything that wasn't a basic necessity.

You dreaded opening the mailbox, because of bills. You dreaded running out of something because that meant you had to go to the store. You lived in fear of your car making a strange noise because that might mean a repair that you couldn't afford.

The last week of the month, the omnipresent stomach cramps and lower backache became more pronounced. You had to actively try to distract your mind from fixating on the $1^{st}$.

Rent.

Rent.

Rent.

And forget about sleeping. You tossed and turned all night in REM sleep, your nightmares not even bothering with the subtlety of symbolism and metaphors. Every subconscious scenario involved being homeless, destitute, without food.

And sometimes when you woke up, there would be a momentary reprieve from reality because in those hopeful early morning hours, your mind had convinced itself that the problem was eradicated. For the briefest of moments, you felt at peace and then when reality resumed its forefront position, the shortness of breath and tightness across your forehead began the daily dance of debt.

Financial difficulties were the primary cause of relationships ending in North America. And it was hard to dispute that. The internal tension that the external tension of poverty caused was pervasive. And once your own physical body and your psyche could no longer contain the malignant growth, that malevolence had to have somewhere to go. And it was usually in the direction of the person closest to you.

Whether they deserved it or not.

Dinah was covered in dog fur and had shit under the thumbnail of her left hand. After she was furloughed from SkyQuest in April – the new hires went first – she had tried in vain to find another flying job. But there were thousands and thousands of pilots who also suddenly found themselves unemployed where two months earlier, they held the aviation industry hostage. And many of them had many more hours and much more experience than Dinah.

Going back to flight instructing was out of the question. Nobody wanted to be in a small aircraft, shoulder to shoulder with another person. And nobody had any extra money for flight training. And most importantly, anybody with half a brain knew that the world of aviation was not going to be a sage career choice for an exceedingly long time.

It was heartbreaking to Dinah, to see all the lifeless planes, sitting inanimately at the airports or worse still, indefinitely relocated to one of the many desert boneyards that voraciously increased in size with each passing week. Her illustrious uniform hung limply in the back of her closet. Even if she could have afforded to have it dry-cleaned, there was no point.

After striking out with flying jobs, Dinah had attempted to get temporary work at one of the grocery stores. She didn't care about the risk factor. She needed the income so desperately. It had temporarily slipped her mind that, with her being laid off, there went her health insurance as well. So, for the sake of a minimum wage job, if she got sick, she would have literally been better off dead.

None of the stores she applied at would hire her. They all said she was overqualified.

Why was that a detriment?

When she pointed out that these were extenuating circumstances and normally an airline pilot would not be applying for a night stocker position at Walmart, the blue-vested manager then stared at her as if she were behaving like a snob.

She texted the pudgy pilot in New York, where he lived, to see what he was – or wasn't – living off. He told her she was sweet for checking on him and that he was fine. He had investments.

Why did every other person seem to have investments?

The pudgy pilot told her that a lot of his friends were signing up to be dog walkers on *Rover.com*.

"You can charge whatever you want," he explained. "And you make your own hours. If you don't want to work a certain day, you don't. Plus, you get to work with dogs. Dogs are better than people."

That was a fact. Dogs were better than people.

But people didn't set the bar very high, did they?

Dinah quickly got one elderly client who had a poodle. But as soon as she arrived at his trailer, she realized that she had priced herself too low at $15 a walk. The poodle was yappy yet easy to walk but his Grandpa Walton-type owner consistently trapped her in endless conversation both before and after the walk. He was lonely. She understood. But at the same time, she empathized with the poodle, who must have also felt like a trapped animal.

Other clients emerged but nobody who employed her on a regular basis. So many people were laid off or outright terminated or fortunate enough to be able to work from home, that not a lot of people needed help with their pets. One beefy guy with wrist tats and a soul patch didn't even have a dog or cat when she arrived. He just wanted her to sit with him and his parakeet, Dagmar, and watch *Blade Runner*. It was a million degrees outside, and he had Arnold Palmers and air conditioning and Dinah didn't have the energy to worry about her personal safety, so she stayed.

It wasn't too bad all in all. Dagmar, the parakeet, had belonged to his ex-wife, Amy, so she periodically shouted out abusive epithets at the beefy guy but Dinah kind of enjoyed it. Apparently, Amy had been an English professor at CSUN, so the parakeet had an extensive vocabulary.

"You cretinous oozing corpuscle of crap," Dagmar crowed.

Nice. Alliterative.

"Knock, knock. Who's there? This abject failure," Dagmar pontificated.

Solid. Classic composition.

"I watch you when you sleep," she hissed menacingly.

That last one might have been pure parakeet.

"Just ignore her," the beefy guy said. "More ice?"

When the movie was over, Dinah was kind of disappointed to leave. She lingered at the screen door. Dagmar turned her back on both of them. Dinah read the room.

"If you ever need anyone to testify on your behalf ..." she offered.

\*\*\*

The deejay was home when she got there. Shortly after Dinah finished IOE and began as a lineholder, they had decided to move in together. She put in her 30-day notice with Kristina and the cockroaches and they found a gorgeous 1-bedroom on Via Mindanao in Marina del Rey. It was right on the harbor and a block from the ocean. Dinah walked on the beach every day that she was home. And at night, lying in bed, the sound of the foghorns, gave her goosebumps.

She loved it.

The monthly rent was $3,510 ... plus utilities.

But there were three pools and a spa and a comprehensive fitness center and a restaurant onsite.

And she was an up-and-coming airline pilot and he was a deejay in high demand, so they took it on the very day they looked at it. Then they went to a campy buffet restaurant called The Warehouse that was right on the water and stuffed themselves to the unfamiliar point of physical discomfort. After that they went to the beach and made sand angels.

She was so happy.

For a while.

Now she was back to normal.

Dinah and the deejay had tried to get out of their lease by legal means but the complex was managed by a multi-national company that didn't care about the individual hardships of those unlucky enough not to have a nest egg in case of catastrophe. They enforced the terms of the lease. So, they had no choice but to skip out. They got a U-Haul truck and moved in the middle of the night. Looking down the street, they saw three other trucks and three other parties doing the same.

Dinah felt so guilty about it, despite the deejay advising her not to.

"What if they take us to small claims court?" she fretted.

"They won't. They'll just get new tenants in there. Trust me, these big conglomerates don't have the time or energy for little fish like us."

"It still doesn't feel right."

"Look," he reasoned. "It's not our fault this happened. And yet somehow, we're still accountable. To hell with these people."

"But it *is* our fault that we're bailing," she retorted.

"I'm going to say something to you that might be hard to hear, Dinah. You are a moral and ethical person. That's one of the reasons I fell in love with you. But morals and ethics are not absolutes. They don't exist in a vacuum. We all do our best in life, but ultimately basic needs must come first. Food and shelter take precedence over doing the right thing. It's easy for rich people to stand in judgment but when you don't have a roof over your head or your kids are starving, you do what you must, to survive. You don't have the luxury of considering the moral turpitude of your actions. That's why I fucking despise the wealthy."

Dinah hated people with money too. Or rather, envied them. Vehemently. Hate wasn't the right word. But she wasn't sure she agreed with the deejay's argument. Time and time again had shown that the most corrupt, least moral, and ethical members of society were in fact the wealthiest. She almost felt the opposite. That the economic strugglers clung to their virtue of character more tightly because that was all they had to show to the world. And it was also their richest asset. Perhaps that was why this event had been so traumatizing to her. She felt so dirty and criminal.

The deejay kissed her on the forehead. "Babe don't worry about it. Everybody does this."

Did they?

\*\*\*

Dinah had called Kristina and begged for her old apartment back. And Kristina hadn't been able to rent it yet, so she kindly allowed Dinah to move back in without filing a new lease agreement. Which was good because now her credit was probably compromised.

The feeling that overwhelmed her when she unlocked the door and stepped back inside a space that she never thought she'd see again was indescribable. It was a sensation of futility and melancholy so concentrated that it hurt her body. The pain made it difficult to breathe.

Life made it difficult to breathe.

Of course, the deejay's work had evaporated virtually overnight. Nobody was congregating, nobody was travelling and certainly nobody was celebrating. He had tried to get temporary work as well, delivering for Postmates. But the wave of anti-Asian sentiment that had gripped the country made his job untenable. He had racial slurs hurled at him constantly and threats of physical harm. And in typical American top form, the abuse was non-specific regionally. He was told to, "crawl back to Chinatown," and one customer said he wasn't taking delivery from that, "Kim Jong-un son of a bitch." His favorite was a middle-aged emaciated man who accepted his hot wings but just as he was closing the door said, "We still remember Pearl Harbor, you know."

After that, he quit and furthermore seemed to quit looking for any other type of income. He sat day after day on the sofa, playing "Assassin's Creed Odyssey" on his PS4. And eating. Eating a lot. But not doing dishes a lot. Not cleaning a lot. Not doing laundry a lot.

When Dinah arrived, the sink was full of dirty dishes and the coffee table was similarly adorned. The deejay was at his usual post on the sofa, eating a slice of pizza from a large box. Dinah took a long inhale followed by a longer exhale.

Nope.

"Hey, have you been home all day?"

She knew he had.

"Self-quarantining," he said with a mouth full of food. "You should have a shower before you touch anything, babe."

Dinah walked over to the coffee table. She was so hungry. Despite reeking of dog and desperation, she still had an appetite. The deejay had ordered the three-meat special … pepperoni, sausage, and ham.

He knew she didn't eat meat.

"Is that a large?" she asked passive-aggressively.

"Yup," he said with a soupçon of challenge in his tone.

"You know we can't afford takeout right now."

He tossed the slice aside. "We don't have any food in the house."

"Then why didn't you go grocery shopping?" she asked.

"With what? My charm? I was waiting for you to get back with your bank card."

Okay.

Okay.

Okay.

"Okay, just make a list and I'll go. But hon, could you please tidy up while I'm gone?"

The deejay had taken another piece and was about to bite down. "Look, it's bad enough that my girlfriend has to support me. Please don't make me feel even more emasculated by asking me to be a housewife." And he took a big bite, masticating the pizza like he was punishing it.

Okay.

Okay.

Okay.

"Okay, as I've told you before, it doesn't matter to me who pays for what. But we're a team and we need to divide up the work so it's equitable for both of us. And the fact of the matter is if I'm working outside the home more then you need to work inside the home. It's the only way for things to be fair."

"Fine."

He got up and stomped over to the sink, where he began rinsing dishes under the tap and then placing them soaking wet into the cupboards. Dinah knew that she was going to have to wash them again. Should she say something?

"Thank you," she said.

"Can you get Frosted Flakes?" he asked.

She hated Frosted Flakes. They got soggy when you poured the milk on. The slimy consistency made her gag.

"Sure," she said. Dinah grabbed a slice of pizza and started picking all the meat off it. "I'm going to go back out right now so that I only have to disinfect once."

"Great. Thanks." It seemed like their exchange had ended but then he threw in one more sentence, like an afterthought. Except that it wasn't. "Hey, I know you've been resistant to it, but have you given any more thought to contacting your old boss? I mean, it's got to be worth a try, right? He might have some flights for you, and it would certainly pay better than walking dogs."

They had already had a heated discussion about it. Dinah had explained to the deejay the many reasons why she did not want to have anything further to do with the owner. She couldn't believe that he was bringing it up again. She had been so supportive about the Postmates debacle.

"There's no point," she said. "He won't have any work. Nobody in aviation does."

He turned the tap off. "Here's the thing. I kind of emailed him using your account, and he responded. And he *does* have flights."

"What?"

"He said you could have your old job back."

Not okay.

Not okay.

Not okay.

## Chapter Twenty

Cat and Chrystal.

That was the only reason that Dinah returned the owner's email. They were interested in booking a flight, but they only wanted to fly with her. When the owner had told them that it might be a better option to fly on an airline, Cat told him that under the present circumstances, that wasn't going to be possible.

So, Dinah swallowed her pride and gratefully accepted the return to service. The owner was more gracious than she would have given him credit for. He simply said that he was sorry things hadn't worked out at the airlines and that he was happy to have her back.

Was it possible that she had him wrong?

And she arrived at that conclusion as someone who was not presently at *her* best. She was short-tempered, depressed and battling a one-woman pity party. That's why Dinah rarely decided how she felt about someone when things were going well for them. It was easy to be a good person when life was on your side. It was when things started to go sideways that a person's true character emerged. If your life was a flaming dumpster fire and you could still behave like a decent person, then you *were* one.

Maybe he had more integrity than she had given him credit for?

Cat had been quite definite – she told Dinah that she and Chrystal would meet her at the plane. And not to worry if they were a little bit late. Their lives were somewhat "hectic" presently.

Dinah was surprised that a Lincoln Town Car drove out onto the ramp and pulled up right beside the aircraft. The rear right door opened, and Cat got out first. She ran around to the other side just as the driver opened the left rear door. A pair of crutches emerged first. Followed by a deathly pale and gaunt, Chrystal. Dinah swallowed a gasp when she saw why the crutches were necessary.

Chrystal no longer had her left leg from the knee down.

She rushed over to offer her assistance.

"We're good," Cat said, propping her daughter up on the crutches.

"Ma'am?" the driver asked.

"She won't let anyone help her so don't waste your time."

"Yes ma'am." The driver tipped his hat and accepted a large wad of bills from Cat. He pulled away from the plane and exited through the security gate.

Cat smiled painfully at Dinah. "Let's get her in the plane and then we can catch up."

Chrystal was ahead of them and turned. "*She* is right here, and *she* can hear you."

Cat cocked her head. "I'm sorry, did you hear something Dinah? No? Must have been a plane backfiring."

"Speaking of hot air ..." Chrystal began but felt no need to finish. "I assume I've earned the shotgun position in perpetuity?"

Cat raised both her eyebrows. "Well, well, well, someone has been using their Google thesaurus feature on the reg."

"A lot of my time has freed up since I stopped playing volleyball recently."

Any awkwardness that Dinah might have felt in those establishing moments was instantly eviscerated. And her unadulterated adoration of this mother-daughter team grew tenfold.

Once they were en route to Phoenix, Chrystal began to share details. Dinah had been respectful of her privacy and had made no inquiries, but Chrystal and Cat were both open books ... and wonderfully so. Dinah wished she had half their fortitude and resilience.

"So," began Chrystal. "The next time that someone tells you *not* to go to Daytona for spring break, you should probably listen."

"I actually told you not to go anywhere," Cat argued.

"Uh-huh. Anyway, I got a blood clot."

"She's lucky to be alive," Cat said to Dinah.

Dinah turned to Chrystal. "I'm so sorry, Chrystal."

Chrystal stared out the window for a few moments. "Thank you, Dinah. You know when I first woke up and saw … you know … this … I wanted to die. I really did."

Cat cleared her throat. "She did. She said, 'Mom, why didn't you just let me die?' She did."

"And do you remember what you said, Mom?" Chrystal asked.

"I said, 'Because think of all the money we're going to save on shoes!' I did," Cat said.

And they both laughed.

These women were sensational.

They were going to Phoenix because they had a vacation home there. And most importantly, that vacation home was a ranch-style bungalow so Chrystal wouldn't have to deal with stairs. They also had an appointment with a prosthetics specialist.

"I'm getting a fancy new foot," Chrystal bragged.

Cat nodded. "It's supposed to be quite something. Extremely flexible and tensile. After she gets it, she should be able to give *herself* a kick in the ass, so I won't have to!"

Chrystal narrowed her eyes. "You'd better make sure you're six feet away, Mother. I would hate for those butt implants of yours to go to waste if I can make contact!"

Dinah loved these women. Where was the anger, the resentment, the self-pity? Where was the blame, the dolor, the regret? Their strength was inspirational and frankly utterly flabbergasting to

Dinah. Wealthy, entitled white women from Orange County were the last people on Earth that Dinah thought she would be admiring and aspiring to be at this point in history.

What a wonderful thing it was to be surprised by human beings in a positive way when you felt so jaded – so deluged, by predictability.

***

After they landed at Phoenix, Cat wouldn't hear of Dinah flying back to Santa Ana, especially since it was almost ten o'clock at night.

"At least stay with us tonight, and go back in the morning," she urged.

"Better yet, stay with us forever," Chrystal encouraged. She stuck her tongue out and pressed it against the window.

"Crystal's still on some pretty heavy medication," Cat explained.

"It's the very least they can do," Chrystal stated.

Dinah agreed wholeheartedly.

"Thank you both. I would love that. Let me just give my boyfriend a quick call," she said.

Everything stopped and all their attention was focused on Dinah.

"What boyfriend?" Chrystal asked.

"You have a boyfriend?" Cat asked.

"Yes, yes, I'll tell you all about him when we get to the house," Dinah promised.

She called the deejay with reservations, certain that he would make her feel guilty about having a nice night out with the girls while he suffered in squalor in the Valley. But he sounded surprisingly upbeat when he answered.

"Sure thing, have a great time and thanks for letting me know."

"Are you sure, it's okay?"

"Babe, you're a grown woman, you don't need to ask my permission to do things."

That wasn't what she thought was doing.

"Okay, well you have a good night. Did you get something for dinner?"

"I sure did! Frosted Flakes!" He chuckled.

"You're in a good mood," Dinah noted.

"I might have a line on a gig up in San Luis Obispo," he said. "I'll know more tomorrow."

"That's great!"

That *was* great.

\*\*\*

After they arrived at the stunning five-bedroom, three-bath Spanish bungalow, with wraparound balconies and an infinity pool, Cat got Chrystal onto the sofa and tucked under a blanket. Then she went off to make pomegranate margaritas.

"*Who* just happens to have the ingredients for pomegranate margaritas, lying around?" Dinah asked.

"I'm sorry, have you met my mother?" Chrystal teased.

"I think your mother is fantastic," Dinah commented.

"Tell her I said so and you're dead, but I agree," Chrystal affirmed.

Dinah stretched out on a vintage bamboo chaise longue. "How is your dad handling all of this?"

"What do you mean?"

"Your dad?"

Chrystal adjusted the pillow she had placed between her legs. "There's no 'dad'." She suddenly crowed. "OMG, did you think good old Cat was a trophy wife?"

Dinah blushed to the core of her being. "No, I mean, I, no -"

Chrystal leaned forward. "You did! You totally did!" She folded her arms smartly across her chest. "My mother happens to be in the top 7% of commercial real estate brokers in North America."

"You're kidding."

"I am not. Before I was born – sperm donor by the way – she worked as a waitress at Denny's. She built all this completely by herself. She specializes in hotel and resort properties."

Dinah felt a sense of deep, deep shame.

Because the only thing as deplorable as underestimating yourself as a woman, was underestimating another woman.

And it happened all the time.

When Cat returned with the drinks – virgin for Chrystal, the medicated wunderkind – they put Dinah on the spot regarding the new man in her life. She felt a trifle protective of him, and she wasn't sure why.

"Well, he's a deejay," she began.

"Sexy," Chrystal said.

"Oh dear," Cat said.

"Or rather, he was. There's not a lot of deejay work right now."

"Let me see a photo," Chrystal demanded.

Dinah found the most flattering one she could and handed her phone to Chrystal. Cat leaned over to take a peek as well.

"Asian guys are so hot, and they have very little body hair," Chrystal stated.

Cat threw up her hands in despair.

"I give up," Cat said. Then she addressed Dinah. "What *is* he doing for work right now?"

"Um … not too much. But he might have a gig coming up," Dinah said hopefully.

"Who cares? He's hot," Chrystal repeated, taking a big swig of her virgin beverage. It left a nice red mustache on her upper lip.

"Hot doesn't pay the bills," Cat said.

"You should know," Chrystal retorted.

"I'm going to let you have that one because your birthday is coming up," Cat said. Then she turned to Dinah. "Seriously though, don't let this guy treat you like a doormat."

"No, no," Dinah protested. "He's a good guy. He wouldn't do that."

"Or a sugar mama," Chrystal added.

Dinah laughed. "I don't think I even qualify as a sugar second cousin."

"Hmmm … sugar … let's bake snickerdoodles!"

\*\*\*

Later that night, Dinah couldn't sleep and after staring at the flickering pool lights until they hypnotized her, she decided to get up and dip her feet. Chrystal had elected to stay out on the sofa and Cat had obviously been similarly plagued with insomnia.

The entire back of the house was glass and Dinah sat at the side of the pool and watched Cat bring her daughter another blanket. Chrystal awoke when she put the throw on her. Cat gently stroked her hair and leaned in until their foreheads were touching. She whispered something unintelligible to Chrystal and they both began to cry quietly. They held this posture for some time before Cat drew away and rose to head back to bed.

Their parting words were louder, so Dinah was fortunate enough to hear and appreciate them.

"I love you, Mommy."

"I love you, sweet girl."

And then Dinah began to weep.

## Chapter Twenty-One

Dinah thought that they should drive to San Luis Obispo, but the deejay argued that it was too far and then they'd be out the cost of a hotel room. Plus, the owner had generously, and again, uncharacteristically offered them the use of the SR-22 for just the cost of fuel. No rental fee at all.

She had definitely misjudged him.

Dinah was still seething about the betrayal of the deejay usurping her email and posing as her in a professional capacity. But truth be told – and he would never know this – she was grateful to have her job back and it seemed as though recent events had radically changed the owner for the better. And perhaps more importantly, the deejay seemed to be back to his old self. He made a special San Luis Obispo mix and sang along at full volume to Boz Scaggs and Ambrosia as they flew up the coast.

"What's the underlying track on this?" Dinah asked.

"N.W.A."

"Very cool."

An incongruous and yet somehow appropriate mix of "Fuck Tha Police" and "Lowdown" serenaded them through Oxnard. Just before Oxnard was Point Mugu which was an Air Force base. The deejay looked at the Avidyne display chart on their instrument panel.

"Hey, don't forget you have to be above 3,000 feet over Point Mugu," he reminded her.

"Look at you, keeping me from busting a restricted airspace!" Dinah said appreciatively.

"What can I say? Chivalry!" he returned. He followed the pink line with his finger that indicated the flight plan that Dinah had input all the way to their destination. And then he frowned. "Are we landing at San Luis Obispo Airport?"

"Well, yeah, that's the closest one."

The deejay hadn't told Dinah much about the gig, just that the client owned a winery and lived just north of San Luis Obispo. San Luis Obispo was a renowned area for vineyards and also famous for the Hearst Castle – which was in San Simeon. It was built by publishing magnate William Randolph Hearst, originally for his family but ultimately it was where he housed his mistress of many years, actress Marion Davies, while his wife and kids were tucked away in New York. The construction began in 1919 and continued until 1947, when he became ill and had to leave for Los Angeles, never to return. Upon his death, the Hearst family gave the castle to the State of California, and they operated it as a museum. Marion Davies, who had a daughter with Hurst, publicly acknowledged as her niece, hosted parties for the likes of Charlie Chaplin, Greta Garbo, Cary Grant, Clark Gable, Jean Harlow and Charles Lindbergh – the first aviator to fly non-stop over the Atlantic from New York to Paris. After he died, she was not even permitted to attend William Randolph Hearst's funeral.

One of the most interesting aspects of this majestic bucolic paradise, was that the architect that Hearst hired was a woman, named Julia Morgan. She was a trailblazer in her field, the first woman to be granted entry to the École des Beaux-Arts in Paris and the first female to have her own architectural practice in California as well as the first to win the American Institute of Architects Gold Medal. Hearst was hugely supportive of Julia Morgan's talent, unlike her previous boss, famed architect John Galen Howard, who appreciated her ability but bragged about how little he had to pay her because she was a woman.

And he didn't have to pay her anything at all when she left and started her own successful firm.

Dinah had toured the castle a few years ago on a layover. It was incredible – 19 sitting rooms, 42 bedrooms, 61 bathrooms, 127 acres of gardens, indoor and outdoor swimming pools, tennis courts, an airfield (only one fatal crash in 1938 that claimed Lord and Lady Plunket) and at one time the world's largest private zoo … though that might have been a cheeky reference to the celebrity guests of the roaring '20s.

She was confused by the deejay's reaction to landing at San Luis. Had she misheard the destination?

"It's just that, I've always wanted to land at Oceano," the deejay said. Oceano was this tiny uncontrolled airport that was literally right on the beach, open only from dusk to dawn and the views were breathtaking. The runway had an east-west designation so when you took off, you flew right over the water. "I've heard it's straight-up gorgeous."

"Okay, well, it's a bit further to travel then after we land," Dinah said. "And the runway is only 2,300 feet long."

The deejay rubbed her shoulder. "Which is no big deal for an ace pilot such as yourself."

She smiled at him. "Just remember that when you're swimming for shore." Dinah modified the flight plan in the navigation programming. The pink line disappeared momentarily and then reappeared, ending at Oceano instead of San Luis Obispo. "Okay, Oceano it is!"

***

After they landed, with a lot less runway to spare than Dinah was comfortable with, the deejay called for an Uber.

Their first driver, Ruth, refused to let them get into her silver Prius. When she saw that the deejay was Asian, she quickly locked the doors and drove away. The app charged him for a cancelled ride.

He was enraged. "Absolutely not!"

While he spoke with Customer Service, Dinah ordered another ride on her phone. This time it was a maroon Chevrolet Traverse, driven by a Somali gentleman. He pulled up and hopped right out to help them with their gear.

"Dinah?" he asked, taking a mixing board from her.

"Yes, thank you," she answered.

The deejay got a refund and filed a formal complaint with Uber. Dinah couldn't help but think that *he'd* have a better chance of action being initiated than the many women who had been sexually assaulted by Uber drivers. Every single time she called for an Uber or a Lyft late at night, she felt palpable anxiety, every single mile that they drove. On one occasion, a driver had taken a remote shortcut in Houston one evening in the early hours, due to construction. Dinah had every expectation that a heinous act was going to be committed against her and was steeling herself to defend her own safety when suddenly he turned back onto the freeway.

This driver was charming. He had been a physicist in Mogadishu, but his doctorate wasn't transferrable to the United States and he couldn't afford to go to school in America.

"But even if you could, I mean honestly, would you want to start all over again?" Dinah asked.

He looked at her in the rearview mirror. "Oh yes. Beginning something new is not starting over. No offense, miss."

"None taken! No, you're absolutely right," Dinah acquiesced.

The deejay was actively working to calm himself down. "Somalia ... isn't that where Iman is from?"

The driver lit up. "Yes!"

"She's beautiful," the deejay said.

The driver beamed. "Thank you!"

\*\*\*

The driveway up to the client's retro-fitted farmhouse was long, circuitous, and lined with olive trees. It was exquisite.

The driver whistled. "This is your house?"

Dinah laughed. "I wish!"

"I wish for you as well!"

The deejay became quieter and quieter the closer they got to the house. He seemed extraordinarily nervous about the gig. Maybe it was because he hadn't performed in quite some time. And private gigs were always a crapshoot. You never knew what to expect.

He told her one of the first private gigs he ever did was in Palos Verdes, a very affluent, predominantly white enclave. It was in this gorgeous glass and concrete post-modern home up on a cliff overlooking the ocean. When he arrived, he saw that his oldest audience member was four years old. It was entirely preschoolers. Willow, the surgically enhanced soccer mom who had booked him had confused him with a children's entertainer. She attempted to discuss a refund, but he refused. So, she obliged him to set up and do two full sets while she put *Frozen* on for the kids. He played for hours while the children ignored him, and Willow and the other soccer moms sipped sangria and stared balefully at him. About an hour in, one little boy got up and attempted to dance but was quickly hustled back in front of the wall-mounted HD television.

It was always a crapshoot.

"How did you get this client again?" Dinah asked.

"He knows one of the managers of the club in Vegas," the deejay said.

Dinah looked up at the second-floor windows, which were surrounded by purple clematis. "Is it odd that the gig is in the middle of the day?"

"Not at all."

"What's the occasion?"

"Don't know. Come on." He grabbed a carton of albums and walked up to the door.

Something wasn't right.

The door was answered by a middle-aged man with curly blond hair in cargo shorts and a shrimp-colored golf shirt, holding a tumbler full of ice and something amber-colored.

"Hey! Thanks for coming! Come on in!" he said in a welcoming tone.

The deejay paused for just a second. "Thanks, man. Is it cool if my pilot hangs while I play?"

His pilot.

The vintner looked over the deejay's head and acknowledged Dinah with delight.

"This is your pilot?! Sweet! I need to fly more often! Absolutely! Bring her in!"

Everything he said seemed to end with an implied exclamation point.

Dinah helped carry the rest of the deejay's gear inside. The vintner didn't help but chatted animatedly with them the entire time. He led them into a beautiful sunroom with grey slate tile floors and mullioned windows. There didn't seem to be anyone else in the home.

The vintner drew some floor to ceiling white silk curtains that enclosed the room.

"Thanks," said the deejay. "The sun can really cause a lot of damage to my equipment. I appreciate it."

"Absolutely!" He turned to Dinah. "Can I get you a drink? We put out a lovely Cabernet!"

"Thanks, but I have to fly him back still," Dinah answered.

The vintner slapped himself in the forehead. "Duh! Of course, you do! You're a pilot! How about an iced tea?"

"That would be great. Thank you."

"Sweetened?! I'll bet you like it sweet!"

"Unsweetened, thank you," Dinah said.

"You got it! Why don't you grab a comfy seat out by the pool, and I'll bring it to you!"

He hustled off to parts unknown.

Something wasn't right.

Dinah looked at the deejay. He was just standing there, not setting anything up.

"Do you want some help?" she offered.

"No, babe, I got this," he said. "In fact, why don't you just hang by the pool until I'm done. It's going to be really boring."

He always loved having her in the house whenever he played.

What the hell was going on?

Where was everybody?

Dinah really wanted to get to the bottom of this, but she also didn't want to cause waves. The deejay was clearly feeling better about himself with this opportunity to earn some income. And it was broad daylight for goodness' sake. At a winery. And the guy was wearing a shrimp-colored golf shirt.

She was probably overreacting.

So, Dinah gave him a kiss and made her way out to the patio. She sat on a wicker sectional with bright yellow upholstery under a cedar-hewn pergola. The pool was a deep azure, clearly saltwater and not chlorinated.

The vintner brought her a crystal glass filled to the brim with ice and the tea. He also had a tray with some nacho chips and salsa. She was worried that he would tarry but he seemed eager to leave her to her own devices.

"I'd better get back to the action!" he exclaimed. "Let me know if you need anything at all!"

He opened the door to the sunroom, closed it and drew the curtain across. Now Dinah had no visibility whatsoever into the room.

After a few minutes, the thump of bass emanated through the tempered glass.

Dinah sipped her tea and munched on a few chips and salsa. Both had evidently been made from scratch. They were delicious. Before long she had polished it all off. She got out her laptop and started doing her flight instructor renewal course or FIRC for short. Every two years a flight instructor had to recertify their credentials by either doing an online course or attending a two-day workshop in person. If you let it lapse, then you were no longer a flight instructor and you didn't have to do the training again, but you had to take another checkride. Dinah couldn't even imagine putting herself through that again. The CFI – Certified Flight Instructor – ride was on average 10-12 hours long and only had a 40% pass rate the first time. Her own CFI ride had lasted 11 hours, and she had passed on the initial attempt. It had been the longest, most grueling day of her life. There was no way she was ever going to let that CFI certificate elapse. Even if she never planned to flight instruct anymore. She had worked too damn hard to get it to ever let it go.

She had barely finished the first unit of thirteen and successfully taken the review test when the music stopped. The curtains were all opened, and the deejay waved at her. It had barely been an hour.

She logged out of the program and hurriedly got to her feet. The deejay opened the door and came out onto the patio.

"Are you done already?" she asked.

"Yup – easy peasy," he answered.

"I'll help you tear down," she offered.

"Already done," he said. "Called a Lyft this time and it's out front, everything loaded."

"Oh, okay," Dinah said awkwardly. "I'll just say goodbye to our host."

"He's not here. He had to slip out for a meeting."

The deejay led her back the way they had come in and out the front door to the waiting car. She didn't see or hear a single person along the way.

When they got to the airport, they loaded everything into the plane and then ran across the street to Old Juan's Cantina for fish tacos and chiles rellenos. The deejay insisted on paying. And Dinah made a big deal out of it, because she felt it was important to him.

"Will it bother you if I have a couple of Coronas?" he asked.

"What do you mean?" Dinah asked.

"Well I don't want to be a dick because you can't have one. You know, on account of having to fly."

The FAA rule for alcohol blood content in pilots was 0.04%. There was a popular colloquial saying, "eight hours bottle to throttle", which essentially meant that if you didn't drink for eight hours before a flight, generally you'd be fine. Dinah never drank before or during a flight. It wasn't worth it.

"Go right ahead. Honestly, it won't bother me at all. I'm fine," she said. "I am however, getting an extra side of guac."

"Fair enough."

While they waited for their food, Dinah tried to find out more about the gig they just came from. "So, who was the gig for?"

The deejay squeezed a lime into his bottle. "Just a few of the guy's friends. I don't know, I guess the winery does business with them."

"So, he wanted like, background music?"

"I guess. You know what, it was painless, and I got paid. That's all I care about." He grabbed her hand and kissed it.

Dinah didn't ask him how much he got paid. Discussing money made her uncomfortable. Which was ironic considering how much it obsessed her morning, noon, and night.

She gently stroked the side of his face. "Okay, well I'm glad you're pleased with how it went. And I can't wait to destroy these chiles rellenos!"

The food arrived – takeout only – and they carried it over to a picnic bench and gorged themselves. The deejay received three texts while they were eating. All from the vintner.

"He's just really stoked with how well things went," the deejay offered in the way of explanation. "He got great feedback from his friends. Says there might be more gigs. You know, on a regular basis."

"That's phenomenal, babe." Dinah said.

Something wasn't right.

## Chapter Twenty-Two

Dinah and the other pilots hadn't been the only casualties at SkyQuest. A large number of flight attendants had also been furloughed, including Fatima. The two had stayed in touch after Dinah had passed her line check. Fatima had been planning to settle in Chicago but now wasn't sure. For the time being, she was staying with some friends in Sherman Oaks.

They chatted on a regular basis and met once a week at Lake Balboa Park to have Boba Tea and keep each other's spirits up. They sat at neighboring picnic tables, Dinah with her Honeydew and Fatima with her Strawberry Matcha.

"Have you heard anything from the union?" Fatima asked.

"They're estimating that this will be until at least the next quarter. They might start bringing people back in then but it likely won't be until the new year at the earliest. If ever."

"It'll be even worse for the flight attendants. At least some of the pilots are just throwing in the towel and taking early retirement. Those grizzled old veteran FAs are going to have to be dragged out kicking and screaming by their support hose." Dinah laughed, guiltily. "I'm not kidding! I swear on one of my last flights I saw an actual sarcophagus in a silk scarf demo the oxygen mask!"

The park was so empty that they felt they could speak freely. With the birds chirping and the nice breeze, it was easy to forget for a few moments. Sometimes the paradigm shift was insidious ... like the new absence of jet engines departing Van Nuys Airport every few minutes.

"I can't believe that they cancelled our health insurance *and* our flight benefits," Dinah said. "The least they could have done was let us hold onto those. Especially considering the circumstances."

In addition to medical coverage, employees of SkyQuest, from pilots to flight attendants to dispatchers to gate agents were awarded flight benefits. That meant that, in addition to flying standby for free to work, they could also fly standby for free for fun, anywhere in the world that the airline flew. Many of the airlines had reciprocity agreements with each other as well. So, a Delta employee could still fly on a United flight – they just had less priority than a Delta employee. Under certain circumstances you could also sign up friends and family to fly in a complimentary capacity. This privilege was a huge attractor for many potential employees and one of the mitigating factors of low-paying jobs in the industry.

"I know. The irony is that now I have time to travel and I can't!" Fatima lamented. She took a long sip of her tea. "Actually, that's not entirely accurate. If I leave the U.S. now, I won't be able to get back in."

"Because of the travel ban?"

Fatima shook her head. "When they furloughed me, they cancelled my work visa."

Dinah's eyes widened. "Oh no! How long can you stay without it?"

"28 days." Fatima sighed.

Dinah drained her tea and used the straw to try and skewer one of the tapioca bubbles. The calendar was already way past 28 days since they'd been furloughed. "What will you do?"

"I'll stay. I know it's risky, but I'll just try to keep a low profile and see if something else pops up."

Dinah sensed she shouldn't ask the next question, but she did anyway. "Is there any possibility of you going back home? At all?"

Fatima pursed her lips. "No. It's not possible."

There was a pregnant silence as Dinah waited for Fatima to elaborate and then realized that she wasn't going to.

Dinah filled in the gap. "Fatima, I wish there was something I could do to help."

"Want to get married?" Fatima batted her eyelashes. "I swear I'll make it worth your while."

Dinah groaned. "You have no idea how tempted I am! My own domestic situation is far from idyllic right now."

"I'm sure it's just because we are in 'unprecedented times'," Fatima said dramatically.

Dinah laughed. "Never get tired of hearing that!"

An alarm went off on Fatima's phone. She looked at it and started.

"Oh shoot, I almost forgot. I'm sorry – this is so terribly rude – but the people I am staying with, their daughter Allie, is doing a Zoom dance recital today and I promised that I'd watch. Do you mind? They've been so kind to me."

Dinah rubbed her palms together. "Bring it on. My viewing experience as of late has been limited to reruns of *Firefly* and watching my boyfriend trash-talk adolescent virgins from Nebraska while he plays 'Call of Duty Modern Warfare'."

Fatima got her tablet out of her purse and placed it on the picnic table, positioning it so that they could both see the festivities. It was adorable. Each little girl was dressed in a pink tutu and matching leotard with a pink glitter heart on the front. They had their own screen and when the music started, they tried their best to sync the choreography from their own homes with each other.

The dance numbers were grouped according to age, so each class got to perform two numbers. Allie's age group, six to eight, were up first in the running order. The music for their opening number began. It was Robin Thicke's "Blurred Lines."

An odd choice for children.

But not as odd as the dance move choices.

There was an inordinate amount of pelvic thrusting and gluteus maximus gesticulating.

"Who choreographed this?" Fatima asked. "They look like a bunch of tiny strippers."

Dinah nodded uncomfortably. "It *is* a little much." She winced. "I kind of feel dirty just for watching it."

Thankfully, it ended a few bars later with them all doing the splits. Their second number was after a costume change. Now they were in cute little dungarees and t-shirts – pink again, of course. Fatima breathed a sigh of relief.

"Good. At least this one's not going to be slutty."

The accompanying song was Lee Dorsey's "Working in the Coal Mine."

And the choreography was thematic.

Watching little six-year-olds act out what it must have been like to toil away below the earth, sixteen hours a day was more than Dinah could take. She covered her mouth but couldn't stifle her mirth. She gazed at Fatima in shame.

"I'm so sorry. They really are good little dancers. It's just …"

"Don't apologize. This is beyond profane! What are these teachers and parents thinking?!" She peered at the screen. "What is happening right now?"

Dinah took a closer look as well. "I think they've got the smallest one pretending to be a canary."

"I can't watch anymore." Fatima snapped the tablet shut. "What am I going to say when I return to their house?"

"Just lie. Say you didn't get a chance to see it," Dinah offered.

"Then they'll sit me right down and do an impromptu viewing."

"Right. Shit. Okay, okay, what about this? Just say, that Allie was the best one. People love to hear that their kid is better than other kids."

"That's good. How do you know this? I thought you didn't have kids."

"I don't. I don't know, I guess people always like to think that they have excelled above others. Isn't that what it's all about? Survival of the fittest?"

Fatima frowned. "That kind of makes us sound like animals in a pack all vying for supremacy."

"To be fair, the animals are kind of killing it right now," Dinah observed. "It's the humans who are screwing everything up."

Fatima threw her empty tea container in a nearby trash bin. Dinah waited until she had enough social distance and then did the same.

"I can't argue that. I guess I always hope that our higher thinking skills distinguish us. That gives me hope."

A look of alarm crossed Dinah's face. "I'm sorry, are you aware of what country you're in right now?"

Fatima smiled wryly. "I know. I know. I just meant, people in general." Dinah nodded in agreement. "I always hope that we as a species are ultimately evolved enough to feel empathy and compassion for each other, even at a personal detriment, where other species can't. I have to believe that, or what's the point?"

Dinah considered her words. "Do you think people are basically good or basically evil?"

"Are we still talking about that dance recital? Because that was pure evil," Fatima said.

They both laughed.

"That will haunt me for a long, long time," Dinah said. "Especially the part when the canary started gasping for breath."

Their laughter turned to hysterics. Fatima wiped her eyes and got control of herself.

"Seriously though, I don't think that good and evil are that simple. Human beings are much more complex than that."

"So, you believe that we all have the potential to be good and to be evil within us?" Dinah asked.

Fatima put her head in her hands. "How did Boba Tea and a dance recital lead to such an existential conversation?"

Dinah shrugged. "It's the end of days, lady."

"In that case, I think we all need to admit to ourselves that we are capable of acts of great kindness and acts of great malevolence. All it takes is the right circumstance."

"Like, if someone pushes you too far?" Dinah asked.

"Perhaps. I mean we all have our breaking points. My hope as a member of the human race is that if I behave badly then I can learn from that and grow as a person. Which ultimately might lead to a greater act of good in the future."

Dinah was dying to probe deeper into Fatima's past. She sensed based on their conversation that this woman had had an eventful life. And perhaps a past not without its fair share of trouble. But she also wanted to respect her boundaries and not jeopardize what was growing into a wonderful friendship. Dinah was not a proponent of the "tough love" school of camaraderie.

Instead she asked, "What would you have had the girls dance to?"

Fatima tapped the side of her temple. "The Talking Heads – 'And She Was'."

"Nice. Tina Weymouth is one of the most underrated bass players of all time."

"Undebatable. What song would you have chosen?" Fatima asked.

Dinah didn't get a chance to answer the question because her phone screen lit up.

It was the border agent.

"Sorry," she said to Fatima. "Just give me a sec."

She answered the call and didn't even get a chance to voice a greeting. The border agent sounded far away and flustered.

"Dinah?" he said. "Can you come get me?"

"Where are you?"

"Imperial."

"I don't know where that is."

His voice began to crackle. "It's just north of the Mexican border. About 120 miles east of San Diego. Can you come?"

Dinah did some mental math. "Okay, I'm in the Valley so I'll have to drive down and get the plane and then fly it to you. Is there an airport there?"

"Yup – a small uncontrolled one. And it's better if you pick me up at night. I'll be waiting."

What was going on?

"Are you okay?" Dinah asked but he had already hung up.

"You have to go," Fatima stated.

"Yes, I'm so sorry. I've enjoyed this so, so much."

Fatima waved her off. "The pleasure has been mine. Truly."

"I wish there were something more I could do to help. If anything comes up, I swear, I'll reach out right away."

"I know you will."

Fatima stayed seated and made no indication that she intended to leave as well.

Dinah grabbed her bag and started across the grass towards her car, which was parked on the street.

Just before she reached it, she turned back and called to Fatima.

"'I'm Every Woman' ... and not the Whitney remake ... the original Chaka Khan."

Fatima raised her arms to the sky.

Dinah did likewise.

## Chapter Twenty-Three

**W**here the hell was this airport?

It was pitch-black out in the middle of nowhere and it was a moonless night with cloud cover. Surely there must have been a commercial flight the border agent could have jumped on. Or he could have driven.

Imperial Airport was an uncontrolled airfield that sat just to the east of El Centro Naval Air Facility and ten miles directly north of Mexicali and the Mexican border. El Centro NAF was the winter home of the Blue Angels. Dinah had checked her charts to find out the hours that the restricted airspace around the base were active. She knew she was fine but just to be sure, she called air traffic control and asked if the zone was "hot." It was not. Some airspace was restricted all the time but a lot of it had specific days and times that you weren't allowed to fly through it.

She was about ready to call it a day and turn around when she saw the flashing beacon. It flashed green and white, signifying a land-based airport. Water airport beacons were yellow and white, and a military airport beacon flashed white twice in rapid succession followed by green. Since Imperial was an uncontrolled airport, Dinah self-announced her intentions on the common frequency and based on the winds and the fact that it had now started to rain, made the choice to land on Runway 14. The runway was slippery with mud that formed quickly from the massive amount of dust that was prevalent in the area.

Imperial, even though it was a desert region and below sea level, was chiefly an agricultural area, thanks to the irrigation canals that led from the Colorado River. Daily temperatures were between 116-120 degrees Fahrenheit. Imperial County produced two-thirds of the winter vegetables for the U.S. It was all about the alfalfa. Despite the burgeoning agricultural scene, unemployment was one of the highest of all the counties in the U.S. The city was in the northern half of Imperial

Valley. The southern half was in Mexico and the border ran right through the middle. And the entire area sat over the southernmost part of the San Andreas Fault so was vulnerable to earthquakes. But the news wasn't all bad. The nearby Algodones Sand Dunes was where some of *Return of the Jedi* was filmed.

So, there was *that*.

Imperial Airport was an Essential Air Service (EAS) airport, which "essentially" meant that no airline wanted to fly there so the government had to entice them by paying them millions of dollars annually. They had had a series of different service providers over the years but presently the only way to get in and out commercially was on a Mokulele Airline flight. Mokulele was a Hawaiian airline who were looking to expand into the mainland, which was always difficult. Shockingly, established airlines generally weren't too keen on having a new kid in town to share the profits with. Flying an essential services route gave them a good foot in the door. Mokulele did 3 flights a day between LAX and KIPL with their Caravan 208s – which sat 9 people in an unpressurized cabin. If you missed out, then a Greyhound bus was pretty much your only other option.

Unless you knew Dinah.

She started to skid on the runway and got her feet off the brakes right away, letting the aircraft roll on its own for a few feet. After she regained control, she taxied off the runway and over to the parking area. There didn't seem to be anyone around.

Dinah really did not want to get out of that plane. She looked at her phone.

No service.

Essential or otherwise.

She decided that she would wait 15 minutes and then she was out of there. She felt like a sitting duck. And the rain was steady. Of course, the average annual rainfall in this region was less than three inches but she was there for two of them.

Out of the corner of her left eye, she saw a light flash several times. Then stop. Then flash again. Jesus Christ, was someone trying to signal her by doing Morse Code with a *flashlight*?

What kind of wormhole had she just flown through?

Was she about to be fired on by a P-38?

This was one of the many times Dinah wished that planes had horns like cars did. Cause she would have honked it. Loudly.

Instead she just popped the door and yelled out into the night, "It's me, Dinah!!"

The light extinguished and a dark, hooded figure ran towards the plane and then around to the right side. Dinah leaned over and opened the door, hoping if it was an airport serial killer instead of the border agent, that it would be over quickly.

It was the border agent.

He was covered in dirt and when he unzipped his jacket and threw it in the back, Dinah could see that his shirt underneath, in addition to dirt, had red stains on it.

"Is that blood?!" she asked.

He ignored her question. "I think we'd better get out of here."

"What's going on?"

"Let's go!"

He had never used that tone with her before. It was a tone that military and law enforcement personnel used. It was a warning tone that let you know that it was in your best interest to comply. Or else.

Dinah got them back on the runway and took off, turning right after takeoff to head back out to the coast. It was raining hard now, and she put the heat on to prevent icing. Even in the summer months, if there was enough moisture in the air, at a few thousand feet, you could get ice. And these types of aircraft had no de-ice or anti-ice equipment. If ice formed on the plane's critical surfaces – for example, the wings – eventually it would lose lift and quite literally fall out of the sky.

*Jarhead* and *The Scorpion King* had also been filmed there.

So, not *all* bad.

***

"Are you going to tell me what happened?" Dinah asked, about 20 minutes into the flight.

"Probably best if I don't," the border agent responded.

"Are we talking professional breach of protocol or identification by dental records here?"

No answer.

Finally, he opened his mouth to say something. Then he closed it again. Then, "I'm not officially on duty right now. This was an independent project. I did this on my own."

"Did what on your own? Exactly?"

No answer.

Then, "What needed to be done. Can I turn this heat down? I'm broiling."

"No."

"Fine. Look, you're not in any trouble. I would never place you in jeopardy."

"Okay," Dinah said. "Are *you* in trouble?"

"No. I just got a little carried away and before I knew it, I was across the border. Which is outside our jurisdiction."

Dinah whistled. "How did you get back?"

"I walked."

"You walked? Over ten miles?"

"What? I don't look like I could walk ten miles?"

"No, of course you could. My question is, why would you want to?"

The more Dinah queried him the more obfuscated the situation became.

"The manner in which I crossed into Mexico was not an option on the way back," he intimated.

All sorts of scenarios were racing through Dinah's mind … thrown off a truck … left at gunpoint by the side of the road … dead donkey … thrown off a donkey.

"Okay, I don't need to know what happened."

But she really wanted to.

"Uh-huh. It's better for your own protection that you don't. Just know that it was for the greater good."

She *really* wanted to.

And she would. In time. But for the present, she knew to let it go. This border agent was a completely different man than the thin-skinned bundle of nerves that she had gotten to know already. It was discombobulating but not unique. Some people just had completely different personas at work. Dinah was pretty much the same person no matter where you plopped her down.

Was that an attribute or a detriment?

"So, what's new with you?" she asked jovially.

"Very funny. Listen, I was sorry to hear about your airline job."

"Thank you. It's *so* not fair," Dinah confessed.

"It isn't. It really isn't. I don't know if this helps at all or is something you might even be interested in …" Dear God, this guy was suddenly the narrator from *The Mystery of the Sphinx*. Spit it out. "And obviously I probably shouldn't be doing any actual flight training right now but I'm eager to learn more. As I said before, you really changed my life. I did a little research and there's a flight school at John Wayne that has a simulator. How would you feel about doing some simulator sessions with me? That way I can get a head start on training and then when it's safe to fly again, I'll be ready to go!"

This guy was worried about the safety of flight training *now*?!

After what he had just described?!

"Which flight school?" Dinah asked.

It was the one that was home to the spilled ashes incident.

"I talked to the owner and he said that he's totally comfortable with having an outside instructor come in and train me. So, I would pay him for the simulator rental, and I would pay you directly for the instruction. What do you say?"

Dinah wasn't sure. She really needed the money. But she also suspected that the border agent might have feelings for her and that this was all just a subterfuge. It wasn't uncommon for students to get crushes on their instructors. You were literally responsible for their lives and that impacted. It was kind of like, Stockholm Syndrome in the sky. She didn't want to take advantage of him, and she also didn't want to create a situation that would be difficult to extricate herself from. In her experience, spurned suitors were dangerous.

"Let me think about it," she stalled. "But thank you for thinking of me, though."

"Of course." He seemed satisfied enough with that answer for now. "Listen, it's going to be far too late for you to drive home by the time we land. Let me pay for a hotel room for you."

"No, no. That's fine – I appreciate it though. Besides, it's hard to find a hotel that's still open right now."

"I never even thought of that. So, you'll stay with me. I've got a guest room with its own en suite bathroom."

Dinah was immediately wary of the invitation. But the border agent was right. It was going to be after one in the morning when they landed. And Dinah was exhausted. And tired of getting into situations that necessitated sleeping in her car.

It would be fine.

"Okay, let me call my boyfriend after we land and let him know. Just so he doesn't worry. I appreciate it."

Hopefully, that did the trick.

"Oh sure, sure. And you're more than welcome. I appreciate being airlifted out of there!"

\*\*\*

It *was* fine.

Maybe Dinah had misinterpreted the border agent's intentions. He was friendly and completely nonthreatening. When they got to his place, he showed her the room, got her some towels that actually looked less than 20 years old and an extra blanket and said goodnight. The next morning, when she woke up, he was already gone. He had left a note with some breakfast options and details on how to lock the door by turning the handle.

He also left a wad of cash for her.

For some reason, counting it didn't seem right. In her mind she was doing him a favor. She hadn't really expected to get paid but in retrospect it was probably better that he did pay her. It kept things professional. But her curiosity got the better of her.

$500.

The deejay had been parking his car in her designated spot at the apartment, so Dinah had to circle, looking for street parking when she got to Van Nuys. She saw a car pull out right in front of her building and sped up to lay claim to it before someone else did. There was a man walking a wiener dog into the building when she got out of her vehicle and locked it. Her car had already been broken into twice. The first time they took the loose change she had in the cupholder. The second time, they took the travel mug she had in the cupholder. Now there was nothing left to take but the cupholder itself.

Dinah did a double take when she realized that the man walking the wiener dog was none other than the baggage handler ... yet another victim of airport-related layoffs.

"Well, well, well, what is this?" she asked with great pomp and circumstance.

He turned and smiled when he saw her. "Don't 'at' me."

"Not at all. But I do have questions. Name?"

"'Pinkie' – after Pink's Hot Dogs."

"Hilarious and appropriate. How are you able to have her here?"

The baggage handler looked around furtively. "She's an emotional support animal."

Pinkie was the furthest thing from an emotional support animal. She was pulling on the leash and chewing on a piece of the hallway carpeting.

"I see that. Yes," said Dinah.

"You can get anything online these days. I have a printed certificate."

"And Kristina was good with that?"

"Nothing she could do about it. It's state law."

Dinah leaned down to scratch Pinkie under the chin. Pinkie barked at her and snarled.

"Oh yeah. There's not a person alive that wouldn't benefit emotionally from being around this animal. Where did you get her?"

The elevator had arrived, and they were both fighting to get Pinkie on it. But there was no way that dog was going. They gave up and decided to take the stairs. Pinkie refused to climb them, so the baggage handler picked her up and carried her.

"Ines found them in the dumpster out back. What kind of asshole throws dogs in a dumpster?"

"Wait. *Dogs*. Plural?" Dinah queried.

The baggage handler paused on a step to catch his breath. "There were three of them."

"Wait. Do you have *three* dogs in that apartment?"

"As far as Kristina is concerned, there's *one* dog. They all look alike so I just make sure to only walk one at a time. And I call them all, 'Pinkie'."

Dinah cackled. "You must be exhausted!"

The baggage handler leaned on the railing. "I'm walking wiener dogs all goddamn day long."

"Okay, let me dump my stuff and I'll come help you."

"Gracias. Ines is working a double."

Dinah frowned. "I hate that she's doing that. Her health is so fragile already."

"I know. I know. But people are too scared to work. Plus, now we've got three little mouths to feed. Which we do constantly - mostly to keep them quiet because if Kristina hears all that barking, we're gonna get bounced out of here."

They got to the baggage handler's door and he did some acrobatic twisting in order to get inside with one Pinkie without letting the other Pinkies out.

Dinah's cell rang just as she was about to turn the corner to her hallway.

"Hello?" she said.

"How would you feel about repossessing a plane?"

## Chapter Twenty-Four

The plane was a Beechcraft Duchess – the same aircraft that Dinah had gotten her multi-engine rating in. But she hadn't flown a Duchess in several years. That didn't faze the owner, at the other end of the phone, at all.

"It's muscle memory. It'll come back to you in a jiff. Just remember 'fly, identify, verify, feather'."

That idiom pertained to what you did if you lost one of the engines in a twin-engine plane. Because you suddenly lost power on one side, the entire plane would torque violently into the dead engine. So first you were taught to "fly." That meant get control of the aircraft and straighten it up, using the rudder pedal – which required so much foot pressure in training that Dinah's bum was up out of her seat. The "identify," referred to ascertaining which engine was out, which sounded simple enough, but it was amazing how flustered a pilot could get in that situation. Which led to "verify," which meant making sure that you knew you had the correct engine failed because if you did the last step to the wrong engine, then bonne chance. "Feather," referred to a process wherein you adjusted the propeller knob on the dead engine to position the blades in order to provide the least drag – in essence, "feathering" it.

"I don't know," Dinah hedged. "You can't do it yourself?"

"I would but my dad was just hospitalized, and I really need to stay close by," the owner said. "It pays $1,500 if that makes a difference."

It did.

"I'm so sorry to hear about your dad," Dinah said. "Where is the plane?"

"It's in Bakersfield. All I would need you to do is get yourself up there, fly it to San Bernardino and park it. The bank will take it from there."

"And this is all legal?" Dinah asked. She had never repossessed a plane before, so she didn't have a clue. She did know however from speaking to other pilots that the reality shows about repossessing aircraft were complete and utter fables. There was no scaling walls and cutting through barbed wires fences in the middle of the night. And there certainly wasn't any gunplay or spaghetti western-style scrapping. That was all fabricated for the sake of ratings.

Which distinguished it from all other reality shows on television. Clearly.

"Absolutely. The bank has notified the plane owner of the foreclosure. Apparently, he's had a bunch of warnings and assured them he could make payment and then nothing."

Dinah still had misgivings. "So, he knows this is happening?"

"Oh yeah. In fact, he's agreed to meet you at the hangar with the keys and make sure that you have the maintenance logs and everything. Good, good?"

The deejay wasn't home, which was surprising but not entirely unwanted, so Dinah didn't have anyone to ask for advice on this. And really, she shouldn't have needed to anyway. Sometimes she annoyed herself. Much of the time she still felt like a child hiding in an adult body. Honestly, if someone had told her to go to her room, she probably would still oblige.

Enough.

"That sounds good. I'll grab a flight from Burbank."

"Awesome – save your receipts," he said. "I'll email you the foreclosure notice. Just slap it on the plane when you get there."

Dinah went online and looked at the flights from Bob Hope Airport to Meadows Field Airport. There was one in three hours. She also booked a rental car in San Bernardino. It would be about a 75-mile drive back to Van Nuys from there. Then Dinah threw a change of clothes and her toiletry bag in a knapsack – just in case – printed the notice and sped out the door. The deejay hadn't let her know where he was, so she didn't feel that guilty about doing the same. She'd text him if she had time from the airport.

On the way up there, Dinah was surprised to reconcile the fact that she didn't feel sorry for the owner of the Duchess. Every time that she saw a foreclosure sign on someone's front lawn, she felt awful for the family. But a plane was different. A plane wasn't your home. And a lot of these guys bought toys on credit that they couldn't afford in the first place. It was time to check their privilege.

That was going to make her job easier. It was harder when emotion got in the way.

*** 

The problems started as soon as she arrived in Bakersfield. She got off her commercial flight and walked across the tarmac to the hangar where the Duchess was stored. But the hangar was locked and there was no one in sight.

She called the owner.

"Hey, are you sure the plane's owner is coming?" she asked him.

"That's what he said," replied the owner.

"Well, there's no sign of him."

"I was afraid that would happen. Okay, can you get into the hangar? Because legally he doesn't have to be there when you take the plane."

Dinah examined the hangar door. "The hangar is locked."

There was a sigh at the other end of the phone. "Shit. That complicates things somewhat."

"How so?" A pit was starting to form in Dinah's stomach.

"Well, if the aircraft is out in the open, then legally you can grab it. But if it is locked in a hangar and you take it, then that's technically breaking and entering, which you're not supposed to do. You'd need to get a court order for that."

"Okay, how long would that take?" Dinah asked.

"A long time. Not really viable at this point. Is there any way you can get into that hangar? Anybody around with a key? Maybe a maintenance guy?"

He wasn't overtly saying to use her feminine wiles, but the intimation was there.

It was always there.

She groaned inwardly. "Let me have a look around and I'll call you back."

"Roger that."

Ugh. She hated when people used aviation terminology outside of flying. She used to reprimand her students when they did that. It just felt so lame. There was also flight jargon that was anachronistic that GA pilots used because they thought it was cool. It was not. When air traffic control – ATC - reported traffic in their area, if a pilot couldn't see the other plane, they were supposed to respond by saying, "looking for the traffic." But a lot of these amateurs piped up with the phrase, "no joy." "No joy" was a military term from the war that fighter pilots used when they hadn't successfully spotted enemy aircraft. No pilot in Southern California, flying to the Waypoint Café in Camarillo for a $100 hamburger (that was $8.50 for the burger and $91.50 for fuel) needed to be enthusiastically spewing "no joy" over the radio.

Well at least that internal diatribe had passed the time while Dinah was trekking back across the ramp to the terminal. She asked at the counter, but the agent didn't know anyone connected to the hangar. There was a maintenance center, but it was closed.

Now what?

There was no way that she was breaking into that hangar.

Dinah decided to use the restroom while she considered her options.

The ladies' room was quite lovely. The sinks were painted ceramic and there was a basket on the counter filled with toiletries. A wicker chair in the corner looked very inviting. She wondered how long she could sit in here before arousing suspicion.

After availing the basket of a wet wipe and some travel-sized mouthwash, Dinah wandered back into the waiting area. Which was perfect timing because a Ford Mustang had just pulled up in front of the hangar.

She sped across the tarmac, waving as she went. The man who had emerged from the vehicle, stopped, and waved in return. That must be the owner of the plane, she thought. And he didn't look pissed so that was good also.

"Hi," she said breathlessly. "Are you the owner of the Duchess?"

The man, an athletic looking, 40-something in gym gear, shook his head. "No, I own the Cessna 182. It's a double hangar."

Bingo.

"Is there any chance you could let me in?" Dinah asked winsomely.

"Depends, are you his ex-wife?" he laughed, and Dinah joined in.

"Better. I'm his girlfriend!"

"Which one?"

More hilarious laughter. And during this witty banter, the athletic guy, pulled out a key, and unlocked and raised the hangar door.

There it was.

"How long have you had your 182?" she asked.

"About two years. I lucked out with this hangar arrangement – a lot cheaper than a single."

She tried the plane door. It was locked. Damn.

She tried to peer unobtrusively through the side window. The keys were dangling from the ignition. Dinah moved farther back to the tiny luggage door. It was unlocked. She was going to have to crawl through it and then climb to the front. But technically that wasn't breaking and entering.

Was it?

"Hey, you wouldn't happen to know where he keeps the maintenance records would you?" she asked without much hope.

The athletic guy pointed at an old scratched wooden desk at the back of the hangar.

"Top right drawer. I always tell him he should keep those locked up. If you lose your maintenance records, you're screwed. Good luck ever selling your plane!"

Dinah walked over and opened the drawer. The records were there. Which was extremely fortunate because unless a mechanic showed up, that was the only way for her to ensure that the plane was airworthy and legal for her to fly. Without the records, she would have had to obtain a special permit from the FAA to do a ferry flight.

"Thanks."

The athletic guy hadn't really been paying attention up to this point but when Dinah removed the binders from the drawer, it alerted him.

"Hey, what are you doing with those?"

Dinah put them into the luggage compartment and smiled at him. "Taking this girl for her annual."

Every aircraft had to have an annual inspection – not just by an Airplane & Powerplant mechanic but rather a mechanic who had an Inspection Authority designation, which was a lot harder to get. Consequently, there weren't as many of them.

"That's weird. Usually he does that here."

"I know. I know. But he found a cheaper guy down at Brackett."

The athletic guy frowned and crossed his arms. "You know, that's so like him. What a slimeball – always trying to get a better deal. Do you know that even though we split the hangar, I still pay more than he does?"

Dinah shook her head sympathetically. "That is *so* like him!"

She had grabbed the tow bar from the luggage compartment. The athletic guy rushed over to her.

"Here, let me give you a hand with that!"

He waved her out of the way and fastened the bar around the nosewheel of the plane and then pulled it forward until it was clear of the hangar.

"Thank you so much! This Duchess weighs a ton!" Dinah said thankfully.

"Yeah, but she's got a great personality!"

"That she does. That she does."

Now what?

The athletic guy started like he had suddenly remembered something.

"I'd better skedaddle." He opened the door of his plane and extracted a set of golf clubs.

"You're not flying today?"

"No. Shooting a round with a buddy and forgot I left my golf bag. Do you need anything else in here before I close her up?"

Dinah shook her head. "I'm good to go. Thanks again for your help."

If only he knew exactly how much help he had been.

She waited for him to wave goodbye and roar off in his muscle car before she opened that luggage door and crawled in ... with more than a little difficulty. Her right pocket got caught on the hinge and she heard a ripping sound.

She was going to invoice for that.

Once she got into the backseat, she reached in front and unlocked the pilot side door. Then she got out of the backseat, exited the plane, and re-entered it from the front. Enough of the crawling and wriggling.

She had a good look at the logbooks before she started up the engine. Everything looked up to snuff. The Duchess was on a progressive maintenance program which meant that certain procedures were spread out over the course of the year so that everything that was required didn't have to be done at once. It was a good cost-effective measure.

But obviously not good enough.

The engines started right away, no problem, which meant that the aircraft had likely been flown recently, which was also a good sign. And speaking of signs, she taped the foreclosure sign up inside the rear window just in case anybody showed up with an attitude.

Dinah went through her checklists and listened to the ATIS. Then she looked at her route of flight. She didn't want to go over the mountains, so she was going to follow the Number 5 Freeway south to the Valley and then cut across Burbank and pick up the 210 and fly along it to San Bernardino. She called and got her taxi instructions and then got herself out to the run-up area beside Runway 30R. While she was going through the run-up checklist, she saw a pickup truck out of the corner of her eye. It was rocketing towards the run-up area.

That wasn't good.

She quickly called for takeoff clearance which she was immediately awarded. Tower control mustn't have noticed the Ford in the "no movement" area. A big guy in a ball cap was already getting out of the truck.

Dinah got the power up quickly and got the Duchess on the runway. She didn't stop but instead kept it rolling. Once she was on the centerline, she added full power. In the moment it took for the Duchess to respond to the power input, the guy in the ball cap, appeared on the runway off the right wing.

Holy shit.

As the plane picked up speed, he chased it. His ball cap was blown off.

Dinah knew he wouldn't be able to catch the plane, but she was concerned that he would be shredded by the propellers.

Should she abort?

The guy without the ball cap was wearing cowboy boots, which were not ideal footwear for chasing planes in. A couple of yards later, he took a header and faceplanted on the runway. That was going to be some wicked road rash.

Dinah kept going. She reached rotation speed and pulled back on the yoke. Still tower control didn't say anything. Maybe *everybody* thought that the guy in the ball cap was a slimeball. Or maybe this was a typical Tuesday in Bakersfield.

As she climbed, she looked back down onto the runway. The guy in the ball cap had gotten up and was limping back to his truck. He turned and shook his fist at her, like an agrarian Ed Rooney in *Ferris Bueller's Day Off*.

Dinah didn't feel fear.

She didn't feel anger.

She felt complete and utter exhilaration.

## Chapter Twenty-Five

The argument escalated so quickly that it almost caused whiplash.

The deejay had booked another gig up at San Luis Obispo. Dinah was fine with flying him up there a second time, but he was being adamant about landing at Oceano Airport again.

"It doesn't make any sense to land there. San Luis Obispo Airport is so much closer. It was such a long drive to the winery last time. Plus, you've already landed there once and seen what it's like."

"I don't care. I really like it there. That's where I want to land."

"But it doesn't make any *sense*."

"Why does it have to make sense?" He was shouting now. "Why does everything have to make sense to you? Why can't you just do it? Why can't you just accept that your boyfriend would like to land at Oceano and because you love him, you're going to do it? What does it matter in the grand scheme of things?!"

What did it matter indeed?

Why was that airport so damn important to him?

Dinah ultimately gave in because the deejay's face was turning a shade of purple that was concerning her. But she also decided that if there were any more gigs after this one, it was San Luis or bust.

The flight up there was noticeably quiet, except for the engine. Dinah didn't understand what he was sulking about. He got his way.

Nevertheless, she didn't like uncomfortable silences so she attempted to initiate a conversation using a teaser that she was certain the deejay wouldn't be able to resist.

"Is this 'My Sweet Lord'?" she asked.

He nodded. "George Harrison. With The Sugarhill Gang underneath - 'Rapper's Delight'."

"Did you know that George Harrison lost a copyright infringement lawsuit for that song?" Dinah inquired.

"Against The Chiffons, right? For the song, 'He's So Fine'."

"What do you think about that?" she baited.

"Well, you've got to admit, the melodies are virtually identical. But I don't think Harrison did it on purpose. In fact, the Court ruled the same thing – that it was unintentional plagiarism."

"So, like collective unconscious, kind of."

"What's that?"

"It's Jungian – he basically thought that all human ideas are collectively shared in the subconscious mind."

"So, like, everyone basically thought of the song, 'Monster Mash' but only Bobby Pickett wrote it down and recorded it."

Dinah shrugged her shoulders. "Maybe."

"You know, those poor girl groups didn't make a dime anyway. They were totally exploited. And there were so many of them ... The Chiffons, The Shirelles, The Dixie Cups, The Exciters, The Ronettes."

Dinah cringed. "Those names alone should be litigable. It's interesting how much has changed with how music is disseminated since the '60s and '70s. You know, with streaming and sampling. It'd be much harder now to win that kind of lawsuit."

The deejay held up his hands. "Hey, I pay for *my* music."

"I know you do. You're one of the good guys," Dinah praised.

"Okay, but did *you* know *this*? The song that was playing on station KLIF in Dallas when Kennedy was shot was The Chiffons' 'I Have A Boyfriend'?" he said smugly.

"Wow. Before and after," Dinah acknowledged.

Before and after.

***

After they landed at Oceano and before the Lyft arrived, Dinah told the deejay that she was going to wait for him at the airport.

"I'll just hang out on the beach until you get back," she said.

"Are you sure? It might be a while," the deejay reasoned.

"I'll be fine. That winery guy kind of gave me the creeps."

"Really?" he said, sounding surprised. "I didn't get a creeper vibe at all. I thought he was pretty chill."

Dinah was worried that he would think her decision was retaliatory and be annoyed with her, but he seemed somewhat relieved that she didn't want to go with him. He gave her a long kiss goodbye and waved to her as he got into the Lyft.

She locked the plane up and grabbed her knapsack, as she headed for the sand. Dinah spread out a towel and pulled a cherry chocolate KIND bar and a bottle of water out of her bag. Then she sank down and stared at the water, cerulean blue with lots of whitecaps. The beach wasn't busy so the sole sound of the waves crashing on the shore became white noise and that in harmony with the warm sun, knocked her out.

A distant shout woke her up about half an hour later. A parachutist was just about to land on the beach. It was a square chute, striped black and yellow like a bee. He fell backwards on the sand and had some trouble deflating the chute. It started to fill up with air again and drag him along behind it. Dinah ran over and grabbed the right toggle handle, pulling it as hard as she could. The skydiver regained his composure and cut himself loose. As she helped him pack up the chute, she got a good look at him and was startled by his age. He must have been 70 if he was a day.

"Whoo – got blown a little off course there. Thanks for the help!" He pulled out his phone and texted someone. "They'll have to come and fetch me in the truck." He winked at her. "They almost always have to come and fetch me in the truck."

"Who are *they*?" Dinah asked.

"The good people over at Skydive Pismo Beach," he responded.

"How long have you been doing this?" Dinah asked.

"What time is it now?"

"Seriously!" she chided him.

"I am serious! This is my fourth jump!" he explained. The skydiver looked over to his left. "Ah good, here they are. They must have been tracking me. Well, ta-ta for now."

He bundled up his gear and turned to walk to the waiting truck. Dinah stopped him.

"Hold on. Can I come with you?"

*\*\*\**

At Skydive Pismo Beach, they explained to her that normally they did tandem jumps, which meant that you were strapped to an experienced diver for at least the first few times. That way you could enjoy the ride without worrying about having to do anything in the way of preventing your own demise. But under the present conditions, that wasn't feasible, so they had temporarily switched to "clear and pulls."

Her *jumpmaster* – a legit title – explained how a "clear and pull" jump worked.

"You see this belly pouch that attaches around the waist of the diver?" he asked. Dinah nodded affirmatively. "Well inside that is something called a 'pilot chute.' You throw the pilot chute out and that triggers the main chute."

Dinah pointed to the handles that rested slightly higher up the chest. "So, you don't pull those?"

"No. Those are for the reserve chute. If the main chute fails to deploy then you pull the reserve chute. But I'll tell you something. The main chute is square, which makes it a lot easier to control directionally and makes for a softer landing. The reserve chute is the older circular style. There's a good chance you'll break your ankle landing under that. Even D.B. Cooper wouldn't jump with one of those old military-style round chutes."

Dinah grappled with the reference for a moment. "D.B. Cooper ... that was the guy who hijacked that plane and then jumped out with a bunch of money, right?"

The jumpmaster nodded. "Yeah, there was a really good movie about it in the '80s with Treat Williams."

Dinah snapped her fingers. "*The Pursuit of D.B. Cooper.*"

"That's the one."

In November 1971, the night before Thanksgiving, a man named D.B. Cooper got on a Boeing 727 to fly from Seattle to Portland. Once in the air, he notified one of the flight attendants that he had a bomb and demanded $200,000 (which would be over $1.2 million today), 4 parachutes and enough fuel to get to Mexico City. When they landed in Seattle, D.B. Cooper had everyone deplane except for the pilot, co-pilot, flight engineer (back when they still had them), and one flight attendant. They refueled the aircraft and loaded the ransom via the aft stairs and then D.B. told the pilot to cruise at 10,000 feet so that they wouldn't need to pressurize the cabin. After takeoff he put all the crewmembers in the cockpit and closed the door. About 30 minutes into the flight, the warning light indicating that the aft staircase had been deployed, flashed. Two hours later, when they landed in Reno, Nevada to refuel again, D.B. Cooper was gone.

The F.B.I. never found him or the money.

"Do you think he died jumping out of the plane?" Dinah asked.

"I don't know. I *do* know the weather that night was brutal. He jumped in a heavy rainstorm. But I also think that D.B. Cooper was ex-military – maybe a pilot – because he seemed knowledgeable about aviation and skydiving. After all, they tried to give him one of those round chutes and he sent it back for a square one. And he knew a lot about the 727."

Dinah wrinkled her nose. "Does it make me a bad person to kind of hope that he got away with it?"

"Nope – cause I kind of do too!"

Dinah grinned. "Okay, so speaking of 'knowledgeable,' what makes it a 'clear and pull'?"

"In this case, you're not really freefalling. I'll hold onto the pilot chute and as soon as you exit the plane – i.e., 'clear' it, then I'll let go of it – that's the 'pull' part - and your main chute will deploy." He held up a battered pink helmet. "And see this? It's got built-in headphones so we can stay in radio contact with you the entire time. We can guide you directionally by telling you which toggle to pull." He paused to let all that sink in. "So, what do you think?"

What *did* she think?

"How much does it cost?"

"$199 per jump."

That was a lot.

"Okay."

He led Dinah into a classroom where she filled out some information forms and signed a contract, indemnity waiver and a medical waiver. Then she was shown some training videos and after that her jumpmaster had her get up and put the gear on. And then they simulated exactly what was going to happen.

"The hardest part is the landing," he said. "That's where most people get hurt. They look straight down and flare way too high."

"How do I flare?" Dinah asked.

"Grab your toggles there," he explained. "Okay good. Now pull them all the way down. That deflates the chute."

"It's just like landing a plane," she said.

"Exactly right. Have you ever flown a plane?" he asked.

"No." She didn't feel like having that conversation.

"Well it's exactly the same principle. Look at the horizon and when it comes up to meet your eyeline, then you flare."

"Got it."

"Alright. What do you say? Should we go for it?"

"One more question," Dinah said. "How long do I wait to pull my reserve chute if my main one doesn't open?"

"Excellent question. I always count, 'one Mississippi, two Mississippi, three Mississippi,' and if it hasn't opened, I pull the reserve. Now in reality, it's a two-step process. You have to cut away the main chute first, by pulling this handle." He demonstrated. "Otherwise the two chutes will get tangled up. After the main chute is gone, *then* you pull the reserve handle." He demonstrated that as well.

Dinah looked a bit stressed. "That sounds kind of complicated."

"It does, doesn't it?" he said cheerfully. "That's why on all our student gear, the reserve chute deploys automatically at 1,000 feet whether you pull it or not. Shall we?"

\*\*\*

They went up in a gutted Cessna 172. The seats had all been removed, except for the pilot's seat. Dinah and her jumpmaster knelt on the floor of the plane while the skydive pilot climbed up to 5,000 feet.

He wasn't wearing a chute. He was wearing a brown leather bomber jacket.

Her jumpmaster leaned in to talk to her. "For the tandem jumps, we usually climb to 13,000 feet but because you'll be on your own, we don't go as high."

Dinah nodded. "Understood."

"Okay, just like we practiced. Your cue will be when you hear the engine throttle back to idle. He'll hold the plane steady while you climb out and hang off the strut. That way you'll already be in the correct posture. I'll come out too and lean against the strut facing the opposite way. When I yell, 'go,' you let go of the strut as smoothly as you can, and I'll release your pilot chute. Okay? And then they'll start talking to you on the radio as soon as your main chute opens."

He gave her the thumbs up and she gave it back.

"I'm nervous."

"Good, you should be. It's not normal for human beings to jump out of a perfectly good aircraft. If you ever come up and you're *not* nervous, then don't jump. That means that something is wrong."

"Got it."

"Okay. One last thing – you can change your mind at any point up until you begin to exit the aircraft. At that time, it's no longer safe for you to come back in. It endangers you, me, and the pilot. So, know that I'll toss you out. I'm five foot seven and one-sixty and change and I threw a three-hundred-pound construction worker out of here two weeks ago. Got it?"

"Got it."

Jumpmaster!

Dinah heard the engine go to idle and she tried to get up, but her legs had gone to sleep. The jumpmaster helped her to her feet and over to the open doorway on the right side of the plane – the original door had been removed. She was shocked how hard she had to fight to get out of the aircraft. Even at idle speed, the wind was hellacious. She got herself positioned on the strut, but she could feel her fingers slipping off. The jumpmaster was only halfway out the door when she lost her grip. He let go of the pilot chute immediately and waved goodbye.

One Mississippi.

Two Mississippi.

Three Mississippi.

Suddenly she was pulled up violently – it felt like the world's worst wedgie - and there was a colossal whooshing sound, like a huge sail. Dinah looked up and saw yellow and black stripes. She inadvertently squealed. It was cold as hell up there, but the view was outstanding. It was a completely different sensation than flying. This was so quiet and peaceful and solitary in the most sublime way. She felt like the only person in the entire world. And it fit like a glove.

Shortly after the chute opened, the guy on the radio started giving her instructions so that she could steer herself left and right. And he told her when to flare, but really, she already knew. Two other guys ran over once she was on the ground to ensure that her chute didn't re-inflate, like the guy's parachute on the beach had. Apparently, it could start dragging you backwards up to 120 mph, and people had been killed in that scenario.

The plane landed shortly after she did, and her jumpmaster rushed over to shake her hand and congratulate her.

"So …. did you love it, or did you love it?"

Dinah grinned at him. "How many more jumps before I can pull my own chute?"

***

The deejay was pacing furiously when Dinah arrived at the airport. He was absolutely livid. Even his inanimate gear looked pissed.

"Where have you been?! I've been waiting here over an hour!"

What was going on with him? He was habitually late himself and usually didn't pay any attention to the clock.

Dinah decided not to bite.

"I was jumping out of a plane."

She grabbed one of his bags and started towards the Cirrus.

"Yeah sure." She turned and stared him down. "Wait, are you serious?"

"Serious as fuck."

His mood transformed instantly. "Holy shit. I mean, holy shit! That's so insanely badass, babe." He stared at her in rapture. "That is ... OMG ... I ... I don't even know what to say. That is so hot!"

"You're right. It *is* hot." She opened the plane door and got in, leaving him to load the rest of his gear. "Don't ever forget it!"

## Chapter Twenty-Six

Dinah had agreed to meet Fatima at three o'clock at the park but thought she should cancel.

Around lunchtime she had received a phone call from Nell, the Cancer Society volunteer who had driven Sherry to and from chemo. The news wasn't good.

"Hi, Dinah, it's Nell from the Cancer Society," she began.

"Oh Nell. Please tell me you're calling because you want to make sure that I filled out my census."

"I wish, hon. It's about Sherry. She's passed on."

Dinah thought that was a lovely way of characterizing her demise. When her parents had been in the accident, the police notified the general manager of the dealership and he came right over to where she was detailing a car and said, "Your parents died." She'd never forgotten the indelicacy … the insensitivity of his delivery.

Breaking bad news to people took a special quality in a person. She'd never had to do it before and she hoped that if she ever did, that she would have the grace and warmth that Nell, unfortunately, had probably had the practice to perfect.

"I'm so sorry to hear that, Nell. Thank you so much for knowing that I'd want to be apprised. Not an easy phone call to make and I really appreciate it."

"Of course. Sherry was quite a magnificent woman and I figured that she would have wanted you to know."

Dinah felt a lump forming in her throat, so she spoke quickly. "Can you let me know when the funeral will be?"

There was a pause. "There isn't going to be one. As per Sherry's last requests. She said that she didn't want any kind of memorial or funeral. The only request that she had was that her entire estate be left to the Pacific Marine Mammal Center."

A sob caught in Dinah's throat. "How completely and utterly perfect. True to herself to the very end."

"There are going to be a lot of happy seals out there," Nell ventured.

"I already have a visual image of them honking and clapping."

"I can think of no better tribute, honestly."

\*\*\*

After the call, Dinah cried for a while and then felt depleted and lower than she had in quite some time. She lay down on her bed and stared at a water stain on the ceiling. She was so tired. So tired all the time. Every day seemed like an eternity. An interminable uphill battle with no clear objective or goal.

What was the point?

Dinah wondered if everyone else felt like Sisyphus too.

Clearly the organic buzz from her skydiving had worn off in a big way.

By the time she decided that she just didn't have the energy to drag herself to the park, it was too late to let Fatima know – she'd already be on her way there. Dinah didn't want to be inconsiderate, so she got up and splashed some water on her face. Experience had taught her that the torment of just showing up was less than the shame of being rude to someone.

Fatima recognized that something was off right away.

"Did you have a fight with your boyfriend?" she asked tentatively.

"No, no, nothing like that," Dinah reassured her. "I just got some bad news. An acquaintance of mine lost her battle with cancer."

She immediately wished that she hadn't phrased it in that manner. Nobody lost a battle with cancer. Every day that a human being survived with that insidious invader inside their body was a victory. Mind over matter was a limited and finite concept. Dinah always envisioned people versus cancer as a sort of symbolic arm-wrestling match. But it was nothing like that. It was like innocently wandering into a hornet's nest. There were so many of them and only one of you that it was impossible not to be overrun and overwhelmed, regardless of how strong you were or how fast you could run.

"I'm so terribly sorry to hear that," Fatima said. "How sad."

"And you know the worst part?" Suddenly Dinah felt like talking about it. "There's not even going to be a funeral. Not because there can't be one right now but because Sherry didn't want one."

Fatima watched a gecko scurry across the grass and then disappear under a shrub. "You know, I always think that funerals are for the living and not for the dead. The dead already have closure."

"You don't think it's selfish?" Dinah asked.

"I don't actually. I think that it's the final choice that someone can make for themselves. Most of us don't get to control how we die. And we certainly have less control over our lives than we'd like. But at least we can control what happens at the end. It's the ultimate exercising of the human will, I would say."

Dinah drummed her fingers on the picnic table as she considered Fatima's words. "I've never thought of it that way. But what about people's need to grieve?"

"None of that is predicated by a formal ceremony. It takes much longer than a few hours or even a few days for emotional pain to find a reprieve. What are those five stages of grief that people talk about?"

"Elizabeth Kubler-Ross ... the psychiatrist ... she was a real pioneer in her field. Let's see, there's *denial, anger, depression, acceptance*. Wait, I'm missing one." Dinah counted on her fingers.

"Bargaining," Fatima supplied.

"That's it. So, *denial, anger, bargaining, depression* and *acceptance*." A smile crept across Dinah's face. She put her hand up to cover it. "Jesus, I just realized that those could also be the five stages of a relationship."

Fatima hooted. "You are as wise as you are witty. What stage are you at presently?"

Fatima was extremely perceptive.

"I think I'm transitioning from *anger* to *depression*." Which seemed odd to articulate because in Fatima's company, Dinah's mood had measurably improved.

"Perhaps we should do away with funerals when a person dies and save them for when a relationship dies," Fatima proposed. They both laughed wickedly. "In all sincerity though, I am so very sorry for your loss, Dinah."

"Thank you, Fatima. Sherry was an exceptional woman."

"We cannot afford to lose an exceptional woman. We need all of them. The world needs all of them."

"Agreed," Dinah got to her feet. "You know something? I never ate lunch and I'm starving. Humble Bee Café? My treat?"

"My pleasure. But you're not paying," Fatima said.

They walked towards their cars.

"We'll see about that," Dinah said.

"I can pay for my own lunch!"

When they reached their vehicles, Dinah glanced reflexively at her own, to make sure that a "smash and grab" hadn't taken place and then did the same for Fatima's. She was shocked to see the interior of

Fatima's Chevy Malibu. The backseat and passenger side were filled with boxes, garbage bags and hanging clothes.

"Fatima, are you living in your car?"

***

Over lunch, Fatima initially denied being homeless, but Dinah eventually wore her down. Over iced teas and two black bean omelets, Fatima admitted that things had not worked out at her friend's place and she'd been obliged to leave without a contingency plan.

"I don't understand," Dinah said. "How could she just kick you out? Knowing that you had nowhere to go?"

"It wasn't her fault," Fatima justified.

"How was it not her fault?" Dinah demanded.

"Her husband ... there was an incident ... "

"What kind of incident?"

"He'd been drinking, you see," Fatima said.

Dinah dropped her fork loudly. "Wait, hold on a minute. Did he try something?" Fatima became overly interested in her omelet. "Are you kidding me?"

Fatima looked around with embarrassment. "Please keep your voice down."

"So, you have to sleep in your car because her husband is a douchebag?!" Dinah's face was red with rage.

"Please, I need you to calm down. Really, it's not that bad. There are some quiet residential streets in Sherman Oaks to park on at night. With the doors locked, I feel perfectly safe. And my car has more square footage than some of the studio apartments in Los Angeles."

Dinah's hands formed fists and she pushed her plate away from her, her omelet half-eaten. "It's not funny, Fatima."

"It's also not the end of the world and it's not forever. It's temporary and a lot of people are far worse off. It's fine."

Dinah stood up abruptly and pulled her wallet out of her purse. "It's the furthest thing from fine. Get your stuff and follow me to my place." She extracted a Bank of America debit card. "And don't even think about paying!"

\*\*\*

Dinah drove past an empty parking spot a few yards past her building and indicated that Fatima should pull in there, by opening her window and waving. Then she did a U-turn at the next stoplight and parked on the opposite side of the street. Dinah had a dolly in the back of her car for the deejay's gear, so she grabbed it and wheeled it across the street to help Fatima with her belongings.

Mercifully, Kristina was on her daily bank run when they entered the building so Dinah didn't have that to contend with, but truthfully, in her present state of mind, Kristina wouldn't have stood a chance. They hustled everything onto the elevator and Dinah pressed the button for the third floor.

Fatima looked extremely ill at ease. "Are you sure this will be okay with your boyfriend?"

"Absolutely."

"But this will be such an imposition. You are in a one-bedroom, right? I'll be completely in your way."

"It's a large one-bedroom, we have a fold-out sofa and you can stay as long as you like. My home is your home. End of discussion," Dinah concluded.

Fatima grabbed Dinah's hand. "Thank you."

Dinah could only imagine how much more difficult it was for Fatima to accept a generosity than it was for her to give one. Offering help made a person feel good. Accepting help made a person feel the antithesis of that. That's why so many people just suffered. Because the swallowing of pride and self-respect that it took to change their situation was too great a sacrifice.

"It'll be great to have you here. I love your company. So, thank *you*."

Dinah was hoping that the deejay wouldn't be home so that she could get Fatima settled in on her own. But when they reached the apartment door, she could hear swearing and gunfire on the other side.

Great.

She opened the door slowly.

"Hey, babe!" the deejay called without turning away from the screen.

"Should I wait out here?" Fatima asked Dinah in a whisper.

The strange voice caused the deejay to turn and when he saw Fatima, he paused his game and got up.

"Hello? Sorry, I didn't know that Dinah was bringing a friend home."

Dinah delivered all the pertinent information like a manifesto. "This is Fatima. She worked at SkyQuest with me and she's going to be staying with us."

"For how long?" the deejay asked.

"For as long as she needs to," Dinah replied.

Fatima was already trying to retreat down the hallway. Dinah stopped her by laying her hand on her arm.

"Great. Can I speak to you privately?" he asked.

"Sure." Dinah looked at Fatima. "There's room in the front hall closet for your things okay? You go ahead and get unpacked and then we'll get you situated. I'll be right back."

She followed the deejay into the bedroom, and he closed the door. Dinah knew what a wasted effort that was because the cheap plywood wouldn't give them any privacy whatsoever. Fatima would be able to hear every word that they said.

"This is not a good idea," he opened with.

"Why not?"

"Because it's a one-bedroom apartment. Where am I supposed to play my games with her sleeping on the couch?"

"We can move your PS4 into the bedroom."

First point deflected.

"But how well do you know this person? You said that you just worked with her. What if she steals from us? Or gets us involved in something? She could be a drug addict for all we know."

"I've known her longer than I've known you. And I trust her completely. Fatima has not brought any of her misfortune on herself. She's just experienced an unlucky turn of events. Like almost everybody else. We need to offer her the same kindness that we would hope others to offer us if we were in the same circumstances."

Second point deflected.

"But we're not. Which is also not our fault."

"But we could be. We have no safety net. We could be homeless ourselves at the drop of a hat."

The deejay folded his arms across his chest and rested his weight on one bare foot. "You should have checked with me first. No, I'm sorry but I'm just not okay with this. I have to put my foot down."

He moved to exit the bedroom and Dinah held him back with her arm extended. "You're right – as a courtesy, I should have let you know that Fatima was coming to stay instead of just arriving without any notice. For that, I apologize. But understand this, she is staying. The lease is in my name and you're not on it. She has just as much of a right to be here as you do. So, it really doesn't matter if you want her here or not. I do. If you're not comfortable with the living arrangements, then you're welcome to leave."

Third point.

Dinah opened the bedroom door. Fatima was hiding in the bathroom with the door closed and the fan going. The deejay stormed passed her and out the door, stubbing his toe on one of the boxes.

"I need some space," he fumed.

"Okay, but can you pick up some milk?"

He didn't respond.

## Chapter Twenty-Seven

After the first few days of incubation, Fatima settled in quite nicely to their household. She was so vocally appreciative and every time that Dinah turned around, she was cleaning and tidying. On Day Two, fresh tulips appeared in a green glass vase on the dining room table and there was some sort of fresh bouquet every single day after that.

Even the deejay warmed to Fatima. Dinah returned from walking one of the Pinkies to see him tucking into a big plate of eggs Benedict.

"You gotta try this, babe," he exuded. "Fatima's a freaking awesome cook!"

"I use crumpets instead of English muffins, so all of the sauce and the yolk gets caught in the nooks and crannies," Fatima explained.

"Nooks and crannies!" the deejay repeated with hollandaise sauce dribbling down his chin.

So, when the border agent texted her for the third time about setting up a SIM training time at the flight school in Santa Ana, Dinah felt confident that she wouldn't return home to a murder-suicide. She really didn't want to drive all the way down there but the money from the repossession had gone to rent so there was nothing left. The deejay had offered to contribute but she told him that the vintner money should be their fallback plan. Partly this was out of altruism and partly because she wanted to maintain control of her domestic situation. The more he invested, the more he had *invested*.

She confirmed with the border agent for 2 p.m. the next day.

At 6:52 a.m., the phone woke her up. It was the owner.

"Hey, I need you to go to Mexico with me."

None of his usual flirtatious banter and cajoling. He was direct and demanding.

"Um, I going to need some more information," Dinah said. She was getting better at not just blindly agreeing to do flights. Even in her present predicament she was becoming more assertive and discerning.

"I might have a line on a contract with a company out of Monterrey," he elaborated.

"What kind of contract?"

"Flying medical supplies," the owner said.

Dinah was impressed. "That's great, actually. But why do you need me to go with you? I don't speak Spanish, like at all."

He seemed in a hurry to get an answer from her. "Yeah, but you told me that your airline flew into Monterrey on a regular basis, right? I've never been there before, and I'd just like to have someone with me who knows the lay of the land."

The fact that he had freely admitted that he didn't know how to do something was nothing short of revelatory. He was definitively winning Dinah over. But she was older and wiser than a few months ago, so she decided to do some negotiating.

"Okay, but I want to do all the flying down there. And you need to defer to me – Monterrey is tricky to get in and out of."

"Yes, ma'am! Can you leave right away?"

"I'm supposed to meet the border agent this afternoon."

"Just reschedule. He'll understand."

Would he though?

Dinah called him and was quite sure she woke him up.

"Hi, it's Dinah. I'm so sorry but I have to reschedule for this aft."

"Everything okay?" His voice was gruffer than usual.

"Everything's fine. I just have to go to Mexico unexpectedly for work. Could we do Friday at 2 p.m. instead?"

"Mexico? Where in Mexico?" he asked.

"Monterrey," she answered. She already knew what his response was going to be.

"Monterrey! That's not the safest place, you know," he cautioned.

"I've been there before. I know where to go and where not to. I'll be fine."

He sighed deeply. "Okay, well, stay alert. And if anything happens, you've got my number."

"I really appreciate it. See you Friday?"

"See you Friday."

***

Flying into another country, was a special kind of challenge. You had to file an International Flight Plan and you couldn't deviate from it. For most flights, regardless of your final destination, after crossing the border you needed to land at an airport with a Customs and Border Patrol center (CBP) for inspection. You remained in the plane and they came to you, usually with a drug-sniffing dog. They scoured the plane and your paperwork before you were permitted to deplane. It was intimidating and stressful.

One of Dinah's classmates had been flying a man with a pacemaker to Ensenada in his private jet. On the way, he had a massive coronary and died. They landed in Mexico with a dead guy in the back and when the officials inspected the aircraft, they discovered that the deceased had an unregistered firearm in his suitcase.

No está bien.

The classmate spent two nights in a Mexican prison cell before he could get the American consulate to intercede. He had never been back. And he was one of the luckier cautionary tales.

The other issue with flying into Mexico was the physical protocol of it all. Mexican air traffic controllers handled their business a little differently than American air traffic controllers. For one thing, in the U.S., a controller would start descending you from your cruising altitude down to the destination airport pattern altitude.

In Mexico, it was the pilot's onus to ask. Otherwise, they would let you cruise right over your destination airport at 37,000 feet. They refused to spoon-feed.

Dinah kind of admired that.

The other thing that was idiosyncratic was how long they waited to clear you for specific arrival and approach procedures. And it was rarely the arrival or approach procedure that you had filed in your flight plan and programmed into the plane's navigation equipment. So, you'd inevitably find yourself scrambling to find the new procedure in your plane's database while you played beat the clock.

"So, here's what I do," Dinah explained to the owner. "Cause, I know they're going to screw me with a last-minute change. I ask if I can 'expect the Notal Bravo Arrival,' well ahead of time so that I know."

"Very savvy," the owner complimented. "What's the city of Monterrey like?"

"It's kind of like the Detroit of Mexico," Dinah characterized. "It's a manufacturing hub. A couple of years ago it was much more dangerous. SkyQuest stopped flying there because one of the flight attendants was abducted one night from the hotel and held for ransom. But it's better now. The police reined in the crime because it was costing the city too much revenue since nobody wanted to travel there."

"Jesus."

"Yeah, I mean, I still wouldn't venture too far from the airport. I booked us into the Hilton Garden Inn. I've never had any trouble there and the hotel staff work their butts off. The rooms are spotless, and they put out a wonderful buffet breakfast every morning. And it's literally five minutes from the airport."

"And for dinner?" he asked.

Dinah had to admit to herself that it was kind of nice to be the docent in this situation. And the owner seemed to really be relying on her expertise.

"There's two really nice restaurants on either side of the hotel. The food is good at both but at one they rip you off on the exchange rate."

"So, we'll eat at the other one," he decided.

The aircraft was just crossing over the mountain range to the northeast of the city.

"Agreed," Dinah said. "Okay, now as soon as we get over the Sierra Madres, we're going to chop and drop because the airport is pretty much right there."

"Noted."

Dinah chuckled. "Oh, and one other thing. There's often bad windshear coming down over the mountains or climbing out, like we'll do tomorrow. And nine times out of ten, the controller will only issue the advisory in Spanish – even though they're all bilingual. So, any flight crews who just speak English hit it completely unprepared."

"That's kind of a dick move," the owner noted.

"Not really," Dinah contradicted. "You should hear how the American pilots talk to the Mexican controllers. It's disgusting. They're rude and condescending. In English. Which for most of them is the only language they speak. Which they are speaking in another country where English is *not* the mother tongue."

"So, respect, then."

"Respect."

***

They landed at Monterrey without incident and waited patiently for Customs to board. The airport personnel were courteous and efficient. Dinah had always found them to be incredibly professional. None of them took their jobs for granted. They reminded her how lucky she was to have a job. In her chosen field no less.

After they were cleared, they got the airport shuttle in front on the terminal. Then after a quick check-in and unpacking, they reunited in the lobby to go to dinner. The restaurant to the right of the hotel had been a Mexican icon for 40 years. It was called, Los Fresnos – "the ash trees," and it was always packed. In the lobby hung a portrait of the founding couple, a gregarious-looking gentleman, and his stern-looking bride, who clearly never had to worry about laugh lines. At least three waiters hovered over their white linen tablecloth with water and a crumb brush. Dinah had a delicious charro and rice combo and the owner had Cortadillo – a traditional beef stew with tomatoes and spices. Every dish came with at least four side dishes and their table ran out of room quickly. Dinah loved the frenetic, communal energy in the room. Eating was an occasion here.

"This is the best beef I have ever had," the owner claimed.

Dinah believed him.

After dinner they strolled back to the hotel. The three-hour time difference had left them both exhausted. Even though the streets were quite busy with foot traffic, Dinah never stopped scanning.

The owner noticed. "I thought you said this area was safe."

"It is. But I'm always vigilant, no matter where I am. You don't get nervous walking at night?" she asked.

"Not usually," he said. "You do?"

"I have never left my home once in my entire life without being at least a little bit nervous."

"Really?!"

"Welcome to being a woman."

***

The next morning, the owner had arranged for the two medical reps to meet him in the hotel dining room. Dinah offered to join, but she really wanted to sleep in so she was relieved when he said he could handle it alone.

"Are we taking stuff back with us on this flight? Because I'll have to do a flight manifest before we go. Everything will be inspected."

"No," he answered. "This trip is purely exploratory. I didn't want to commit to anything until I meet these guys and check them out."

The owner texted her when he was done, and Dinah went down to the lobby.

"How did it go?" she asked.

"Good, really good. I think we're going to do an inaugural flight in the next week or so. Just need to hammer out a few more details."

The owner waved goodbye to two men in pinstripe suits with slicked-back hair as they exited the lobby. Most of the other guests and occupants were blue collar – in construction clothes or plaid shirts and jeans – so the pair looked awfully incongruous.

Were those the two medical reps?

They grabbed the shuttle back to the airport and got their clearance to El Paso, Texas. That was the first airport after crossing the U.S. border that had Customs and Border Control on site. After clearing customs, they'd continue on to Southern California.

They had absolutely no problems at all - at either end - and Dinah found that she was surprised how much she enjoyed flying with the owner this time. This trip was a stark contrast to the Aspen fiasco. She didn't think he would need her help after this flight since she had familiarized him with how to do things. But she thought she'd offer anyway.

"Hey, if you need a second crewmember for any future flights here, I'm sure I could free myself up."

Dinah scrutinized his face, but the owner didn't give anything away.

"Honestly, I'm surprised to hear that. I didn't think you'd be on board with this."

"The Mexico thing? I'm totally comfortable. Ever vigilant but comfortable!" She laughed.

She shouldn't have laughed.

## Chapter Twenty-Eight

On Thursday, the deejay told her that he had another San Luis gig on Friday.

"I'm so sorry, babe," she said. "I can't take you. I've got a SIM session."

"Can you reschedule it? Please?" he asked.

"I really can't. I've already cancelled once on him. Can you drive?"

"No."

"Why not?"

"I just can't, alright?"

Dinah could feel her irritation mounting. "No. Not alright. I want to know why!"

The deejay grunted in exasperation. "Because I got a DUI, okay? I can't drive!"

His license had been reinstated *months* ago.

Dinah put her hand over her mouth. "What the hell? When did this happen? Why didn't you call me for a ride?"

"I don't know. You were away," he said.

"Or take an Uber?" she asked.

He narrowed his eyes at her.

Right.

"So, can you reschedule?"

"I really can't. What about this? What if we ask Fatima to drive you? We could pay her for her time."

The deejay shook his head. "I wouldn't be comfortable with that."

"Why? I thought you guys were BFFs now."

"She's actually really cool but that's a seven-hour round trip by car. I don't know her well enough. It would be awkward. Please, babe?? It's so humiliating. Please, can you just help me out here? I can call your student and explain." He rubbed her back.

And so, Dinah had rescheduled on the border agent yet again. She couldn't tell if he was mad or not. He told her he'd try to change the booking at the flight school and let her know. For sure that flight school hated her guts by now.

The only benefit to flying the deejay up there was that she could do another jump. This time she didn't even raise the issue of which airport they were going to land at – she went right to Oceano. He went off to the winery and Dinah headed straight for the drop zone. She knew that she couldn't justify the expenditure but for once she didn't overthink it.

She just did it.

This time, her jumpmaster wadded up a piece of yellow tissue paper and stuck it in her belly pouch. He told her it was to replicate the pilot chute. He would still throw the real pilot chute, but he wanted her to throw the tissue paper so that she could show him she was collected enough to do it for herself.

Dinah let go of the strut and then looked down and grabbed for the yellow. She probably whipped it much harder than was necessary, but she got the job done. And she stuck the landing. She landed on two feet. At the same time. Simone Biles would have been envious.

Her jumpmaster told her that next time she could pull the chute herself.

***

When the border agent got back to her it was to let Dinah know that the flight school at John Wayne had notified him that their SIM was down for maintenance. She took that explanation at face value. The only entities that went down for maintenance issues more than SIMs were planes themselves.

She thought that let her off the hook, but the border agent had hatched a contingency plan.

"There's a flight school in Van Nuys that has a simulator – Mach 1 Aviation? Anyway, it's available and they were fine with us using it," he said.

"But that's an awfully long way for you to go," Dinah replied.

She wasn't sure how she felt about him being in her hood. But that feeling was dominated by the feeling of relief that she didn't have to drive all the way down to Santa Ana.

"It's no problem. I've got a meeting up there, so I'll already be in the area."

What meeting? Nothing good ever resulted from a meeting in Van Nuys. The arrival of the ATF habitually resulted from a meeting in Van Nuys.

"Okay," she said. "And again, I apologize for the other times. I promise you, even an earthquake won't be a deal breaker this time!"

"Well, Mach 1 is on the 2nd floor so let's play that by ear."

***

Mach 1 was just down the street from Dinah's apartment, so she walked there. It was kind of cool. They had extended Runway 16R in 1957 and built an underpass on Sherman Way so Dinah walked underneath planes that were landing right on top of her. The original incarnation of Van Nuys Airport was opened in 1928. During Prohibition, they stayed afloat, by smuggling liquor in from Mexico. Also, during those years, famous female flyers like Bobbi Trout, Pancho Barnes and Amelia Earhart broke speed and endurance records flying at Van Nuys. But perhaps the *most* celebrated female denizen was a young Norma Jeane Dougherty, who was photographed working on an assembly line at a military factory there in 1945 for a story in *Yank* magazine. And secured a screen test shortly thereafter. And also changed her name to Marilyn Monroe.

So, two women were famous for speed (Amelia at 184 mph and Pancho the next year at 196 mph), another was famous for endurance (Bobbi, in the air 12 hours, 11 minutes without refueling) and one was famous for being pretty.

Dinah met the border agent on the second floor and the receptionist directed them to a small room at the end of the hallway. The simulator was quite straightforward, and the flight school had kindly printed out step-by-step instructions on how to fire it up and use it, so Dinah didn't feel like too much of an idiot. She had the border agent take off and then gave him some headings to turn to and some altitudes to climb and descend to. She also had him practice some steep turns. He got a little flustered on the first two but the advantage of practicing on a simulator was that you could press "pause."

She genuinely thought he had done quite well and didn't feel like she was blowing smoke when she told him so.

"This was a good idea," she admitted. "I think these sessions are going to be really advantageous to you."

"And the best part is … no wind!" he declared.

"Oh, I can program in some wind. This time I went easy on you. Next time get ready for *The Wizard of Oz*!"

They went back out to the front and the border agent paid for the simulator rental. Dinah refused to take any payment for the instruction.

"Not a chance. Not after cancelling on you twice. I appreciate your patience and your perseverance."

He put his wallet back in his pocket. "Okay, well at least let me treat you to a Subway sub. I was going to grab one for myself anyway before I jump on the 405."

\*\*\*

The Subway franchise across from the airport was always busy that time of day. As usual there was quite a lineup. There weren't a lot of other options in the immediate vicinity, so they voted to wait.

"They're really good here," Dinah assured the border agent. "The line will move quickly."

Just then, out of the corner of her eye, she saw a woman crossing the parking lot, heading straight for Subway.

No, no, no, no, no.

It was Fatima.

Dinah tried to subtly wave her off, but Fatima didn't notice. In fact, when she saw Dinah, she hastened her pace and yelled out her name. The border agent turned when he heard her.

No, no, no, no, no.

"Dinah! I thought that was you!" Fatima said.

"Hi, Fatima," Dinah responded. "What are you doing here?"

As in, what were the odds of this exact implosion?

"Your fella wanted a sweet onion chicken teriyaki sub."

No, no, no, no, no.

"Are you kidding me? You are being way too nice to him. He's taking advantage of you."

Fatima smiled. "Not at all. I felt like a walk. And I wanted to pick up a few things at Food 4 Less anyway. We're out of Frosted Flakes."

The border agent was listening to this exchange with rapt attention.

"Your boyfriend has another woman getting his sandwiches for him?" he asked cagily.

Fatima laughed. "It's all completely innocent, I can assure you. I'm their houseguest at the moment."

Dinah introduced Fatima and the border agent to each other.

Why was the line moving so slowly?

"We were just grabbing a quick bite before I have to go back on shift," the border agent explained.

Dinah could see the puzzlement on Fatima's face.

"On 'shift'?" she asked. "Are you a paramedic?"

He smiled. "Nothing that admirable, I'm afraid. I work for U.S. Customs and Border Patrol."

Fatima visibly blanched before she had a chance to collect herself.

The line crept forward a few inches.

"Wow, that sounds interesting," Fatima managed to throw out.

"What about you, what do you do?" the border agent asked her.

Dinah could see that Fatima was struggling to control her breath, so she jumped in. "Fatima and I both worked at SkyQuest. She's a flight attendant."

Another few inches forward, to the next tape mark on the ground.

He addressed Fatima. "You must love to travel then as much as Dinah."

"I do. Yes."

He stared at her. "Where are you from?"

Dinah had known it was coming.

They were inside the store now.

She could see the wheels spinning, both in Fatima's head and the border agent's head.

"Well I was planning to settle in Chicago until we got laid off so for now, I guess I'm a Valley Girl!" Fatima said that all in one breath. No exhale.

The border agent was next in line to order.

"No," he said. "I meant, where are you from, originally?"

No, no, no, no, no.

Fatima looked up at the menu, studying it intently.

"Buffalo."

Dinah fervently hoped that the border agent had never seen *The Usual Suspects*.

"Ah, the snow belt," he said. "You ever try the wings at Anchor Bar on Main?" Now all three of them were in the store. The border agent insisted on paying for Dinah and Fatima's orders and relayed them to the Subway employee. "So, have you? The Anchor Bar?"

"I'm a vegetarian, so that would be a 'no'."

Yes, yes, yes, yes, yes.

The border agent rolled his eyes and pointed to Dinah. "Not another one! I'm overrun by vegetarians. You're everywhere!"

Dinah grinned at him. "Welcome to Southern California, pal!"

She did a quick visual check-in with Fatima. Fatima was mesmerized by the tv set mounted behind the counter. She started pointing frantically.

"Your neighbor! Your neighbor is on tv!!"

Fatima had quickly joined the ranks of the Pinkie walkers and had become quite good friends with Ines and the baggage handler.

"What?!" Dinah exclaimed.

Ines was being remotely interviewed by the new and improved Ellen DeGeneres, who seemed overly excited, which struck Dinah as incredibly odd.

"That's your neighbor?" the border agent asked.

They both nodded.

He paid for their orders and distributed the sandwiches. They didn't want to leave but the store was crowded, and their business had concluded. As they left the store, Dinah walked backwards so that she could keep watching. The sound was off so she couldn't hear what they were saying, but now Ines was holding up a portrait of Ellen, done in *The Scream* theme.

Ah.

Dinah decided to capitalize on the opportunity that the moment had provided. She grabbed Fatima's arm.

"We'd better hustle home and get the scoop on this!" She gestured to the border agent with her bundle. "Thanks so much for lunch. See you next week?"

"Yes," Fatima piped in. "Thank you as well."

"My pleasure ... oh boy, I'm going to butcher this. Is it *Fa-teem-ah*?" The border agent stumbled over the word.

Fatima laughed. "*Fat-em-ah*. I know, it's a tough one. When I was growing up, people always struggled with it. You can call me by my nickname if you like."

"What's your nickname?"

"Tammy."

## Chapter Twenty-Nine

Tammy had not had an easy time of it. But she chose the modern tenet of blaming herself for her hardships. Every time there had been a fork in the road, she had ridden the gravel shoulder. Or careened off the road entirely into the nearby gulley full of brambles.

Her parents had done everything they could to prevent her from flying the plane left to her by the farmer. They tried hiding the keys. She'd had a duplicate set made. They tried selling the plane. She relocated it so that the potential buyer was shown an empty barn for his troubles. They tried locking her in her room. She climbed out the window and shimmied down the drainpipe, tearing the drainpipe away from the side of the house.

When they ultimately threatened to contact the local authorities and report her for flying without a license, she laughed in their faces.

"Go ahead," she challenged. "I'm a minor. Who do you think will be held accountable for my actions? Legal guardian to my left and legal guardian to my right."

Tammy was indomitable.

They finally acquiesced and decided instead to focus their parental energies on her grades. With high dividends. Tammy got admission to all three universities that she applied to – University of Toronto, Queen's University in Kingston, and McGill University in Montréal. She received a partial scholarship to U of T and full scholarships to Queen's and McGill.

Her parents wanted her to go to U of T.

She chose McGill.

Because it was the farthest away.

Scholarships were an extremely rare and coveted occurrence at McGill University. The cut-off grade for even being so bold as to apply was 95%. Tammy's average was 98.9%.

McGill University was founded in 1821 and was opened to women in 1884. The first degrees to women were awarded in 1888. And McGill's graduates included Prime Minister Justin Trudeau, Star Trek Captain William Shatner, and Governor-General (and former astronaut) Julie Payette. Even though McGill was in the heart of Montréal, actually at the foot of Mount Royal, it was predominantly English-speaking and the only faculty that required a working knowledge of French was the Faculty of Law. Tammy's major was engineering.

In addition to the lack of proximity to Kapuskasing, Tammy was further attracted to McGill because of their strong support of gay, lesbian, bisexual and trans students. As early as 1972, Student Services had started an offshoot initially called, "Gay McGill," and later modified to "Queer McGill" to provide guidance and direction to their sexually diverse students.

Tammy's parents still had no idea about her sexual orientation. In high school, she never went to student dances or senior prom, effortlessly using her studies as a convenient excuse. She played a season of Girls Field Hockey, which mostly entailed standing in the middle of a deserted field, chewing gum and, occasionally getting whacked across the shins by a hormone-addled teenager. But it was just enough to placate her parents, who for some reason seemed concerned that a lack of physical activity was somehow going to result in meningitis.

Escaping to McGill was the best thing that could possibly happen to Tammy, who was pining to have her first girlfriend ... away from prying eyes. She was also very much looking forward to getting plastered at the Peel Pub. The drinking age was 18 in Montréal so she probably would have gone there even without the scholarship.

Even though McGill was a Canadian university, it had a healthy number of international students, including many Americans. It was located close to the borders of Vermont and upstate New York. And a Canadian university's tuition was about a third of an American university's tuition. Tammy went all in and decided to live on campus her first year. She was accepted into Douglas Hall, in the Upper Residence or "Upper Rez." "Doug" was built in 1936 and the dorm rooms had a lot of character, as did the cafeteria, with exposed timber ceilings.

She met Lucinda while she lived at Doug.

Lucinda – never Lucy – was majoring in political science, or "poly sci." If an undergraduate could shorten a term or a name, they would. She was from Burlington, Vermont and she smelled like maple syrup. Tammy wasn't actually sure if she smelled like maple syrup but as soon as she heard, "Vermont," the power of suggestion was insurmountable. Even in present day, Tammy couldn't face pancakes, waffles, or French toast for breakfast. The pain was palpable.

Lucinda bore a striking resemblance to Lucille Ball – which was probably why no one was allowed to shorten her name - and Lucinda was officially *out*. Which was thrilling and inspiring to Tammy. But also evoked great contrition in her own situation. Tammy conspired for months to make her move. She thought that the Montréal Jazz Festival would be the perfect site for seduction. Every July, the city hosted the world's largest jazz festival – 3,000 artists from over 30 countries and 650 concerts. Much of the downtown core was closed for concerts throughout the ten-day event. Tammy had scored a summer job in Montréal so that she didn't have to go home. She worked at Café Santropol on rue Saint-Urbain. They had an unusual and stunning menu of sandwiches and blended drinks, along with the vastest tea selection that Tammy had ever seen in Canada. The front of the restaurant was a restored rowhouse and the back opened into the most bewitching courtyard. It was Tammy's favorite place in Montréal besides the Notre-Dame Basilica. Not for the religious ceremony – that would have killed her parents quicker than the lesbian thing – but because every December they staged a free performance of Handel's "Messiah," and the acoustics were unparalleled. The experience evoked epiphany. The first time she went, the vocal beauty was so insidious, she got goose-bumps on her arms.

Lucinda was splitting her summer between Vermont and Québec. She spent some time at home but also was on a sailing team in Montréal. The most affluent "Anglo" region of Montréal was called

Westmount and most of their residents were well-versed in the term "regatta." Lucinda had distant relatives who lived there and got her onto a team.

"What do you do exactly?" Tammy asked.

"I wear blue and white stripes and shout a lot," Lucinda detailed. "And whenever someone yells, 'Ready about,' I duck."

So, Tammy didn't know Lucinda was in town one evening while she was devouring her favorite sandwich on break – a concoction of green olives, pecans and cream cheese heaped on fresh dark pumpernickel. Lucinda strolled into the courtyard and after just a few minutes of preamble, leaned across the table and kissed Tammy right on her cream-cheese-encrusted mouth. Tammy didn't even care that she was robbed of making her move on rue Sainte-Catherine in front of Taj Mahal. This was just as perfect as perfect could be.

"Why did you do that?" Tammy asked.

"Because I knew that you were never going to," Lucinda said matter-of-factly.

"No, I was going to do it right in front of Taj Mahal!" Tammy protested.

"In India?"

"No. You know what, never mind. Kiss me again."

\*\*\*

From that point on, Tammy and Lucinda were an inseparable and very public couple. Beyond the novelty of having companionship and romantic love, Tammy allowed herself, for the first time, to present a true self-representation to the world and not a heavily censored persona. The word "freedom" didn't even begin to encompass the liberty she felt. That summer was the first time Tammy could remember not feeling like there was a physical weight on her chest.

The two dated all through sophomore and senior year and then a decision had to be made. Lucinda had only enrolled for a three-year bachelor's degree, so she was graduating. Tammy was in for another year because she was doing an honor's degree. And she hated the thought of it. Engineering was a horrible program full of testosterone-fueled hazing rituals and misogyny. At parties, they waited for classmates to pass out drunk and then shaved their eyebrows off and drew new ones on. Every weekend, some poor hungover soul would wake up looking surprised, whether they were or not. And the rumors of roofies and rum punch ran rampant. Tammy was happy that they all knew she was lesbian because it removed her from "the pool." The worst she had to contend with was the occasional drunken "Durometer Dyke" slur.

It was clever because it was esoteric.

Tammy really relied on the strength and support of Lucinda to stay in the program and she couldn't even conceive of being there without her. So, when Lucinda suggested that she blow off her last year and come with her to Burlington, she didn't have to ask twice.

"Look, do you really want to be an engineer?" Lucinda asked.

"My parents really want me to be an engineer."

"What do *you* want to be?"

Tammy didn't have to think about it. "I want to be a pilot. Well, really, I want to be an astronaut, but I'll start with pilot and work my way up. I'm realistic."

"So, come with me and do that. I've got that great policy analyst job lined up so I'll do that, and you can flight train full-time."

Tammy's heart felt like it was going to explode.

But then.

"Wait. I can't come and live in the U.S. I'm Canadian."

"I thought you were Sri Lankan?" Lucinda queried.

"My family got our Canadian citizenship a few years ago," Tammy explained.

"So, get a green card."

"How?"

Lucinda kissed Tammy's nose. "Same-sex marriage is legal in Vermont."

Tammy's heart felt like it was going to explode.

But then.

"My parents. I'll have to tell my parents."

So, she did. At the age of 21, she phoned her Sri Lankan parents back in Kapuskasing, Ontario and told them that she was getting married. To a woman.

And that phone call was the last time she had spoken with them.

Their choice.

***

At first, Vermont with Lucinda was dreamlike. Tammy was able to get a student visa right away for flight training and she would apply for a green card after the wedding. She got herself set up at the Vermont Flight Training Academy and settled into the Burlington lifestyle.

The Burlington lifestyle was white, extremely white. Of course, Burlington was perhaps most notorious for being the birthplace of Ben and Jerry's, but their ice cream wasn't the only thing that was vanilla. The population was over 85% white. Tammy never felt like she fit in. People were nice, but she always felt like she was being stared at. And not because she was a lesbian.

Then Lucinda started dragging her heels on the wedding. She said she wanted to do it *right*, but she was so busy at work, she didn't have any time to plan it.

"I can plan it," Tammy said. "I love that kind of stuff!"

Lucinda laughed out loud. "You hate that kind of stuff!"

"But I love you."

And still nothing with the wedding progressed.

Tammy successfully passed her private pilot checkride and her instrument rating and started on her commercial license.

Then Lucinda made dinner one night.

Lucinda never made dinner.

There was somebody named Terri. At work. It was nobody's fault. It just happened. She never meant for anyone to get hurt.

Tammy's heart felt like it was going to explode. Again.

And there she was – living all alone, in another country, with no source of income and a student visa that was going to expire in a few months. And going home wasn't an option.

She couldn't move forward, and she couldn't go back.

She started looking online for any aviation-related job that might allow her to stay in the country on a work permit. The flight training would have to wait for now.

And that's how Fatima saw the ad for a corporate flight attendant.

## Chapter Thirty

Dinah wasn't really counting on the owner to contact her about any more flights to Mexico. She knew that his business was hanging by a thread and that he really didn't need her to tag along. The owner's father was still in the hospital. He wasn't expected to recover, which saddened Dinah greatly. He had always been so lovely to her. And she really didn't know how long the owner would be able to stay in business without his father's financial and organizational support. He had been the one that kept his son on track.

So, she was surprised to get a text asking if she could do a Monterrey run in two days. Fatima and the deejay were getting along famously – Fatima had made it her business to learn to love "Call of Duty," and now Dinah had two lumps on the couch where she had previously had one. That Fatima was a wise woman ... she also never won a battle. Smart.

And the trip wouldn't conflict with any simulator sessions she had with the border agent. Their next one wasn't until the following week.

So, the stars were all aligned.

The owner had paid her $300 a day plus expenses for the first trip and offered the same for this trip, with the understanding that they'd be flying down and returning on the same day. Dinah knew that he was trying to save money on meals and hotels, so she didn't press the point. And she also didn't know if Fatima was completely comfortable staying alone in the apartment with her boyfriend. She trusted them both implicitly but there was just always an awkward dynamic when any man and woman had to share a sleeping space platonically. She had once had to stay overnight in Truckee with her male flight instructor due to a magneto issue and he couldn't afford his own room, so she offered to get a room with two twin beds. He was so paranoid about his new bride finding out, that he slept in the plane instead. He agreed to showering and changing clothes in the room, but Dinah had to wait downstairs in the lobby.

The owner let Dinah fly down and then he wanted to fly the leg back to John Wayne from Monterrey. She filed all the paperwork for him though. As he explained, she was just so much quicker at it than him. It would have taken him hours. And she *did* want to help him out. She felt badly for him with respect to his dad and how much stress his business must be causing him.

On the way down in the King Air, Dinah told him the jaw-dropping story of her neighbor, Ines, who had been "discovered" by Ellen DeGeneres. Well, initially discovered by some nameless production assistant and then up the food chain it went.

"Wait, so she paints celebrities' faces, and they're screaming?" he asked incredulously.

Dinah nodded. "They're based on that famous Munch painting."

"That's outrageous! I love it. Good for her."

"They're really quite good. They remind me of the kind of stuff Andy Warhol did – kitschy and clever."

"So, what happened after she was on the show?" the owner asked.

"Well, apparently, it went viral. One of the producers created a website for her and so many people ordered commissioned pieces that the website crashed. I guess since so many folks are at home right now, the timing was perfect. Ines is doing the paintings full-time now. She was able to quit her job at Target."

"Wow, that's stellar. Nice to hear some good news these days."

*\*\*\**

When they arrived at General Mariano Escobedo International Airport – Mexican airports were all named after military generals – the cargo was already waiting to be loaded.

It was just one small pallet with only a few boxes on it.

"Is this it?" Dinah asked.

"Yup, yup," the owner said somewhat dismissively. "We wanted the first run to kind of be a trial thing. The volume of the loads will grow as we go."

"Okay, sounds like a plan."

That was an awful lot of time and fuel for such a small load.

Dinah really hoped that the owner's father made a full recovery ... soon.

They switched seats and the owner got ready to taxi out and take off. Even though Dinah had flown *and* done the radio calls on the way down, he asked her to still do the radios on the way back.

"I'm ashamed how much trouble I'm having with understanding their accents," he admitted embarrassedly.

Dinah really didn't mind so she got their clearance from their filed flight plan and their taxi clearance out to the runway. They were told they could take off without delay and so they did. And as per usual, they got tossed about climbing out over the mountains. Dinah looked out her window at the most well-known one in the region, Saddleback Mountain.

"It really *does* look like a saddle," she observed.

"What?" the owner said, distractedly. "Oh ... yeah."

As soon as they had passed over the mountain range, there was a flattening of the topography near Vallecillo. The owner started banking the plane towards it, away from their course.

"What are you doing?" Dinah asked him.

"I need you to cancel our flight plan, real quick," he said.

"We can't cancel our flight plan. They're expecting us in El Paso."

"Just need to make a quick detour. Go ahead. Quickly Dinah, before we reach the border." She didn't respond. "Do it now!"

Dinah didn't want to get into a contentious situation in the air, so she cancelled with the Mexican controller. She'd deal with it once they were on the ground. Speaking of, where was he planning to put it down out here? The owner was clearly descending with the intent to land but there were no airports in the vicinity.

Then she saw the field. There was a large white Econoline panel van parked in the middle of it and two wiry men with rifles were leaning on the grille at the front of it. One of them spotted the aircraft and waved to them, pointing to his left.

The owner put the gear down, reduced power and started extending flaps.

What had he gotten them into?

She was frightened and furious with him but still had to begrudgingly admit to herself that he did a decent landing. Always a pilot. He rolled it to the end of the field and then did a 180-degree turn and kept the engine running.

"What the hell is going on?" Dinah demanded.

The owner unbelted himself and moved back to open the door.

"I need you to stay put."

The doors at the back of the panel van opened and people started getting out.

People were getting out of the van!

There were seven of them. Five adults (three young women and two older men) and two children – a boy who looked to be about ten and a little girl about five. The little girl was holding onto a stuffed Dora the Explorer doll. It was positively filthy. They all looked dirty, sweaty, and absolutely petrified.

One of the armed men stayed by the van and the other one walked them over to the plane. They boarded youngest to oldest and the owner directed them where to sit. The women belted the children in and then themselves. The men just sat there. The second gunman yelled at them in Spanish and then they did their seatbelts up.

The owner gave the "thumbs up," and the first gunman sneered at him but they both backed away from the door and allowed him to seal it.

Then he returned to his seat up front.

"Who are these people?" Dinah demanded.

"Medical personnel," he offered.

"Bullshit! I didn't sign up for this!"

"What are you talking about? You said that you were fine with the 'Mexico thing'," he said.

"I didn't think you meant *this*!"

"Oh Dinah, grow the fuck up!"

***

After a very bumpy takeoff, the owner turned the aircraft due west away from the border. He never revisited the flight plan issue. They simply flew without one. They stayed on the Mexican side of the border. Their passengers sat in terrified and exhausted silence. Dinah tried to turn several times and give the little girl a reassuring smile but each time, her attention just caused the poor thing to shake more. So, she stopped.

She needed to do something, but she didn't know what.

Round about the Arizona/California border, the owner began to turn north and crossed over into the U.S. in the middle of an extremely isolated area of desert. Dinah fervently hoped that they weren't being tracked but who knew? They had cancelled their flight plan, so they weren't on record, on either side of the border. And they weren't using *Flight Following* so no one could track them on *FlightAware*.

But she wasn't sure.

"Where are we going?" she asked.

"Imperial."

Imperial?

That was the airport where she had picked up the border agent. On one hand it was good because it was uncontrolled. They could fly in without alerting anyone. Hell, they could fly in without even self-announcing. There were still some planes out there that didn't have radios and they flew into uncontrolled airports all the time. On the other hand, Dinah wasn't sure if Imperial had been a one-off for the border agent or if he was there on a regular basis.

Did he know about the King Air?

"Why Imperial?" she asked.

"They'll blend in and there are jobs waiting for them. On a farm."

"Isn't it risky being so close to the border here?"

"No, the opposite. Most people try to travel by land across. Nobody is expecting them to fly in."

She had no more questions, so Dinah just sat there paralyzed, watching it happen. The owner brought the plane into the airport pattern and landed it, taxiing off the runway. Not a single radio call was made and luckily, the airport wasn't busy, so nobody seemed to notice. He taxied the aircraft over to a remote transient tiedown area and shut down the engines.

"Now what?" Dinah asked. She was scanning the entire airport, nervously seeking out the familiar physique of the border agent.

Was she hoping he'd be there or not? Would he recognize the plane? Would he see her?

She wisely decided not to share any of this information with the owner.

After a few minutes, two black Ford Expeditions pulled up. One parked by the main cabin door and the other one parked diagonally across the front of the plane, blocking the view of it from the terminal building.

The plane's occupants deplaned quickly and quietly. They were all loaded into one SUV, which drove away without any further delay. The other SUV remained behind. The driver popped the trunk door and the owner, and the driver unloaded the pallet of boxes from the aircraft and into the SUV. They took their time and made sure that their actions were highly visible.

Dinah stayed in the plane. They didn't ask her to help and she didn't offer.

When they were done, the driver presented a clipboard to the owner and he signed something. A copy was torn off and given to him and then the driver of the other SUV departed.

No money exchanged hands.

Once the owner, secured the door and returned to his seat, Dinah unfastened her seatbelt. She wanted to get out so badly. She wanted to walk away. But what if someone saw her? What if the border agent was there?

"What are you doing?" the owner asked her with narrowed eyes.

"Nothing." She did the seatbelt back up.

"Look, wherever your morality lies, we just helped those people. They're going to have new lives because of us. They didn't have a chance back there. Here they *do*."

\*\*\*

Usually extracting payment from the owner was like pulling teeth, and eventually Dinah had to deal with the dad, unless the client paid her directly. But immediately after landing back at Santa Ana, the owner opened the storage compartment between the seats and extracted a brown manila envelope, folded over several times, and fastened with an elastic band.

"I know that you're not going to want to take this," he started. "But take this." Dinah took the envelope and put it in her purse before she got out of the plane. As she was walking away, he called to her. "And I'm sure I can count on your discretion."

A statement. Not a question.

Dinah sat in her car for a long time, completely numb.

She felt stupid.

She felt naïve.

Should she have known?

Was she an idiot?

Finally, she opened the envelope. There was $2,000 in it.

Dinah drove to the nearest bank and got a bank draft. Then she went to the Catholic Charities of Orange County Immigration Services office on 17th Street in Santa Ana and donated it all.

She thought it would make her feel better.

It didn't.

## Chapter Thirty-One

Curled up in a fetal ball in bed for the next two days, was the limit of what Dinah could handle. She told Fatima and the deejay that it was the flu.

"Are you sure that's all it is?" the deejay asked with concern.

"I'll be fine. I just need to rest," Dinah assured them.

Nevertheless, NyQuil, acetaminophen and a thermometer appeared. Fatima took her temperature.

"It's okay," she reported to the deejay.

On the third day, she was thinking about how much work a shower was going to be when she got a call from Cat. She wanted to let it go to voicemail, but she was worried something had happened with Chrystal's condition.

"Hi Cat. Are you still in Phoenix?" Dinah asked.

"We are. That's why I'm calling. We're so excited – Chrystal's prosthetic leg is ready. They were going to ship it but she's so eager to get moving …"

"Where is it?"

"Salt Lake City. Could I possibly impose on you?"

"Of course, Cat. It would be my honor." Dinah had a sudden thought. "Hey, would you mind if I brought a friend along?"

\*\*\*

And that's how Dinah and Fatima ended up flying to Salt Lake City to pick up a foot. Fatima had been delighted to be included and the deejay looked pleased to have a few days to his own devices. Dinah was the most grateful. She didn't think that she had to strength to leave the apartment without someone with her. She wanted to confide in Fatima so badly, but she was prevented partly by not wanting to implicate her and partly by not knowing how she would react. Fatima had become such a good friend Dinah just couldn't risk losing her.

So, instead they talked about pretty much everything else.

"Salt Lake City ..." Fatima wondered out loud. "Wait. Wasn't that the site of the infamous cheese plate incident?"

Dinah gasped and then laughed. "You're right. That asshole jet owner! I remember now – he made you go and pick up that fancy cheese plate for that broker that he was trying to do business with. He was being so anal about it. 'It's gotta have Brie. It's gotta have Brie!'"

Fatima picked up where she left off. "And then of course the man didn't even touch it, the entire flight. And we were both so ravenous."

"And the asshole sat there after we landed and bogarted the entire tray. Ate every single morsel."

Fatima smiled wryly. "Well Mother Nature exacted her revenge, so we didn't need to."

Dinah nodded. "What a horrible way to find out that you've become lactose intolerant."

"You know I still can't even look at a piece of Brie."

Dinah giggled. "I feel badly that that's what I'll always think of now when I think of Salt Lake City."

Fatima frowned. "Okay, we have to fix that. Salt Lake City has so much more to offer."

"Like Mormons?" Dinah added. "Oh hey, I forgot that I was going to ask if you wanted to do a little of the flying?"

Fatima lit up. "Really? I would love that!"

"Okay, your controls."

"My controls."

"Your controls."

Fatima looked positively giddy. "Salt Lake City is surprisingly progressive. Of course, the Latter-day Saints make up a large component of the population but there is also a strong LGBTQIA+ demographic there."

"You're kidding."

Fatima shook her head. "Salt Lake City is considered one of the top gay-friendly places to live in the U.S. And the Utah Pride Festival is one of the biggest – 3 days and over 50,000 people."

"I would never have known that." Dinah watched Fatima work the controls for a minute. "Hey, you've got excellent instincts. Have you ever flown before?"

"I've taken a few lessons," Fatima admitted.

"You should get your license. You're really good." Fatima looked pained rather than pleased by the compliment, which made Dinah feel awful. She attempted to deflect. "So, tell me what other wonders Salt Lake City has to offer."

Fatima recovered. "I almost forgot the most important yearly event … Pony Com!"

"I'm afraid to ask."

"The annual convention for the cartoon show, *My Little Pony*. Attended by over 800 bronies."

"*Bronies?*"

"Male adult fans of the show. There's a compelling documentary about it," Fatima added.

"I actually love that," Dinah decided. "I like it when men aren't afraid to put themselves out there, to not care what other men think. I think it's incredibly brave to show your true self to the world." She looked at Fatima. "I think you're brave."

Fatima laughed. "Why am I brave?"

"Because you show your true self."

"Trust me, that's a lot easier to do here in Canada and the U.S. than it would have been back in Sri Lanka or other parts of the world. Those are the truly brave ones."

"What's it like there, if you don't mind me asking?" Dinah inquired delicately.

Fatima considered her answer carefully. "Well, we left when I was quite young, but at that time, it was illegal to be homosexual and you could be jailed up to ten years."

"Oh my God."

"Generally, the law wasn't enforced but the police beat people up and harassed them, even extorted them on a regular basis."

"Is it still that bad?"

Fatima sighed. "It's convoluted. Now, there are anti-discrimination laws regarding the workplace and housing and the military, which is good. But marriage is still not legal, adoption is not permitted, and the original Constitutional law still exists."

"Your parents must be so relieved to have you away from all that." Fatima didn't answer. Dinah gleaned a lot from her silence. "Ah." They were starting to descend from the mountainous terrain. Dinah could see the glittering Great Salt Lake in the distance. The airport lay just on the other side of it. It was a clear, bright, glorious day and Dinah felt grateful to be distracted from her problems temporarily. "Well, as I said, I think you're brave."

"Dinah, we're all brave."

***

When they got to Atlantic – the FBO they'd been directed to – there was a package waiting for them. Dinah signed for it, while Fatima was using the restroom. She was surprised to see that the young fellow working the counter had to get it from a locked safe.

"Is it worth that much?" she queried.

He glanced at the paperwork. "It's insured for $120,000, ma'am."

Holy crap.

Fatima returned to join Dinah. Dinah looked at her with huge eyes. "I think we're picking up a bionic leg."

"Why?"

"This thing's worth over $120,000!"

Fatima's eyes bulged as well.

They both suddenly became incredibly nervous and ran out to plane with the package, bobbing and weaving as they went.

Fatima had packed a lunch for them – no Brie – and they munched along as they flew straight to Phoenix. Both kept periodically glancing in the backseat to make sure the box hadn't moved.

When they landed at Phoenix, they taxied over to Cutter – which was another FBO – and took an airport taxi over to the house. Dinah clutched the box tightly on her lap the whole way. On the outside of the box was a logo that said, "Ottobock," and then the product name and description, which was, "X3 Waterproof Prosthetic Leg."

"I can't wait to see this thing," Fatima admitted.

"I know! Me too!"

At the house, Dinah was surprised and delighted to see that Chrystal answered the door herself. She was looking much healthier. Much stronger.

"My leg is here!!! Gimme!!" She grabbed the box from Dinah and hopped away with it.

Dinah made all the introductions and then they congregated in the living room to watch Chrystal like a kid on Christmas morning.

"So, this is made by a German company, based in Berlin," Cat explained. "These prosthetics were originally developed for the American military."

Chrystal pulled it out the box. The leg was comprised of an inner shaft, covered by a sleek black shell. "This is so fucking cool!"

Fatima looked at the instructions. "What is a Genium microprocessor exactly?"

"So, it's got this sensor technology," Cat said. "It allows it to respond in real time, like a real leg would, whether you're walking, running, climbing stairs, etc."

"Amazing!" Fatima enthused.

"Not only that, look at this!" Chrystal grabbed her phone and showed them the screen. "You can download this app that allows you to pre-program different settings for different sports and recreational stuff."

"Now I understand why it was so expensive," Dinah mused.

"Only the best for her little princess," Chrystal teased.

Dinah thought Chrystal was the furthest thing from a princess.

The furthest.

They all stared in veneration at the leg. Cat came to first.

"Honey, why don't you try it on."

Chrystal sat on the floor and snapped the prosthetic on with no problem at all. Dinah and Fatima both moved to help her stand up, but she waved them off.

"I got this." She braced herself on the coffee table and rose to her feet. Then she took a few tentative steps.

Cat applauded. "My baby's first steps!"

Chrystal gave her a dirty look. "Remember I have power of attorney."

Fatima looked a little shocked by their exchange, but Dinah was well-used to it by now and laughed gleefully.

Chrystal moved around a little bit more, becoming more agile and confident with each passing minute. She did a little catwalk. She did a little twirl. She did a little moonwalk. By then she had reached the open patio doors.

"Easy does it, baby," Cat cautioned to deaf ears.

"You wanna know the best part?" Chrystal asked them. "It's completely waterproof!"

And without any further ado, she disappeared off the patio and leapt into the pool. Cat shrieked and ran over to edge, followed closely by Dinah and Fatima. Chrystal languished below the surface for longer than any of them were comfortable with. Finally, Cat couldn't take it anymore. She jumped in with her beautiful pale pink silk sundress on. At that exact moment, Chrystal floated effortlessly to the surface.

Cat splashed her. "You brat!"

"I love you Mommy!"

Dinah heard another splash and realized that Fatima had jumped in too, completely clothed.

"It just looked so inviting," she offered in the way of explanation.

To hell with it.

Dinah cannonballed in her jeans and sneakers, never one to pass up a good invitation.

\*\*\*

Later, after they had all dried off and changed clothes, Cat got the blender going with the margarita of the day – watermelon. She had graciously put out all the ingredients for them to make their own personalized pizzas and they each set to the task with great relish.

"What a wonderful idea, Cat, thank you," Fatima said.

"Your friend is the best," Cat said right in front of her.

"Your friends are the best," Fatima volleyed back.

Chrystal, for her part, was studying the selection of toppings that Cat had put out on the island counter, a grey Carrera marble that complemented the charcoal cupboards beautifully.

"Fine, fine, but if anyone even thinks about committing the abomination of putting pineapple on theirs, they're dead to me."

Cat grabbed a big handful of pineapple morsels and scattered them across hers. "So, tell me more about your neighbor, what was her name, again?"

Dinah and Fatima had been filling them in on the recent stardom of Ines. Dinah loved boasting about her success. She had basically told anyone she encountered about it.

"Ines. So, I'm thrilled for her of course, but she's done so well that they're moving out of our apartment building."

Fatima nodded. "They've bought a lovely home in Encino."

"I'm so happy for them but I'm also going to miss them so much!" Dinah opined.

"But now the Pinkies will have their own backyard!" Fatima exclaimed.

Cat laughed. "The trifecta of wiener dogs has me dying! And her paintings are emulations of Munch? What was he? Austrian?"

Dinah shook her head. "Norwegian."

Chrystal had tuned out and was now sitting on a bar stool doing a kicking routine with both feet, like a Rockette.

"Is Ines Norwegian?" Cat asked.

"I think she and her husband are Mexican," Dinah posited.

Fatima supplied the correct answer. "They're from El Salvador. It's quite an amazing story. They escaped from the death squads during the civil war in the '80s. I guess they were quite an affluent family in San Salvador, and they gave up everything - spent every single dime they had – to get to the U.S. And they were two of the more fortunate ones. They had the money to get out legally. Many didn't."

Dinah didn't know any of this.

"That's astonishing!" Cat marveled. "Well, I definitely want one of those paintings. With *my* face on it."

That got Chrystal's attention. "Mom, she only does *famous* women's faces."

Cat feigned defensiveness. "I will have you know I am quite the cause célèbre within the Southern California Realtors Association."

"That's like bragging that you're the skinniest person in the Midwest," Chrystal quipped.

Cat very calmly got up from her seat and opened the oven door. Chrystal's pizza was cooking on the top rack. She grabbed the bowl of pineapple and dumped it all over the pie.

Chrystal screamed and everyone else collapsed in gales of laughter.

Dinah wished that she could stay in this cozy coven forever.

## Chapter Thirty-Two

The respite her trip to Phoenix had provided, quickly wore off once Dinah got back to Van Nuys. She found herself increasingly consumed with anxiety and paranoia about the Monterrey trip. Every time she left the apartment, she was worried she was being watched. Unknown numbers calling on her cell, quickened her heart rate and she dreaded hearing from the border agent, still wondering if he had seen anything or heard anything. One evening there was a knock on the door and Dinah nearly jumped out of her skin.

The deejay gave her a weird look as he got up off the couch. "Jesus, babe, relax. It's just Postmates. I wanted Sugarfish."

A few days later when he pestered her about yet another gig up in San Luis Obispo, she readily agreed. She was grateful to get out of town for a spell. Dinah wanted to ask Fatima to come with them but with the deejay's gear taking up the backseat area, there was no room for her.

"Please don't clean anything while we're gone!" she beseeched her. "Do something fun and relaxing. For yourself."

The edges of Fatima's mouth curled up. "Oh, don't you worry. I'm planning to spend every minute beating a certain deejay's high score."

The deejay crowed gleefully. "Dream on, sister! I was born a champion!" He strutted around the living room like a rooster.

Dinah watched him disdainfully and then said to Fatima, "What is wrong with men?"

"Nobody knows."

***

Dinah had every intention of going to the drop zone, so she headed for Oceano Airport. But as each nautical mile flew past, she had less and less desire to go. She reasoned that she didn't want to spend the money. She rationalized that she was nervous about going because it was going to be her first solo jump. But the truth of the matter was, that joy of the adrenaline rush that she got from taking the risk, had turned sour. Her personal paradigm had completely altered since the last time she was there. Now Dinah felt like going grocery shopping was more of a risk than she could handle.

"Aw, you're not going to go?" the deejay said, disappointedly. "But I was really looking forward to hearing all about it. And seeing it too. They film it, right?"

"Yeah, I still don't feel 100%," Dinah said. "Maybe next time."

"What about this? What if, I go and do the gig and then I go to the skydiving place with you? Maybe some support is all you need."

Dinah definitely needed some support, but she didn't want him out there. The skydiving was *her* thing – something that was entirely hers and hers alone. It made her feel strong and independent and impervious. She needed to be selfish with that. She needed to protect it.

At all costs.

"That's sweet of you but honestly, it's fine. Next time."

She kissed him on the cheek.

"Well do you want to come to the winery with me?"

"No, that's okay. I'll just hang out on the beach. Maybe sleep a little."

The deejay put his hand on Dinah's forehead. "You're kind of warm. I'm a little worried about you. You haven't been yourself lately."

That set off alarm bells in Dinah's head. She couldn't afford to have people notice that she was behaving abnormally. She forced herself to smile with some energy. "I'm good! Really! As I said, just a bit tired. Now go – by the time you get back I'll be back to my old self. You've been warned!!"

The deejay didn't delve any further and set off for the vintner's place.

Dinah walked over to a bench beside the runway and sat down. She had only intended to rest for a moment or two but couldn't raise enough energy to motivate herself that few feet farther to the beach. It was a nice day, overcast but the clouds were quite high, so the air was still, and it wasn't too hot. She watched a couple of planes practicing takeoffs and landings in the pattern.

Just for kicks, she got out her iPad. There was a fantastic feeder site called, *LiveATC.net*. You could stream live air traffic control communications from all around the world. All of Dinah's students, without exception, struggled with learning to speak on the radio. The vernacular was aviation-specific, and the jargon was hard to retain. And everyone spoke so quickly, it was easy to miss calls or misunderstand calls. It was also not uncommon to get "performance anxiety," and freeze up on the radio when it was your turn to speak. She always recommended that her students listen to *LiveATC*. It was a great way to familiarize yourself with aviation communication without the pressure and multi-tasking of doing it in real-time in a noisy, vibrating aircraft.

There were a lot of older aviators flying today. She could tell by the timber of their voices and the plenitude of "no joy" calls. The older guys also loved to crosstalk, which colloquially-speaking, meant that they didn't keep their radio communications, strictly professional. There was a lot of casual conversation and general chatter. Sometimes that wasn't a big deal but a lot of the frequencies were shared over large geographical areas so it kind of sucked to see another plane heading straight for you on a collision course and not be able to give a position report because someone was relaying their Quizno's order to another pilot. Dinah used to admonish pilots verbally on frequency, but she'd been called the "C-word" a few times so now she used a different technique called "blocking." Each time a pilot tried to make one of those superfluous calls, Dinah would "key her mic," which meant, simply, that she pressed the button to transmit but then didn't say anything. What that accomplished was to block whatever the other pilot was trying to say and instead there'd be silence. Sometimes it happened by accident when two pilots transmitted at the same time and someone would say, "blocked," and then each would take their turn. But in this case, Dinah did it repeatedly, every time that pilot tried to transmit until she was sure she could picture the vein pulsing on their forehead in mercurial rage.

It was the little things.

Today there was a pristine older biplane in the pattern, the seminal one of course, being the Wright Flyer. This one looked like a Sopwith Camel, with the open cockpit and the wood frame and canvas coverings. Dinah was always so humbled by these older planes. The complete and utter vulnerability of flying in those types of constructions. She could just make out the cap and goggles of the pilot as he (or she!) taxied past her on the way back to the runway.

The reason Dinah couldn't determine if the pilot were male or female was simply because the plane wasn't equipped with radios, so the Camel pilot wasn't making any calls. That's why the older planes generally stayed at uncontrolled airports. Most controlled airports required working two-way radios for all aircraft – except for in an emergency and a few other exceptional conditions.

The sun had begun to peek out and it was directly in Dinah's eyes, so she slid down the bench a few feet. Something was nagging her at the back of her mind, but she didn't know what. That biplane had triggered it.

Why?

She pondered.

And pondered.

And by the time the deejay pulled up in front of the airport, Dinah had arrived at a conclusion.

And she hoped she was wrong.

***

Dinah didn't say a word while they were loading the plane.

Until she saw the bag.

It was a dark green REI hiking backpack.

In the entire time that Dinah had known the deejay, he had never once gone on a hike.

And the bag hadn't been there on the flight up.

"What's in here?" she asked him.

She moved towards the bag and he started.

Yup.

"Just a couple bottles of wine that the guy gifted to us. Nice swag, huh?"

"Yeah, really nice. What kind? Red or white?" Dinah bent down to unzip the bag.

"Don't!"

It was full of money.

Dinah didn't react at all. "How much is in here?"

The deejay seemed to physically deflate right in front of her. "Three hundred grand."

"What's it for?" No answer. *"What is it for??!!"*

He raked his hands through his hair. "I don't know, babe. I swear to God, I don't! I just take it back to Van Nuys and then I deliver it to the bartender at that club around the corner from us on Woodley."

"Valley Strip? Across from the Flyaway?" Dinah demanded. The deejay nodded miserably. "What do you exchange it for? What do you bring back?"

"Nothing! I have no idea what the money is for. It could be for something completely legal."

"Bullshit. That's why you were so stubborn about flying into Oceano and not San Luis Obispo, wasn't it? Because Oceano is uncontrolled – there's no control tower tracking your comings and goings. So, there'd be no record of us landing here."

He hung his head.

"I'm really sorry I didn't tell you. But I was trying to protect you. That way if anything happened, you'd be completely innocent."

Dinah climbed into the plane and slammed her door. The deejay scurried around to the other side and did the same.

"I'm calling the police," Dinah stated, pulling out her cell.

The deejay grabbed for it. "No, no, no, babe, you can't do that!"

"Okay, well, this stops right now. Get out and take the money back to him."

"I can't."

"Then I'll do it." Dinah cracked her door.

"No!"

She was so sick of the prevarications and the puerile behavior. Dinah grabbed the bag and he lunged for it. They both tugged on it, struggling for control.

"I can't go back!" he yelled.

"Why not? Are they threatening you?"

"No, but ..."

"Then why?? Why??"

"I can't! I can't go back!!! I can't go back!!! I can't go back!!!" The deejay was completely hysterical now, sobbing and rocking himself, repeating that same phrase, like it was a mantra. "I can't go back. It was so fucking awful! I ate once a day. I was always so hungry. And that fucking bus I took. Two hours each way and it fucking smelled so bad! I can't ever go back to that. Fucking ever!! Do you understand me???!!!

The way people treated me. Like I was nothing. Nothing!! *I can't go back to that."*

Unfortunately, Dinah understood.

All too well.

## Chapter Thirty-Three

**B**y the time Dinah got the deejay home, she had managed to calm him down. They discussed their limited options. One thing was for certain, she told him, she couldn't continue to use the owner's plane to conduct this type of business. Dinah neglected to tell him what type of business was being conducted in the owner's *other* plane.

"It's too much of a risk to drive," the deejay decreed.

"I agree," Dinah concurred. "How hard would it be to completely extricate yourself?"

He held his head in his hands. "I don't know. This guy has seemed really reasonable so far. But I don't know. People can change without warning, you know?"

No kidding.

"Maybe you could say you have to go back to South Korea. Or you could tell him that the police came and questioned you and he should use someone else because they're watching you."

They decided to think about their next course of action and the dynamic at home was tense to say the least. Fatima didn't comment on it – she probably just assumed it was more of the same ... Relationship Problems 101. She could tell that Fatima wasn't a fan of the deejay even though she never said anything. So, Dinah found herself going out of her way to make excuses for him, citing how difficult his life had been. But deep down, she knew that an adverse existence didn't give you the right to treat others badly.

Fortunately, beyond the bellicose boyfriend issues, Dinah had other sources of extreme stress to distract her. Namely, the border agent and Monterrey. He had his next SIM session coming up and Dinah went back and forth on whether to cancel. She didn't want to antagonize him. But she didn't want to give him an opportunity to pry.

She didn't want to raise his suspicions by cancelling. But she desperately wanted to avoid dealing with him.

Ultimately, she arrived at the conclusion that it was better to continue on … business as usual. She met him in the downstairs lobby at Mach 1. The main level was housed by the FBO, Atlantic, one of the good ones, and a freshly baked batch of chocolate chip cookies had just been put out. The border agent had one in his mouth and three in his right hand.

The dispatch desk agent glared at Dinah when he saw her join the border agent. "Are you with him?"

"I am," she answered.

"Well those cookies are for Atlantic customers. *Not* the upstairs tenants."

"Sorry, he didn't know," Dinah apologized. The border agent looked guilty but satisfied. She took one of his cookies. "Come on! You're going to get me in trouble!"

He mumbled through the crumbs. "Cookie police! How do I get *that* job?"

***

Back in the SIM room, Dinah booted up the simulator while she explained to the border agent that she was going to teach him how to do "holds" today.

"Is that the racetrack pattern thingy?" he asked.

"Exactly! Sometimes you need to hold for spacing, when there's a lot of aircraft for ATC to handle at once. Sometimes you might be holding because the weather is bad at your destination and you're waiting for it to clear. It depends."

Dinah drew a diagram for him outlining the layout of a typical holding pattern. On the left lower corner, she drew an asterisk.

"What's that?" the border agent asked.

"That's called the 'holding fix.' When you cross that point, that's the official start of the hold. Usually you do turns to the right. But if you need to go left, ATC will let you know, or it will be depicted on the chart."

Then she showed him how to time one minute on the outbound leg, turn around and then time how long it took to fly the inbound leg and cross the holding fix again.

"Okay," he noticed. "It took one minute to fly out and then a minute and twenty seconds to fly in. What gives?"

"Good catch!" Dinah praised him. "That means that we need to shorten the inbound leg by shortening the outbound leg to accommodate it. It's the inbound leg that matters. I added some wind in – that's what affected your times."

"Aha, very clever."

"I warned you last time, didn't I? No empty threats from this camp!"

Dinah started to relax a little bit. Nothing seemed to be out of the ordinary. The border agent was acting as he normally did. There were no strange looks. He hadn't said anything. It was going to be okay.

"I always hear how hard these are, but this is pretty simple," the border agent observed. "You just fly in a circle."

"Well, flying in a circle is harder than it looks," Dinah joked. "Once you're in it, you're fine. It's getting into a hold that is challenging."

She grabbed the diagram again and divided it into three sectors. Then she wrote, "D" on the largest piece of the pie, "P" on the second largest and "T" on the remaining piece.

The border agent studied the diagram. "I withdraw my previous comment."

Dinah explained to him that these represented the three different entry procedures into a hold: direct, parallel and teardrop.

Depending on which direction you were flying towards the holding fix from, you had to choose which of these entries was appropriate. A direct entry meant that you were able to fly right over the holding fix and start the hold. A parallel entry was when you were basically travelling to it from the opposite direction. In that case, you crossed the holding fix going the wrong way, flew outbound for one minute on the inbound track and then did a big loop to your left and tracked back to cross the holding fix going in the correct direction. A wonderful aviation homage to Abbott and Costello. The teardrop entry was more or less when you were approaching the hold from the southwest (bottom left for non-geography fans) direction. You would cut across the holding fix at an angle, fly outbound on that heading for one minute and then this time loop around to the right to pick up the inbound track.

Who's on first?

"The best way to figure it out, is to draw it," Dinah said. "Back when we used paper charts more often, I would draw it right on the chart. Now I just draw it on a piece of paper on my kneeboard."

"Wait a minute here," the border agent said. "Do you mean to tell me that in this day and age that you still have to figure this out yourself? That there's no software that allows planes to calculate the entry method intuitively?"

Dinah folded her arms across her chest. "Oh, in the larger, more technologically adept aircraft that I fly, you betcha. I don't have to figure out a thing. I just sit back and let the airplane do all the work. But you my friend ... you are at the bottom of the aviation barrel, no offense. You've got to do it all yourself. You've got to walk before you can run. True story."

The border agent sat and thought about this for a moment. "Okay, okay – I'm a smart guy. I can do this. Give me another hold instruction and I'll come up with the right entry procedure, all on my own. No help."

Dinah refused to give him a direct entry – too easy – so she set him up to have to do a parallel entry. She gave him the fix and the heading to the fix. He thought about it and then drew the course and the correct hold entry line.

"Which is it?" she asked.

"It's a parallel."

"Good! That's right! Let's fly it. But this time, don't time the legs. Let's fly ten-mile legs. So, ten miles out, turn around and then ten miles inbound."

It started to take longer than Dinah had anticipated. She should have given him five-mile legs. After a few moments of concentrated silence, the border agent made an observation.

"You know, this is really interesting. These holds, I mean. It always ends the same."

"What do you mean?"

"Well they're like certain situations in life. No matter, how you get in – and there's a lot of different ways – you can only come out one way. It's the same result every time."

Dinah's vision blurred and she suddenly felt faint.

He knew.

\*\*\*

The lesson ended quickly after that. The border agent never addressed anything overtly, but the suggestion was there. On the way out to his car, he thanked Dinah again for "helping him out that time."

"The blood that you saw was from an injured burro. This family had tried to ride it across, and it got tangled in some barbed wire. I put the poor thing out of its misery and advised the family to go back."

"I figured it was something like that," Dinah breathed.

He squinted at her. "No, you didn't." He rested against the trunk of his car. "My job is important to me. I don't have a wife or kids or a hamster. My career is my life. And I take it very seriously."

"I understand."

"I can never allow myself to be swayed by my personal feelings ... regardless of how strong they are."

"Of course."

And then he confirmed their lesson for the following week, and he drove out of the parking lot.

Dinah couldn't even remember the walk home. She had completely left her body by this time. She needed to be alone. She needed to think.

But when she arrived, it was a full house. Ines and the baggage handler were moving out and he came by to say goodbye and to drop off some presents. He had some frozen steaks for the deejay that wouldn't survive the trip, he said. Which was very sweet because Encino was all of ten minutes away. There was a card in an envelope for Dinah and a special large rectangular package for Fatima.

"I wonder what this could be!" Fatima said excitedly.

The sound of obnoxious horns blaring cut the conversation short and they all promised to get together for a housewarming as soon as it was safe.

Dinah distracted herself by watching Fatima tear open the package. She knew that if she saw the baggage handler disappear around the corner, that she would start crying.

Instead, her emotions turned to mirth.

"Who is that?" the deejay asked, scrutinizing the portrait.

"It's Indira Gandhi," Fatima said.

"Indira Gandhi?" Dinah said. "Wasn't she ... "

"Prime Minister of India. Yes, she was," Fatima finished for her. "Do they think that I'm Indian?"

"Well, at least it's the right continent," Dinah offered kindly.

The deejay scoffed. "Personally, I can't believe that junk qualifies as art. It really busts my hump that she's making all that dough off these things. I mean, she's not even creating anything original. She's just borrowing from another artist."

Dinah and Fatima looked at each other and waited for him to understand what he was saying.

Nope.

"Well, I love my paintings," Dinah said. "I will cherish them always!"

"Babe, you should sell them. You too, Fatima. Now that Ines is so popular, these will be worth a fortune!"

Fatima responded carefully. "I think that sometimes the sentimental value of certain items outweighs their monetary value. There are some things that are so important to me that I would never sell them."

"Me too," agreed Dinah.

Just then, she remembered that she was still holding the unopened card. She slit the envelope with her finger and pulled the card out. It was a generic Hallmark-type "thank you" card, with a drawing of a bunch of wiener dogs linked together to form a chain of solidarity.

Cute.

The handwritten message inside said, "Dinah, you are one of the kindest, most decent and welcoming people that we have met since we came here. When we think of 'America,' it's you that we see."

And in the card, was the $200 that she had given them for rent, repaid in full.

## Chapter Thirty-Four

Events accelerated very quickly after that, like a snowball travelling downhill. But a special sticky snowball that picked up every little piece of excrement it rolled over along the way.

The deejay, after several heated discussions, had eventually agreed to tell the vintner that his courier days were over. He and Dinah mutually decided that if he were pressured or threatened as a result, they would go to the police.

"You can tell him I found out about it and I'm the one who wants to go to the police," Dinah offered. "That way, it's not on you. It looks like your hand has been forced."

"That's really awesome of you, but I don't want him to see *you* as the threat. He might retaliate and I don't want anything to happen to you. I'll just be straight with him," the deejay stated.

As for the owner, Dinah genuinely wanted to walk away from that situation completely. But they needed the money so badly. She decided she would tell him that she would only fly the Cirrus clients. No more flights in the King Air, especially south of the border. And in the meantime, she would start looking for another source of employment.

Not sporadic dog walking.

She hadn't slept well, what with all these problems marinating in her subconscious and when she finally managed to crawl out of bed, late morning, both Fatima and the deejay were nowhere to be seen. Perhaps he had finally beaten her self-respect down enough to go to laser tag.

Then the music started. It was Katy Perry's "California Gurls." Dinah sped over to the window and looked out.

Goddamn it.

That bloody woman was doing the cycling classes again in the pool.

And the pool was closed indefinitely.

The gall of this chick!

Dinah threw on some yoga pants and a t-shirt and went down to the rental office. She knocked on the plexiglass window and rang the bell and Kristina appeared.

"Hi, Kristina, I was wondering, is the pool open again?"

"No, closed until further notice." Kristina looked to her left and saw the babes with bikes. "I keep the blinds closed in my office to block out the sun, so I didn't see that. I'll take care of it. Thank you for alerting me."

"My pleasure." Dinah turned away smugly.

"It's good that you dropped by. I noticed that you have two people staying with you. They've been here more than two weeks so they will have to be added to the lease or they will have to leave, yes? Let me know."

And the plexiglass window slid shut.

Then Dinah's phone vibrated. She must have forgotten to turn the ringer back on. It was a voicemail from the guy with the verbally abusive parrot. He wanted to know if she could come over and watch *Escape from New York* with them.

"We have Funyuns," he dangled, while the bird screeched something halfway intelligible about impotence in the background.

While she was listening to the voicemail, another call came in.

The owner.

She didn't want to answer it.

"Hello?"

"Hey, beautiful, I'm in a bit of a jam."

Dinah gasped. "Were you arrested?"

"No, no, nothing like that. I just, I need you to do a Monterrey run for me day after tomorrow."

Dinah took a deep breath. "Look, you're going to have to do it yourself from now on."

"No, you misunderstand. I don't want you to come with me, I need you to go instead of me," he clarified.

"Are you crazy?! Absolutely not!" Dinah was on the verge of hanging up on him.

"Hold on, hold on, hold on. Look I know it's a big ask but my dad … the hospital just called … he's only got a few hours left. I can't leave right now. And our colleagues in Mexico have a schedule that can't be modified."

"Have you talked to them?" Dinah asked agitatedly.

"Yes. It can't be modified."

"Okay, I appreciate your difficulties and I'm so terribly sorry about your dad, but you created this situation yourself. And you need to fix it yourself. I am never doing one of those flights again." She thought she was done, but she wasn't. "In fact, I'm tendering my resignation effective immediately. I'll email you in a few minutes with a written notification." The owner didn't say anything. "Hello?"

"I'm here. Dinah, I've tried to be a nice guy with you, but I'm done. You *will* do the Monterrey flight. And you know why? Because on the last trip, it was *your* name on the customs paperwork. And *you* filed the flight plan. And it was *your* voice doing all the radio calls. As far as I'm concerned, *I* wasn't even there."

"Fuck you!"

"No Dinah, fuck *you*. You think I'm an idiot, don't you? I see the way you look at me and talk down to me. Well, guess what? I'm smarter than you are, you dumb bitch!"

He finished the conversation by telling her that he had shared all her personal information with their Mexican colleagues, and they would be expecting her. He would hear about it if she were even a minute late.

She sat down on a chair in the lobby, hoping that Kristina hadn't heard any of the conversation. She wanted to go back to the apartment, but she couldn't make her legs work. Inertia was her only friend at present.

Her phone rang again, and she was about to decline the call, thinking it was the owner calling back but when she looked at the screen, she saw that it was the deejay.

"Where are you?" she answered, with annoyance.

"San Luis Obispo. Babe, you've got to help me!" He sounded frantic.

"What the hell?! How did you get there?"

"I got up early and drove up here. I just thought it would be better if I did this face-to-face, you know?"

"I wish you had talked to me first." Dinah could feel her panic magnifying.

"I wish I had too. The thing is ..." He started to cry. "Dinah, they're going to kill me."

"What?!" She wasn't sure if she had heard him correctly.

"They're going to kill me if you don't come!"

"Why?" She still wasn't connecting the dots.

"They want you to come and get the money and take it back to Van Nuys. Once they know it's been delivered then they'll let me go. Please!"

"I'm calling the police!" Dinah said.

"No, no, no – no police! Dinah please just do as they say, okay? They want you to come Wednesday morning. Please, babe. I'm so scared! I'm so fucking scared!!"

And then the call was cut off. Dinah called back but it went straight to voicemail.

She knelt down on the floor and rocked herself. She couldn't breathe. She couldn't get enough air in her lungs and her entire body was trembling.

That's how Fatima found her a few minutes later when she returned with a bag of groceries.

Fatima left the groceries and half-carried Dinah back to the apartment. She got her settled on the couch and went back downstairs to get the bag.

The groceries were gone.

Viva Van Nuys!

Fatima didn't have time to investigate further so she returned to the apartment quickly, not wanting to leave Dinah alone for long. When she got back, she held Dinah tightly and rubbed her back until the anxiety attack had passed.

And then Dinah told her everything.

Everything.

"I don't know what to do!" Dinah cried.

"That's alright," Fatima responded. "I do."

***

And so, that very afternoon, Fatima did something she hadn't done for over five years.

She went home.

Dinah understood that she needed to do that. And there was no dissention. She loved Fatima. This woman had become the best friend that she had ever had.

On Wednesday, Dinah got up at the crack of dawn and drove down to John Wayne to pick up the King Air. She flew straight to San Luis Obispo Airport. The runway at Oceano was too short for the King Air so she didn't have any choice. Even though landing at a controlled airport heightened the risk considerably, she knew the day would be over before it started if she didn't.

She got a car to the vineyard and marched up to the door, her legs shaking. The vintner answered immediately.

"Hey, Dinah, right?" He was as affable and easygoing as the first time she had met him. What was this guy's deal? "Thanks so much for doing this! I really appreciate it!" He was talking to her like she'd offered to drive his kid to soccer practice. "Wait right here and I'll grab it for you!"

"Hold on! Is he okay?" She didn't know if she should demand to see the deejay or not.

The vintner dismissed her concerns with a wave of his hand. "He's good! I'll be right back!"

Dinah stood in the foyer and left the front door open. She needed to know that she had a quick means of escape. The entrance was dark and cool, but she was still drenched with sweat.

And then she heard a splash.

Was the vintner swimming?

She edged into the next room, which looked like a study – lots of dark wood and leather-bound books - and peeked through a part in the drapes.

The deejay was in the pool. He swam towards the ladder, hauled himself out and toweled off. Then he plopped down on a chaise and took a sip of the frosty Arnold Palmer that was waiting on the table beside him.

Dinah could hear footsteps, so she hastened back to the foyer. The vintner appeared carrying the green REI knapsack.

"Is it the usual amount?" she asked.

"Far as I know," he deflected. "Hey, next time bring your swimsuit and we'll have a barbeque! Don't be a stranger!"

And he stood in the open doorway and waved until she was tucked in the backseat of the car, like she was leaving home to go back to college after winter break.

***

Back at the airport, Dinah secured the bag on the seat behind her and opened her flight plan from San Luis Obispo, California to Monterrey, Mexico.

She took off and tried to calm herself down. But she was alone with nothing but time on her hands. Never a good combination. She started thinking about how hard she had worked. And all the sacrifices she had made. And about how much she used to love flying and now every plane that she got in felt like a prison. She yearned to escape its cocoon, like a chrysalis changing form.

And then she thought about her parents. She thought about how supportive they were. How proud they were of her. About all the sweat equity they had put into that dealership so that she could benefit after they had gone.

Dinah thought about all the times in her life that she went along when she shouldn't have. Because she didn't want to be difficult.

All the times she didn't *speak* up for herself.

All the times she didn't *stand* up for herself.

She had never held her ground.

*Never drawn a line in the sand.*

And she felt a profound anguish, deep down to her toes. It burned like a white-hot flame all the way through her. It consumed her … mile after mile … inch by inch of her body … until she couldn't bear it any longer.

Somewhere over New Mexico, high over the Rockies, where the nearest town was a place, ironically called, Truth or Consequences, Dinah opened her mouth wide.

And she screamed as loud as she could.

She screamed one word repeatedly.

And that word was, "No!"

And while she was screaming that word, Dinah turned the aircraft directly towards the face of the Black Range Mountains.

And flew straight at it.

And when the aircraft collided, it exploded into a ball of flames.

## Chapter Thirty-Five

Anyone who saw the plane crash into the side of the mountain in that remote area, would have likely been spellbound by the fire and smoke. They would have reported this visceral image to emergency services. It would have taken some time to get a rescue team out there. And then longer to pinpoint the exact site in such inaccessible conditions. And then perhaps weeks before a ground team could reach the area. And by then, who knew what wild animals might have done to ruin the integrity of the crash site and what remained amongst the debris.

Anyone who saw that plane, probably didn't notice the lesser spectacle of two parachutes that opened shortly after the plane impacted. One chute was round, and one was square. And they were both pale blue, which made them hard to discern from the sky around them.

And anyone who saw the chutes probably didn't have a good enough viewpoint to ascertain that the round chute didn't have a human being attached to it. Rather, it just looked like a bag of some sort.

The square chute *did* have a human being below it. A human being who had never actually done a legitimate solo jump before. And after that human being tossed the pilot chute out and then with expectant hope saw the glorious main chute unfurl itself above, that human being felt considerably better. And once, safely on the ground, in a field that offered the cover of scrubs, that human being watched the knapsack land, a couple of hundred yards away and dashed over to cut it loose and hugged it tightly while scurrying back under the bushes .

And then neither the human being nor the knapsack were visible from the air.

\*\*\*

A short time later, the droning of a single-engine plane could be heard approaching. Anyone looking up to spot it probably would have assumed it was part of the search-and-rescue mission. It was an older Cherokee with a strange tail number. All American-registered planes started with the letter *N*. This plane's tail number started with the letter *C*. The Cherokee circled down above the field and then looked as though it was going to land right there.

And it did.

It was a beautiful, soft field landing.

The human being who had been crouched beneath the scrubs, darted out, carrying the knapsack and ran over to the waiting plane.

The pilot reached across and opened the passenger side door for the jumper.

They smiled at each other.

"Need a ride?" Fatima asked.

"Thought you'd never ask," Dinah replied.

**NOW**

## Chapter Thirty-Six

**H**er landings were improving.

But she could do better. She knew she could.

Dinah had only been flying seaplanes for a few months and it was a shockingly different skill set from land-based aircraft. For one thing, the sight picture was completely different. Because of the pontoons, you sat much higher up. At first, Dinah felt like a baby in a highchair and she was all discombobulated. The other challenging aspect was timing the landings in between swells – on the lee side – or worse yet, when the conditions were calm and glassy, trying to eke out some depth perception.

But it was intoxicating.

She flew the Twin Otter, an amphibious aircraft, which meant it had both water and land capabilities. Sometimes Dinah picked up and dropped off passengers at the dock right in front of the Canareef Resort and sometimes she went to the Gan Airport, which was on Addu Atoll, the southernmost part of the Maldives.

The Maldives had had an extremely tumultuous history, at one time or another being ruled by just about every Tom, Dick, and Harry out there. They had been under Dutch rule, Portuguese rule, Indian rule and of course the ubiquitous Brits. Eventually it became a republic – just in time for the tsunami to hit it in 2008. The region had had a long battle back to functionality, but tourism was back on the rise and Dinah had been hired almost immediately as a pilot for the resort. She ferried guests back and forth and did island tours on demand and loved it. People who were on vacation had a unique mindset. They were generally relaxed and ready to have some fun. And they were open to new experiences that they normally wouldn't be in their everyday lives.

She got to see people at their best.

And the setting for that couldn't have been more idyllic. The Maldives were a group of small islands called "atolls" (technically coral reefs), that lay in the Indian Ocean, southwest of India and Sri Lanka. And the views were breathtaking. It was truly paradise. The official language was Dhivehi, which was related to the Sinhala language of Sri Lanka, but most people spoke English. Even still, Dinah enjoyed studying it on her days off. She was enthusiastic about immersing herself in the culture of this diverse, resilient community. This place resonated with her.

She felt at home here.

Dinah taxied over slowly and delicately to the dock. Twin Otters didn't have a lot of maneuverability in the water but who cared? Nobody had anywhere to be.

As she was tying the plane down – tightly with a sailor's knot – otherwise it would be gone with the tide, the resort's dive boat pulled up to the dock. A darkly tanned man with green eyes, a broad forehead, and a mess of curly brown hair, threw her a line. She pulled the boat closer and tied it up.

"Thank you for that," he said.

"You're most welcome," she returned.

After the boatful of sunburnt divers and snorkelers had gathered their things and struggled onto the dock and were ambling back to the resort, the dive instructor jumped off the boat and gave Dinah a big kiss.

"Are you done for the day?" he asked.

"I am. I was going to head home and have a shower. Get ready for tonight."

The head concierge, Mari, was turning 30 and the staff had planned a party for her. Here in Addu, a birthday ending in a zero was considered an accomplishment not a death knell. Dinah wore an extremely casual uniform, that consisted of cargo shorts and a monogrammed white golf shirt, but she still wanted to change into an airy and comfortable dress. And to wash the insidious salt out of her hair.

The dive instructor was from Christchurch, New Zealand and he lived at the resort. But Dinah had her own place. A charming little condominium with water views that a certain real estate impresario had invested in as a vacation sublet. Cat had let her buy it outright and Dinah knew for a fact she had not paid even close to market value.

Dinah retrieved her scooter from the parking lot and just as she was about to start it up, her phone rang, and a call went through to voicemail. It was Fatima. She'd call her back when she got home.

Fatima was still back in the U.S. She was enrolled in flight training full-time in Atlanta, Georgia. A recent mysterious donor had generously gifted her the financial means for her studies and she was well on her way to an airline job.

But up front this time.

Where she belonged.

As Dinah pulled out of the parking lot, she couldn't help but take mental stock. A call from Fatima always pulled her back, but not in a negative way. Dinah was in such a better place, both literally and figuratively. She loved flying again and she was enjoying her new home and her new situation. The dive instructor was quite shy, and Dinah had been the one to ask *him* out. He had been raised by a single mom and had two older sisters and they had definitively influenced the kind of man he had become. The very first night they went out on a date, she noticed immediately that even though he was considerably taller than her, he shortened his stride so that he could walk beside her and not get ahead of her. Dinah had a moment of realization that every other man she had been with had walked slightly ahead of her, while she followed hurriedly behind like an obedient pet. He was supportive without being didactic. And he didn't dominate yet also managed not to be an emotional incubus. Dinah liked who she was with this man — namely herself and not a version of herself.

He was a part of her life but not her whole life. She had her own goals and aspirations, her own interests and friends and her own home. She would never share a residence again. She adored living alone. And adored not worrying about rent even more. The dive instructor was a positive addition to her life at present but if at any time that changed, then he would cease to be allowed the privilege of being in her life.

And that was the way it should have always been. Dinah wished that she could fly a banner across the sky, letting all women know that they had been bamboozled from birth. Richard Gere wasn't coming to whisk you away from your streetwalking ways. Tom Hanks wasn't going to meet you at the top of the Empire State Building. No one was coming to save you ... neither of the two Ryans and none of the Chrises. And frankly, women didn't need saving. And they didn't need a Prince Charming either.

Her message to them was clear and concise:

Cinderella needed to kick off that other glass slipper and go back into that ball.

Rapunzel needed to give herself a cute, pixie cut and knock down that door.

Snow White needed to wash her fruit.

Dinah's eyes filled up at the mere thought of what women could accomplish if only they knew from inception that they were the heroes of their own stories.

Because they were.

*Women were the heroes of their own stories.*

It was only a short distance to the condo from the resort and her phone screen lit up a second time as soon as she dismounted her scooter. It was Fatima again, but this time she had sent a text. She must be trying to avoid studying, Dinah knowingly guessed. It was hard not to become myopic in those training programs. But Dinah had every confidence that Fatima would be a ground-breaking success in aviation with respect to her gender, her cultural background, and her sexuality. She knew she was going to cry when she saw the first photo of Fatima in her pilot's uniform. And she couldn't wait to see this strong, intelligent woman excel.

The text was about the dive instructor. She wanted to send them both a Christmas card and she couldn't remember his name.

Dinah texted Fatima back.

His name was <u>Michael</u>.

# Glossary

**A&P** - Airframe and Powerplant

**ADS-B** - Automatic Dependent Surveillance-Broadcast

**AFSP** - Alien Flight Student Program

**AME** - Aviation Medical Examiner

**ATC** - Air Traffic Control

**ATF** - Bureau of Alcohol, Tobacco, Firearms and Explosives

**ATIS** - Automatic Terminal Information Service

**ATP** - Airline Transport Pilot

**CA** - Captain

**CBP -** United States Custom and Border Protection

**CFI** - Certified Flight Instructor

**CSUN** - California State University, Northridge

**DPE** - Designated Pilot Examiner

**DTS** - Data Training Simulator

**E6B** - Flight Computer or "Whiz Wheel"

**EAS** - Essential Air Service

**FA** - Flight Attendant

**FAA** - Federal Aviation Administration

**FBO** - Fixed Base Operator

**FIRC** - Flight Instructor Refresher Course

**FO** - First Officer

**GA** - General Aviation

**GFS** - Graphic Flight Simulator

**IACRA** - Integrated Airman Certification and Rating Application

**IFR** - Instrument Flight Rules

**ILS** - Instrument Landing System

**IMC** - Instrument Meteorological Conditions

**IOE** - Initial Operating Experience

**KABQ** - Albuquerque International Sunport Airport

**KASE -** Aspen-Pitkin County Airport

**KCM** - Known Crewmember

**KIPL** - Imperial County Airport

**KMCE** - Merced Regional Airport

**LAX** - Los Angeles International Airport

**LCA** - Line Check Airman

**LOFT** - Line Oriented Flight Training

**NAF** - Naval Air Station

**NGPA** - National Gay Pilots Association

**PF** - Pilot Flying

**PIC** - Pilot in Command

**PM** - Pilot Monitoring

**QRH** - Quick Reference Handbook

**RNAV (GPS)** - Area Navigation Using the Global Positioning System

**SIM** - Simulator

**SOCAL** - Southern California

**TAWS** - Terrain Awareness and Warning System

**TFR** - Temporary Flight Restriction

**TSA** - Transportation Security Administration

**UCLA** - University of California, Los Angeles

**U of T** - University of Toronto

**USCIS** - United States Citizenship and Immigration Services

**VFR** - Visual Flight Rules

**VMC** - Visual Meteorological Conditions

## Acknowledgements

**T**hank you first and foremost to my mom, Pat Lince, who in addition to being my strongest advocate, was also my editor and proofreader on this book. She didn't charge me but if you want to hire her, expect to pay through the nose.

Also, thanks to Gina Sorell, a wonderful author who has a novel called *Mothers and Other Strangers*. She was kind enough to guide me through the publishing process.

Justice Wainwright, a brilliant writer, artist, and comedian, designed my book cover and my website and has extended much generosity to me over the years. In return, I took him to Boise, Idaho. So, we're even.

Brian Rosenfeld and the gang at Baymark Aviation have always given me a home and a place to train and flight instruct. They are a fantastic company that operates out of Van Nuys Airport in the Los Angeles area. Tell them Laura sent you. It won't help you at all.

The two best bosses I've ever had in aviation, are Michael Hodgson and Kris Conrad, both Chief Pilots at ExpressJet. They are kind, funny, and incredible mentors. And they never once told me that I flew like a girl.

And much appreciation to both my aviation community and my entertainment community for your help and encouragement; as well as, my super supportive immediate and extended family members. I am lucky to have so many people in my corner ... on the ground and in the sky!

If you are a male pilot and you'd like to correct any technical errors that I have made, we welcome your input. Send a message to feedback@notarealemail.com

## About the Author

Author Photo by Paul Landry, Paul Landry Photography

In addition to being an alumna of The Second City Theater, Laura has an Honors Bachelor of Arts Degree from The University of Western Ontario. In Canada, Laura has written and performed on CBC RADIO and at the Just for Laughs Festival in Montréal. Her one-act play, entitled *Joyride*, won the Special Merit Award in the 7th Annual National Playwriting Competition. It has been performed in Vancouver, Orlando, and Chicago. Another international credit for Laura was an all-female stage version of *Reservoir Dogs* entitled, *Reservoir Bitches*. *Reservoir Bitches* premiered in Toronto and then played at the DR2 Theater in New York City. *Reservoir Bitches* received a Canadian Comedy Award Nomination for Best Play and has since been produced by theater companies in Halifax and Minneapolis. Laura's television writing credits include the *2001 Canadian Comedy Awards* – which aired on THE COMEDY NETWORK and CTV. She was nominated for a Gemini Award for this project. Several years ago, Laura decided to start a second career in aviation. Laura became an Instrument and Multi-Engine-Rated Commercial Pilot as well as a Certified Flight Instructor. This past year, she acquired her Airline Transport Pilot certification and was a First Officer at United ExpressJet Airlines. Originally from Toronto, Canada, Laura now lives in Los Angeles with her rescue dog, Gary Cooper. Follow her exploits and web series, on her website, *www.lady-pilot.com*

Made in the USA
Coppell, TX
13 July 2022